FACE OF FEAR

C. Marry Hultman

1

WISCONSIN
-NOIR-
WISCONSIN

Acknowledgements

The book that you now hold in your hands, or on your e-reader, whatever the case may be, has been a work in progress for many years. It has gone through many stages, from a mere idea, to an exercise in writing, to an exciting venture and finally a full-fledged tale. I do have people to thank through all of these stages, and I am eternally grateful to all who are present in its essence.

Firstly, this story came about when I saw several mashup drawings of Golden Age comic book heroes. The images conjured up certain characters and inspired me to use versions of them in my work. I would therefore like to thank Tim Ellis of CKRTLAB Toys for drawing those figures and allowing me to draw from them. Find him here; http://www.ckrtlabtoys.com/

Secondly, I have to thank those who have helped me along the way by simply being inspirational people; Emil Haskett, Vuyo Jama and Fredrik Olsson. You have all been an intricate part of my growth as a writer.

Last but not least, my family and friends, who have stood by me through the process and especially my wife Marie who has believed in me even when I did not. This book is as much yours as it is mine, I love you.

CHAPTER ONE

Tony wasn't nervous. That was what was odd about the whole thing - he just wasn't nervous. Throughout the preparations and the decisions leading him to this point, his heart had been racing. At night, when he lay on that lumpy mattress on his wrought iron bedframe and the light from the neon sign filtered through the Venetian blinds, perforating the darkness of his studio apartment, the pulsating of his blood played on his eardrums like an old man plays a kendang. At first, the lack of sleep and the stress of it all had affected his work, causing several notices to be late, him to lose his train of thought when reading the news, and his colleagues to suspect him of having caught the flu. It had even gotten so bad that the station manager, Mr. Linden, had called him into the office to have a word with him. A weekend of R&R and the blowhard Johnny Summers filling in for him and he had been right as rain.

The past week had seen him back to his old self, managing to balance work, training and putting the final additions to his suit. He had finally figured out what to do with the twin kalis he had used. Traditionally the sheath, or warangka, stuck in a warrior's belt, but he had found that the wave-shaped blades only fell out when he moved about. Instead of constructing dual warangkas into the suit itself, he placed them on his back for easy access.

He leaned his back against one of the many thick stone pillars that kept the three levels above from crushing the lower level of the parking structure, and he slid down to a seated position. He placed the mask on the concrete floor next to him and sighed. The Face looked back at him. That grin with its fangs protruding from the lower jaw, the red eyes and the horns on either side of the crown. It was as if it was challenging him.

You do not have the fortitude for this endeavor. You do not have what it takes for what is coming, it seemed to say, and he looked away in response to this attack on his person.

Then there was a sound. The unmistakable noise of a car reverberated through the empty structure. He swung his head around the pillar, making sure most of his body remain hidden behind the safety of the manmade stone. Two round headlights cut through the sparsely lit area and headed for the center of the structure where they came to a halt. The engine cut out, and the lights faded as three men exited a Chrysler Imperial and headed to the front of it. They were all wearing trench coats and hats. It was hard to tell, but he was fairly confident that at least two of them were hiding machine guns, and the other man would be armed as well, he had no doubt.

His fingers were twitching; he was ready to pounce, but he had to bide his time. Then it came, the sign he was looking for; another vehicle cast its headlights through the gloom of reinforced concrete and painted outlines. It was larger than the Chrysler was - the sound bouncing off the walls told him so - and it headed towards the waiting party, only fifty feet from where he was hiding. He cracked his knuckles and twisted his head from side to side; he had limbered up for a good hour earlier, but the wait had stiffened him some, and he hoped it would not hinder what he needed his body to do in the coming moments.

As the truck swung around and stopped, facing the Chrysler, he grabbed the mask and pulled it over his head. He gently flattened it out over his scalp and tugged at the chin to make it sit comfortably, and to make sure it appeared flawless - like his second skin. He moved his jaw and the mouth of the face moved as his did, and he could see perfectly clearly through the eye sockets, heightened in fact. It was time. He gently patted his outside thighs for luck and bounded up the pillar to the rafters

CHAPTER TWO

Hammer killed the Chrysler's engine, and Peterson, Anderson and Camp climbed out. Anderson pulled a pack of smokes from deep inside his grey coat, and Camp mimicked the action, but instead producing a handful of chew. Peterson regarded them both and raised a critical eyebrow. With a thumb, he pushed the fedora from his forehead to take in the full view of the parking structure.

Hammer climbed out of the driver's seat and leaned on the hood trying to impress his elders by rolling his own cigarette. He fumbled.

"What the hell're you doing?" Anderson snarled at the young man, as his cigarette dangled from his lips. "You're getting most of the tobacco on the floor."

Hammer took off his flat cap and scratched his head. "My Pa always makes it look so easy," he replied, flustered. "But I can never get the hang of it."

Anderson held out his pack of Lucky Strikes and offered it to Hammer, who accepted it, pulled one out and lit it.

Camp patted the side of his coat, finding the hard surface of an automatic carbine under the fabric; Anderson was carrying a shotgun, while Peterson, the point man, always favored revolvers. The kid was probably carrying something as well. Camp didn't care. He was not fond of the little punk; just some goon Peterson had saved from the streets. Apparently, he was a former hockey player—and a failed one at that. Trying to make his fortune on the ice, he lacked the skills and spent more time in the penalty box than on his skates. At least, that was the word on the street. What was *the business* coming to when a kid could be picked off of the streets and welcomed with open arms? No questions asked. Camp spat on the ground with a snort.

Peterson plucked the pocket-watch from his vest. It was just about one a.m., and everything was going according to plan. He tapped his wing-tipped shoes against the stone floor and scrutinized his companions. "These late-night pickups will be the death of me." He ventured a smile in Anderson's direction. "We sure ain't as young as we used to be, are we, Rosy?"

Anderson shrugged his shoulders and lit another cigarette on the butt hanging from his thin lips. A wet splat echoed through the desolated building, and Camp wiped his mouth with the sleeve of his beige coat.

"So, when's the merch coming?" he asked when he noticed the others watching him.

"Well, if everything goes according to plan, and they don't get ambushed by the cops or any of our rivals, they should be here any minute," Peterson replied.

Before Camp could chide their tardiness—he'd rather be home with his wife and five young kids than standing in a dank parking garage waiting for some micks—he heard them approach. Anderson dropped his cigarette and stepped on it, placing a hand inside his coat while Hammer snapped to attention and scuttled to the passenger side of the car for cover. Peterson remained, with a calm that can only come from twenty years' experience in back-alley drop-offs and pickups. In the corner of his eye, he could have sworn he saw movement in the dim recesses of the garage but chalked it up to the regular jitters caused by clandestine, illegal activity.

A truck, resembling an old farm truck from the 1930s, stopped in front of them, its headlights illuminating their forms and casting ghostly shadows on the back wall. Peterson fingered the snub-nosed revolver holstered in the small of his back. The headlights might blind him, but if shit hit the fan, he was damn well going to take some of those bastards with him. The lights switched off, blinding the men once again, their eyes now unaccustomed to the darkness.

Three figures appeared as their sight returned to normal, two from the front and one leaping off the bed of the vehicle. They were all dressed in black slacks with suspenders over white dress shirts and caps on their heads. Peterson rolled his eyes and whistled at the walking clichés. The driver extended his right hand in greeting and scratched the red stubble on his chin with his left.

"Hi there, buddy," the man said in a low voice. Peterson nodded and gripped his outstretched appendage. "Name's Flanagan and those guys are Norwood and Connors." He threw a thumb toward his companions, who touched their caps to acknowledge the introduction.

Peterson returned the favor, using their assumed names. "Hello. Call me Baz, that's Rosy, Asa, and the guy behind the car we call Maury." Flanagan nodded at each of them in turn.

He pulled a chewed cigar from above his right ear, placed it between his teeth, and smiled. "Baz, huh?" The crow's feet around his eyes instantly aging him. "I've heard of you."

"Most people this side of the underworld have." Peterson smiled back, secretly hoping he was not revealing his own age. "You got the stuff?"

Flanagan nodded and gently waved the trio forward. He backed up with his eyes squarely on Peterson and moved toward the bed of the truck. Norwood and Connors climbed in the back, where a cloth tarp was concealing most of its contents. Flanagan snapped his fingers, and Norwood pulled back the cloth to expose wooden crates. Peterson eyed the boxes and then looked at Flanagan.

"You wanna check the contents?" Flanagan asked, producing a crowbar from beneath the tarp.

Peterson took it and handed it over to Camp, who jumped up to the crates. With some effort, he opened the top of the box closest to him. It let out a groan that reverberated through the building. Anderson tossed him an electric torch, and he dug amongst the straw hiding the contents of the carefully constructed container. He found what he was looking for, weighed it in his hand, and brought it up to his eye to assess it. Peterson whistled to catch Camp's attention. When he got it, he threw him a questioning shrug. Camp tossed the object back into the crate and gave a thumbs-up.

"Well it seems everything is in order," Peterson said to the Irishmen, this time offering his hand.

"Completely," Flanagan responded. "Everything's in exact order."

Peterson called Hammer and the two others over to help unload the crates; they had a truck of their own waiting on the second level. Once the truck bed was empty, the men congregated around the stack of wooden boxes, wiping the sweat from their brows with handkerchiefs. Anderson lit another cigarette.

Suddenly, a soft thud caught the men's attention. The truck dipped, and, in unison, they turned to it.

The murky light of the garage made it impossible to make out what they were seeing. Once their eyes were able to focus, they saw a shape that appeared to be a person in hues of red and blue stooped in the center of the bed. As the springs of the truck slowly stilled, the form rose to a standing position. Anderson froze as the figure, dressed in a red-and-blue bodysuit with a spiked belt, moved. Its face made his blood run cold. Crimson eyes, fangs and horns stared at them and, before he could get a closer look, the micks opened fire.

The creature somersaulted over them as bullets tore through the back of the vehicle. Camp and Peterson quickly turned around with weapons at the ready. The beast's eyes intensified with red fire that roared at them, briefly paralyzing them all. Flanagan and Peterson, grizzled vets, were the first to recover, but it was too late. In a flash of steel, Flanagan fell backward screaming as his severed right hand landed on the ground, still clutching a Smith & Wesson. The demon-faced creature slid across the floor and clipped Peterson's legs from beneath him with a swift kick, slamming him into the floor. The men left standing spun on their heels as the creature leapt to a crouching position. Two lightning-quick strikes later,

Norwood and Connors collapsed to the floor with nasty gashes on their torsos and faces. Blood soaked their crisp white shirts. Anderson could smell the pungent aroma of human waste as guts spilled on concrete alongside teeth and was that part of a tongue. Camp let a cry escape his lips and, with brown chew flying everywhere, he unleashed his automatic rifle in a vicious spray at the enemy. Anderson followed with his revolver, but the figure flipped around, avoiding every single bullet. It stepped off one of the pillars, spun in the air, and planted a boot on Anderson's forehead. It sent him flying a short distance through the air, and he landed hard on his back, knocking the wind out of him. Camp reloaded his rifle as Peterson stirred on the ground, and Hammer came running from behind the Chrysler, revolver raised and firing as he moved forward. The figure dropped to one knee and swung his weapon low, slicing Hammer's lower leg clean off, sending the appendage one way and the owner of it another. The smoke from the gunfire enveloped the figure as it rose and turned at the same time, revealing two wavy swords, one in each hand, blood dripping from the point of the one in his right. Peterson threw his revolver to the ground and came at it with a baseball bat that he grabbed from the bed of the truck. He swung at the head, but the figure parried with the left blade and let the right one separate Peterson's head from the rest of his body.

Without hesitation, Camp unleashed another barrage of bullets that tore through Peterson's body as it fell limply to the floor, but the figure was already gone. It landed behind the inattentive gunman and let sharpened steel pierce him through the back.

Anderson, still on the floor, flat on his stomach, fired his gun and struck the figure in the arm, only grazing it. He continued to pull the trigger, but without results, and soon he was out of bullets. The figure walked towards him, the eyes glowed at him, and it felt as if they were burning two pinholes through his skull.

There was a shriek and Anderson was no more.

CHAPTER THREE

It started, as it always did, with a shipwreck. This one occurred in Indonesia, off the coast of Bali, in fact. Jonathan Hill, who had been in the British Navy, was a confident swimmer and easily saved his wife and their infant son, and they crawled onto the beach drenched in salt water, covered in sand and into the arms of the Dutch rulers of the island. Luckily for the Hills, they were headed to Bali as Mr. Hill had been sent there as a cultural attaché, so once they were cleaned up and leant dry clothes they were presented to the ruler of the Dutch East Indies. They soon moved the family, which consisted of Jonathan, Patricia, and little Anthony, into one of the finer homes on the islands. Made from local wood, with a wraparound porch and a straw roof held up by intricately carved pillars, the house, situated on a grassy knoll, was shortly after their arrival dubbed Busut-Busut. Busut being Indonesian for Hill. Mrs. Hill would sit in a rocking chair on the veranda gazing at the sun reflecting in the meeting of the

Pacific and the Indian Ocean. It was a perfect existence for her; the climate, the culture, the native servants there at her disposal. She even loved the food, which was surprising because of her sensitive digestive system. It was a very different lifestyle than she was accustomed to, but she had become more comfortable with it following her marriage. She was of a lower class than her husband, who came from a long line of barristers and whose family was in great standing in London. Enjoying the kind of existence, she had only read about as a little girl. Watching the men and women of high society get in and out of their cars and into fancy restaurants or hotels while she and her sisters glumly sauntered home from trying to make extra money for their ever-growing family.

Mr. Hill spent most of his days in Batavia in close proximity to the Governor-General, assisting him in administration, but he saw his wife and son more than other government officials did. Overall, warmth, love and tropical adventure filled the first years of young Anthony's life.

* * *

Garfield Teague stepped out of his car and tried to straighten out his coat in the process. He had never understood why his wife kept insisting he had it pressed when it always creased as soon as he climbed into his vehicle. He removed his hat and ran a hand through his red hair, trying to make sure the part was in place - he had been very generous with the Brylcreem this morning to ensure his coiffure stay in position. He fished a silver case from inside his blue pinstriped suit jacket, but he thought better of it before producing a cigarette and so let it slide back into the recesses of fabric. He walked over to the parking structure on the corner of Main and seventh and halted by one of the three black and whites parked on the curb, blue lights flashing almost indistinctly in the morning sun. Teague gently placed the fedora on his head and followed it by stroking his neatly cropped beard as his hand slid into a pant pocket.

"Detective Teague!" A young officer called him over to the parking garage entrance.

"What have we got here, Officer Boden?" Teague asked as he approached, and he realized that he had taken out the cigarette case again.

"Well, it seems to be some kind of mob hit, sir." The young man eyed his notebook. "Lang was first on the scene and is still down there. All I know is that there is blood everywhere, casings all over the floor, and one survivor."

"Got it," Teague replied and headed through the glass door and down the stone steps, ignoring anything else the officer might have to say. His black patent leather shoes echoed in the stairwell and were slowly drowned out by chatter from the lower level. He toyed with the case and flipped it over in his hand, a nervous tick he had developed the same week his dying father had placed it in his palm. As he descended, he watched his hand turn it from the back with its fleur-de-lis pattern to the front with his father's initials: R.T.

Another beat cop opened the door for him when he reached the basement floor and gave him a quick two-finger salute, touching his digits to the brim of his cap. Teague did not return the gesture, maintaining his reputation as arrogant. Various lamps and floodlights illuminated the otherwise sparsely lit the lower level. In the center, stood two vehicles - a well-cared for Chrysler and a not-so-well-tended truck of unknown make. They faced each other, like two lovers about to share a kiss, and the symbolism made Teague miss his wife. The closer he got, the more sinister the scene before him became; officers and medical personnel surrounded the silent cars, both riddled with bullet holes, and six white sheets littered the floor. Stains of various shapes and sizes covered a large area, reminding him of one of those Jackson Pollock paintings he had seen in the paper once. He wasn't much of an art connoisseur, and most of what he had seen on field trips as a child had never tickled his fancy, but that painting, Cathedral they called it, had spoken to him. It forced him to think, like a crime or mystery that needed solving. He liked it, but the splatter across the grey concrete created a very different mystery.

"It's one hell of a scene, Teague." The voice woke him from his trance-like state. It was Detective Greg Glade, a rotund man with a nervous disposition who wore his brown beard and hair cropped to the same length, giving him an even rounder silhouette.

"Glade." Teague forced a smile. He had never been especially fond of the younger detective, whom he found trying - mainly due to his defeatist attitude. "Were you the first detective on the scene?"

"Yes, sir. It looks like we're working together on this one."

"Great." Teague turned to the rest of the scene instead and tried to survey the area.

"We've got six bodies laid out both here and there and that goes for the different parts of them as well." Glade snickered as he mentioned that tidbit. "Most likely a mob hit or a drop off gone awry. Maybe the buyer and seller couldn't agree on a price?"

"So, they took each other out?" Teague rounded the truck and inspected the crates. Bending down, he removed a bloodstained sheet from a body. He quickly rose and stepped back and dropped the fabric back on the headless shape. "Doesn't seem likely." He stifled his urge to vomit. "The crates being left here would maybe indicate that, but this man was decapitated, and unless you have found a sword, machete, an axe or a large kitchen knife here, something else is going on. Have you found such an item?"

Glade thumbed through his notebook. "Not that I can see."

"Well then, something sinister is going on here. I would assume that all these guys pissed off the wrong person and paid a high price for-"

"There is one survivor," Glade interrupted. "He's at St. Mary's, I guess."

"Right." Teague flipped his cigarette case over in his hand again. "Not much more to do here. You stay and spearhead the investigation on the bodies, and I'll head to the hospital."

* * *

Tony Hill stepped into the offices of WRJN News Radio Station at 11:30 a.m. He often thanked his lucky stars he had found a job that checked so many of his boxes: It was fun, challenging at times, allowed him to start later in the day, and became a vital piece in the puzzle he was trying to lay. He slung his coat across his right arm and removed his hat, quietly placing it on the coatrack, followed by his coat.

"Good day, Mr. Hill." The sweet voice of the leggy Lindsay Jones greeted him as he turned around. "Here is the sheet for the five o'clock broadcast. Big things happening today." Tony raised an eyebrow and grabbed the piece of paper. "A shooting downtown, several dead."

"Well, our listeners will get their money's worth today. Is there any possibility of getting a representative from the force into the studio for a word?"

"I don't know," Miss Jones replied. "I will get right on it, Mr. Hill." She hurried off at a quick pace, making sure he got an eye full as she did so.

Tony kept his eye on her for as long as he could until she rounded a corner and was out of sight. He glanced at the paper again and ran his fingers through his blond hair, making sure everything was in order.

"Hill!" A burly man in a tight-fitting beige suit and vest with a red and white tie askew stepped in front of him and slapped him on his arm. Tony tried not to wince as the ham hock of a hand hit the spot where the bullet winged him the previous night. Vic Linden was the station manager of WRJN and answered directly to the owner. His management style was often times described as rabid, and his conversation always came screaming with a side order of saliva. "I see they've handed you the five o'clock newssheet already. This is a big deal. Shit is hitting the fan. Mark my words; we will have a war on our hands - micks and scandihoovians."

"You think so, sir?" Hill replied while keeping his eyes on the sheet. Linden's visage would cause a nauseous reaction in anyone who stared at him too long. A face full of craters, a constant sheen of sweat, and a tie that was never tied properly because he was unable to fasten the top button of his shirt.

"Details are still coming in. We don't know exactly who has been killed, how many or why, but sources at the precinct say it's a bloodbath, and that can only mean one thing: the mob." Linden put a cigar in his mouth and tried to light it, but he couldn't get his Zippo to ignite. He looked at Hill and shrugged at him expectantly, but Tony shook his head to show he didn't carry a lighter.

"Anyway..." the station manager said in a frustrated tone. "You need to present this report with all the gravitas it requires. Dig deep, speculate, you know, that whole spiel."

"I have sent Miss Jones to inquire about the chief of police. To have him on the show."

"Excellent! We'll have them glued to their sets as if it were the President's State of the Union." Linden once again attempted to light his cigar, met with the same difficulties and then flung his Zippo into a nearby garbage can. "Make this good, Hill. I'm counting on you."

Tony waited for his boss to head down the corridor and then walked in the opposite direction towards his own office. Having the chief on the news would serve him two ways. One, it would be great for the ratings, improving numbers that would already be stellar for the show based on the content alone, and two, it would give him the answers he needed to pursue his next move. It was all going to fall into place.

CHAPTER FOUR

When young Anthony was four his mother fell ill. It wasn't unusual in those times for the western elite to come down with some form of tropical disease, more often than not fever, and the outcome was often uncertain. They might survive, but they might just as likely succumb to it. It began with a coughing fit one morning during breakfast. The night had been rough, tossing and turning in the humidity, wrapping around her form like a damp blanket. It was as if something had stuck in her throat - like food had lodged there and refused to go down or come up. She had appeared paler than her normal western visage at the breakfast table, with an oily complexion, swaying, as her eyelids seemed to be exceptionally heavy. Blood on the linen napkin in her hand confirmed that something was not quite right, and the staff called for Mr. Hill and the doctor.

They sent Mrs. Hill to bed and there she would remain for the remainder of her life, except for the odd venture out on her beloved porch when her declining strength allowed. Every doctor who visited to the islands reported to her side to give their opinions but to no avail. They could not figure it out, and she grew weaker and weaker as the days turned into weeks and the weeks into months. Finally, a year had passed without improvement. Mr. Hill stayed by her bedside as much as he could without neglecting his duties, and the Governor-general allowed it. Little Anthony, who had already been assigned a governess - a mild-mannered young local girl the family named Patrice since her true name was too difficult to pronounce - spent all his time away from his mother because his father could not bear to see the horror in his son's eyes every time he saw her. This was the reason for her powering through and walking, with the support from the family butler, to her rocking chair so she could watch her son play with the native kids and his beloved Patrice.

As time passed, the doctors failed, and the crimson stains on the sheets became more frequent and greater in size. The staff whispered in the hallways and service areas. They knew what it was and how it would end, and Patrice became more attentive of the young master, to make the imminent separation less traumatic. Anthony was oblivious to the goings-on in the house, only noticing that his mother was more absent than usual and his father taking her place. The spring morning Mrs. Hill did not wake up, and she was forever gone from his life, sent immense ripples through it.

* * *

Peter Swann was not your typical chief of police. He was tall and slight of frame, had a full head of tightly curled brown hair, wore a wispy mustache under a pronounced beak of a nose, and dressed only in various shades of brown. Added to this was the fact that he lived a clean life: no smoking, no drinking, he exercised regularly and was a vegetarian. A habit, he told Teague, he had picked up on a spiritual journey to the Far East, whatever that meant.

When he spoke to people, he never became agitated or raised his voice; instead, it more resembled an inner monologue that those he addressed were privy to than an actual conversation. He was the sort of man who let nothing get him down, and he always had a smile to share with those around him. It made him a joy to be around - for those on the force as well as the various city officials.

As Teague stepped into the station with his hat in hand, he was approached by the Chief who slowly sauntered over to him while scratching his chin and sporting a concerned look. Teague hung his coat on the rack but placed his hat back on his head and produced his notepad, preparing for the debriefing.

"Garfield, welcome back." He motioned for Teague to follow him and turned to walk towards his office, expecting the detective to fall in. "What have you got for me so far?"

"Not much, sir." Teague leafed through the papers. "Six bodies found, some cut and some in various forms of dismemberment - mostly a limb missing here or there. We have identified one of the victims, a man known as Baz Peterson. According to our records, he is an infamous, high-ranking figure in the Lehman crime family - or was that is. Seeing as how the Lehmans were eradicated a few years back, and of course, Mr. Peterson is now deceased."

"So, have the Lehmans returned and are maybe trying to regain their position in the city?" Swan pondered.

"Unclear. We have not managed to identify any of the other bodies. We can't tell if we are dealing with rival gangs fighting over goods or one gang being taken out by another. One that left no trace. The men were all sliced up like some butcher handling a side of beef, and that is unlike anything we've ever seen before."

"A gang wielding sharp instruments. The Yakuza? Here? But why?" Swan was now deep in his own head. "It doesn't make any sense that the Japanese would venture to this part of the country, but who else would use blades to attack a gang of men with firearms?"

"If I may, sir," Teague interjected. "The crates are en route to our storage facility on Spring, and once they have been opened, and the contents analyzed, we might have a better idea of what happened. But there is another detail."

"Is that so?" Swan replied and turned to look at Teague.

"There was a survivor. Medics rushed him to St. Mary's before I arrived at the scene. I tried to talk to him, but he was well guarded and has refused to speak to anyone but you, sir."

Swan raised an eyebrow and looked Teague over. His eyes fell on the cigarette case that had, for some reason, ended up in the detective's hands again.

The chief sighed and opened the door to his office. "You'd better step inside, Garfield," he said, entering his office. After Teague had passed him, he closed it and pulled the shade down over the window that bore his name. "Listen, Teague." Swan proceeded with more focus than he usually managed. "There is more to this case than there appears to be on the surface. The man at St. Mary's who refuses to talk to you is one of our own."

Teague raised an eyebrow in surprise.

"His name is Martin Lindquist, and he has been undercover for the past year. When the Lehmans went under, there was a void within the criminal underground, and we began to hear from the FBI that someone had stepped in to fill it.

Through our own clandestine investigation, we found that Baz Peterson and some of Lehmans' former cronies had jumped ship to this new organization, but we knew little more than that.

Lindquist was fresh out of the academy and had the necessary Scandinavian heritage to attract mobsters of a similar national background, so we decided to send him deep undercover before he even set foot on these premises. He was clever enough to infiltrate the group through Peterson, and he checked in with his contact a couple of times, but we were never given any meaty information."

"So, Lindquist is the key?" Teague scratched his beard.

"He may very well be. I will send word to him at the hospital to ensure that he talks to you." Swann sat down at his oak desk, moved a statuette depicting a meditating Buddha, and pulled out a piece of paper and a pen. "We best be quick. It may be that whoever eradicated the mobsters might come looking for him as a means to eliminate witnesses."

He began writing as the door to his office gently opened and the head of a young dark-haired girl with horn-rimmed glasses appeared in the doorway.

"Chief?" the head said.

"Yes, Hannah?" Swann replied while scribbling.

"A representative from WRJN is on the phone and wants to know if you can be a guest on the five o'clock news to answer questions regarding last night's killings?"

Swann looked at Hannah, then at Teague, and then at his paper. "Sure, tell them I'll be there."

He winked and smiled at her, then looked back at Garfield. "Hand this to the secretary at the front desk of St. Mary's and they'll give you free passage, and then show it to the two officers standing sentry outside the room. Once inside, call Lindquist by his real name, and then he will start singing like a canary."

"Will do, Chief." Teague grabbed the paper once Swan had finished writing.

* * *

The windows of the empire suite located on the top floor of The Racine Hotel were wide open, and a warm breeze had blown in from the lake. It caressed the face of Paul Geert and lightly played with his tangle of light brown hair stained with the occasional streak of white. He was still wearing his nightshirt, but he had managed to pull on a pair of grey pinstriped suit pants, and his suspenders were hanging lazily from the waist. He rarely rose before noon as a rule. A lifestyle filled with expensive drinks, lavish meals and women of questionable morals took its toll, on not only his ever-expanding waistline, but his routines as well. A young runner had knocked on his door at around eight a.m. - an act he did with some trepidation since rumors abounded that they had fished last man who had done so out of the river a few hours later - and informed him of the bodies in the parking structure.

The information had caused him to wake right up, but not to actually get up. The effects of the escapades of the previous night also came knocking, and it had taken several hours and three strong cups of black coffee before he was ready to put his feet on the walnut floorboards.

Now the fresh lake air and the sounds of traffic below him soothed his nerves, and he could begin to think more clearly. The hours Geert had spent awake in the king-sized bed, between the satin sheets and staring at the ceiling, caused him to reflect on the information he had received. It had made his head spin, more than the champagne and Cuba Libres. He could not quite wrap his head around what might have transpired down there in the concrete structure.

It was supposed to be a routine pick up, albeit with those Irish thugs from the other side of the tracks. They were nothing if not unpredictable, but from what the youngster had told him, the micks had bitten it too. If there was a third party, Geert, in the role as one of the main figures, in one of the main crime organizations of the city, would have heard whispered rumors of it. This had not happened, so he assumed that something else was in the works. What he did know was that, whatever the explanation, his boss was not pleased, and the thought of that made him perspire.

Geert wiped the beads of sweat from his brow and slipped out of the nightshirt and into a clean white daytime version - avoiding the top button due to the width of his neck. After pulling up the suspenders, he put on a red tie, hoping it would cover the open collar. It never did. Another knock indicated that his driver was waiting outside, and he quickly slipped on his jacket, hat and downed a now cold Cup of Joe.

The black Lincoln smoothly drove into traffic, and Geert fanned himself with his hat as he checked his pocket watch. It was close to one in the afternoon. Not great. The boss had not called on him, which was common practice, but Paul knew he expected him, since news traveled fast in the underworld, and an explanation was in order. This particular deal was his baby, and he had arranged for his best and most experienced man to spearhead the pickup. He had laid the groundwork, made all the calls, and planned every minute detail so that Peterson could easily step in and get the stuff.

His informants had told him that one of Peterson's guys had survived and was now being treated at St. Mary's. That was something he was going to have to deal with before the police, ones not on his payroll, got to him. Geert pulled out a small mirror from his breast pocket and examined his blood-shot eyes, his unkempt hair, his damp forehead and untrimmed beard. He looked more like the bums who lived under the Sixth Street Bridge than the second in command of a major crime network.

He had tried to present himself in a more favorable countenance, but the lifestyle that came with his position made Spartan living difficult. His family had originally emigrated from the Netherlands in the 1840s, following Father Van den Broek, and had settled in the Midwest. From being farmers, they had moved to the cities to work in factories and harbor towns until the depression came.

Geert knew all too well what it was to go hungry. His family was Catholic, and he had been one of ten siblings sharing a three-bedroom house, clothes and shoes. It was a miserable childhood and no matter how much his mother valued education; she would send the children out to make money any way they could.

When his father passed away - at least that is what they thought happened to him. He walked out one winter morning to shovel the walks of the people on Main Street and never returned - Paul was 16 years old, and as a middle child, he had a difficult time knowing where he fit in when it came to the grand scheme of the family. His older brother, Jan, introduced him to the Lehmans, and so began a life of crime. It came easily to the young man. He started out as a runner, and he soon found that he could provide for his mother and siblings. Now he shuddered when he thought of those days. It made him colder and hungrier, and he found that it was a chill and hunger that no amount of duvet covers, or food could satisfy.

The Lincoln swung into an empty parking lot placed outside a red brick building and parked underneath one of the big, thick glass windows that divided by lead mullions. He stepped out on the faded blacktop pocketed with sprouting plants and cracks from neglect since the twenties. Geert adjusted his jacket and snuck through the arched doorway. It took a moment for his eyes to adjust to the dim light of the defunct factory, but having been through the building on several occasions, he was well aware of its layout. Once he could see clearly, he had already reached the main factory floor - an area filled with debris, scattered obsolete machinery, and worn out conveyor belts. He scanned the place to look for activity but there was none. Instead, a noise came from the upper regions of the room. He spun around and raised his gaze to the balcony lining the upper echelon. In the south-west corner sat an office structure made from the same red brick as the outside. The solid walnut door open and in the light that shone from inside the office stood a slender figure looking down at him. Paul moved slowly across the floor, kicking up the dead leaves and papers littering his path until he came to stand right below the figure, straining his neck to see them properly.

"Mr. Geert. I was expecting you'd show up."

CHAPTER FIVE

The months and years following the passing of his mother were pivotal in Anthony's life. Initially, his father catered to his every need- a way for Mr. Hill to work through the pain of losing his wife. His towheaded son with the blue eyes, pale skin and sharp features was the spitting image of her, and by staying by his side, reading to him, and watching him as he slept, it made it seem as if she was still in his life.

After the first month had passed, Mr. Hill was forced to go back to work in the capital, and left Anthony in the care of a new governess, a young woman who had lost her own son two years previously. The young boy was melancholy most of the days, only showing emotions when his father left in the morning, crying and screaming, tugging at the man's pants legs in an effort to keep him at home, and in the evening when he returned.

After two weeks, Patrice returned to give Anthony a semblance of normalcy and it worked. She eased him into the transition of a new governess, and she even gave the woman a

Christian name: Charlotte. Charlotte and Anthony bonded with each other through their common denominator of loss - his mother and her child. They became each other's surrogate, and before Patrice knew it, the two strangers had formed a bond reminiscent of a mother and son.

During this entire process, Mr. Hill became increasingly absent. His days in the capital grew longer, some of it due to the demands of his office and some, in part, due to an unease he felt when gazing upon his child. He was beginning to heal after six months, but when he came home and the car approached the house, he could see Anthony sitting in his mother's rocking chair. For a mere second, he would swear it was his dead wife come back to life.

His heart would skip a beat, and his palms would get sweaty as he exited the vehicle, and then a wave of disappointment would wash over him, as his son would leap off the stairs and into his arms. The first time it happened he dropped him, his limbs refusing to raise up in the obligatory embrace. He had also begun feeling other, natural urges. His wife's sickness had made the marital bed reserved for care and little else. This had left the widower with a pent-up frustration that now began to rear its ugly head once the hole in his heart was becoming smaller.

The Governor-General and several members of staff, all of them close friends of Mr. Hill, were now urging him to remain in Batavia and attend the various illustrious parties thrown in the honor of assorted dignitaries from around the globe. Once he relented and attended one of the soirees, it hooked him. To unwind with other adults of the western caste was something he realized he had been craving. To have real conversations about real things and to laugh again completely altered his reality. Mr. Hill had never been a great drinker, taking the odd snifter of brandy at the end of the day, champagne on his wedding day or a whiskey and cigar whenever he entertained, but now the libations flowed, and he concluded that he quite enjoyed it. Another aspect he enjoyed were the local Balinese girls who would come around and offer their services to the men of the governing class. He had not paid much attention to them while his wife was still alive, but now, when his body ached for a human touch and the warm embrace of the supple skin of a woman, he could not ignore them. All too often, he would wake up in one of the guest rooms of the Governor-General's annex with a different girl, and he would feel the pang of guilt course through his veins. Nevertheless, the following evening he would repeat the pattern of drinking and womanizing, and his voracious appetite became legendary among the islanders.

As his father was sinking deeper and deeper into a spiral of debauchery and he saw less and less of him, young Anthony his governess introduced him to Balinese culture. Charlotte first brought him round to her small village and family after a year had passed, and their relationship strong. At first, her husband, a tall and menacing warrior, was skeptical, but once he saw how his wife and the white child had formed a close relationship, and how much she needed the child, he relented and welcomed Anthony into his

home.

Since he spoke no English and barely any Dutch he communicated with the boy in his native tongue, and the child replied, for Charlotte, who spoke poor English herself, had incorporated Bali in her speech early on in their relationship.

Anthony would stay with the couple and their tribe days on end without issue since his father was away more and more often, and he did not care about where his son was. Many a night, as the boy lay in the hand-carved cot they had made for their own child, they discussed how a parent could abandon their own flesh and blood for such lengthy periods.

The village elders came by and clucked their tongues at the attitudes of Westerners. And so it was that after a year had passed, Anthony Hill had lost both his biological mother and father and managed to replace them with an entirely new pair.

* * *

3...2...1.

This is your radio friend, AM 1400 WRJN! Welcome back to the news at five, with your hosts Tony Hill and Gabe Posen.

"Welcome back, dear listeners. My name is Tony Hill, and this is the five o'clock news" Tony's voice took on the familiar tone of the common radio host.

"And my name is Gabe Posen" Gabe was an expert in the art of seamless linking - much of it due to his twenty years in the business. "Our top stories tonight: Mayor Gothner addresses the city in regards to the constant road work in our city, and a preview of the game of the week as the Raiders look to capture their first title in BSFL. But first, this."

Tony jumped in. "A grisly scene was discovered this morning by city police at a parking structure downtown. An undisclosed number of men dead in the lower level of the structure in what police call a bloodbath of a proportion seldom seen in our peaceful town. Here to give you, our listeners, the latest inside information about what some speculate is related to organized crime is Chief of Police Peter Swan."

Tony swung his chair to the right of the mic stationed above the desk in front of him, allowing Chief Swan to push his chair closer. The cramped booth normally hosted the two regular news anchors - and then when weather and sports joined in, one had to hold one's breath so that the doors could even be closed. "Chief Swan, what can you tell our listeners about this horrible event?"

"Well, Tony," Chief Swan began in his very careful dialog. "To be quite honest, we are not at liberty to divulge any specific details of what has happened. This is in part because we just don't know everything yet. We have victims, and we have a scene reminiscent of one you might see in a horror show, but as to the why and how, we are still working on those aspects."

"Chief Swan, there have been rumors abound concerning the number of victims and their alleged alliances," Tony continued.

"Certainly."

"Our reporters on the street have heard numbers ranging from four to as many as twenty."

"Well, I can tell you that numbers ranging in the teens and upwards are highly exaggerated. What is important to point out is that, even though the incident is a gruesome one it is far from the scene the media wants to paint. If that were true we would have some form of mob war on our hands and that is just not the case. Moreover, we at the moment have a body count of six men."

Tony hesitated at that answer. He was sure that there had been seven armed men down there. Chief Swan's reply indicated that there was a survivor or Swan had forgotten a victim, but the chief of police was not the sort of man to forget details - not if the stories about him were correct.

He replayed the events of the previous night in his mind. The bullets flying, him dodging, bouncing off walls and ducking behind the truck. One, two, three men fell and then four, maybe five or six? He couldn't quite recall. It had all happened so fast, he was in the moment at the time, not thinking, just letting it happen.

His body began to travel back to that moment, and everything visualized itself in slow motion. Too late he realized that he had let a full minute of dead air fill the airwaves and Gabe jumped in to make the save. "And what of the rumors that the victims all belonged to local mob gangs?"

"That is an interesting aspect, Mr. Posen." The chief swung around, placing himself between the microphone and Tony so that he could face Gabe. "Several of the victims are known to the police from earlier crimes, which might not be a surprise seeing as how men in this line of work tend to end their days violently. What they were doing in the parking structure, downtown late at night and what precisely happened to them, as well as the why, is still a mystery to us."

Tony popped out of his fugue state as soon as Chief Swan began talking, and he quickly regained his composure. "There have been speculations, especially in the early edition of the Journal Times, that this might have been the Lehman family once again staking its claim on the city. Care to comment?"

"That is a distinct possibility, I guess, but nothing we have uncovered in the past year has pointed us in that direction."

"So, this might be some other crime family attempting to control the city? Maybe by taking out minor criminals in the area?"

"That is also very possible. This is nothing that I am comfortable commenting on at this time. We have yet to uncover if these criminals killed each other in some form of trade that might have gone south or if a third party murdered them. It is just too early to tell. We are looking at various scenarios and in the end, it is all very early in this investigation and wild speculations from the press doesn't help."

"So, for our listeners out there what can you say?" Tony pressed. "Should they stay indoors and avoid the downtown area or even to venture out at night?"

"Tony, Gabe, and the good folks out there in the ether." Chief Swan maneuvered his chair so that he sat squarely before the microphone attached to the desk. "You may trust that the police have the situation at hand. As we speak, investigators and homicide detectives are on the case and no stone left unturned in an effort to solve this. Our primary goals are to keep you safe in your beds at night, and to ensure that you may venture out on our streets without worry. It is also important to note that our fair city is nothing like Chicago or New York. It is true that there have been incidents in the past caused by organized gangs, but those days are in the past. This media attention is making it appear to be very different. There is absolutely no need to panic." The chief looked over at Tony and nodded.

"Well, thank you, Chief Swan. I am sure our audience will sleep easier tonight. Next on the five o'clock news hour, we will hear from the mayor, but first, a word from our sponsor. This is WRJN, your radio friend."

Teague turned the volume all the way down, shutting off the radio. He had just finished listening to Chief Swan saying nothing on the Five O'clock News, and he had little interest in hearing what the mayor had to say. He was quickly approaching St. Mary's anyway and needed to focus on parking his car, a task he always had trouble performing.

After taking ten minutes to get the car squarely in the parking space - it had to be perfect - he approached the grand building. It was a red brick structure, in that classical Danish industrial style, that looked as much like a school as it did a hospital. He walked through the doors, passing doctors and nurses on their way to and from work and even the odd patient, silently sauntering along the white walls. There was an officer standing in the foyer who threw him a glance, but Teague flashed his badge and the man tipped his hat and nodded at him to pass.

He stopped at the reception desk and asked the young woman seated there where he possibly could find Mr. Hammer, the name Chief Swan had given him, and she directed him to the fifth floor. Tipping his hat and managing a smile, he ventured down the hall, stopped at the elevators, waiting a few seconds before deciding to take the stairs. He was getting out of shape; his wife kept telling him as much.

Once he had reached the fifth floor, he realized his mistake. In truth, he had realized it after the first flight of stairs, but he had pressed on, and now he could feel the sweat drip down his spine, making his pants stick to his thighs. He had to stop and catch his breath at the top, almost leaning on the statue of the Virgin Mother stretching out her arms invitingly towards him as if she was saying, *Come, let me comfort you, my child.* He did not heed her.

The stark white walls of the narrow corridor lining the narrow corrido gave him a sterile sensation. With the overhead light tubes bathing the space an equally cold glow, everything appeared clinical and chilly. Every few feet hung a nondescript painting of some landscape or a black and white photograph of an ancient doctor. It did nothing to thaw the sensation Teague got upon listening to the echoing of his footsteps bouncing off the walls.

Past the corridor, he arrived at a large open area with a hexagonal high counter in the middle, like some form of command center. Several nurses were busy moving files, answering phones, and speaking with doctors. From the epicenter, several doors and corridors led to other parts of the floor, like spokes on a bicycle wheel.

He sauntered up to the desk, removed his hat, and placed it before him as he leaned up against the hard wood. A woman wearing her dark hair in a bun and her horn-rimmed glasses placed low on her nose met his gaze and gave him an inquisitive look.

"Detective Teague here to see a patient by the name of Hammer," he said and tried out his best smile.

The woman smiled back and then looked over Teague's shoulder and called out a name that he couldn't make out. No sooner, a burly officer stepped up beside him with his hands on his hips.

"What seems to be the problem, Esther?" He looked down on Teague from a height of near seven feet.

"This gentleman wants to see Mr. Hammer in room 506, and I thought I'd run it by you first, Bill." Her voice was chipper in the presence of the giant.

"My name is Detective Garfield Teague, Officer...Billy?" Teague cut in with an as authoritarian voice as was possible whilst staring into the barrel chest of the boy in blue. "And, yes, I am here to interview Mr. Hammer - the only survivor of the massacre downtown this morning. I believe he may have vital information,"

"Well, sir." Officer Billy mused ay his superior position. "I can't allow that. Strict orders from the chief of police himself. No one is to see Mr. Hammer."

"Well, Billy boy..." Teague took out the handwritten letter from Chief Swan and handed it to the officer. "I have here written permission from the chief that I am allowed access to the witness. So, we can stand here and debate it, or you can show me to room 506 and let me in."

The towering Billy glanced at the paper and then at the receptionist Esther. She clucked, he shrugged and motioned Teague to follow him, which he did after picking his hat off the desk. They walked around the reception area and headed down one of the sterile corridors. This particular one had a faulty fluorescent bulb and it flickered on and off as if it was speaking in Morse code. It strained Teague's eyes, and he placed his hat back on his head and pulled the brim down so that the flashing became no more than

reflections in the hardwood floor.

The corridor ended with a glass window overlooking Grand Avenue, and another police officer leaned up against the window holding a shotgun. He wondered if the officers knew what they had behind those doors. Was he anything else to them than a cut up thug or were they aware of his identity? At any rate, the chief was taking no chances, even if, at the moment, no one actually knew that Lindquist was still alive.

"Detective Teague here is green, Chuck" Officer Billy said to the man carrying the shotgun and was met with a smile and a nod. Then he turned and opened. "Through here, sir."

Officer Chuck was the same height as Officer Billy, but he was almost twice as broad across the shoulders - a linebacker to Billy's lean wide receiver.

The room was as stark white as the corridor and sparse in its interior decor. There was a dresser at one end of the room, a bed in the center of it against the wall, with a small table on the right side, and above it hung a painting of Wind Point Lighthouse on a summer's day. The room, dimly lit with the only light coming from a window facing the street outside, and it cast shadows from the blinds that hung in front of the glass.

"Martin Lindquist?" Teague inquired cautiously.

"Who's there?" the figure in the bed replied, mimicking the tone of the visitor. He moved his hand over to the table and turned on the lamp. The light shone on his pale face, deep-set eyes encircled by dark rings and greasy dark hair. "How did you get past the officers at the door? What have you done to them?"

Lindquist started squirming, trying his best to move from the confines of the sheets, but he kept tangling himself in the white fabric, trying to reach for something that could act as a weapon.

"Calm down, Officer Lindquist." Teague approached the bed in slow, measured steps and put his hands up, palms towards the nervous man. "My name is Garfield Teague. I am a detective with Homicide. I Chief Swan gave me permission to speak with you. I know you worked as an undercover cop, and I want to talk to you in that capacity." Lindquist settled down and cautiously scooted himself to a seated position, raising a suspicious eyebrow and biting his lower lip.

"How can I be sure that you are who you say you are and that you haven't come to take me out?"

"Well, I guess that is difficult to say, but I have here a handwritten note from the chief with his seal on it, if it would calm you down?" Teague flung the paper, now badly crumpled, onto the foot end of the bed. Lindquist, with some difficulty, leaned forward, grabbed it and looked it over. Once he had done so, he placed it on the table and appeared to relax.

"One can never be too cautious," he said with a sigh of relief. "Detective Teague, was it? Why don't you pull up a chair, sir?" Lindquist pointed to a shiny metal stool that stood off to one side, and Teague grabbed it and sat by his side.

"How are you doing, kid?" He changed his tone now that most of the irritation was out of the way, and he could do his job. "I wanted to speak to you this morning, but I was denied that privilege."

"I've definitely been better, sir." Lindquist smiled. "I narrowly escaped being shipped off to the Pacific, and then this happens. Injured at home instead of dying on some Godforsaken beach is a blessing in itself, I guess."

The man lying there seemed to be in his mid-twenties. He must have escaped the draft with more than a narrow margin, Teague thought, but he did not mention it. The war had taken its toll on him, just like it had on many others, and he disliked even thinking about it. The nights haunted him enough.

"So, can you tell me what happened this morning, Martin?" He moved on to the questioning, instead, to quieten his mind.

"It started close to a year ago, sir," Lindquist began. "I had been appointed by some form of task force - a combination of the Federal Bureau, the Police Department here, and the Sheriff's office. There had been rumors of groups of gangs trying to move in on the city in the wake of the Lehmans' disintegration."

"I see." Teague had brought out a notepad and was jotting down words for his own use. "Why you?"

"I had just recently graduated from the academy. I was a late bloomer academically, and being from Michigan, they knew I was an unknown in the area. So, the perfect man for the job: Midwestern, unknown and of northern European descent. My family is from Denmark."

"So, they moved you here, and you were just picked up by a criminal syndicate?"

"Pretty much. I started hanging out in seedy bars on the east
side, and I made myself available when jobs needed doing. You'd be amazed how much work the bar owners have for an eager young man. After a couple of months, I was approached by one of the regulars in one of the bars I frequented, Henry Peterson-"

"Commonly known as Baz Peterson, one of the Lehmans' stooges," Teague interjected.

"Right. He heard that I was looking for work and easy money, and I had questionable morals. He was in need of a driver for some runs."

"That's it?"

"He took a shine to me for some reason. I did have to do some dirty work for him, things I would rather not talk about, but it was for the greater good as I saw it. Soon I was allowed to sit in on meetings he had with his boys and join him on more advanced jobs."

"So, Peterson was the head of the entire operation?"

"Not at all. He was some lower-tiered boss. He was in charge of finding men to do various tasks. He reported to some big fellow who they never mentioned by name."

"Was he the leader, then?"

"I don't think so. It seemed as if that guy took orders from someone else. I never heard a name there either. The only thing I ever heard was The Black Diamond, but that was in reference to... I don't know. Maybe I would have if last night hadn't happened."

"Let's talk about that. What did happen last night?"

"Baz came to me for a routine pick up, of drugs I'm thinking. I was really only informed about these things after the fact. We were trading with the micks - I think they referred to themselves as the Lonergans - anyway, one of the newer criminal families in the area. This was going to be the first time we did a deal with them, so we were supposed to be extra cautious. Baz brought some of his top guys, men with loads of experience, so that made four of us all told."

"And then something went wrong during the drop-off, I gather?" Teague scratched his head with the pen to show some kind of concern.

"Yes, but not from the Irish. They came with their own boys, probably just as worried about the unknown factor we presented. No, there was something else there."

"What do you mean something else?"

Lindquist's voice had begun to quiver, and it fascinated. Teague.

"We arrived first, and then they came with their truck. Everything was running smoothly or was going to I should say. Just as Baz was going to inspect the crates, a thing was there, standing on the bed of their truck."

"A thing? Like a creature?" Teague let out a scoff.

"I don't know." Lindquist started shaking as he tried to recall the morning's events. "It must have been a man, what else would it have been? He was dressed in a red and dark-blue skintight costume in some strange pattern, and he carried two strange looking, almost wavy, swords. It was the face. The awful face of the thing that was the most horrifying. That is what will keep me from sleeping for many nights to come. That face almost makes me wish that I'd be lying on some beach in the Pacific cut down by the Japs."

Teague put his hand on Lindquist's to try to calm him down, but the young man recoiled instead. "There, there." He tried to act empathetic, but he felt as if he failed. "I am going to need you to attempt some kind of a description."

"I think I only saw it clearly for a minute or so. Gosh, the whole thing was over in a couple of minutes; he moved so fast. The face was also red and blue with some horrible bulging eyes that peered at you with a horrible crimson glow. Like it peered into your soul. It had a high brow, without eyebrows. In fact, the head was completely bald, and fangs stuck out of the mouth and horns stuck out on either side above pointed ears."

"And it, or he, killed all of them? Are you telling me that all those thugs with guns and experience never managed to hit him once?"

"He moved so fast. Leapt over our heads, ducked our shots, and came so close that he could cut us down easily. We didn't stand a chance. I came at him, and he just ducked and took my leg clean off. I don't know if he thought I was going to bleed out, which, thank God, I didn't. He let me live. I don't know why. In truth, I think I passed out after he cut my leg off."

Teague looked in his notepad. He tried to draw Lindquist's description while he listened, but the horrid image he now had before him was too unbelievable to be real - although that could come down to his drawing abilities.

"So, you want me to believe that a monster - or rather a man dressed as some form of demon - attacked and killed all the men down there with you?"

"That is what I recall, sir," Lindquist answered with complete sincerity. "I know what it must sound like, but it's all I know. I haven't even been able to get to the bottom of the criminal organizations in the city either, and that is going to bother me just as much. Now, I only have one good leg, and my career as a cop is over. I'm going to have to sit behind a desk for the rest of my life."

Teague leaned back, realizing just in time that he was sitting on a stool when a nurse came through the door.

"I am sorry, sir, it is time for the patient to take his medicine and then to meet the doctor." She was very polite, and Teague had no reason to argue. He rose and took Lindquist by the hand.

"Thank you for your cooperation, bud." He winked at him. "It will probably help a great deal in our investigation. Feel free to contact me at the station if you remember anything different."

"Will do." Lindquist smiled and winked back.

Teague put his notepad in his inside pocket and placed his hat back on his head. It was getting late, and his wife would be wondering where he had gotten to. He had a feeling that there would be several late days ahead of him, and with that, quite a few arguments about that fact.

CHAPTER SIX

Time passed on the island, and young Anthony became in need of a tutor. His father realized this when the governor-general's wife one day inquired about how his son's studies were coming along. That day, Mr. Hill hurried home to find his son sitting on the porch with his governess, who was teaching him about the folklore of Bali. It didn't bother him - in his alcohol-addled mind, any education was a good education - but a few days later, a Mr. Mahr was standing on the porch dressed all in black with a silver-handled cane in his hands, a stern bespectacled look on his face. He had come over from Batavia where he had been teaching the society women English. Mr. Hill offered him a substantial sum. Not only to educate Anthony, but also to fill in the blanks created from years of academic neglect.

Mr. Mahr brought a semblance of order and structure to the young boy's life and a male role model that complimented what he received from Charlotte's husband. An intellectual piece of the puzzle to add to the physical ones already given him. Despite his hard exterior, the old tutor took a shine to the boy. Maybe it was his advancing age and the sense of nostalgia that came with it, or the fact that he had spent too much time with people set in their ways and unwilling to change their point of view that was the cause of it. During his time as a headmaster at a boarding school his affinity for the switch, but he was as sweet as honey to Anthony and often referred to him as 'my boy'.

Most weekday mornings Anthony would stay indoors learning his letter and numbers, this due to the fact that Mr. Mahr, had a weak constitution and was particularly sensitive to the humidity of the Indonesian mornings. After lunch, though, they would venture outside, wander the island, and learn from each other. The tutor would point out trees, flowers or animals and give both their English and Latin names and Anthony would give the Balinese version he had picked up. They would converse about science, inasmuch as the young boy could comprehend it, or the folklore of the region. Sometimes Mr. Mahr, being a rational man, would scoff at the naïve beliefs, yet other times he would halt, look up at the sky or crouch down, and consider a flower and give the idea its rightful time to marinate in his mind.

In the evenings, Anthony went to the governess as Mr. Mahr needed time to study the curriculum and grade whatever exams his pupil had handed in. He claimed the rocking chair on the porch and would sit there and soak in the island atmosphere with a good book, and the spirit of the late Mrs. Hill would wash over him, she would place her hands on his shoulders and gently whisper inaudible words in his ear and he would smile although he did not know why.

Anthony spent his time with Charlotte in the wild or in her village playing with the local children, speaking to them in their tongue, and during the weekends, he would even spend the night.

The days did not only entail roughhousing with native islanders, Charlotte's husband, the seasoned warrior who had traveled the Indonesian islands, also taught the boy the art of unarmed combat - feeling satisfied that his knowledge was being passed down. At night, he would go to bed in his hut with a grin on his face secure in the fact that he was passing his family legacy on to someone. Even if it was not his biological son, Anthony had become his adoptive one.

* * *

Tony slipped out of his suit jacket and placed it carefully on the bed. He walked over to the window with its view of both Seventh and College, the intersection where the two streets met. The sun was still setting over the city, and the lights had flickered on only moments prior. He pulled at the tie around his neck, and it easily loosened so he could slip it over his head. It messed up his perfectly curated hair, but it didn't matter much now. He moved to his closet and carefully hung his clothes on their appropriate hangers.

The apartment was a two-room affair, perfect for a bachelor.

such as him. In fact, the entire complex housed single young men, and the odd widower. It was central enough for his needs, close to the radio station, and the goings-on downtown.

It was his second residence since moving to the city. The YMCA was not private enough - even though the training facilities were a boon. He still exercised there - swimming, gymnastics and weightlifting - but coming and going at all hours of the night would have led to far too many questions, and he wanted to avoid that.

In his undergarments, he entered the closet to dig out the trunk that lay at the back of it. To most who saw the object, it appeared to be your garden-variety travel trunk; something an ancestor might have brought on one of the great ships crossing the Atlantic. In a way, it was true. The trunk had a small, yellowed note glued to the inside of the lid that read:

Property of James Mahr
Essex, United Kingdom
1929

It had contained the life belongings of his old tutor and he had inherited it, as well as its contents, when the ancient educator had passed away in 1944. He always stored the trunk as far back in the closet as possible, and he covered it in old blankets and pillows. If anyone, in an unlikely scenario, were to rifle through his apartment, the indistinct pile of laundry might go ignored.

He carefully opened the lid to expose the contents to the light of his apartment. Tony had always felt like the trunk, the property of his intellectual keeper, guarded the tools he had received from his moral tutor.

There was a full bodysuit in red and blue, made from a stretchy material with a near silk-like quality. He had managed to find an old tailor in the Chinatown district of Chicago who had been willing to make the outfit to his specific needs. It had resulted in three suits that she made by hand for a substantial sum that also included her silence in the matter.

Tony returned a year later to find that she had passed away, leaving her family a sizable inheritance. They subsequently spent the money on the opening of a restaurant outside the neighborhood. Beneath the suit lay a pair of gloves and a set of boots matching the color scheme of the rest of the outfit. There was also The Face - the fanged and horned mask. It lay between the hilts of several blades - twin kalis, the swords and two matching kris, the daggers – placed in their sheaths, or warangkas, and the mask seemed to stare at him with its red glowing eyes, daring him to pick it up. He did so, gingerly, and placed it on an end table next to his bed before slipping into the suit.

The stretchy material eliminated the need for a zipper, and he glided into the neck hole and pulled it upward. After he had put on the boots and gloves, he slung a kalis over his shoulder, so it hung across his back, and stuck a kris in his belt, leaving The Face where it was. He turned off the lights in the room and walked over to the window, staring out over the downtown area.

It was closing in on eight p.m. and the police station closed for most of the duties by now. At most, a skeleton crew would be working there. He had no time to rest; he needed to begin the investigation in earnest. He wanted to know what was in those crates that were on the truck and where they came from. To find the underlying cause of the burgeoning drug trade in the city, he needed to move quickly before the police picked up the scent. He couldn't stall anymore and needed to move out. He went over to the end table, picked up The Face, and pulled it down over his head. With a couple of tugs at it, he moved it into place. He flung the window open by moving it upward, and then he deftly swung his legs over the windowsill and out into the night.

* * *

The black Lincoln was still running as it stood there, the headlights cutting through the darkness of the unlit parking lot, illuminating the gravel and climbing up the red brick wall of the factory.

Geert was sitting in the front seat on the passenger side and was trying to monitor his breathing, which came out in wheezy spurts through his nose. He found it embarrassing and tried to hide it from his chauffeur by holding it, but the strain was too much effort, and he often erupted in a coughing fit. Whenever this would occur, the driver would react as if woken from some form of slumber. Once realizing what was happening, he would eye the boss and then return to gazing out the side window, quietly puffing on a

cigar.

A figure stepped out into the glow of the headlights, dressed in what appeared to be a duster and hat, smoking a cigarette of his own. It cast a long shadow against the wall creating the illusion of two persons - one smaller and then a bigger counterpart. The driver opened his door and stepped around the Lincoln to open one of the doors to the back seat. The figure slid into the back, pulled down the brim of his hat to hide his forehead, and pulled a scarf over his nose to hide the lower part of his face. It was mostly for show since Geert

53

knew exactly who the man was, but since he was of a paranoid caste himself, he understood the idea. He decided not to engage the man's face in the rear-view mirror and kept his eyes on the illuminated brick wall that the driver was leaning against now, smoking his cigar.

"So, what have you got for me?" Geert asked the man.

"Not much at the moment, Mr. Geert." The man was obviously trying to mask his voice by keeping it lower and raspier than it was. "I have tried to stay in the loop, but for some reason, the lead investigator is playing this one close to his chest."

"Can you tell me anything, or is my investment in you an enormous waste of my dollars?"

"Not at all, sir." There was a nervous tinge to the voice now as if it was on the verge of cracking. "I can tell you what we are working on and what is believed."

"Then do so; my time is valuable." It wasn't. He only had a soiree to attend back at the hotel.

"What the others have revealed so far is that it appears to have been someone else who whacked the micks and our boys. Someone cut them up good."

"Cut them up?"

"You know, knifed them, or something like that. Whatever crew did this; they wanted it to be messy and used some form of blade."

"And the goods?" Geert temporarily ignored the information.

"They're being kept safe in the police impound lot, awaiting investigation."

"Is there anything on that truck or in those crates that might lead to us?"

"Not that I'm aware, but I'd have to check it out to be sure."

"I suggest you get on that immediately then. Were there any survivors at all?" It was getting chilly out there now Geert observed as the driver slipped on a pair of fingerless gloves and rubbed his arms. "Any of our boys make it out?"

"None of the Irish guys survived, but from what I have gathered, there was one who avoided being killed, but I have no clue who it was."

Geert's heart sank. He had experienced people dying, even seen it with his own eyes, When he was younger, he had even murdered some, especially during the end days of the Lehman gang, but the prospect of his long-time friend Baz Peterson biting it had hit him hard. Now there might be an outside chance that he had survived. "Maybe Baz?" he said with the shiver of anticipation in his voice.

"Could be, I guess," the man in the back seat replied. "If anyone could come out of that massacre it would be him."

"I need you to find out. Also, check out those crates so that we come out clean. The contents we'll have to replace some way, but we need to cover our asses in this."

"Got it, Mr. Geert, sir," the man said.

"Report back to me as soon as you have any more information; time is of the essence. Now get out!" Geert waved his hand to signal that the meeting was over, and then he waved at the driver to approach. The rear door opened, the man vanished into the cold night air, and then the driver positioned himself next to him again.

"Where to, boss?" he asked as he flung the cigar out the window.

"We need to head to the West side," he said through gritted teeth.

"What about your thing back at the hotel?" The sound of astonishment in the driver's voice was palpable.

"I don't have time for that, at the moment. I need to find some guys, and then I need to talk to The Black Diamond."

"Right you are." The driver shifted gears and drove west.

* * *

The police impound lot was surrounded by a tall chain-link fence, and around the top, rusty barbed wire snaked around to deter anyone who might think to enter. It was a large gravel yard with cars lined up in neat rows in the center, a large garage-like structure made from sheet metal stood off to one side, and on the opposite end, where the gates were, stood a smaller wooden building that served as the guardhouse.

The glow of electric lights shone from the single window that faced the entrance, signaling that the guard on duty was in. Tied up to one of the posts that held up the roof above a low porch were two vicious-looking German shepherds, one pacing and the other sleeping with one eye open.

Tony was crouched low atop the roof of one of the nearby buildings surrounding the lot. He surveyed the scene while he was pulling at his gloves to make sure they were snug on his hands. The building he was on was too high up from the garage to be able to leap from, and the sheet metal would most likely make too much noise for such a maneuver. He needed to use another method of entry. He crawled over to the edge of the roof and swung over it, hanging from his fingers. He hugged the brick wall, searched for a foothold, and he eventually found it - a window ledge. He let go of the roof and found his balance. He glanced behind to find that the ground was still too far off, and he gazed below him. There was another window there and, by all accounts, it appeared as if no one was home or at least not in the room it belonged to.

He let his feet come off the sill and fell toward the ground, catching himself on the top part of the window frame below. Now his entire body was covering the window, and he dared a look inside. It was a perfectly normal kitchen with a table placed before the window, a sink, and a white refrigerator. Though the lights were off in the room itself, he could see a faint glow through a doorway and shadows interrupted it from time to time.

He peered over his shoulder again and then bounced off the windowsill, sailing through the air, and flipping over so that his head was facing downward. As he did so, the guard dog, still awake, turned its ears towards him and began to bark. Tony pulled a vial out of his spiked belt and released it from his grip. It shattered a few feet from the animal's paws. The dog went silent, tilted its head to the side, and proceeded to whine.

The vial contained a tincture of Balinese flowers so pungent to animals that it masked his scent while also confusing them. He landed, in a crouching position, with his hands to the ground. The other dog, the one that had been sound asleep, startled by his friend's barking began a whole tirade of his own.

The door to the guardhouse opened and a middle-aged police officer walked out on the porch. He pierced the darkness with his flashlight; first, the beam shone around the lot and then on the dogs, who were both pacing in a worried manner. He sighed while unhooking them both and walked out into the lot. It was uncommon that people tried to break in or trespass. The few times it had happened, it had been young whippersnappers daring each other to run through the area without getting caught. Whatever it was it was definitely a person, since he had trained the dogs to ignore cats, squirrels or raccoons.

He unsnapped his holster - just to be on the safe side - and raised his hand again to scan the cars as he passed them. The dogs sniffed around wildly, but they seemed unable to pick anything up. Instead, they whined and tried to rub their noses against the gravel or pawed at the snouts.

Tony was hiding only a car's width from the officer, behind a blue vehicle. He controlled his breathing as the officer shone the flashlight through the windshields and down the rows. He silently moved around so that he ended up behind the man, carefully maneuvering so as not to allow the gravel to grate against each other. He wanted to avoid injuring the officer, but he realized he might have to if it came down to it.

The officer moved towards the garage where Tony also needed to go. From above, the structure had appeared solid, but down on the ground, he could see that one of the sides was completely open, making for easy access. When the man reached the building, he let the dogs run the length of the chains and then popped his head inside the darkness. As he did so, Tony quickly ran down the side of the garage and flattened himself against the sheet metal.

Unfortunately, he was now hiding in the only area that was open since the opposite side lined up against the fence. If the officer turned the corner, it was over, and as he pondered this, he saw the light approach. This was why detailed preparation by way of scouting was so important, he realized. Before he could even consider his next move, his legs had bent and then straightened out to send him up to the roof where he clung to the edge as the man rounded the corner. He raised his legs so that they were perpendicular to his hands to avoid his feet touching the guard. Once he had passed, Tony straightened out and by hand over hand movement got himself around the same corner. Dropping down in front of the entrance, he then walked inside.

The streetlights from around the lot had lit it enough for him to see what he was doing but not much more. Here, surrounded by three walls and a roof, it was nearly pitch-black. He knew that if he produced his own flashlight the officer would see it all too well, so it forced him to move around as best he could. What little light escaped into the garage gave him enough illumination to make out the shapes of vehicles placed therein.

There were cars, buses, motorcycles and even boats, and there - against the far wall - was the truck, loaded with crates, wrapped in yellow police tape.

The floor here was concrete, and he could more easily move in silence, so he swiftly headed for his goal and swung himself up on the bed, trying not to make the springs of the truck move at all. He investigated the crates, made from unfinished pine and could see that a few were already open. The police had started their investigation, just as he knew they would.

In the distance, he heard the door to the guardhouse close. Now he could safely produce his light and more easily see which crates had been opened and where. He took out his kris, the wavy dagger that looked like a smaller version of his kalis and slid it under a lid. It came off easily. He just moved it a bit out of the way, so that he had enough room to feel around in the torchlight.

The pine box contained packages made from brown paper secured with twine. He picked one up and moved it around, shook it and weighed it, but he needed to satisfy his suspicions. He cut into the brown wrapping with the kris and once he withdrew it, white powder coated the blade. He plucked a small leather pouch from his belt, and with one hand, he opened it and produced an envelope. Gently, he tapped the powder off the blade and let it fall between the papers. Sealing it up, he placed it back in the pouch.

After having put the lid back on, it was time to analyze the crates. He moved in close to the pine and held the flashlight near. At first glance, it looked as if the wood was completely unmarked, but when he let the light shine from an angle, some form of stamp was visible. He touched it with his gloved hand and felt ridges, but he had a hard time making out what it was.

From his pouch, he grabbed a pencil and began rubbing the lead against the mark. Slowly an image began to emerge - it was a skull placed inside a diamond. The kind of symbol one might find in a deck of cards. A quick once over some of the nearest crates revealed a similar mark in the same spot, the lower left-hand corner. It was what he had been looking for.

Spinning around so that he faced the exit, it was once again time to head into the night; he had more work to do and some dogs to avoid.

The Lincoln traveled down Washington, and the yellow glow of the streetlights reflected in the window as Geert stared at them. He watched the buildings pass by and slowly turn from homes to storefronts. The car drove across Ohio before it stopped in front of a building made from the same red brick so common in the city. It was an Italian restaurant with a bright neon sign proclaiming it to be 'The Pizza King'.

The western part of the city was home to the Danes, who had emigrated there between 1870 and 1950. While most of the other ethnic groups had declined that population had skyrocketed.

Since the Scandinavians, as a rule, are not known for their cooking, most of the eateries were run by Greeks or Italians. The driver opened the door and helped his boss out by giving him a hand and supporting his weight so that he wouldn't trip. In an ungrateful gesture, he yanked his forearm out the hands of the driver, straightened out his jacket over his dumpy frame, and glared at the man. He indicated that the driver should wait by the car, and then he opened the glass doors to enter.

The interior was dark - mostly due to the dark wood paneling throughout - but not gloomy, thanks to the white walls above it. The counter and the booths constructed from the same brown wood, and the seats covered in brown faux leather. A man in his mid-thirties with dark, greasy hair slicked back and a wispy mustache under a pronounced nose, stood at the counter arranging baking sheets. It was near closing time and he seemed eager to close up shop. He gave Geert an annoyed stare when he saw him, but he gave a polite nod and a halfhearted smile.

"What'll it be, sir?" He asked in a monotone voice, with a hint of an Italian accent.

"Just a coffee, Joe. I need to speak to my associates over there." Geert tilted his head in the direction of a booth occupied by three dapper men in pinstriped suits. He would have much rather have ordered a brandy old-fashioned to compensate for not being able to go back home, but the Protestant church ladies who had made this neighborhood their home had forbidden the distribution of alcohol on the west side, to the ire of the restaurateurs of the area.

Joe gave a slight nod and sighed as he bent down to fetch a cup and saucer from beneath the counter. Geert walked over to the men in the booth, who were the only patrons in the place.

"Gentlemen," he said. "I thought I might find you here." He sat down in the only seat that was open.

Jensen, Charles and Thorne always dressed the same, even if they were not triplets. In fact, they lived on opposite sides of the city, but they somehow managed to coordinate their outfits perfectly. Today, they wore, in addition to the black pinstriped suits, white shirts and black ties. One could really only tell them apart by their facial hair. Jensen was clean-shaven, Thorne wore a mustache, and Charles had a full beard, but they were all redheads, most likely due to their Danish heritage Geert philosophized.

"What can we do for you, Mr. Geert?" Thorne asked as he sipped a cup of coffee of his own. The trio were freelancers and not directly under his organization. Therefore, they often skipped the traditional "boss" moniker others used.

"Well, boys." Geert paused as Joe placed his coffee in front of him. "I need you to investigate something for me."

"All right, I guess we can squeeze you into our busy schedule." Jensen snorted and lit a thin cigarette. "Your money is always welcome here. What do you need?"

"You have no doubt heard of the incident downtown that took place this morning?" The men nodded. "And as you might have guessed, it involved my organization and the Lonergans. We don't really know who is to blame yet, but we are pretty sure it wasn't the Irish, and it sure as hell wasn't us."

"Okay, so you want us to find out who done it?" Charles chimed in. "We can do that. A bit of detecting sounds easy enough."

"Not really." Geert cautiously blew on the hot liquid in the cup, but then set it down again before tasting it. "While most of the guys involved perished in the garage, there appears to have been one survivor. One of our men. He most likely holds the answer to the question of, as you so eloquently put it, who done it. I need you to find out that person's identity so that we, in turn, can identify the guilty party."

"All right." Thorn felt his face; a touch of stubble was beginning to form on his chin. "So, you want us to investigate so that it can't be traced back to The Black Diamond or you, yourself. The easiest way to do so is naturally by eliminating the problem."

"You could put it that way," Geert was beginning to sweat. They had seen through his not-so-clandestine plan. "You would be paid handsomely, of course."

"Of course." Jensen smiled. "And if we can get the survivor to spill his guts about what happened?"

Geert knew exactly what he was alluding to. For their ability to interrogate witnesses, the trio had become quite famous. He nodded slowly.

"Let us confer, my friends," Thorne said to the other two, apparently taking the lead on this deal. "If you could excuse us."

Geert rose, downed the coffee in one gulp, and headed to the counter to settle the bill. "I'll pay for the gentlemen as well, Joe," he said and Joe nodded and gave him the total. Geert handed him a five-dollar bill, which was more than enough, and Joe smiled and thanked him. Once he turned back to the trio, they were standing in a row before him, all carrying black hats with white bands.

"We'll do it," Jensen said as he leaned past Geert and stubbed out his cigarette in an ashtray placed on the counter. "It's going to cost you twice the standard fee." It was steep, yet still a good price for keeping his name out of it.

"Agreed," Geert said and put forth his hand, the men each shook it in turn.

"It's always a pleasure doing business with The Black Diamond and yourself," Thorne said. "I hope this isn't as big a risk as we all think it might be. It would be sad if our relationship would have to end due to one of us dying."

Geert tried to act unconcerned, but he could feel beads of sweat forming on his upper lip. The men left in single file.

"We'll be in touch," Thorne said before placing his hat on

his head and exiting.

CHAPTER SEVEN

When Anthony had turned six, his adoptive father, Wayan, came to the hut one Saturday evening carrying a gift. He carefully tiptoed into the common area where they had gathered around the open fire for dinner, and he gently placed an oblong object on the floor before the young child's feet. Wrapped in red and blue fabric, intricately sewn together like a very detailed quilt. As Anthony tilted his head and considered the present, the warrior told him to unwrap it. With care, he did so and revealed four scabbards lying within, two smaller and two larger. With big eyes, he watched as Wayan unsheathed the wavy blades. Wonder filled him when he saw how the light from the fire glinted in the steel and cast golden reflections in wonderful patterns on the walls. The weapons were the *kris* - a traditional dagger of the region, originally from Java - and the larger one was a *kalis* - a double-edged sword from the Philippines.

Being the infamous warrior that he was, Wayan had traveled and battled all over the islands as a young man, and through this, he had amassed quite the collection of weaponry. He informed Anthony that it was time for the next step in his physical education. Whatever concerns Charlotte might have voiced went unheeded.

The decision was made to, initially, keep the training with the blades on weekends and keep them in the hut so that the servants at the house would not see them and report to Mr. Hill. It was difficult for Anthony to keep the training out of his mind once he returned to his home and the tutelage of Mr. Mahr. During the first week, he found himself drifting off in class, dreaming about parries and strikes, twists, turns and evasions as well as gutting the imaginary demons of Balinese folklore.

His teacher would stare at the boy when he gazed off through the window in the direction of the village. He knew then that the boy was more Balinese than he would ever be Western and that it was fine. He, of course, knew nothing of the violence that occupied the mind of the child with the serene smile, and it is quite likely that it had not mattered at that moment. He quietly stood there and wondered what the future might hold for such a child.

Anthony was very much innocent of what was going on in the world outside the rise of fascism in Europe, militarism in Japan, and the general hate in the world. It was the reason Mr. Mahr had moved around so much the previous years. Somewhere along the road in his career, he had become despondent when it came to educating the future. Frequently, he had asked himself if it was worth trying when it all seemed so bleak. Teaching proper English, French or Latin to high society women were at least mind-numbing activities where he surrounded himself with inane chatter.

His contact with Anthony Hill had changed his outlook on life. The innocence of a child so completely removed from the cruelty of the world, and clueless when it came to his own father's proclivities, had caused him to try to envision the world in a similar fashion. It had worked, and he felt he was a better man for it. Therefore, he let him drift off from time to time for he believed the boy dreamed of the wonders of the world when in actuality he dreamed of slaying demons.

* * *

It was one of those mornings. The sun shone right through the window on to his face. He had forgotten to pull the drapes when he got in, or to be more precise, he had been so off-kilter that he more than likely hadn't bothered to do it.

Geert turned over, with some difficulty because of his large frame, and wiped the drool from his chin with the back of his hand. He lay flat on his back and stared up at the ceiling without any concept of time. After his talk with Jensen, Charles and Thorne, he had hurried back to the hotel and had played catch up with the socialites there. He soon caught up and surpassed them. He felt now, as he wondered what time it was, that he might have overdone it, both food and drink wise.

"Good morning, Mr. Geert," a deep voice said, startling him and making him sweat at the same time as ice ran through his veins. He scrambled quicker than he had ever moved before and instantly shuffled up towards the headboard, getting his feet tangled in the sheets.

The sunshine streaming through the tall windows blinded him, and he tried to squint to let his eyes adjust. He tried to focus through his blurred vision, and slowly shapes became sharper and the scene grew out of mere distortion.

By the window stood a round table on one ornately carved leg, flanked by two armchairs. He would sit in them from time to time to drink his morning coffee. Otherwise, they mostly filled the role of storage for discarded clothes. Something other than his wardrobe now occupied the left chair. In the light of the morning, it was no more than a silhouette, but one that was all too familiar to him.

The Black Diamond, for it was he, cut an impressive form: straight back, wide shoulders, a body poured into a black suit and hair carefully combed to create a part on the left side. He rose and picked up a cup and saucer from the table next to him, and as he moved towards the bed, he became more of a person than just a black form. Now Geert saw the black suit with the matching tie, white shirt and the pin on the lapel shaped like a diamond with a white skull in the center - the symbol of the organization that bore his name.

The Black Diamond's age had always been difficult for Geert to ascertain, having that forever youthful appearance, and the domino mask that covered the upper portion of his face, naturally made things difficult. That coupled with the fact that the man seemingly had arrived in town, unannounced, one day and taken control of the vacuum left by the previous mob family, made him a figure steeped in mystery.

It wasn't the first time Geert had been startled by his boss. He had an uncanny knack for popping up at the most inopportune time. However, at the same time, he always knew when something was afoot.

It was no surprise that he now stood before Geert. Not after the events of the other day. The fact that The Black

Diamond himself could walk through the hotel and past the guards, men who were tried and true in their loyalty, was no surprise either. Most of the men at this level, ones who were closest to Geert, knew The Black Diamond and recognized him on sight. They would have gotten out of his way had he walked down the hallways of the house.

"A busy night I take it, Mr. Geert," The Black Diamond said in his baritone. "And although I would have liked to avoid waking you at noon, there are pressing matters that need to be attended to. So, if you would please rise from your place of rest and slip into a robe, I have ordered breakfast through room service so that we may do this in an orderly fashion." He handed Geert a blue and white striped bathrobe and turned away. Geert gingerly rolled off the edge of the bed, the preferred method on any given day, but more so on a day like this.

"So, what do you have for me?" The Black Diamond was back in the armchair with one leg slung over the other and the cup and saucer once again in his hands.

"Well, sir," Geert began, and he lumbered over to the opposite seat. "My source within the police department had very little information to give when it came to the case. It seems as though they are keeping the lid on tightly on this one, but he is working on unscrewing it. What we do know is that the attacker used some form of knife to hurt our guys, as well as the micks, and that there was one survivor, but I don't know who yet or where he is for that matter."

The Black Diamond nodded as he listened to the information, but he did not move a muscle in his face to indicate any emotion. He was silent for a moment and stared into his teacup before speaking.

"And what measures have you taken to make sure that we find the one or ones who perpetrated the attack on us, as well as the Lonergans?" He asked while still keeping his masked gaze on the cup.

"I have enlisted the aid of three freelance gentlemen who I have used previously." Geert was feeling more confident now, especially since he believed he had covered his bases. "They have been instructed to find the identity of the survivor, and through doing this, it should give us a lead on the killers. I believe that the survivor is none other than our most experienced soldier Baz Peterson, and he would surely point us in the right direction."

"I am sorry to have to rain on your parade, Mr. Geert, but this information is not new to me." The Black Diamond rose and put down the cup. Geert began to sweat, the kind of dirty perspiration that forced itself out one's pores the morning after. His boss had always had the ability of being several steps ahead of him. It always made him wonder why he was kept around at all, but somebody needed to be the eventual fall guy, and as long as Geert was swimming in women, food and drink that possible future didn't bother him. He managed to cover his own ass often enough that he was safe from any real danger.

"Excuse me, sir?" Geert said with a cracked voice.

"The survivor of the attack was a man using the name *Hammer* - someone your precious Peterson had recruited some time ago. I assume you know the name?"

Geert nodded thoughtfully.

"Well, it appears his real name is Martin Lindquist - a young police officer from Michigan - and he had been tasked with infiltrating our little band of merry men. He is currently under the care of the good doctors at St. Mary's Hospital, and he has already started talking to local law enforcement. It could potentially lead them to us, depending on what Peterson revealed, but he is also sitting on valuable intelligence about our new-found enemy if that is the case."

"You want me to call off the search? Geert made ready to catapult himself into action.

"No, that has already been taken care of. I have taken the liberty of rerouting your trio of freelancers. We will know whatever the infiltrator has revealed to the police through sources other than yours but seeing as he most likely is sitting on quite a bit of information, elimination is vital. I am leaving it to you to make sure that he does not leave the hospital other than in a body bag."

He walked into the hallway that inevitably led out of the room. "And, Geert..."

"Yes, sir?" Geert said in his hoarse voice.

"Pay the men handsomely, out of your own pocket, of course, when the job is done."

"Yes, sir."

The Black Diamond turned around and left the room unceremoniously, and Geert, once he was convinced his boss was not going to return, he relaxed, and the rum began to spin. He started to feel queasy and a low rumble emanated from his stomach. He tried to suppress the urge to throw up, but it became too much, and he ran to the bathroom and vomited up last night debauchery, with a side order of fear.

* * *

Tony sat in the office he shared with Gabe Posen tapping a pencil against the notes for the evening's broadcast. According to them, there was nothing more to report in regard to the shooting downtown. He picked up his cup bearing the WRJN logo and sipped the now cold beverage. Why was cold coffee so unpleasant in flavor when it was essentially the same thing as the warm counterpart? Peering over the rim, and with his lips still pressed to it, he let the liquid trickle back into the cup. Instead of dwelling on the question, he leaned forward, tented his fingers, and stared out over the busy city through his window.

The contents he had brought with him from the police impound lot had proven to be cocaine, just as he had suspected - so far so good - but who was it for? The Lonergans were obviously selling it, but they were merely the intermediaries in the transaction - he had established that earlier. The product must have come from down south, crossing the border and then traveling through Texas, changing hands in Chicago where the Irish gang had its home base. He would deal with them and their leader Aiden O'Shea later, but first, he needed to halt those who would spread it throughout the city first.

He picked up the notepad and viewed the image he had drawn there. It was a replica of the brand stamped on the crates. A diamond with a skull placed in the center of it. He wouldn't win any awards for his artistic abilities, but if he could show it to a few of the city's criminals they might know something, they might point him in some direction. Then there was the matter of the survivor.

Chief Swan had mentioned six victims, but Tony had thought back to the events of the night. He had concluded that seven men had fallen to his blade. If the chief counted six bodies that must have meant that one survived, badly injured, but alive, nonetheless. That person was sitting on valuable information and somehow, he needed to get in touch with him for questioning. The horror of the mask would help him with that no problem, but he needed to figure out how to find the name.

He spun around in his office chair and faced the door that led out of the office; the Police Station would have the information he sought. He would have to go there, right after the news, and break in tonight. That's what he would do. He put his hands behind his head and sighed with an amused look on his face, so much so, in fact, that Gabe Posen, who happened to walk into the room at that moment, raised a confused eyebrow.

* * *

St. Mary's Hospital was one of the largest buildings on the block - as it needed to be since it serviced most of the citizens of the city. It stood six stories tall and spread out over the entire block with its red brick hiding behind the young oak trees that lined the sidewalk. Two wings stretched out on either side, like a horseshoe, mimicking a welcoming embrace to those in need of assistance. A white stone staircase led up from the sidewalk to the glass doors, only six or seven steps up, but enough to hinder those infirmed to climb them without a helping hand, which was an odd juxtaposition against the warm openness of the form of the structure. A thick stone railing flanked the stairs, the kind of resting place for statuesque lions, but instead, nurses or medical students would sit there in order to gossip and grab a quick smoke.

It was a state-of-the-art facility, and there was many an aspiring doctor who wouldn't mind being sent there for their final work practice before having to face the real world.

Three men in gray suits covered by light brown trench coats stood on the sidewalk in front of the hospital. They were leaning against their car while listening to the radio as the five o'clock news came on. They were all smoking cigarettes and conversed with each other in low voices, hushed, almost like whispers as they watched people enter and exit the building. They paid special attention when two police officers walked past them, both of them carrying shotguns over their shoulders. If the officers had been on the job longer than the mere year they had logged so far, they would have paid special attention to the men. One of the young men would later tell guests around a Thanksgiving table that he had always lived with the regret that he never questioned them that day. Thorne tipped his hat and smiled at the men who acknowledged him in return. When they disappeared behind the glass doors, Jensen fished a pocket watch from his vest and looked at it, and Charles quickly bounded up the steps and sat down on the stone railing next to a young redheaded candy striper so that he a had a clear view through the doors. She giggled at some crude joke he whispered to her and plucked a cigarette from his pack.

According to Jensen's watch, it took fifteen minutes for two other officers to exit the hospital. They too were armed - one carrying a shotgun in his arms and the other one with an old-fashioned looking repeater rifle resting across his shoulders. Charles stroked his chin and leaned over to the girl, seemingly continuing conversing with her in a soft voice. Thorne gave the new officers the same courtesy he had shown their colleagues and they responded in kind. The officers climbed into a police car parked down the street and drove off.

"So, it seems to me," Thorne said, dropping his cigarette on the sidewalk and stepping on it, "that two officers at a time is the limit of resources spent on this guy."

"It takes fifteen minutes for them to switch, and I guess that entails briefing each other regarding any news," Jensen replied, flicking ash on the ground. "Intervals of four hours so far. It seems doable for us - of course, depending on what the security situations is on the inside, at least at night."

"Well, we did see five security guards enter this morning and three leave. So, I'm guessing they run a skeleton crew at night."

Charles came towards them with a big grin on his face that only grew wider as he came closer. He reached into his coat, produced his pack of smokes, and lit one after having placed it between his teeth.

"So, what's the score?" Thorne asked.

"Well, apart from the fact that I'm picking her up at seven on Friday?" Charles showed all his teeth in his big smile, his buddies shrugging in unison. "From what she gathers, the police officers always go to the fifth floor, that's where they keep patients who have come out of surgery and need to be monitored. She doesn't get to help out there - only nurses do - but she has heard rumors from the ladies in the building that room 506 is the room that is heavily guarded. Two officers at a time, armed at all times."

"What of security? The regular hospital security, I mean." Thorne asked.

"According to her, they only have three older men patrolling the hallways at night, but most of the time they hang out in the reception area on the first floor playing cards. There are a few doctors on call, but they are most often in the basement area where emergency cases go at night. Nurses sit on each floor, but only two per area. She is also pretty certain that the officers do the rounds every hour on the hour, so the reception is most likely unmanned at those times."

"Excellent!" Thorne's grin was almost as wide as the one Charles wore. "Fellas, this may just be the easiest cash we ever made. We sneak in after midnight. If need be, we take out the nurses and whatever guards we may encounter on the way, and then we deal with the officers - they are likely the ones we have to be careful with. We take them down after the nurses and then finish Mr. Hammer in his bed."

"Easy as pie," Jensen mused. "So much nicer than having to investigate the guy's identity. Now we just have to snuff him. Then I propose we take an extended vacation. We will be in high demand from the law after this."

"Right you are," Thorne replied. "Now let's scope out the building so that we know what we're dealing with tonight."

"We don't need any unnecessary surprises," Charles chimed in, and they left their car and walked towards St. Mary's Hospital in order to get the lay of the land.

* * *

The first floor of the police headquarters was bustling with activity. The main command center an open space with desks littering the floor. These, in turn, littered with files, papers and coffee cups. Secretaries, police officers and plainclothes detectives were running around handing papers to each other, talking on the phone, or just standing in front of chalkboards going over current cases. At the far end, right opposite the big mahogany double doors that led to the hive of activity, was a dais and on it stood a desk, like a podium, that stretched from one side of the room to the other. Behind it stood secretaries and older police officers who barked orders, answered phones, and handed documents to young boys, runners, who made sure the information went to the right person. On the left side of the command center lay Chief Swan's office, with the door closed and the blinds drawn.

Tony walked over to the dais and tried to avoid bumping into those running around him. In his hands, he was carrying a box of donuts from Bendtsen's bakery on Washington, and several times he was forced to lift it above his head so that it wouldn't be sent flying across the room, landing on some unfortunate detective's desk.

Once he reached the overlook area, he turned around and

exhaled. He thought the offices at WRJN could get busy at times but working in this atmosphere every day would most likely kill him in the end.

"May I assist you in some way, sir?" a cautious voice asked behind him, and Tony spun around to find a young, bearded man dressed in an ill-fitting tan suit. With his dark brown hair, cut the same length as his facial hair, the man looked like a disheveled grizzly bear. Having this figure looking down on him made Tony feel more than uncomfortable.

"I am here to speak to Chief Swan, if possible," he said. "I brought donuts," he added and held up the box.

"I see," the bear-man said and looked to a middle-aged woman wearing horn-rimmed glasses with a shawl covering her shoulders. "Angie, is Chief Swan in?"

The woman looked at him over the rim of her glasses and sucked her gums in a distasteful manner. She then turned her judgmental gaze at Tony and raised her eyebrows in a quizzical expression. "Who is here to see the Chief?" Her voice had all the nasal properties of a true Midwestern native, most likely from the northern part of the state. "Does he have an appointment?"

"My name is Anthony Hill," Tony said with his best smile, one that could melt even the coldest of hearts. "You might recognize my voice from the Five O'clock News on WRJN, Your Radio Friend?" He adjusted his voice to make it sound like the radio version of his regular diction.

"Mr. Hill?" The woman looked skeptical and riffled through some papers. She was obviously not impressed. "And what is the purpose of your visit?"

"I would like to speak to the chief in regard to what we spoke about on the radio, if possible?" Tony's voice went back to its natural tone, and he looked at her with his best puppy dog eyes.

"Chief Swan is busy at the moment, he has a guest... who had an appointment," the woman said and smiled smugly. "Then he has an engagement to attend with The Knights of Columbus, but if you're lucky, you might be able to speak to him the few seconds he is in transit."

"That would be great, Miss. Care for a donut? They're fresh." He opened the box and smiled.

"Mrs. Connors," the woman bit back. "And no thank you. Detective Glade, why don't you show Mr. Hill to the office?"

Detective Glade, the man with the disheveled look, hopped to and circled around the podium and down from the dais to stand next to Tony. "Follow me, Mr. Hill," he said and moved through the throng of people.

"Donut?" Tony tried again and held out the box to Glade.

"Don't mind if I do," Glade replied and grabbed an éclair. As he bit into it, cream filling burst from it and landed down the front of his suit. "Dammit!" He shouted. "Just my luck. This always happens to me. I'm going to clean myself up; this is the office, so I'll leave you here. Is that alright, Mr. Hill?"

"Sure thing, Detective Glade. Thanks for the guided trip." Tony tried to avoid laughing at the slovenly detective as he vanished through the wild landscape that was the police station.

No sooner had his guide disappeared to clean himself up than the door to Chief Swan's office opened and out stepped a man dressed in a dark suit followed by Swan. They both stopped in their tracks when they noticed Tony standing there with his box.

The first man appeared to be in his mid-forties and wore his dark hair in a part on the right side, with a few strands playfully falling over his forehead. Clean-shaven and dapper looking, he smiled at Tony and revealed the slightest hint of wrinkles by his dark eyes. Chief Swan stuck out his hand and Tony took it in greeting.

"Mr. Hill, what a surprise to see you here."

"I thought I'd stop by to discuss some details from yesterday, sir," Tony replied as he let go of the chief's hand.

"Interesting. I am pressed for time, but I can give you a few minutes. By the way, have you met Dr. Benton?" Swan indicated the man standing next to him.

"I have not had the pleasure," Tony replied and grabbed the doctor's outstretched hand.

"Delighted to meet you, Mr. Hill. I often enjoy your news reports," Dr. Benton said in a soft voice.

"The good doctor runs one of the largest pharmaceutical producers in the Midwest, and he has set up base in our fair city."

"That is true." Benton nodded in agreement. "I have always wanted to own a house on the lake. One opened up here, and the harbor in the city is perfect as a base for our operations. Proposed railway connections would make this a hub as well, and it all plays very well into our plans."

"We were just discussing a fundraiser Dr. Benton and his company are holding this weekend to benefit widows of policemen. A very good cause: we need all the funds we can get."

"It's the least we can do for our boys in blue. Have you received an invite, Mr. Hill?"

"I don't believe so." the question surprised Tony. He had always found himself standing on the outside of the higher circles. Being a newscaster, and fairly famous, at least among some people, he had still not been invited into the group that Gabe Posner, Chief Swan or Vic Linden ran in. "Maybe it got lost in the mail," he continued and faked a laugh only to be met with a puzzled look from Benton and Swan.

"Well, consider yourself invited," Dr. Benton said and smiled again, a very infectious one. "Will you be bringing a date?"

"No, sir." Tony almost blushed. "I do not currently have a young lady, and my mother passed away several years ago."

"Well, we'll have to remedy that." Dr. Benton winked at him. "A man of your talents should not stay unwed for long. A card will land in your mailbox shortly, Mr. Hill." Dr. Benton gave a short bow to Tony and Chief Swan. "I must, unfortunately, be moving along - there are pressing matters at hand and a business to run. Good day, Gentlemen."

As they watched Dr. Benton leave, Swan put a hand on Tony's shoulder.

"Step into my office, Mr. Hill. I can give you my undivided attention for five minutes."

* * *

The command center was far from as bustling with activity at night as it was during the daylight hours. In fact, there was no movement at all since the officers on duty who occupied the building after hours always stayed on the lower levels, and the detectives seldom worked at their desks past six p.m.

Occasionally, the phones would ring, only to remain unanswered, the call automatically transferring to the main desk in the lobby. The only light in the room came trickling in from below the great double doors, now closed, from the hallway beyond, and the streetlights that cast a yellow glow across the furniture and made strange shadows dance back and forth. If an unsuspecting visitor might have ventured into the room, it is more than likely they would have died from fright at finding a horrific face hanging upside down in the window, peering in with red glowing eyes as it scanned the area, its hideous grin showing rows of sharp teeth.

Slowly two hands glided down the windowpane and tried to find a possible way to get fingers between the ledge and frame, but to no avail. A knife with a wavy blade appeared and slowly it slid betwixt the wood, and with the slightest crack that echoed through the room, the frame lifted, and four gloved fingers appeared. Luckily, the chill of the night air had caused the wood to contract and it made it easier to slide the window upward so that the figure could pull itself inside.

Tony found that he had to use all his strength in order to keep the window open while simultaneously hauling himself across the windowsill, but he managed and came in with his back towards the floor. Dragging his body up, he landed with both feet against the hardwood and gently let the window slide back down.

Placing the blade back in the wangaraka, he crouched down and looked around for any signs of life. It was deadly quiet and gloomy. The only sounds he could hear was his shallow breath and the beating of his heart. His trip to the station earlier that day had provided him with a lot of information, not so much his discussion with Chief Swan - who had given him the same song and dance from their on-air interview - but he now knew where to find what he was looking for.

He needed to know who that surviving member was and where they were now. The skull and diamond logo were a dead end without another lead to follow, and this man might be able to give him more to work with. He had quickly realized that he didn't have the network to ask around about the symbol and going around to dive bars and doing so would only raise suspicions. Not taking any chances, he continued to stay low as he moved through the labyrinth of desks towards Chief Swan's office. To his surprise, the door wasn't locked, and he quietly entered, still crouching. Once inside he rose since the blinds were down. One could say many things about Chief Swan, but that he was neat was not one of them. By all accounts he was organized, well informed and in the know, but it was most likely not due to his ability, or lack thereof, to keep order in his office.

The gloominess of the room made it difficult to find

anything and with papers piled upon papers, several coffee cups strewn everywhere, and half-eaten bagels and donuts stacked on top of each other, the task wasn't made any easier.

He produced a small electric torch to aid the search, and with a sigh, he began scanning the mountain of objects before him. Several of the taller skyscraper-like stacks were easy to eliminate from the search due to the layer of dust covering them. These covered most of the regular surfaces, like tables, parts of the desk, and even the odd flower pedestal. On the leather couch standing off to one side and the office chair were, what looked to be, newer documents, so he started there. He could quickly put most to rest by looking at the dates of the first paper, so he moved to the piles on the floor. As the electric light passed over the range of documents and some leftover dishes, he noticed the box of donuts he had brought earlier in the day atop a tan folder. Quickly, he moved the box out of the way, noticing that Swan had managed to get jelly filling on the folder, but he opened it anyway.

It was a report filed by a Detective Garfield Teague, and it detailed the facts in the case - or at least what they knew so far. It noted that they now knew the contents of the crates – cocaine - but from whence it came, they had no idea, at this time. The truck and its cargo belonged to a newer crime family by the name of the Lonergans, and they were of Irish descent. Their representatives had all perished down in the parking structure. According to the report, the other victims were under the leadership of Henry 'Baz' Peterson, but he was not the head of whatever group was attempting to purchase the drugs.

Most of the men connected to Peterson, some named and some not, had been killed, save for one. Here was a dilemma – they had blacked out the name of that person. There actually seemed to be two names or one long one. Whichever it was, it was impossible to read. There was no other information, only that the men had not killed each other that day. Teague believed there to have been a third party, whose agenda he did not know, someone who used a blade. That he had managed to find this information could only mean that he had spoken to the survivor - their name still eluding Tony.

He turned the report over in his hands and flipped through all the papers for additional clues. In doing so, he found something written in blue ink on the back of the file. In Chief Swan's beautiful

cursive script, it read *The Black Diamond.*

Tony tapped his index finger on the name. What did it mean? Was this a clue to whomever The Lonergans were working with? Whatever it was, it was a start. He still needed to find the survivor before he died from his wounds or worse murdered by his colleagues, though.

He placed the torch on the desk and was in the process of placing the box of donuts back on top of the file when he noticed something. There was a notepad lying there. It was empty, but the light from the torch shining at it from an angle revealed the indentations of Swan's familiar handwriting. It was a long shot, but he picked it up and shone the light across the bleached white paper.

It was from the day before. A note giving Detective Teague access to a patient at St. Mary's Hospital, room 506. Swan had addressed it to the hospital staff, as well as the officers on duty. There was a name too. Two names in fact: Martin Lindquist and Maury Hammer. It might be a dead end, but it was all he had to go on now. Suddenly, he heard the doors to the room outside the office open. He turned off the torch and sat down by the desk. He slowly crawled across the floor towards the couch and gently climbed the creaking leather, making sure he didn't knock over any piles.

He put two fingers between the lower blinds and peered out. All he could see was a shape. A large frame of a man, wearing a hat, carrying a flashlight illuminating the room. The spare light revealed a hint of a beard and glasses with the rest obscured by darkness. The figure moved slowly from desk to desk, rifling through filing cabinets and drawers very clearly looking for something, or possibly anything that might be of interest.

After having been up on the dais, startled by the ringing of one of the phones, the light targeted at the office. Tony had to think quickly. There was no way he would manage to exit the room without the man noticing him; he would have to hide.

Silently he leapt from the couch, hit a roll and curled up next to the door. The figure stepped inside. This person had more knowledge than Tony of how Chief Swan kept his office, and he ignored the various piles and headed straight for the desk. He moved the donut box and paged through the file but seemed unfulfilled by the contents, keeping his back to Tony. Letting out a sigh, the man opened the box and grabbed a pastry from inside. Taking a bite, the unmistakable sound of custard dripping onto clothes broke the silence, and the figure let out an even bigger sigh before quickly exiting the office and slamming the door behind him, completely ignoring the noise it made.

Tony waited for the double doors to close before he exited the office and headed for the window again. He had a lead, whatever it meant.

CHAPTER EIGHT

Young Anthony's training was rigorous and contained a variety of exercises. His second father would take him out to the jungle to practice the kalis and kris while also teaching him the others skills he might need in combat. It was important for the young man's education to be versatile- instead of becoming overly muscular like some of the Balinese tribesmen who had arms like tree trunks but could not move with the grace of a slimmer man.

Wayan's goal was to mold Anthony in his own image - lean and lithe with clear definition. It was what had made him such a phenomenal and sought-after soldier of fortune throughout the isles. Wayan sent him climbing trees to hone the strength in his legs and fingers, and from the tops, he leaped from milk wood to milk wood. Pushing off, he would grab onto the twisted branches and swing onto the next one and hang upside down for hours, from time to time sitting up to tone his stomach muscles for a strong core was the key to controlling the body.

Some mornings they would venture to the coast, and here Tony would leap from the white cliffs into the clear blue water, repeatedly doing flips, spins and rolls into the deep.

As the years passed, Anthony noticed his body changing from the softness of childhood to the toned solidity of a Balinese warrior. He scaled the trees and rock walls with ease, somersaulted without using his hands, and could avoid the reeds that Wayan tried to slap him with while he tried to slice the sticks placed in a circle around him. As he matured into a young man, he was also evolving into a tanned and toned soldier.

* * *

Entering the building had been the easy part. Everything had been as the information Charles had. The guards were doing their rounds, so they were away from the front desk. It meant they avoided unwanted questions, and whatever nurses who might have been on duty in the middle of the night paid little attention to them as they walked with a purpose.

Thorne carried a snub-nosed revolver in a holster under his suit jacket, while Charles and Jensen each had sawed-off shotguns strapped under their armpits, hidden by their coats. Sure, it would make noise once they offed the police officers and the snitch, but that was how they liked it. At this hour, they would be out of the hospital and long gone before the boys in blue had a chance to get into their cars.

They wanted to avoid the security guards before they reached their destination since they would ask them some uncomfortable questions, and they would be forced to kill them on the spot. They really didn't want to have to do that so early on. It was also the reasoning behind not lighting cigarettes as they perambulated through the offensively white hallways. No need to call attention to themselves. Quickly, they entered the elevator and rode it up to the fifth floor. It landed there with a friendly 'ding', and the doors gently eased open to reveal the corridors of level five.

The first thing that greeted them, and with open arms no less, was the likeness of the Virgin Mary. A full body statue made from red stone stood before them, eyes downcast with a look of sadness on her face. Charles, the religious one of the groups, swallowed hard, which he always did when confronted with his Catholic beliefs. Then he made the sign of the cross as the others passed by with smirks on their faces, Jensen even rolled his eyes. It had always been a sore subject between them, but nothing he was eager to part with. There was some sense of security in the warm embrace of the lord, and eternal forgiveness.

As they moved along the corridor and past several doors, with only the sound of their shoes on the wooden floor, they could hear voices coming from the reception area. Thorne stopped and put his arm up to halt his friends. He listened intently. Two voices - a man and a woman. Probably a nurse and a security guard or possibly a cop. He put his hand in under his coat and cocked his revolver. At the same time, he could hear Jensen and Charles ready their shotguns. He nodded, and they continued to walk.

* * *

Luckily enough, it had not rained the past couple of days, but the night air added its own brand of dampness to the roof on which Tony was crawling. Seeing as how he was still wearing

The Face, it was foolish to try to enter the hospital through the front entrance, and he felt he had gotten quite adept at opening windows from the outside. He walked on all fours, gingerly placing one foot and one hand down at the same time, looking like a camel against the moonlight. He could, of course, have walked upright, the roof of the building was completely flat, but he didn't want to raise suspicions among nightwalkers, who might begin to wonder at the shape atop the hospital in the middle of the night. He had scoped out the structure from across the street before scaling the walls, and he believed he knew where the room was located. Climbing the brick building was not a problem as he swung from nook to cranny and rested on window ledges until he finally swung over the rooftop. He had chosen to move up along the back of St. Mary's, so he had to cross the roof because room 506 was facing Grand Avenue that ran outside. Anything to avoid detection. Once he had reached the opposite end, he leaped down onto a balcony that replaced the seventh-floor level at the end facing the street.

Swiftly he jumped up on the railing, turned so that his back faced the street, and dropped down, only to catch the edge of the balcony with his hands, allowing him to hang from it. He had positioned himself so that he was hanging perpendicular to the window below. All he needed to do, was drop down and catch himself on the sixth-floor windowsill. He also needed to move quickly for the longer he was out in the open the more likely it was that he would be noticed.

He felt his shoulders strain from the pull of the drop and catch, but his toned arm muscles could handle it. He swung from side to side in order to steady himself. He threw a glance below to make sure that there still was a window there. He repeated the previous motion and once again felt the strain as his fingers caught the edge of the sill. He winced; this time it hurt. As he passed the glass, he saw the light from the inside and two police officers standing with their backs to the window.

* * *

As the trio turned around the corner that led from the corridor to the reception area, they saw the big desk and behind it a blond nurse, likely in her twenties. She was engaging in a conversation with one of the elderly security guards who was leaning over the desk and resting on his elbows as the men approached in a neat row.

The guard fell silent when he noticed them, and the nurse soon followed suit once she suspected something was amiss. Whether it was their steely gaze, their determined gate or the fact that three men in dressed in trench coats and hats approaching her was difficult to assess, but something was wrong, she could feel it. The setting was ideal for them; they had met their first obstacle exactly where they had wanted it to happen - in the open area of the reception. The hallways would have been too narrow to maneuver. They had a clear view of the corridors that branched off from the hub as well as the two adjoining washrooms. The guard straightened up and pulled his pants up by way of tugging at his belt, unclear if it was supposed to look menacing or not. He grabbed some gray hairs that had fallen behind his right ear and moved them across the bald spot atop of his head.

"Hello there, fellas. What do you need?" He asked in a quivering voice, placing his right hand on the pistol at his hip.

There was perspiration on the top of his lip, and his fingers twitched.

"We're here to visit a buddy." Thorne took charge. "Hammer in room 506."

"Visiting hours are over," the nurse said with quite the decisive tone as she picked up the black receiver of the internal phone.

"I think we'll see him anyway." Thorne shrugged and looked at the others.

"We have special permission," Charles added.

The nurse went for the numbers on the telephone as the guard unholstered the pistol. "I'm going to have to ask you to leave," he said in a harsh tone.

Thorne's revolver barked loudly as he fired at the nurse. She turned towards him and in that instant, with her finger hovering above the call button, the bullet hit her squarely in the center of her forehead, sending a spray of blood, skull fragments and gray matter behind her. Limply, her body collapsed to the floor, bouncing off the desk first. The movement of leveling the weapon at the now-expired woman had caused Thorne to stand sideways. The guard aimed his weapon at him, but before he could squeeze the trigger, a blast from the right of Thorne caused the lower half of the guard's body to explode in a wave of red. The shotgun blast from Jensen had nearly cut him in half, and he was now gasping for breath in a pool of crimson and innards. Once the ringing in their ears had stopped, they could hear the footsteps of the police officers approaching.

* * *

Tony hadn't quite figured out how he was going to enter the building. First off, he hadn't scoped out where the police officers watching over the man would be standing. In his ignorance, he had figured they would be in room 506, but they were standing outside and that complicated things. He quietly cursed himself for being so ignorant. He really needed to prepare better, one did not go into battle without the proper equipment and knowing the lay of the land was one of the most important aspects.

He looked to the left, where he assumed the room was located, but there was no window there. He was just about to swing to his right when he noticed the officer moving down the corridor at some speed. Tony pulled himself up so that he was resting on straight arms, unsheathed his kris with his right hand while balancing on the left, and then slid the blade under the window frame. He pushed down on it, and the window opened. To avoid having to go through it again, he quickly shoved his fingers in the crack before it fell back down. The kris fell and he saw it tumble down to the ground below. He cursed again. He'd have to recover it once he was done.

With some effort, he pushed the window upward while still balancing on his left hand and swung both his legs over the sill so that he could slide inside. He heard shouting and the unmistakable sounds of gunfire coming from down the hall. He unsheathed the kalis, brought it around, and shook his arms to get the blood flowing through them. He felt unprepared for whatever might lie ahead, and he was not too keen on the prospect of a fight with rubbery, lactic-acid-filled limbs. He noticed that he was standing outside room 506, and he slipped behind the door instead.

The room was dark except for the machines that lit up the

form of the young man who lay in the bed, covered by a single sheet. His eyes were open, the noise from outside most likely had woken him up, and Tony could see two tiny pinpricks reflected in the orbs. It was tense. The man obviously could not quite see him as he stood there, a silhouette against the light that escaped the door.

* * *

The old man let out one final ragged breath and shuddered as Jensen walked over to him. He had wanted to end it with another blast, but he didn't need to bother wasting another shell. Suddenly, one of the bathroom doors burst open and another elderly guard appeared, gun held high. This one had a flat top haircut and a barrel chest reminiscent of a marine. At the same time, the two police officers came around the corner, both aiming slide action shotguns at anyone who might be in their way and screaming at the trio to drop their guns and get down on the ground.

This was exactly what the trio lived for, this action. The adrenaline coursing through their veins as they tried to defy the odds. That was why they tried to avoid doing things in the dark. Out in the open and with as much danger as possible, that was their thing. Even so, Jensen became confused at where to focus his attention being that he was in the middle of two threats, and Charles could not use his weapon for fear of hitting him as well. Thorne took out one of the officers by firing three rounds into his chest. The police officer's body fell and skidded across the floor leaving a trail of red. At the same instant, the guard fired at Jensen, who tried to spin out of harm's way, but the bullet caught him in the shoulder. He dropped to a knee, just as the second officer fired sending shots his way and blowing his hat off and scraping his scalp.

It gave Charles the opening he needed and aiming high he sent a hail of shots towards the head of the second officer, who, catching several pellets, dropped his rifle and doubled over. The guard, still standing on the threshold of the bathroom, and leaning against the door to hinder it from closing on him and forcing him to move, pointed his gun at Jensen who was still kneeling in the lake of blood. He squeezed the trigger, but the thug had already rolled forward in a tumble over the dead body of the other guard causing his coat to become soaked in red, coagulating liquid.

Charles was busy reloading his weapon, thinking to himself that he should have brought something capable of firing more than two shots at a time, rather than going for an item with the destructive power of his double-barreled sawed-off piece.

Thorne spent his remaining two bullets in his revolver on the guard who vanished back into the bathroom with the door taking the hits as it swung back and forth on its hinges. Thorne cursed and tossed his weapon to the side and headed over to the downed officer.

Jensen rolled to his feet in front of the wounded police officer who was clutching his face after the pellets had dug themselves into his skin, and he shoved the double barrels of his gun into the man's chest. Firing, he blew right through the man's upper torso, coloring the ceiling a deep red and making parts of lungs, the heart and bone fragments rain down. Jensen used the man's body like an umbrella, still supporting the body with his shotgun. After the raining body parts had stopped, Jensen dumped the body to the side and rose, covered in blood and gore. He turned to Thorne, who had just ripped the weapon from the hands of the other police officer and was joined by Charles whose shotgun was locked and loaded.

"We're wasting time!" Thorne claimed. "We need to get on with it. The mark needs silencing, and the guard in the bathroom needs to taking care of so that we can get out of here. I'm sure we've made enough noise to alert the authorities."

"If nothing else, these guys have already used their radios to call the station." Charles pointed to the police radios attached to the shoulders of the dead men.

"I'll take the old man in the toilet," Jensen said as he reloaded his shotgun after pulling it out of the dead body. "You guys take care of that Hammer kid." He went for the doorknob of the bathroom but found that it locked. He sighed and nodded to the others to go.

* * *

Martin Lindquist lay paralyzed in his hospital bed. A feverish dream had woken him, glowing red eyes coming at him in the dark. There was running outside his room, and he slowly came to the realization that his days were numbered. He knew enough of organized crime, and the one he had infiltrated in particular, to know how these things usually went down.

He had once been part of a similar incident when going out with Baz Peterson. A minor dealer had threatened to blow the whistle, to go to the cops, and the big boss had wanted him taken care of. Baz, Martin and some guy referred to as Rosy

Anderson went uptown to meet the man. He ended up dumped off the Sixth Street Bridge and into the Root River with several bullet holes in his body. Rosy had wanted to torture and string him up as a warning, but The Black Diamond, whoever or whatever that was, wanted no trail. Nothing that could lead to questions. Even though Martin had taken no part in the killing, he had witnessed the cold action by the two men. They had given no quarter, just entered his apartment, pulled him out and emptied their guns into his body. He hadn't even gotten the chance to defend himself. This was what awaited him. Sure, the police officers on duty might be able to delay the inevitable, but if the men coming for him were anything like Peterson, they didn't stand a chance.

The door to his room gently opened, and he steeled himself for what was about to come, but instead of the barrage of bullets that he was expecting to riddle his body, a figure slipped in through the small opening. It happened so fast and the light from the outside temporarily blinded him so that he couldn't make out the figure clearly.

As his eyesight slowly adjusted back to the darkness of the room, he stared at the person, who remained at the door seemingly listening for what was going on outside. It looked as if the figure was naked. As he concentrated, Martin could see the shape of boots on the feet and gloves covering the hands and the head... the head had a strange shape. Not the type of irregular silhouette created by backlit hair but caused by something else, and when the figure looked at him he saw the red glow of two very familiar eyes - it was the thing from his dreams. He started to squirm and as he did, the thing quickly moved towards him. In its hands, it carried that nasty, wavy blade it had used to separate Martin's leg from the rest of him. He began to shudder and opened his mouth to scream when a gloved hand covered his mouth. The light from the little lamps on the machinery next to his bed lit the beast partially, and they showed a figure dressed in a skin-tight blue and red suit, a spiked belt at the waist and a terrible, angular face with fangs and a sharp nose with piercing red eyes staring right through his very soul.

The figure slowly raised the blade to its closed mouth so the fangs protruding from the lower jaw were the only thing visible. "Be silent," it hissed in the voice of someone wearing a mask, a man. "I'm not here to hurt you, I need your help, but we don't have time to talk now." The sounds of battle had ceased, and Martin could hear two sets of feet come closer to his room. "Hang a pillowcase in the window outside your room if and when you want to talk so that we can take this organization down."

Martin nodded and the dressed-up man slowly backed towards the door.

* * *

Down the hall, Charles and Thorne could hear Jensen trying to force the bathroom door open by shouldering and alternately kicking it, but he wasn't having any success, and he wouldn't want to waste another shell by blowing the lock off.

With their weapons at the ready, Thorne grabbed the door handle of room 506 and turned it. Without warning, the door flew open with force and knocked Thorne over, crashing into his head. He rolled over to the wall and tried to find his bearings. His hat had flown off, and there was a deep gash in his forehead causing blood to trickle down his face. Disoriented, probably concussed, he attempted to resume his upright position climbing the wall with his left hand. Charles had jumped back when the door opened and had seen his colleague knocked down. Instinctively, he pulled the trigger of his gun and blasted a hole in the door. It swung back slowly, and he could clearly see that there was no one behind it. He sidled up next to the hole with his gun raised and slowly moved his hand towards the handle trying to avoid the crater left from his shot. It caused his arm and the right side of his upper torso to cover the door, but he had no other choice - he wasn't about to become visible through his own handy work. It was still, apart from Jensen working on the bathroom and Throne struggling to get to his feet and breathing heavily.

* * *

Tony had stepped back into the darkness once he had kicked the door open. He had planned for it to catch whoever was trying to enter by surprise, and he was certain it had succeeded. At least, the door had hit a body on the other side, and the shotgun blast affirmed his belief that hostility was behind. As he backed off, he caught a glimpse through the hole and saw a man in a trench coat and dark suit clambering against the wall with blood pouring from a nasty wound in his head. It convinced him that whoever was in the hallway wasn't here in a friendly capacity.

The door moved ever so slightly as if it shivered at the touch from someone on the other side. Tony rolled his shoulders and tried to loosen them up from the strain of the climb. Once the handle began to move again, he flipped the blade so that it pointed towards the floor and then pounced. The point of the kalis dug through the wood like soft butter, and he felt it cut into tissue on the other side. A man cried out, and Tony pulled his weapon free, tumbling backward on the floor and coming to standing position. Reversing his momentum, he ran forward, and, like a long jumper, he leaped into the air and planted both his boots on the door, sending it flying off its hinges. He landed on his back, relaxing his body to avoid injury and the risk of losing his breath.

* * *

Just when Charles had reached the handle of the door, he felt a sharp, biting pain in his shoulder blade. He had always prided himself in not showing weakness when hurt, but the pain from whatever it was now digging into his body was too much for him to bear. It was white-hot and ice-cold at the same time as steel cut through muscle, sinew and tissue, grinding against bone and then the intrusion vanished tearing at his flesh as it moved away, but the pain remained. He slumped against the door, feeling the warmth of his blood freely flow under his suit, down his entire body, and pool in his shoes.

Thorne had risen and was leaning against the opposite wall, his friend's cry of pain had jarred him, and now they were staring at one another, both bloodied, both breathing heavily, and both furious. He could see it in Charles' eyes. A fiery rage there usually spelled the end for those who might try to oppose them. They had both been hurt before as it was nothing new to people in their line of work. They had powered through it and always ended up on top. That was how you stayed relevant and in demand, and it was not going to be any different this night.

Whoever was hiding in that room, be it Hammer, another cop, or something else, they were going to meet their maker, and it was going to hurt. Everything seemed to move in slow motion as Thorne cocked his revolver he had managed to recover from the floor. It was sticky with his blood, but it would serve its purpose. Before he could make another move, the door flew out once again, this time off the frame itself, most likely due to its integrity already compromised. Charles flew off his feet and flew like a rag doll across the hallway, crashing into the same wall Thorne was leaning. Sliding to the floor, his body left a bloody print on the white paint tracing his trajectory. Thorne stared into the opening left by the missing door and saw a pair of red dots in the dark and a figure that slowly rose from a crouching position. As it unfolded, a long wavy sword appeared at its side. He raised his revolver and fired, but the figure was no longer there. Instead, it was next to him. A quick movement before Thorne's face and the revolver clattered to the floor with his hand still clutching it. He stared at his hand as it bounced on the floor, and he blinked at it in disbelief and then looked up, staring into a horrible face with huge incisors, red piercing eyes and a nasty snarl. Then he faded into darkness.

* * *

The man Tony had seen through the hole in the door, now lay on the floor next to his own hand, and they united in a macabre heap. Another man, dressed exactly like the first one, lay against the wall, blood flowing in a constant stream from somewhere. Tony assumed it was the one who had been behind the door the second time.

The man was panting heavily and staring at him in fear. Well, at The Face to be more precise. He briefly glanced over to his right, and Tony followed his gaze to a sawed-off shotgun. He kicked it down the hall, and the man shook in fear at what was going to happen next, but Tony let him be. He needed survivors, and in the next instant, he heard a shotgun blast and the sound of splintering wood coming from the reception area. He hurried off, leaving the two men to their bleeding.

* * *

Jensen felt fed up with trying to break down the door by physical force alone. He was wasting time, and the law would arrive at the scene at any moment. He needed the witness done with and out of his hair, so to speak.

There was commotion over by room 506. His colleagues were seemingly running into more trouble than they had bargained for, but he was convinced that they would deal with it accordingly. One shot from his gun was all it took to blow the door open. He aimed for the lock and half the door and some of the frame sent splinters flying both through the bathroom out into the hallway. His ears played that familiar ringing tune in his ears that only a well-played shotgun could produce.

The door swung out on its hinges followed by a couple of desperately fired bullets that passed through his coat, the hint of a pistol quickly visible round a corner. He stepped back, loaded another shell into the spent chamber, and walked inside to the bathroom. The sinks were to his right, and on the opposite side were three stalls, all of which had their doors

102

shut tight. This was going to be both easy and fun for him. He chuckled as he took careful steps forward, and then he caught something in the mirrors hanging above the sinks. It appeared to be a figure in a tight-fitting red and blue suit. The thing that had first caught his eye were the two points of light emanating from two eye sockets situated above a ghastly grin.

He spun around and fired a round back from where he had come, but the doorway was empty, and now he stood there with only one round left in his smoking shotgun. The figure stepped into the doorway again; Jensen was relieved that his mind hadn't played a trick on him. It stood at least six feet, was lean and muscular, dressed in skintight fabric, and that awful face was obviously a mask now that he got a good look at it with its fangs, protruding red eyes and horn-like appendages.

The man, for a man it was, held a wavy sword in his right hand, slick with blood. Jensen didn't think, he acted and fired his second shot at the man who slid across the floor to avoid the blast and caught his shin with his boot. Jensen toppled forward, gun flying, and would have landed on his opponent had he not rolled straight past him. He landed hard, losing his wind and becoming tangled in his coat.

After what seemed like forever, he managed to get to a standing position. In the process, he had fished his switchblade from his back pocket. The man in the mask was also up, standing with his sword at his side, facing Jensen who was crouching with his own blade at the ready. He lashed out aiming for the man's abdomen. He wanted his death to be painful and slow.

The figure sidestepped, and Jensen jabbed at thin air. As he hyperextended, he left himself open to a knee to the ribs.

Once again, the wind went out of him, and he felt the wet snap of bones breaking in his chest. Struggling for breath, he moved sideways and fell against one of the stall doors, one hand on his torso and the other still clutching the knife. The figure strode towards him with great calm, the blade still held at his side. Jensen thought he could hear the sounds of sirens in the distance, and he coughed as he tried to take a deep breath. He furrowed his brow and let out a gargled scream as he flew at his enemy.

* * *

Tony sidestepped the man, also dressed like the two he had already combated, who came at him while trying to scream - although it more sounded like the gurgling sound someone makes when drinking from a bubbler. He blocked the switchblade coming at him with his left arm and then pierced the man's gut with the kalis, pushing his entire weight back so that it went clean through and dug deep into the door behind. The man's eyes went wide, and Tony could see his pupils dilate as he struggled with the reality of his newfound situation. Blood bubbled up through his mouth, and his hands struggled to grab The Face in one last desperate attempt at winning the battle.

Tony quickly released him by pulling the kalis out, free from the door and the soft tissue of the man's abdomen. With a final gasp, his eyes went blank as he slowly slid down to the tiled floor and lay in an unnatural pile.

Tony had also heard the sirens outside, and he decided immediately that he dared not take a chance at talking to Lindquist when the police more than likely were bounding up the stairs. To go out through the window he came in would also be madness. So he ran back to the reception area, calculated in his head where the streets outside lay from his vantage point, and then moved through another room where an old woman lay petrified with her covers pulled up to her chin as he flung the window open and vanished into the night.

* * *

Geert waited in his black Studebaker across the street from the hospital. He had been a bundle of nerves as he saw the three hired guns walk in through the glass doors. Having brought a sandwich, because he always ate when he was nervous, he dug into it almost immediately, but he had eaten it slowly as he strained his ears to hear the sounds of gunfire. He knew far too well that Charles, Jensen and Thorne would refuse to perform their task quietly. No, they wanted the world to know what they were doing. After a good ten minutes, he believed he could see the muzzle flashes in the windows of one of the floors. He sighed and remembered to once again chew and swallow.

After another few minutes had passed, he once again slowed his progress on the snack. The men should have been done by then; they should have done the deed and then sped off into the night. To make matters worse, he now thought he heard sirens in the distance. Something seemed to have gone horribly wrong; he flung the sub out the window and stepped on the gas, speeding down Grand Avenue as the police cars came around the bend.

CHAPTER NINE

Even though Bali was under the imperial rule of the Dutch, it was a peaceful place. The natives had never made much noise and lived out their existence in their villages without a care for their European rulers. Therefore, the Dutch had never seen the need for a true military presence, like the one that they had on the other islands. Instead, 600 native soldiers and a few Dutch officers, led by Lieutenant Colonel W.P. Roodenburg, made up Korps Prajoda.

Wayan had been asked to join the corps - mainly because of his fighting prowess, but also, in part, due to the fact that he had served in the Royal Netherlands East Indies Army, stationed in Batavia. He had gracefully declined the offer, no one knew why, and vanished into the wilderness. When the war in the Pacific broke out, the government in Batavia panicked. It became increasingly clear that the Japanese had their sights on the Dutch East Indies, and Anthony's father claimed, over brandy in the governor's sitting room, that the days of Dutch imperial rule were over.

Emperor Hirohito's campaign was successful. Initially he spared Bali. Mr. Hill returned to his mansion on the island and would spend the first few days standing on his porch with a scotch in his hand, trying to figure out if it was time to flee or stay. The airfields in Borneo would not serve their purpose, at least not the Japanese needs, and in 1942, the Imperial forces landed on Bali. Korps Prajoda could do little to stop the superior army, and the island quickly came under Japanese rule. Mr. Hill decided to stay.

* * *

He had to stop beginning his mornings like this, Teague told himself as he removed his hat and stepped past the threshold into St. Mary's Hospital. He was uncertain how many days it had been since the last homicide call; he had barely slept, barely been at home. His wife had found him asleep at the kitchen table. She hadn't even known that he had come home. After waking him, she had placed a cup of coffee in front of him and then given him the telephone receiver. One of the receptionists from the station had been on the other end. Another shooting, this time at a hospital. He had downed the hot liquid, gone to the bathroom and then changed shirts - from his plain white one to one with blue pinstripes to match his dark blue suit. Mrs. Teague had circled him to make sure he was presentable. Even though he had argued that such things mattered little at a murder scene, she had insisted.

"It's important to always look professional," she had said and then kissed him on the cheek. "You sure you don't have time to shave, dear?" He had shaken his head, checked the cigarette case, and then headed out the door.

* * *

The reception area of the hospital was teeming with activity. There were nurses, doctors and police everywhere, and this was only the first floor. A pig-faced older officer came up to him and demanded ID. Teague presented his badge without even looking at the man and his sweaty features. They had met before, around the station, there was something about the man that sickened him. It could have been his pale complexion, bordering on translucent, that turned to pink whenever he was under great strain. This seemed to be mostly all the time. On the other hand, perhaps it was the smell of old sweat that appeared to follow the man like an old, wretched dog.

Teague remembered the time they first met. It had been his first year on the force, and the man had looked close to retirement even then.

Nervous that he was going to make a bad impression on the rest of the men at the station, he had been conscious of an odor. Like a blend of something sour and at the same time sickly sweet. Concerned that he was the one offending those around him, Teague had rushed to the washroom and had, less than attractively, smelled his armpits, undressed, and investigated his clothes, but without result. It wasn't until the second time he and the obese officer crossed paths that he understood what the repugnant smell was. He was now relieved to smell that some things never changed.

"What have we got, Officer?" Teague asked the man, speaking while trying to hold his breath at the same time.

"It ain't here, Detective Teague." The man spoke in a German accent and wiped his pink forehead with a dirty rag, leaving a trail of black against his skin. "The nasty business is on the fifth floor." He pointed upward as if Teague had difficulties with which way that would be.

"Who is on the scene so far?" Teague asked and looked around to see if he could find any familiar faces.

"Detective Glade and Officer Boden were here early on." The man wheezed. "Boden should be around here, and Glade is already upstairs."

"Fine." Teague sucked his gums and furrowed his brow in concern. Boden was an effective young officer that would be going places, but Glade... He needed to get to the crime scene before that idiot messed it up. "Tell Boden that he has the lead on setting up a command center down here. I don't want any friends or relatives of patients coming in. Only authorized doctors, nurses and maybe the odd candy striper - if their identities can be verified."

"Very good, Detective." The officer seemed a bit peeved that he hadn't been put in charge of operations on the entry level. As Teague headed towards the elevators, the man called out to him. "Detective Teague!" Teague halted and looked over his shoulder. "Whatever happened to our Belle City? It never used to be like this."

"I believe crime has always been around us," Teague began. "It was easy to ignore when it was localized to the poor areas, but now it is knocking on our front doors, and suddenly we are afraid." He walked on, ignoring any kind of reply; he didn't feel like engaging in a debate about the socio-economic state of the region.

An acrid smell of gunpowder and blood wafted towards him as the electronic doors of the elevator opened. It was as if the metallic scent lay heavy like mist on a cool summer morning. Teague had never been to war, flat footed, but he had spoken to enough veterans at the bar of The Hobnob on Sheridan Road to imagine what it was like. Here a crimson-stained tiled floor replaced the blood-soaked fields of France, but otherwise, it was probably pretty much the same.

Detective Glade, on the other hand, had been to war, serving on the beach on D-Day, and Teague believed that his experience overseas was what had scrambled his brains. He could hear the hustle and bustle of his colleagues at the end of the white corridor he had stepped into. He followed the sound and came upon the reception area. This was where the repulsive smell became the most offensive.

The tapestry of carnage startled him. He had seen his share of crime scenes, especially during his time as a younger beat cop. Those days he had patrolled the poorer neighborhoods of the city. The recently developed houses beyond Durand, where the streets were little more than mud, and the children of day laborers were forced to play around the water tower and scrap yard. It was a sad situation most of the time. People wandering up from the south in search of a better life, some picking beans in the fields, being subjected to whatever pesticides the farmer spread out, and some doing the odd jobs that might pop up in the area. The lucky ones found work in the factories.

It could tear your heart in two, seeing the aftermath of a drunk husband coming home to a wife, wondering where his paycheck had gone. At night, the images of wives beaten to a bloody pulp while the children were trembling in a corner of the home. He had also seen bodies lying in alleyways after drug deals gone awry, but nothing could compare to what was before him in this moment. Teague noticed that he had frozen in place, his hand tightly gripping the cigarette case so that his knuckles turned white.

Detective Glade sidled up next to him with a pad and pen in his hands. He was silent for a moment, making sure that the detective had time to find his bearings, tapping the pen against the pad.

"Whenever you're ready, sir," the detective said.

Teague sighed and put the case back in the pocket of his jacket. "What have we got, Glade?" He asked.

"We have five victims total," he began, paging through his notes as he spoke. "One mortally wounded and one unscathed. Also, several patients who are visibly shaken."

"So, there are more survivors this time?"

"Right." Glade looked at Teague with a raised eyebrow. "Do you want to speak to them now?"

"It can wait." Teague slowly moved closer to the reception desk, absentmindedly. The height forced him to get up on his toes, in order to peer over the top of the desk. His height had always been a cause for jibes from friends at the academy, but his instructors had convinced him that how tall you were had no bearing on your skill as an officer.

On the floor lay the receptionist. On her back with her body awkwardly twisted so that her back lay flat, but her legs were facing to the right. It was as if she had tried to move when she went down. In her right hand, she was clasping the receiver of the phone that lay in pieces next to her. Her brown eyes were wide open, staring at the ceiling, and her red lips slightly parted. Teague imagined he could hear the last gasp of life escaping her, the moment frozen in time. There was a nasty entry wound in the center of her forehead, and her brown hair lay swimming in the pool that her blood had created, like a halo around the head.

"Her name was Jennifer Woods," Glade informed him. "Twenty-one years old and recently engaged. She started working here about a month ago."

"I'm guessing she would have been the first victim." Teague walked around the outside of the desk, towards the time sheet that hung on the wall, covered in Miss Woods' blood and brain matter.

"How so, sir?"

"Seeing as how she was hit so squarely between the eyes, it may indicate that she had not initially perceived a threat."

"Otherwise, she would have been trying to avoid the bullet." Glade excitedly wrote the information down.

There were police officers and forensic specialists everywhere, and Teague greeted them with nods as he tried to wind through them. Flashes went off at regular intervals, and it distracted his thought process immensely.

Before he could circle the desk, he came across two more bodies. One was that of a guard and the other a police officer. The elderly guard had been little more than cut in half, his blood was splattered all over the walls and spread across the floor, impossible to avoid. The police officer - Teague recognized him as one of the men sent to protect Lindquist - lay crumpled up, clutching his stomach.

"Johnathan Nyman and Officer O'Brien," Glade called out from behind him.

Teague sighed. The officers on the scene had decided not to draw a chalk outline around the two bodies, which would have been impossible to accomplish, due to the amount of blood. He looked around for the chief forensic analyst, but he couldn't see him. He grabbed a young man taking pictures. "Where is Dr. Price?" The youngster pointed towards the washrooms and then continued about his business. Teague followed his directions and stepped over the body of O'Brien to move towards the toilets.

He made a note of the fact that the door to the washroom was hanging off its hinges with the lock obliterated. Splintered wood hung from both the door as well as its frame. Someone had wanted to get inside by any means. He looked down and noticed shell casings strewn in the crimson.

Doctor Price, a round man with wild gray hair and a matching salt and pepper beard, was standing near another body. This one was not an officer or a guard. Teague kept his eyes on the figure as he walked closer. It was a burly man, dressed in a trench coat. The body rested face down on the once-white tiled floor so that the jet-black hair was the only means of identifying the man. Next to Dr. Price, an assistant documented the scene.

"Detective Teague," Price said in a broad Midwestern accent. The good doctor was from up north, a floating geographical area depending on where you were from. In this case, Robert Price had moved down from Door County. He had studied medicine at the University of Madison and then continued his movement to the Southeast. All the while, he retained the characteristic dialect that was the ridicule of so many television shows.

"What is the scoop here, Doctor?" Teague bit his lip expecting the worst.

"Quite the bloodbath if you ask me." Dr. Price pushed his black-rimmed glasses up his nose. "A young woman killed by a gunshot to the head. Two police officers and a guard shot to death by shotgun pellets, and two thugs killed by what I can only assume would be a blade."

"This again." Teague sighed. "I guess it's too early to tell if it's the same blade that killed those thugs down in the parking structure downtown?"

"If I were to venture a guess..." Price grabbed a notebook from the hands of his assistant. "I believe it to be the same weapon. Of course, I would need a closer look, but there seems to be some form of an anomaly with the weapon."

"Continue," Teague said, even though Price had only paused to catch his breath.

"It leaves a very odd cut. I noticed it in the parking garage victims, and I saw it on the body down the hall. The one whose arm was severed."

"His arm was severed?" Teague scratched his head. This was getting bizarre. As if a killer wielding a blade wasn't odd enough, he had to go cutting people's arms off as well. Why couldn't he just stab them like the Armenians?

"He bled to death. This one appears to have been stabbed through the chest." Price pointed to the prone body on the floor, and then turned to the bathroom stall that was behind him. "It looks as if he also was pinned to this door for a moment." The doctor pointed to a visible cut in the wooden door of the stall and a patch of blood that had left a trickling trail down to the floor.

"So, we are dealing with someone with a great deal of strength?"

"It would appear so. To run a blade through a person and then push that weapon through this." He knocked on the solid structure of the door. "And the blade must have been very sharp."

"Razor-sharp," the assistant agreed.

"You guys seem to have moved quite fast. I only counted three bodies out there." Teague gestured towards the reception desk.

"There was no room to maneuver if we hadn't." Price explained. "Added to that, one of the trench coat victims, the amputee, was in the room of the patient in 506."

"The patient in 506?" Teague had forgotten about Lindquist for a moment. He was probably the target of the killer or killers, as the case may be. "Is he alive?"

"Well, he is not counted as one of the victims at this point." Price smiled an inappropriate smile. "He has been moved to the same room, one floor down."

That settled him down a bit, and he made a mental note to take Lindquist's statement before he left for the station.

"So, we have begun the process of moving all the bodies to the morgue. I can't give you any more details until I have examined them closer. It will also give my guys enough room to investigate the scene thoroughly."

Teague nodded, for it all made sense. "I will get out of your hair then, Doc," he said and tipped an imaginary hat, seeing as how he was still holding his real one in his hands. "I will continue to make the rounds here."

Teague didn't have to navigate through the bodies on his way out since the forensic team had already moved them. He could see them being wheeled towards the elevators. Stained white sheets covering them. In his mind, he saluted them. Contrary to popular belief among the upper middle class in the city, violence was common.

Ever since drugs had become more prevalent, brutality had followed. Street justice the criminals called it. Once he had interviewed one of the Lehman brothers. He had tried to convince Teague and Fred West, his partner at the time that the gangs in the region should police themselves. They held each other to a higher moral standard than the government ever could. Taken straight from the Good Book no less. Officials always got it wrong, subject to all forms of bribery. It was why society would fail in the end, the slimy middle-aged gang leader behind steel-rimmed glasses claimed. It was better to let him go, and he could handle it all himself, with the detectives, of course, getting a taste.

To a young police officer with a mortgage and a pregnant new bride, it might be quite the deal. Lehman had winked at Fred at that moment, sending Teague's partner over the edge. He had punched the thug and given him a piece of his mind. Fred was a deeply religious man, and having this smarmy bastard try to claim some form of biblical high ground infuriated him. Because of a lack of evidence and no witnesses to come forward, the man walked, and within a week, Fred West was found floating down the Root River.

Officer Boden ran right into him when he exited the washroom. He was supposed to be setting up the command center a few floors down but was apparently here now. Teague, distracted by the bodies carted off, and he had not been looking where he was going. "Detective Teague," the officer said nervously, causing Teague to raise his eyebrows in concern. Boden looked pale, and he had quite a visible glean of sweat covering his face.

"What is it, Officer?" he asked.

"The third man," Boden began.

"Yes."

"The one who had survived."

"Right."

"He has unfortunately passed away."

Teague tugged at his reddish-blond beard and then smacked his leg with his hat. "Dammit, Boden," he cried. "What happened?"

"I am not sure, sir." Boden paged through the notes as if the answer might hide therein. "It was just reported to me by one of the other officers on duty. Apparently, Detective Glade is with the body. You might want to ask him, sir?"

As if he didn't have enough problems - a secret witness, two dead police officers, a dead guard, a dead secretary, and three dead unknowns - now he had to deal with Glade as well. "Fine, I'll go talk to him."

"And sir." Boden halted him as he turned to walk away. "There is the other survivor." Teague turned around, slowly.

"There is?" he said in a quiet and controlled voice.

"Yes, sir."

"Where is he?"

"He has been taken to protective custody downtown, sir."

"All right. You call down there and make sure no one talks to him until I get there."

"Right," Boden said and grabbed his walkie-talkie. "The third John Doe is in room 502, sir."

"Thank you, Officer," Teague said and headed to the room.

CHAPTER TEN

While the Imperial Army ousted the Dutch rulers from the East Indies, Mr. Hill remained. As soon as the Japanese landed on Bali, he greeted them with open arms. He opened his stately home to them and served a celebratory dinner. Young Anthony was there as well. At that point, he hadn't seen his biological father for several weeks, and he was at first reluctant to go when his tutor informed him of the dinner. Wayan convinced him that it was only right to attend; no matter if you do not agree with your family's decisions, it is the duty of the eldest son to stand by his master.

For the first time in years, Anthony dressed in a full suit. He had taken to running around the jungle in nothing more than a pair of linen shorts, and whenever he was doing his lessons, he donned a white shirt - as not to offend the women of the household.

Mr. Hill impressed the new Asian masters of the island, and they valued his knowledge of the people and the government the Dutch had set up. They decided to keep him on as a liaison in their provincial government. They allowed him to keep his home and granted a stipend. He was not allowed to take part in any actual governing, but he was expected to sit in on meetings in an advisory capacity.

It was odd to Anthony to see his father every day, instead of maybe once a month, but he welcomed it. Most of the time, Mr. Hill stayed in his office and drank - when he wasn't dealing with the Japanese. It was the only vice that was left to him since the nightlife of Batavia had been permanently shut down. The tutor, Mr. Mahr, was also convinced to stay on. He had made his mind up that he would flee once the Japanese made landfall, there was something in the eyes of his young tutee that tugged at his heart. He had not been able to pack his trunk.

At first, the Balinese people had welcomed the Japanese. The Dutch were by no means cruel, but they had a form of paternalistic view of the natives akin to the famed Albert Schweitzer. Soon the act of war requisitions throughout the island, though, made the new masters more resented than the earlier ones.

After an especially violent episode in their village, one that Anthony, fortunately, did not witness, Wayan decided to act. He sought out and joined the so-called Freedom Army; led by the military officer I Gusti Ngurah Rai.

* * *

Tony had caught a couple of hours of sleep the rest of the night. He had felt satisfied with a job well done, but he realized that he needed to make it an early morning also. There would be breaking news, and they would need him down at the station to cover it. Very much like with the police, these things were an all-hands-on-deck situation.

At five in the morning, he had bolted up from his twin bed in a cold sweat. He had forgotten to recover his kris from the bushes below the hospital. He had jumped out of bed and dressed as quickly as possible. It would be impossible to retrieve it dressed in his gear now; the sirens he had heard as he left the scene indicated that the police were on their way, he would have to hope that they somehow would miss the blade. There were certainly other matters of greater importance, but if the police did their jobs properly, they would likely find it.

The sun was already shining quite brightly when he rounded the corner from 15th Street on to Grand Avenue. It was so strong that it even reflected off the dull dome of St. Richard's Catholic Church as it towered against the blue sky. He had parked the car on Villa Street, one block over, as to not arouse suspicion, and because the street outside St. Mary's would most likely be blocked off at this point. He was correct. There were wooden barriers blocking off either side of the street. That is to say, between 15th and 16th Street.

When Tony approached the yellow barrier that read *Police. Do Not Cross*, a young police officer politely told him to move along. Tony had then presented him with his ID, informing the young man that he was WRJN's own Tony Hill, and that he was interested in having a gander so that he knew what to report on later on that evening. At the promise of naming the officer by name, the man let him pass without further argument. Tony wiped his forehead, for the sun and his nerves were making it uncomfortable in his gray pinstriped suit. He wasn't the first member of the press to arrive on the scene. He recognized men from the local newspaper and radio personnel from both Chicago and Milwaukee. He gave them all a slight nod with his head and tipped his hat, but they all gave him callous stares, everyone but the newspaperman clueless to his identity.

There were armed patrol officers standing at the top of the steps with shotguns in their arms, checking the identities of both doctors and nurses. The young candy stripers promptly turned away, as were most of the journalists who tried to sneak inside. Tony scanned the bushes at a distance, in the hopes of catching a glimpse of steel reflecting in the sunlight, but he was out of luck. There was so much life outside the hospital that any attempts at closing in on the vegetation and rifling through it would be seen as highly suspicious. All he could hope for was that no one would trudge through the bushes, maybe that they were too thorny, so that he could return that night.

He also hoped to have a date with the surviving thug; he was in desperate need of a lead. Tony sidled up to his colleague from WRJN, a Cecil Fields, who informed him that they were still waiting for official word from the Police Department. Most of what he had come across was speculation. Nurses and doctors who had been inside the hospital when things started up. There had been gunfire on the fifth floor, and then there had been none.

There was nobody who could give a clear answer to what had happened and to whom. One of the guards on one of the lower levels had decided to telephone the authorities instead of venturing upstairs. A wise choice both Tony and Cecil agreed. Tony turned and walked back to his car on Villa to head to the office. Vic Linden, with his round face and unkempt appearance, would probably need him earlier than the five o'clock news this day.

* * *

"So, what is this? Garfield Teague said, as he looked at the sharp object the police officer held before him. He had subconsciously placed a cigarette between his lips and now it was hanging from the lower one. The dry paper stuck to the wet flesh.

"I'm not sure, sir," the officer said. "I found it in the bushes on the right side of the stairs. I saw it as I returned from sealing off the street. It was sticking out of the ground as if it had just fallen and stuck there."

Teague took out his handkerchief and grabbed the hilt of what appeared to be a dagger. He held it carefully, with the point facing the floor. The hilt was not like most knives he had seen before. Curved and made from thick wood. Designed to look like some form of Asian demon, it resembled something he thought he had seen in one of the museums in Milwaukee. The face of the creature had bulging, almost piercing eyes, large fangs, and long wavy hair. The blade was also wavy and adorned with writing in an alphabet he didn't recognize, and figures engaged in battle. The same demonic face was also visible here.

"What do you think, sir?" the officer interrupted. "Did a professor at the museum on Main Street drop it while visiting?" The young man sneered in jest.

"I highly doubt it," Teague replied mirthlessly. "First of all, there have been no reports of any objects like this missing. Secondly, I have visited that museum many times, and this is not part of the Horlick collection. There is that mummified princess from Egypt, but nothing like this. Thirdly, the odd form of this weapon is very similar to what has caused the wounds on our victims that are currently on their way to the morgue."

The officer nodded as Teague handed the weapon back to him. "It's a beautiful piece," Teague continued. "Bag it and take it downtown. We need to have an expert look at it. Thanks, Officer, good job."

The police officer gave another nod and headed back to the command center that set up by the reception desk.

Teague continued his route towards room 502 - his earlier destination. This might just be a break in the case. Well, at least the portion of the case that seemed to involve a deranged knife-wielding lunatic, dressed in some form of costume. The idea of someone dressed in an elaborate outfit, taking it upon themselves to right whatever perceived wrongs in the world might exist was not new.

He had heard of other such vigilantes in the bigger cities - New York, Chicago, San Francisco and the like - but why such a figure would want to make an appearance in a city of 71,000 was beyond him. The vigilantes were all inspired by the pulp novels, and superhero comics published by Fawcett, Quality and Timely, to name a few. He had read them as a child; his father had owned a small cigar shop downtown, and young Garfield would look in on him after school and peruse the periodicals. It was what had inspired him to become a man of the law, so in a way, he had some understanding of those who chose to take it further.

Black Bat had always been his favorite costumed hero. A no-nonsense hero. A district attorney by day, who when he is blinded by acid thrown in his face his other senses became heightened. Through innovative surgery, he had a cornea replacement while retaining the elevated senses. Dressed in a black costume, resembling a bat, he fought crime at night. Sure, Teague had dressed up as him for Halloween and read all those books written by G. Wayman Jones, but he would never take it upon himself to go out at night and ape such behavior.

The real crime fighters also lacked superpowers, and all succumbed to the very real bullets from the criminals they tried to stop. Even though the craze died down in the late forties, a few men still carried the torch. Teague had always felt that doing the work of the law demanded working within the limits of the law itself, not taking it into one's own hands. To him, the character that had cut up the drug dealers in the garage, and probably the men at the hospital, was just as big a criminal as his victims.

He was about to knock on the door to 502 when it opened and a stretcher holding a body was wheeled past him. An orderly pushing it and gave him a solemn nod as he did so. Teague removed his hat and cast down his eyes in respect. No matter the reason for the man being there, a dead man, cut down in the prime of his life, was worthy of some small semblance of honor. Teague held the door until the stretcher had passed and then snuck inside.

Detective Glade was standing next to an empty hospital bed. The sheets stained with blood, as were his hands. He was clutching his own brown hat and staring out the window. His cropped brown hair was glistening with sweat, and his beard, always unkempt, seemed in more disarray than usual. He must have seen Teague's reflection in the glass, for he turned before his colleague had spoken. He wiped his eyes with the sleeve of his beige coat and put his glasses back on his face.

"Garfield," he said as he snorted. "I'm sorry that we couldn't save him."

"What happened here, Glade?" Teague was not as comfortable using the first name of people he did not see as friends. "We had two survivors, one of which most likely was both perpetrator and victim. He could have garnered so much information. Now we're basically back to square one."

"I came in here to question the man," Glade said. "Before I could get anything from him, he began to convulse, and then I called the nurses and medical staff, but it was too late. He died in my arms. I think he bled out. I tried to stop the bleeding, but I just couldn't do it." Tears started to well up in his eyes again, and he turned away.

"Shit!" Teague surprised himself at his inability to keep it professional. He slapped his hat against his leg and threw the cigarette, still dangling from his lip, across the room.

"Hey, I'm sure we can bounce back," Glade said. "There is so much forensic evidence that something will give us information."

Teague walked over to a chair placed between the window and the bed, pushing the detective off to the side. His entire body sank down in the white, faux leather cushion, and he rested his head in his hands, scratching at his beard. There were so many unanswered questions. The way he saw it, not that many roads that would lead to any answers. Every avenue, while not hitting a dead end, just branched off into more riddles.

Now, he had victims from, at least, two gangs. Where these new trench-coat-wearing men belonged was anyone's guess. There were dead police officers and civilians; one witness - obviously the target of this latest attack; a demonic figure wielding blades, wantonly killing those in his way, who probably left his weapon; and a surviving guard. Then there were the crates of drugs in the police warehouse. Whom did they belong to? It was becoming quite overwhelming.

When the extent of the investigations one had been part of previously all entailed domestic violence and the odd crime of passion, one was quite unequipped to deal with something of this magnitude.

"So, what are you thinking, Teague?" Glade asked in his high-pitched, grating voice. "I can take the lead on this one if you'd like."

He would like that, wouldn't he? Teague thought and bit his lip. Skin had attached itself to the cigarette paper and been torn off as he flung it away. He could feel the tinny taste of blood on his tongue, and the familiar sting of an open wound. "No," he said. "I've got it, Glade. Thanks all the same. I didn't have such a restful night and an early morning." He looked up at him and raised an eyebrow. "How did you get here so quickly, anyway?"

"I was at the station," Glade replied. "I was doing some late-night paperwork. The call came in, and I rushed over with the first responders."

"I see." Teague had fished out his cigarette case again and was tapping it against the metal armrest of the chair. Glade often worked late nights. He was the kind of man who burned the candle at both ends, yet he never seemed to get anything done. His reports were always late - if they even came in. Occasionally, he would get the lead on a case, but he muddled them up so badly that another detective would silently sneak in and take over. The man didn't have enough pride to say anything against it. He must have pushed his buddies in front the day they landed in Normandy.

As a government employee, it had been difficult for Chief Swan to fire the man, but there had been talks of a transfer. Maybe to a smaller station - Caledonia, Franklin or Sturtevant - but nothing had ever come of it. "Well, we have some other leads that might actually point us in some direction," he continued.

"That sounds good," Glade replied.

Teague rose from the seat with some difficulty. "We have another witness." He could see that he had Glade's attention. "A guard survived, I guess. Completely unharmed. Oh, and some other evidence that we have in our possession."

"Nice," Glade said with intrigue in his voice. "What exactly? If you don't mind me asking?"

Teague walked to the door, stopped, turned slightly, and then placed the hat back on his head. "You'll find out at the briefing."

* * *

Paul Geert was already on his third scotch when he finally calmed down. The morning sun shone annoyingly on his face through the tall windows in his room. He could have pulled the curtains, but now, it seemed like too great an undertaking. In addition, he somehow enjoyed the accusatory rays against his flushed face. It was as if the almighty was pointing at him and damning him for his misdeeds.

Since he was a little child, his parents told him he was sinful, and it had carried over to his adult life. Around his regular table in the restaurant of the Racine Hotel, he would jokingly say that it was a self-fulfilling prophecy. His mother had called him a sinner, and so he became one. Not to be a disappointment, he turned into one of the biggest ones in the city. "Look at me now, Mom!" He had called from atop the bar one night. "Look at what your baby boy has become! Are you proud now, Mother?" There was so much venom and spite in those words that he had regretted it long after. Not only thanks to the fact that he had slipped off the bar and twisted his knee.

He was relieved that his mother was no longer around to catch wind of his debauchery. The tinge of pain in his knee that he felt to that very day, he believed, was her way of getting back at him.

As he had sped around the corner, as the flashing police sirens passed him, luckily not paying him any mind, he had realized that he might have been a bit too hasty. Thorne and his friends had assured him that they could do the job, and from previous interaction with the trio, Geert was well aware that they never did things stealthily. No, letting everyone know what was going on was their way. It was obvious that the police would come as soon as the first bullets began to fly. He hadn't told them that he was going to wait for them outside; he wasn't their getaway driver as such. He had just wanted to ascertain that they kept their promise. Even so, it had seemed to Geert that it was taking too long for them to get out. The trio only had to put down two or three persons, maybe a couple more if they were unlucky.

Of course, the matter of sitting outside the hospital late at night would have been difficult to explain had the cops asked him. To get out of there when he did had been best for all. It was closing in on eight in the morning he noticed as he placed his tumbler on the glass table. He should have gotten word from them by now - if they had gotten out in one piece. If everything had gone according to plan. They always sent a note to him on completion, unless... unless they were forced to lie low. When it came down to it, walking into a hospital and killing a witness and several cops was a big deal. Most likely bigger than they had ever done before. It was also very likely that they had left a witness or two of their own. If so, then they would have to flee the state.

The law might not have known Thorne, Jensen and Charles, but their handiwork was infamous. If someone were to go snooping about in the underworld, he would soon dig up information about them. Geert had begun to perspire again, over the old dry sweat already present, and it made him feel even more gross than usual. His huge thighs had already begun chaffing him at the start of the previous evening. Now they were a mass of red blistering skin, he was convinced. He tried to move in the love seat as delicately as he could to avoid them rubbing against the fabric of his pants. The only thing that helped was to sleep naked, with legs spread apart, to let things air out.

He lifted the bottle of scotch that lay on the cushion beside him and opened it to refill the tumbler.

"Is it not a bit too early for such a voracious consumption of alcohol?" The familiar voice of The Black Diamond caused Geert to freeze in mid-action. He looked up from the bottle to see the figure dressed in his fitted black suit, hair perfect and domino mask on his face. His mysterious boss was standing, with great confidence, in the small hallway that led out to the hotel corridor, one hand to his side and the other tightening his black tie monogrammed with a white skull centered in a diamond square. "Rough night?" He continued.

"A tad nerve-wracking," Geert replied in a trembling voice. "But I think everything went off without a hitch."

"Is that so?" The Black Diamond walked over to the other seat, looked it over for cleanliness, and then sat down. "I am not as convinced."

"What do you mean, sir?" Geert proceeded to fill the tumbler. "Care for a drink?"

The Black Diamond shook his head and raised a hand, just to clarify his point. "According to our agent within the police department, our friend in the hospital survived the attack." Geert's veins turned to ice. "In addition to this, our dear friends Thorne, Jensen and Charles were not so lucky."

"They were all killed?" Geert asked before downing the scotch in one gulp.

"Well not entirely," the boss began. "They are all dead now.

One of them was left alive, but we could not have this, so he has been eliminated now."

Thank God for that, Geert thought. "How did it all happen? Were the police ready for them?"

"I highly doubt the police had the wherewithal to be prepared for an attack like this one, even if a certain Detective Garfield Teague appears to have been with the target earlier in the day. No, this was the work of someone else."

"The same gang who attacked and killed Petersen and his boys?" Geert bit his lip.

"That is what I would assume." The Black Diamond's gaze pierced Geert's very soul as he stared at him. There was no real emotion there maybe because of the mask or just the coldness of those icy black eyes, but it was so difficult to read the man's thoughts. "Mr. Geert, it would seem as if we truly have a wild card interfering with our plans."

"That is what I was going to say, sir," Geert chimed in, only to be met with a raised eyebrow from the man sitting opposite him.

"Indeed," said The Black Diamond. "It is unclear what the agenda of this player might be. Currently, we have yet to know if it is a single figure or an organization, and if they want to horn in on our market."

"Maybe it is one of the Lehman's returning?" Geert said enthusiastically. "It is possible that some relative came away unscathed and has been hiding up north for a bit. Now they want to hit us where we live, to bring us down. Maybe that is their only reason for this." He felt he had come across a real explanation for once, one that wasn't silly and completely out of context.

The Black Diamond rubbed his neck for a bit. "That does not seem very likely either, I'm afraid. We have kept an eye on whatever remnants of the Lehman Empire remains. We even eliminated the minor bases that were in existence as far up as Eau Claire. This does not fit their method at that. No, this is something fairly different, and maybe even for another reason than just an attempt at joining the underworld drug business."

He relaxed a bit in the chair, placing his arms on the armrests. "According to our source, now mind you he has yet to give us a full report, whoever killed our trio of hired guns used the same mode of operation as seen in the parking structure."

"The Asians?" Geert spoke while holding the bottle of

scotch to investigate its contents.

"They have never expressed any interest in coming to this state," The Black Diamond answered, and his voice changed from its robotic cadence to one a little bit more human. "They do have a vested interest in Chicago, from where our goods have to be moved through, though. Could be that they are trying to send a message to us. Maybe they are no longer pleased with the fact that we smuggle our goods through their city using their railroad." The Black Diamond actually smiled at Geert. "Could be that you are on to something there, Paul. I will have to investigate."

The Black Diamond rose from the chair in one fluid motion and straightened his suit. "Mr. Geert," he said, back to his monotone voice. "Please clean yourself up and take care of the business here at home while I am away. We still need to deal with our dear Mr. Lindquist, as well as any other unpleasant occurrences that might appear. I will have my man report directly to you, and do not forget our contact downtown." He once again straightened his tie with the skull emblem and exited the room without ceremony.

Geert was unsure what had just happened, but he put the bottle to his lips and downed the last few drops of the amber liquid. A hiccup escaped his throat, and he hit his chest with his fist. The responsibility was nothing new. He had been solely in charge several times when his boss was away on *business*, though never previously to such a degree that the man's aide would report straight to him. Geert rose with some difficulty from his seat. The scotch had taken the desired effect. He wasn't going to die today. He had believed that this was going to be his final failure, but his speculation into the

Windy City Yakuza had distracted his boss enough to let him live another day, or more even.

Now he felt foolish, having tried to dull his senses. The burning sensation from his thighs flared up, and he could feel wetness in the seat of his pants. He had wet himself... again. Gently he sauntered off to the shower to clean up. He needed to get in touch with the inside man. He needed to know what the cops knew so that he could plan their next move.

* * *

"So, Mr. Lindquist." Teague sat down beside the bed and placed his hat on the side table. "It would appear that you once again, are in the thick of things."

Martin Lindquist hazarded a smile at him as he lay there beneath the sheet. "I don't mind telling you, sir," the young policeman began, "that I am awful relieved that I have a catheter."

Teague smiled. It felt good to find something comical in this ghastly business. The instinct to smile meant that he still had a sense of humor.

"It can come as no surprise that we are working under the assumption that they were coming for you," Teague continued.

"You wouldn't be any good at your job if you didn't, sir," Lindquist came back. "They were on their way in here. Well, not here exactly." He indicated his new room: 406. An exact duplicate of the room they transferred him from. Teague was fairly convinced that the same architect and builder had contracted every hospital in the city.

133

"Can you tell me what happened? As you remember it." Teague replaced his cigarette case with a notepad.

"I'll try." Lindquist scooted up a bit, and Teague aided him by propping up his body with pillows. "I was in a deep sleep when it all began. The two police officers on duty had checked on me earlier and then assured me that I was safe. To be honest, no one knew whom I was - not even those tasked to watch over me. A gunshot woke me, then several shotgun blasts. The noise was farther away, so not right outside the door.

The first couple of seconds I didn't want to open my eyes, afraid of what I might see. Once I did, I saw that same figure that had killed the others in the parking garage. Those pinpoints of red eyes stared at me."

"Did he, or it, say anything to you?" Teague interrupted.

"I don't think so," Lindquist said with the slightest bit of hesitation. "No, but it's hard to remember such details. Before he could come at me, for I was convinced he was there for me as well, he moved to the door. He flew at it, and then another blast followed. It blew a hole right through the door. You might have seen it upstairs."

Teague had seen the door in pieces on the floor. He nodded. "Then he did some acrobatic flips or something and was back in the room, only to fly at the door again. That is what I know. There was noise in the corridor, and one of the killers collapsed in my room. After that, all I heard were more sounds of gunfire farther away."

"Thank you." Teague put the notepad in his lap. "It's not much, but at least that confirms that the trench coat men that showed up here were not with the masked man." Teague had taken the dagger found in the bushes and showed it to

Lindquist. It was in a big plastic bag, but the details were clearly visible. "Do you recognize this?"

"Sure." Lindquist turned on the light attached to the headboard and held the bag up to it. "This looks just like one of the weapons the guy was swinging. This is a bit shorter than the other one he had, but otherwise, it's exactly the same." He leaned in for a closer examination of the blade itself. "See this figure on the steel, and the head on the handle?" He showed it to Teague.

"Yes, I've seen those," the detective answered.

"That is what the face of the figure looked like." Lindquist sank back after handing the bag back. "I didn't get a good look last night, but the other night, in the garage, standing on the back of the truck... That's him."

Teague lifted the bag and looked at the wavy form of the blade again. He strained his eyes to read the swirling pattern of figures dancing in some form of merry battle. He then let his gaze fall upon the hilt again. Protruding eyes, fangs, and the demonic stare. "So, this is who we're looking for?" he said and held up the face of the hilt to Lindquist, in jest.

"That's him." Lindquist smiled. "Shouldn't be too hard to find. I understand why he tries to keep out of sight. With a mug like that, it must be difficult to remain inconspicuous." They both laughed, and it felt good.

Teague bid the young man good day and hoped that he had a speedy recovery without further incident. There didn't seem to be any more information that he could give them on the case, so they would arrange that he was sent to a safe house upstate. Green Bay maybe, somewhere that he would be out of harm's way. They might be done with him, but the bad guys didn't know that.

Once he had left room 406, Teague paused a while and leaned against the wall. It was just too much right now, he felt. Young Lindquist had assured him that the figure with the ghoulish face had not spoken to him, but he had hesitated just a bit too long before saying so. There was more there. That was obvious. Teague would put extra officers outside his door, and even a plainclothes cop watching his every move. He may have told Lindquist that the police were done with him, but Teague sure wasn't.

* * *

The bulbous station manager Vic Linden met Tony as he entered the offices of WRJN. He got right up into his face and the stench of cigar, sweat and day-old gin washed over him.

"Where the hell have you been?" he roared at him. "Don't you know it's all hands-on-deck when things like this blowup?"

"Sorry, boss." Tony held up one hand in defense, mostly to shield himself from the hail of his saliva. "First, I woke up late, heard the news on the radio and rushed over to St. Mary's."

"The hospital?" Linden quieted down and looked at him suspiciously. "What the hell were you doing there?"

"I figured it would just be easier to get straight to the scene of the crime, in case you needed a live report."

"Good thinking." Linden turned away and laid a hand on Tony's shoulder in what was supposed to be a fatherly gesture. He scratched his day-old stubble. "That was very well done, Hill, but the coppers are being tight-lipped at the moment. I'm guessing they'll be holding a press conference soon."

"Do you need me to get on that?"

"No." Linden continued to ponder. "I think I'm going to send one of our less articulate reporters to that. One that has a face for radio and a voice for the newspaper. I'll send Boar."

"So, what do you need me to do?" Tony really felt like he needed to get on the inside so that he could plan his next move. "Do you want me to do the play by play updates?"

"I've got Posen on that. One needs a man born without charisma to do such menial work you see. No, I want you to get downtown. I know people in the police department, and they owe me favors. Go to the back door and knock, let's say, four times, and someone will let you in. Once on the inside, you can poke around until they throw you out, but Swan is such a pushover, plus you know him now, that he won't give you the old heave-ho!"

"Can do, sir." Tony did a mock salute, and Linden spat on the floor, hiked up his pants and tightened his suspenders before he stormed down the halls of the station house in a cloud of smoke.

Tony clapped his hands together in an exaggerated gesture.

That went well. Infiltrating the police station as a journalist would most likely give him the information he needed. He trotted off to his office and began rummaging among his notes. He found the piece of paper with the skull/diamond emblem he had drawn. The shipment of cocaine halted this time, which meant that another shipment was imminent. He needed times and a place. That was his next goal. Grabbing the papers and stuffing them in his pocket, he headed out again. He needed to get his weapon as well before it was too late.

CHAPTER ELEVEN

Wayan was very concerned when it came to the Japanese occupation of his island. It wasn't just the requisitioning of goods and services that the invaders did, it was what the outcome of the entire affair would be. He was well aware that the Americans would not stand for the occupied Pacific and that sooner or later the East Indies would be the scene of great battles. He had also had a vision of his own demise, but it was shrouded in such mystery that he could not interpret the how and why. The premonition caused him to act.

One evening, he took his adopted son, Anthony, by the hand and brought him to the small straw hut that served as the village temple - a place he had yet to see. The single room was no more than a fire pit, with constant smoke billowing through a hole in the roof where the straw came together. The smoke stung Anthony's eyes, and forced him to rely on Wayan's strong hands to avoid walking straight into the smoldering ashes in the center of the hut. Once the tears cleared his eyes enough, he opened them and screamed at the horrific sight in front of him. A head hung on the wall. Great bulging eyes, a lolling tongue, a mass of hair, and a jumbled mass of vaguely organic tissue hung in tendrils from what would have been the neck. Wayan grabbed his shoulders and forced him to stare at the hideous visage before him.

"You must be brave, my son," Wayan spoke in his deep voice. "There are those who seek to harm the world, and then there are those who are tasked with putting fear in the heart of such men." He moved Anthony closer to the head. "In our family, we have been given such a task. I give it to you." With a firm grip, he forced Anthony to sit on the trunk of a tree used for seating. Now Anthony could clearly see that the horrible head hung above a small altar. Flanking that altar stood small statues depicting various gods of the Balinese. He had learned about them through his adopted mother and the legends told around the fire late at night. Wayan leaned over the altar and brought out a wooden box elegantly decorated with elaborate patterns. Wayan sat down next to him and placed the box gingerly beside him.

"This," he said, "is the symbol of fear. To men who have evil intentions in their hearts, it is horrible to gaze upon. To those who are innocent, it may still fill them with terror, but they will survive."

Anthony opened the box and gasped at The Face staring back at him. "What shall I do with this, Father?" he asked with his own fear coming through.

"When the time is right, you will know," Wayan replied. "You will wear it as your mark of power, and you shall fight those who seek to harm others. They shall know The Face of Fear."

It had been no great issue to get into the police station. He had sauntered up to the back door facing the alley. He had been forced to wait out a couple of middle-aged police officers who were smoking by the garbage cans, but once they had turned the corner, taking lunch at White Tower on Main Street, he gave the iron door four deliberate knocks. A scrawny cop, dressed in a uniform that obviously a size too big for him, opened the door and motioned to him to come inside and make it snappy.

Once inside, it continued to be smooth sailing. Most of the coppers, secretaries and lawyers ignored his presence. He was dressed sharply enough in his pinstriped suit, that they probably took him for a public servant. It took him a while to understand where he was in the large building. It had the same red brick exterior as most of the buildings constructed in the twenties bore. Completely square, the building looked easier to navigate from the outside than it was on the inside. When he finally found his bearings, by following a young woman carrying folders addressed to Chief Swan, he came to the large command center.

As he passed the large double doors he had sneaked past the previous night, he was amazed that he hadn't been able to hear the commotion from outside. It was quite the stark difference from what it had been at night.

He headed towards Chief Swan's office - the only one separated on this floor. The door was open and inviting to visitors. Tony tried to look as inconspicuous as possible as he traversed the network of wooden structures and bodies. Outside the office of the chief hung a corkboard, and as he drew closer to his goal, he could see that in photographs from the crime scene in the parking garage covered it. He paid special attention to one of the trucks and the crates. A young beat cop was trying to organize the photographs and assorted notes, making room for the stack of new ones that lay on a nearby desk.

One of the pictures already pinned to the board was a close up of the skull and diamond emblem. The cops had discovered that particular detail. He wasn't as far ahead of them as he thought. He needed to pick up the pace. He bumped into a man rising from his desk with papers in his hands. He excused himself, and the man muttered something incoherent. The man was dressed in a dark blue suit and sported a blond beard, which Tony found odd for a police officer. He was shorter than the average law enforcer was, and since he was dressed in civilian clothes Tony took him for a detective. If the desk was indeed his. As Tony moved the last distance to the office, he noticed that the man was following him. Did he suspect that Tony didn't belong there? The man was a cop after all.

Even though the door to the office was open, Tony found it pertinent to knock and as he was just about to do so, Chief Swan appeared in the opening. Tony almost bumped into his second cop in just the span of a minute.

"Excuse me, Chief Swan," he said and backed to the side, so as not to get trapped in between Swan and the man who was behind him.

Swan looked him up and down with skeptical air.

"Tony Hill," Tony said. "From the radio, remember. We've met."

"Right," Swan replied, distracted by the figure behind Tony. "What can I do for you Mr. Hill?"

"I wanted to see if you had any progress to report on the case," Tony probed.

"Nothing I can speak of unfortunately Mr. Hill. "Swan waved the other man over. "This is Detective Garfield Teague, lead investigator on the case." The man nodded to Tony but did not smile. "We have pressing business to attend to. We will have to talk later. You have my number, Mr. Hill."

Swan pushed Tony aside and fell in step with Detective Teague, who carried a plastic bag. His heart sank when he saw his kris through the clear plastic. They found it.

* * *

Just outside the city, due south towards the boarder to Illinois, situated right on the lake was one of the fanciest restaurants in the area. The Hobnob was famous for both its fine dining and elaborate yet contemporary rooms all decorated in a classic supper club style. From the grand ballroom to the more intimate Persian quarter with its fabric covered wall and secret entrance. It had only been open for about a year but had already garnered a reputation for hosting the upper crust of the area. Maybe that was why both Teague and Chief Swan felt out of place, as they were lead through the doors, past the neon sign boasting Food & Cocktails. Swan, due to the status of his office, should have fit right in, but finer establishments like the Hobnob made him uncomfortable and dressing in tuxedos seemed to have some form of suffocating effect on him. Once a year, on their anniversary, he would take Mrs. Swan to one of the high-class restaurants downtown and suffer through the process of attempting to choose wines he could barely pronounce, but that was for her sake and he was fairly certain she felt as out of place as he did. Teague on the other hand, coming from a humble background, never had the opportunity to set foot on such classy marbled floors, polished to the point that they reflected his image better than the mirror in his bathroom at home. Contrary to his chief, this was the kind of establishment he could see himself in one day and he was thoroughly convinced that he was meant to rub elbows with the well-to-do behind the plush velvet ropes. Those who knew him would claim that he acted as if he already was accepted in the exclusive rooms of the supper club, which was just fine by Teague, in fact, he welcomed it.

A tall, wispy, balding man with a thin mustache looked down his nose at them as they approached the podium with the small sign reading *Please wait to be seated*. With a very clear attitude of them not belonging in his establishment the man asked them, in a mock British accent, if he could be of assistance. Now both Teague and Swan were dressed in suits and could easily have fit in with any setting, but there dress was far from high end and this host seemed to be able to sniff it out from quite the distance.

"We are guests of Dr. Benton." Swann replied after a moment's awkward silence. "I am Chief of Police Swan and this is Detective Garfield Teague." The man sniffed in reply, as if the fact that Swan's title didn't faze him. He raised a tentative eyebrow and continued to stare down his nose at the visitors. He let out a sharp sigh, snapped his fingers and a younger man appeared at his elbow, dressed very much in the same style of black dress pants, white shirt and vest. The host whispered something in the other's ear and he ran quickly moved towards the main dining room.

After followed a very awkward silence between the three men. Teague stroked his beard and stared out through the glass doors to the parking lot where the mid-day sun was baking the concrete and black cars. Wavy lines of heat rose from the ground and blurred the vehicles like the static on his TV at home. Swan on the other hand focused more on annoying the host by leaning on his podium and bombarding him with various questions ranging from the menu, the specials of the day and how many patrons the restaurant welcomed in a day. The host became visibly annoyed but struggled to find any reason to leave his designated post. After what felt like several hours, but which was in reality only a couple of minutes, the young man returned and whispered something to the host.

"It appears Dr. Benton is expecting you gentlemen." He said through gritted teeth. "If you would like to follow me to his table." He stepped away from the sanctity of his ivory tower podium and led the way through the dimly lit hallway, without grabbing menus for them, assuming they were not going to eat.

They passed dark wood walls, checkered wallpaper and mysterious doors with brass knobs until it all opened to a bright room were the sunlight shone in through huge panes of windows.

Slung over his shoulder Teague had a cloth bag, very much like one might keep one's gym clothes in. Inside the bag, protected by plastic bag was the weapon they had recovered from St. Mary's Hospital. The make had stumped the forensic experts of the department, but at closer inspection, Swan had assumed the markings and design to be Asian in origin. This had led him to round up all the veterans at the station, specifically those who had fought in the Pacific. Some claimed to recognize the wavy form of the blade, but little more. One aged officer by the name of Paulsen informed

Swan that if anyone would know the origins of the blade it would be Dr. Benton. They had briefly met at the VA- Hall and Paulsen recalled that the good doctor mentioning his interest in artifacts from the various islands liberated from the Japanese.

It was but the work of a moment for Swan to call Benton Pharmaceuticals and get information from receptionist that Dr. Benton would love to be of assistance and instead of meeting him at the factory by the harbor he would like to invite him to The Hobnob for luncheon. Swan accepted and brought his lead investigator for good measure. The thought of entering the high-end establishment made his skin crawl and, even though he refrained from telling Teague, he felt he needed the moral support. Now they were, hat in hands, awkwardly wandering past tables covered in fine linens with silver cutlery worth more than the salary of his police officers. The suspicious stares from the bankers, captains of industry and old money who were having their lunches interrupted by riff-raff seemed to boar right through them as they headed towards a single table situated right by one of the large windows.

Dr. Benton rose from his chair and his soup bowl and stretched out his hand. He was impeccably dressed in a black suit, and he smiled with his entire face.

"I am sorry to interrupt, Doctor." Swan said as he took the man's hand. It was soft and delicate, almost like that of a woman. "Thanks for coming down on such short notice. We know how busy you are."

"Think nothing of it Chief." Benton replied and moved his hand over to Teague. "I will do anything I can to assist in this investigation."

"This is Detective Garfield Teague. Our lead investigator on the case."

"Delighted to meet you sir." Benton indicated that they should sit and snapped his fingers at one of the waiters, telling them that he needed menus. With the risk of seeming rude both Teague and Swan refused the menus as they were brought out. The waiter scoffed as he returned them to the host.

Benton had returned to his soup while they were waiting, placed his spoon down gently, and then dried his lips with a monogrammed napkin. "If you are not going to eat with me we might as well get down to business."

"That would be preferable," Swan replied. "We are working on something of a deadline. If you don't mind of course."

"So how is the investigation coming Detective Teague?" Benton turned his attention from the Chief and lifted a roll from the breadbasket.

"We are treating both the hospital incident and the murders at the parking garage as being interconnected," Teague replied. "The crime scenes have several similarities, but also some key differences."

"The massacre at St. Mary's is such ghastly business." Benton sighed and looked out over the lake from his seat. The water glistened as it reflected the light of the bright sun. "Where is the world coming to when people aren't even safe in a hospital?"

"Well it is what we are trying to figure out sir." Teague followed Benton's gaze over the water and considered how quickly the news had spread about St. Mary's. "What we can say is that it seems to be several groups involved and not only one perpetrator. The modus operandi from the parking garage and the hospital would indicate just the thing, but we don't know."

"If I can shed any kind of light in the dark where you are now located, I will do so." Benton turned to them both with tears in his eyes. "You must excuse me, but the thought of those brave officers and security guards who will not be coming home to their families just gets to me. That was why I jumped at the offer to help. It intrigues me how this might be."

"Well Dr. Benton we would like to know if you might be able to assist us with a find we made this morning at the crime scene," Swan replied and nodded at Teague to pick up the bag he had carelessly slung on the floor. "We heard that you served in the Marines during the war and that you fought in the Pacific."

"That is true."

Teague handed the gym bag to the Chief, who weighed it carefully in his hands, as if he was unfamiliar with the contents. Then he slowly pulled the plastic Ziploc bag from its hiding place and placed it on the table. "This is the object found right outside the hospital this morning. Our experts couldn't identify it, but to me it looks Oriental." Swan slowly pushed the bag gently, indicating that Benton could grab it.

He did, careful not to disrupt any of the flatware and turned it over in his hands. He smoothed the plastic against the hilt and blade to get a closer look at the carvings and markings. He clicked his tongue against the roof of his mouth as he considered the blade intently and then after no more than three minutes placed it on the table again.

"So what is the conclusion?" Teague asked. "Is it Japanese?"

"Not at all," the doctor said with his wide smile. "As you said, I served in the Pacific, fighting the Japanese, but none of them carried anything of this sort."

"So, another dead end," Teague's shoulders slumped.

"Not at all, my good detective," Benton continued. "You see, I have always been interested in history as well as foreign cultures. The East Indies have always held a special fascination. So, as we were liberating the various islands, I came across quite a few artifacts."

"Then you do know what this is?" Teague's eyes lit up like a dog waiting for a treat.

"I do. This happens to be a kris." He patted the blade. "It is a knife, obviously. An integral part of Javanese culture."

"Javanese?" Teague knew of Java. His expression was more one of surprise.

"Well, it is known all over Indonesia - Bali, Malaysia, The Philippines and so on. It does hold more importance on Java and Bali though."

He moved his hand over the weapon as he detailed its parts. "The hilt is known as the hulu and is often sculpted to look like some form of demon. Which this one obviously is. Sometimes made from precious metal, but this seems sculpted from wood alone. Wilah, the blade, usually depicts various legends. As you can see. I'd have to look closer to give you more information on just what story this one is relating, but maybe that should be after it has been thoroughly processed. These waves are called luk, and a kris can have anything from three to thirteens waves - always an odd number though. This one has the traditional thirteen. It severs more blood vessels in the body when used so that a victim will bleed to death faster."

"Gruesome!" Swan exclaimed at this information.

"Indeed," Benton replied. "The kris and the kalis, the sword variety, are lethal instruments of combat, but also have a lot of mysticism and magic to them. People believe it to have a soul of its own, and the pattern, the pamor, imbues the kris with this soul. All the elements of nature are present in a kris: water, wind, fire, earth - represented by iron - and the soul. All are present when forging it."

"That is all very interesting," Teague said as he took the bag off the table to return it to the gym bag. "But why would there be a killer using a Javanese weapon in our city. It's not like we have a huge Indonesian population here."

"The people of that particular area are known as good warriors," Benton added.

"And what would this have to do with our case, Doctor?" Teague replied.

"Not sure," Benton said and scratched his head in an awkward manner. "I was just saying. The warriors of the East Indies have always been fierce fighters. So, if they were having issues with criminal elements in our city, they would definitely spell trouble for anyone getting in their way."

After a moments silence Swann and Teague decided to leave Dr. Benton to his luncheon. They politely rose and thanked him for his help in the case. Benton nodded, but did not get up. Instead, he wiped his mouth on one of the white cloth napkins and made sure that the Chief had received an invitation to the soiree he was hosting.

As the detective and his chief walked back the way they had come. Teague quietly spoke. "Indonesian blades. That just opens up a whole other line of questions."

Swann nodded.

Martin Lindquist had managed to convince the nurses to let him out of his bed for a bit. The mass of police officers and forensic technicians had left the hospital, and the cleaning crew had done what they could to clean up the mess. Occasionally, he could hear the noise of machinery operated on the floor above. They were most likely repairing the damage the various bullets had caused. The nurses had been oddly tight-lipped about what was going on within the hospital walls. He had a difficult time remembering that they had no clue who he was, so they had no real reason for giving up any form of information to him. To them, he was just some gimpy thug - if they even cared to know that much about him.

An orderly had presented him with a wheelchair and had pushed him around the hallways a bit before driving him back, placing him by one of the windows. It wasn't really what he had wanted. In his mind's eye, he had seen them taking a quiet stroll down Grand Avenue, and maybe even visiting a small park somewhere, but alas, the big burly man had other plans. He had remained at the window for only a few moments before he decided to make a move. Most of the morning he'd been in deep contemplation. He was quite aware of the fact that he had escaped with his life intact for the second time in a row. He had not seen who his would be killers were, but he was quite convinced he knew of their identities. The underworld had its own folklore and mythic characters.

The trio of Jensen, Thorne and Charles were part of that lore in the Midwest. Their names spoken in the darkest corners of the seedy bars surrounding the factories. During his time with the crime syndicate, he could not remember them being hired, but Baz Peterson had mentioned them with a whisper. One wanted to avoid them called in to do your job. If that was the case, then you were not performing on the level you needed to be. After said task finished, then a visit from the trio was inevitable. If the masked killer sparing him the first time around was an oversight on his part, then the second encounter was more benevolent. Maybe he understood what Lindquist's role in the whole operation was. This meant that the man was privy to information that most of the cops did not have access to. This also convinced him that the figure was on his side.

Working outside the law was certainly a way to be more effective when it came to defeating a drug ring. Lindquist had thought about it long and hard. He didn't want to work against the police, but it was very likely that Detective Teague and his colleagues would be barking up the wrong tree for a long time to come. The organization, under The Black Diamond, was a labyrinth of people at different levels that by the time the police would make it to the top, would just be another dead end. No, the vigilante tactics of the masked figure were probably the right way to go.

He had also had boyhood dreams of running the streets in a costume, fighting bad guys. His favorite character had been The Blue Beetle. He had even listened to the short-lived radio show at the beginning of the 40s. The Beetle was a cop like him, but Lindquist never came across any power-granting magical scarab.

With the loss of his leg, those dreams were now out the window. That did not stop the possibility of him assisting the masked man, though. He did have information he had not shared with the police. He knew that it was obstruction of justice, but he knew that there was an agent within the police - even if he was in the dark regarding that person's identity.

He had wanted to keep his information under wraps to keep an eye on the situation. After all, he could not be certain that Teague himself wasn't the mole. On the other hand, the bad guys needed to be stopped sooner than later. He wheeled his chair around and headed towards the door. With some difficulty, he rose up on his one leg and opened it. Sitting down heavily, he strained to keep the door open with one hand while turning the wheel with the other. It was if he had to try to thread a needle, but by propping it up with the chair, he managed to scrape through, leaving an ugly mark in the wood.

He had visited St. Mary's a few times during his time undercover. Baz Peterson had an elderly mother, who was in and out of the hospital, as well as there being a fair number of thugs having wounds and whatnot treated.

Seeing as Lindquist was supposed to be attached to Peterson's hip, he naturally went along. He remembered that most of the first floor contained administrative offices, for senior doctors and hospital board members, but there was a cafeteria for those visiting relatives. There was also a library. Most of the time it was used by the medical staff or students who might be doing their internship, but patients, who were being treated for a longer period of time, were also allowed to use it. One of the nurses had even mentioned to him that she could bring him an assortment of novels. He had never been much of a reader, but if the book depository contained books of the more literary kind, maybe it would have other informative source material, not of a medical nature.

Most of the staff were busy with other patients or reading charts, and they ignored him as he wheeled past. He nodded to the two police officers set to guard him. They smiled and let him pass without question. The same with the two others flanking the elevators. It was surprising that the hired guns had even seen a need to enter, weapons blazing, when most of the personnel were completely uninterested in who came and went.

"Where to?" one of the officers asked him when he approached. He was young - early twenties maybe. Completely blasé, he leaned against the wall with his cap cocked back. He

looked like one of those Irish cops from the movies.

"Ground floor, please," Martin said, and he gave the officer and his aged partner a smile. The other cop looked like he was going to fall asleep. He wore a big bushy mustache and had silver hair that protruded from under his cap. Everything about him looked old. His rifle, his faded uniform, and the badge, having lost its luster that he wore on his chest.

The elevator chimed its familiar bell, indicating that it had arrived, and the doors slid open. Martin saluted the men. "Have a pleasant evening, officers," he said. "Stay safe."

"We'll give it a try, citizen," the elder officer replied and barked the kind of cough that always ended with yellowish slime in a handkerchief.

Once on the ground floor, Martin continued to roll down endless empty hallways, each one decorated with paintings of old hospital directors and retired doctors. There were also the obligatory pictures of the Virgin Mother and her child, as well as the Wind Point Lighthouse in all its glory. He had gone there once. On one of those rare occasions when he had a day

153

off. He had thought that the life of a police officer was hard graft but being on the other side of the law was equally as demanding. He had been at Park Inn with Peterson, Anderson and Camp after a successful pick up. Each of them was enjoying a steak and a brew when he spotted a young server by the name of Angela. She reminded him of a girl he knew in high school back in St. Paul. She wasn't overly tall, but she was blond with the kind of figure that one would like to grab onto while sitting on the porch, listening to the thunder roll, and watching the lightning light up the mountains.

Peterson had noticed his interest and nervous speech pattern when she took their orders.

"Why don't you ask her out, kid?" he had said. Martin had blushed at this remark and claimed that there was no time for romantic entanglement. "Don't be silly, kid," was the reply he had received. "Now is the perfect time to play the field. The three of us are so tired of our wives that we make up excuses to stay away from home." Camp and Anderson had laughed at this.

"The romantic aspect might not even be what you're looking for," Camp had added and spit his dip in his coffee cup. "Just have some fun with her."

"Fun time is all over for guys like us." Peterson winked at him. Martin was quite aware that his three mentors frequented the brothels on the outskirts of the city. They were the only places he wasn't allowed to follow them to. They forced him to wait in the car.

"Look here, kid." Baz leaned over to him. "I will give you the night off, and tomorrow too come to think of it. We can handle ourselves; Anderson can drive. Ask her out and show her a good time." He slid a fifty over the table and Martin pocketed it.

Baz had become the father figure he had always wanted. It wasn't like his own dad had been absent from his life, but he had worked in a factory. He had risen early in the morning, before the kids had woken up, repaired machinery all day, and then come home for dinner. Sometimes he was bleeding, sometimes bruised, but every night he covered in grime and oil. He ate in silence, kissed the heads of his kids, and then fell asleep on the couch. Martin and his siblings would at times crawl up next to his snoring form and feel the warmth from his exhausted body. Martin would inhale the very smell of his father: oil, stale sweat and iron.

His father gave all of himself for his family. He worked six days a week and never complained. The security of a home and food on the table was his gift, but he never gave any advice or spent quality time with them. The criminal Baz Peterson became that to him.

He had asked her out, and she had said yes. He picked her up from the house on Yount where she lived with her parents. Still quite unfamiliar with the city, Camp had told him to take her to Wind Point on the North Side. That was where he brought her. They watched the sun set over Lake Michigan atop the checkered blanket he had brought. They drank sparkling wine, ate strawberries, and talked about their lives up to that point. He avoided the truth and said he worked construction for the city and that the men he was with were honorable businessmen. She was skeptical, but she let it slide. She had started working at Park Inn in high school and had decided to continue after graduation while she tried to figure out her next step. Her father worked at Case and her mother, of course, stayed home. Angela was dressed in a polka dot dress and had her blond hair pulled back in a ponytail, gathered up with a red ribbon. She explained that Wind Point was the oldest lighthouse on the Great Lakes, built in 1880. As the sun made its descent, the light came on and lit up the horizon. Martin swore he could see the silhouette of the lighthouse keeper in the beam of light. She laughed, and then he kissed her. He dropped her off at home, and they decided that he would pick her up for work the next day, seeing as he had the day off.

For a month, he called on her whenever he had the time. The days he chose where they would eat, he picked her restaurant. Then they were to make a routine pick up in a parking structure downtown, and now he was here, missing part of his leg. He realized that he had been daydreaming. It had only been a few days, but he missed her more than he thought he would. Now that his three mentors were gone, and his family was back in Minnesota, she was the only relation he had. He looked down at the blanket he had wrapped around himself and thought about his stump. Would she even want him now? That was a question for another time; he needed to get into the library.

It was early afternoon, and the library was empty. There were a couple of people sitting, like him, in wheelchairs, crowding the fiction aisle. He saw a doctor or two with their attention turned to large tomes too heavy to carry. They had placed them on the cherry wood tables and poured over the texts with their brows deeply furrowed. A mousy woman in horn-rimmed glasses and a knitted sweater slung over her shoulders, the epitome of a librarian, greeted him with a smile and inquired if he needed assistance.

"Yes, please," he replied. "I am looking for a book that might have something about mythological creatures. Demons and such even."

"Something in the area of folklore then," she replied. "It would be filed under anthropology mostly. I will show you." To Martin's surprise, she walked behind him and began pushing the wheelchair down one of the aisles. The library itself wasn't very big - basically twice the size of his hospital room - but it was jam-packed with books of varying age. He could see books on the shelves that appeared to be falling apart, covered in layers of dust. He imagined that the library staff was none too keen on letting the cleaning staff roam around their babies.

Just like the tables scattered about in the room, the bookshelves were made from cherry wood, creating a pleasant contrast to the bleached covers of the books themselves. With acute navigational skills, the woman moved him among the furniture, and he was unsure if he would be able to find his own way out. Finally, they came to the section dubbed anthropology. Martin counted maybe ten books in all on the designated shelf.

"So, is there a certain aspect or type of mythology you are interested in, sir?" the librarian asked.

"Not really," Martin answered. "I'm not really sure what I am looking for. Something that might be about demonic beings in various myths."

"I guess something like this would do you then." She picked out a large book and showed it to him. The title read *Illustrated World Mythology*, and the cover displayed various figures carved from wood and stone. Hideous gargoyle faces and with too many arms.

"I think that will work, to begin with," he said.

The woman set him up at one of the tables, in a private corner of the library with a view of the street for maximum light. He began flipping the pages. An idea had popped into his head earlier that day. The mask of the figure that had been in his room the previous night had something very familiar over it. There was something with those eyes and the fangs that hinted at something he had seen as a child. He remembered going to the museum of natural history with his school. There had been a section highlighting different cultures in the world, and the face resembled something he had seen there. He tried to think back to that day. It was so long ago now; he must have only been nine or ten.

The exhibit of world cultures was large, but he wanted to say that this specific area was off the beaten path, more like an afterthought. He continued to page through the book, pausing at various points to look at the illustrations. He quickly moved past the African continent. Nothing there reminded him of the mask. The Asian chapter was more to his liking. There were photographs of what, to him, looked like dogs with the same basic appearance as the one he was searching for. They had similar eyes and grins, but the fangs were missing. The Far East was close.

Then it hit him. The bamboo walls, the blades, the water, tattoos in swirling patterns. It had been the East Indies. There had been wax models depicting the natives of the region. They looked nothing like the man Martin had seen. Muscular with a weathered look on their faces, and their glass eyes watching the horizon with that dreamy gaze that only imitation eyes can produce. He quickly flipped the pages to the chapter that treated myths from that region, and there it was. There was a black and white photograph of a carved statue. It looked like a pillar meticulously reformed to take the shape of a bulging-eyed monstrosity. He let his finger glide down the picture to the text below. *Rangda,* it read. *Queen of the demonic Leyak in Balinese mythology.* He leaned back in his wheelchair. So, the mask was Balinese.

There were some slight differences between the Rangda figure and that of the mask. She looked to have curly hair down her back, though this was hard to tell in the photo. What wasn't difficult to discern was the long tongue that hung from between four fangs. The mask might have had only two protruding incisors, but the tongue was missing. He chuckled to himself when he imagined fighting with such a thing swinging from the mouth. There was an illustration on the reverse page, a drawing of the demonic queen in full. The color scheme was different from the figure he had encountered- where Rangda was mostly white, with some gold additions, the masked man had dressed in blue and red. The additional information regarding Rangda was sparse, only a few sentences covered her. The chapter on East Indian mythology was only two pages at that and mostly pictures.

The leyak were demonic creatures - a flying head with entrails hanging from the neck. In daylight, they appeared as normal humans, but at night, the head ripped lose and they would haunt graveyards, feeding on corpses and animals. Martin was not interested in the background of it. He just wanted the image.

He had asked the librarian if he could bring the book with him back to his hospital room. He was feeling quite tired, after all. He had indicated the stump where his leg should have been, and it garnered the appropriate response.

Once back on the fourth floor, he almost went to the fifth one instead, the nurse had chastised for leaving the room. Then she chewed out the police officers who had just let him pass. He apologized, claimed to be bored and said that he needed some entertainment. Since she didn't seem like the song and dance type of nurse, he had decided to settle on a book.

She had laughed and had then granted his request for glue, a pair of scissors, and some construction paper without question. Arts and crafts had never been his strong suit. His grandmother had always tried to force him to get into it whenever he stayed with her. It had been in the latter days of her life, when her eyesight was failing, and her fingers had become twisted from the rheumatism.

He had tried, but he couldn't get into it. He regretted it now, when she was gone those were most of the memories, he had of her.

He had drawn the outline of Rangda's head on the white construction paper and tried to shape it so that the fangs were visible, by sticking out on each side, as with the horns. He had naturally opted to avoid the tongue. Once the cutout of Rangda's head was finished, he took some tape and fastened it to his window. Then he pulled the little side table in front of it, turned on the reading lamp, and pointed the light it emitted towards the cut-out. It would become a beacon for the masked figure. He remembered reading about something similar in one of his comics as a kid. He was hoping that it would snag the man's attention, and he would know that Martin wanted to talk to him. Once he was satisfied with his message, he crawled onto his bed, brought out his notebook and began writin

CHAPTER TWELVE

Wayan and his mask were quite active in the first year of the Japanese occupation- although The Freedom Army never engaged in open combat with the Imperialist forces; they did make life a bit harder. The Dutch had educated I Gusti Ngurah Rai, the leader of the group. Both in elementary school as well as during his military career. His plan was to gain Balinese freedom by breaking the Japanese from the inside. Wayan and Ngurah Rai met while both serving in the Dutch Military in Central Java and had met up again when the latter had become a second lieutenant in Bali. Ngurah Rai was well aware of the Face that lay in the wooden box, having seen Wayan don it on occasion. He had been the one to ask his old friend to pull it over his head again. He wanted it to be a symbol for the Indonesian people and their fight for freedom. Too long had they lived under the yoke of outside rule. The tribes of Bali had never been able to work together, and the

Dutch had easily exploited their various conflicts. They had swept in and conquered. Now, with Wayan's mask, maybe they could be united, and if the Americans would defeat the Japanese, they might finally have a chance at their independence.

* * *

Detective Glade and Officer Boden had spent most of the night before pushing desks and setting up folding chairs in front of Chief Swan's office. The station was so small and cramped when it came to space that there wasn't even space for a real briefing room. Instead, this was the chosen method. At least cases of this magnitude were quite uncommon. The preferred method used to give out information was to gather the investigators involved around the lead detective's desk. Most of the personnel started filing in around seven thirty a.m. as the time for the meeting had been set for eight. There were five rows of chairs. The first row dedicated to the most important investigators - chief forensics, detectives, and first responders. The rest of the chairs occupied by random police officers, and administrators Teague was pacing back and forth with a manila folder of papers. He had spent the morning pinning photographs to the corkboard and arranging his papers in the correct order. It was not his first briefing, but there were so many angles to this case, so many questions he could be asked that he didn't know the answers to, and that made him sweat.

He had actually gone home at a decent time the previous day, mostly because there was nothing more he could do. Today was the day they would gather their accumulated information to see where they would go next.

By seven fifty-eight there were no seats left, and Officer Boden came up to him letting him know that everyone was there.

"If everyone could pipe down," Chief Swan said, lazily holding a mug of hot tea in his hand, the little string from the bag still dangling from it. "We need to get this briefing going so that we can continue the investigation."

The sounds of murmuring subsided, the rustling sound of people seating themselves followed, and then silence. The ringing of a phone or the movement of an administrator occasionally interrupted this.

"Welcome to the briefing for the case assigned number 312-42, and no we have not given it any other nickname." Some of those present gave a little chuckle. "You all know how this works. I present to you the lead investigator on this particular case. Detective Garfield Teague."

There was a smattering of applause, mostly out of relief to not be the one taking the lead.

"Thank you, dear colleagues," Teague said and nodded to the assembled mass. He had allowed his wife to trim his beard and hair last night as he had soaked in his bathtub and today, he had dressed in his finest blue suit before coming to the office. He felt good. "We have a lot to go through this morning, so there is nothing else to do other than to get started." He picked up the folder and started to page through the papers inside.

"I guess we shall start at the very beginning of this case, or what we assume to be the beginning of it," he began. "Four days ago, at approximately midnight, two groups of known criminals, each with ties to underworld organizations, met up to do some form of drop-off. The place was the new parking garage downtown, bottom level. At the scene of the crime, we recovered a truckload of crates, all of them filled with what we now know to be cocaine.

Something appears to have gone wrong at the exchange as a third party wiped them all out.

"What we were not aware of at the time, is that a police officer had infiltrated one of the groups and was at the scene. He survived, badly maimed, but he survived, nonetheless. He is one of our strongest leads, now. He has informed us that the Irish thugs, known as the Lonergan crime syndicate, were there to drop off the drugs and that the group picking it up are known as *The Black Diamond*. This explains the faint marking we have found on each of the crates." Teague pointed to a photograph of a faint stamp on a piece of wood.

"The victims at this scene that you should be particularly interested in are Asa Camp, Don 'Rosey' Anderson, and their leader, Henry 'Baz' Peterson. These infamous in the underworld, but we have never been able to finger them for any crime. Peterson has run in several circles, and we believe he was instrumental in bringing down the Lehmans a few years ago.

The Irish, led by a man named Flanagan, are of less interest, and I will tell you why in a moment. None of the men appears to have killed one another; instead, a sword-wielding vigilante cut them all down. That is the main person we are interested in." Teague paced back and forth. "We will get back to him.

"Yesterday morning, at about three a.m., three men, dressed in similar attire and brandishing shotguns and revolvers, entered St. Mary's Hospital. This is where our only witness stayed. You remember. The undercover police officer who survived the parking structure attack. We also know these three men from before, although not by name. We call them The Trio and we believe them to be behind numerous murders for a variety of crime syndicates all over the Midwest and the East Coast. It is obvious that they wanted our witness. After killing the secretary Miss Jennifer Woods of Sheridan Road, recently engaged, police officers O'Reilly and Cole and the aged guard Mr. Fish, they headed to room 506. This is where our witness was sleeping.

"This is as far as they got. There were two guards - the deceased Mr. Fish and one Jeremiah Park, who managed to get away without a scratch. The testimony that we have been able to accrue from our earlier witness, as well as Mr. Park, has allowed us to piece together the events that took place within the span of fewer than ten minutes."

As Teague mentioned the names of the various victims, he moved the photographs of their bodies from his folder and pinned them to the board. Even though they were black and white, it was a gruesome display for all to look at. To his astonishment, only a few of the administrators averted their gaze.

"As mentioned, the three men, whose names we still do not know." At this, he hung the three images of the dead men. One missing his right hand, lying face down in a pool of blood, the second one in the bathroom with a deep cut through the chest, crumpled against one of the stalls, and the third one, peaceful in one of the hospital beds. "Both our witness and Mr. Park report, as do several of the patients staying on the fifth floor, hearing gunshots from the reception area. After a few moments, they heard a second round of gunfire, most likely from when officers O'Reilly and Cole left their stations to investigate. After the second volley of shots, Mr. Park emerged from the restroom, where he had been at the time of the attack. He claims to have hit one of the perpetrators since he took them by surprise. He was himself then taken by surprise at the number of people on the other side of the restroom door, and he locked himself back inside. It appears as if the trio split into two groups, and two of them headed towards room 506. From there, we have the eyewitness report from our alleged target.

"Soon after he had heard the second round of gunfire, a figure climbed into his room from the window. This figure fits the description of the killer from the parking structure murders. He describes the figure as tall, muscular and carrying a mask. The mask is of particular interest as it might be the clue that blows this case wide open. We have had our sketch artist draw something up from the eyewitness's testimony."

Teague stuck a sketch done in pencil up on the board. It depicted a horrific-looking face, with red protruding eyes, a gaping maw filled with rows of sharp teeth, and small horns sticking up. It looked like a medieval depiction of the devil - the only reference the Presbyterian artist had. It had been quite the process to translate Lindquist's description through Teague's notes. Then match them up with what little Mr. Fish had seen from his hiding place in one of the stalls. The artist had broken out his colored pencils to add some detail, red and blue, but as no one was sure as to how the colorization looked, artistic license took over. "According to our witness in room 506, this was the figure who attacked them in the parking structure. They claim he carries wavy knives or swords, which would match the wounds on the victims. On both occasions, he was dressed in a skin-tight blue and red outfit with a spiked belt around his waist. He made no contact with our witness, leading us to believe that he was looking to take him out and got interrupted, or that he was never interested in him. Nevertheless, he hindered the entrance of two men, killing one and injuring the other. From there, he seems to have moved on to kill the third man, who had broken into the restroom. After this, the trail runs cold. We have no clue where he might have gone. He could have changed to street clothes and walked out, or he may have left the way he came. We assume he entered the building by scaling the wall only to enter through a window.

"We were able to recover this."

One of the analysts rose from his seat and handed him the plastic bag containing the knife.

"This was found in the bushes in front of St. Mary's. It is a kris, a common blade from the East Indies. Even if the wavy edge is consistent with the injuries to the victims, this particular weapon does not seem to match the dead. This is still though one of our best leads so far. A Javanese weapon is quite the clue. A second clue is a black Studebaker seen leaving from in front of the hospital as the first responders pulled in.

"This is the man we are looking for." He tapped the image on the mask. "If we find him then we will most likely bring down the crime syndicate known on the streets as The Black Diamond as well. Now, we have yet to figure out what his motives are. We are working on the idea that he is a vigilante - a concerned citizen who is looking to stop the influx of drugs to our city. Our second thought is that he is acting as some kind of agent for another criminal organization. To take out the drug flow would leave the market open for another player on the market. Either of these theories would be difficult to prove, but we must try.

"I would now like to invite Dr. Price to discuss the victims." Teague pointed to the chief forensic investigator.

The small man with the giant salt and pepper beard and mass of white hair rose from his seat. He was wearing his white coat and round glasses, carrying papers under his arm. Teague moved to the side and gave the honored doctor a nod.

"I have yet to perform an autopsy on the latest victims. In fact, I have only given them a quick glance." Dr. Price pushed the glasses up his nose. "The victims of the Main Street Parking Garage murders were all cut down with the same type of blade. After examining the knife found at the scene, I can say, with some certainty, that the killer used a similar weapon. The cuts are consistent with the wavy form. The design of these blades is to make more damage to the internal areas of the human anatomy.

"An initial investigation of the victims from St. Mary's similarly shows that a weapon very much like the one in the bag was used." He indicated the kris in the plastic bag. "But without a full-on forensic analysis, I do not wish to say too much on that score. The two officers and the guard succumbed to gunshot wounds, as did Miss Woods. The body of the third killer, the one found in the restroom, was also wounded in the shoulder, which coincides with Mr. Fish's account of events."

Dr. Price removed his glasses, placed them on a desk, and then walked over to the corkboard.

"The one thing which does not really fit here is our second killer." He pointed to the photograph of the dead man in the bed. "We were interested in this man since he was given his own hospital bed at St. Mary's. He had sustained trauma to the head, but he received no life-threatening injuries, otherwise. Yet, he died in his bed mere hours after place in custody. Detective Glade has told us that the man began convulsing and that blood came bubbling for his mouth before he died."

Detective Glade, who was standing next to Chief Swan, nodded and stared down at his feet in apparent embarrassment.

"As I said, this is not consistent with the other deaths. From what I can see, there should not have been enough trauma to cause brain swelling, and there were no injuries allowing him to bleed out. The only thing I could guess, and which would be consistent with the descriptions from Detective Glade, would be that the weapon was poisoned. The only snag in that assumption is that no poison has been found in the system of any other victim."

Dr. Price looked over at Teague, indicating that he had nothing more to say. Teague thanked him and resumed his place in

front of the board.

"To summarize," he said. "We have a dozen victims over the course of three days, nine of them allegedly killed by one and the same man. We have two eyewitnesses describing him as a tall, slender man of muscular build. Dressed in a skin-tight red and blue costume, with a spiked belt around his waist and the mask of a demon. We know this person to be incredibly athletic - this is stated in the testimony from our undercover man, which is in the open case archives. His preferred weapons of choice are Javanese swords and knives.

We are working on two angles: The first one being that we are dealing with some sort of vigilante, and the second one that this is some kind of hired assassin in the employ of another crime syndicate. Therefore, while we are working this case, we need to be mindful of certain aspects as we do our questioning around the city.

"In the first scenario - the Vigilante one - we need to look for citizens who recently have spoken out against crime in the city. Specifically, drug use and organized crime. Most of us know that the people of this city are unaware of what goes on among the poor, or that there even are poor, so someone who has tried to bring this to our attention. Scour the papers for any op-eds on the subject or any interviews from the radio. Anything where a person might have been outraged.

"The second angle is the assassin one. This killer uses highly unorthodox methods. The use of blades instead of guns is so different that, if this person has been active before, there should be records of it in other parts of America. I am putting Detective Hansen on the task of contacting other precincts and searching the database for deaths by wavy bladed swords." He nodded towards a blond man in his forties, who smiled and nodded back at him. Hansen was one of the precincts best investigators, and by all rights, this case should have been his - if one were to go after his record. His wife had become sick earlier in the year and she had spent time in and out of the hospital. Taking care of their young twins had drained him, on a detective's salary considering a full-time nanny was out of the question, and without any grandparents alive, he had to do everything himself. A desk job, sifting through archives, or at least in charge of administrators doing the same, was perfect for him, at this time.

"We are also interested in the black Studebaker Commander that sped from the scene of the crime." Teague stroked his beard. "Unfortunately, it was not seen as important at the time, so no information about it was registered as it happened. Officer Boden will be in charge of asking around regarding a similar vehicle at other crime scenes. We did recover another car at the scene, most likely one that belonged to the mysterious trio. At first look, it appeared empty, but we sent over to Dr. Price's department for a closer examination. This might yield some answers to who these men were, and that, in turn, might lead us to who they were working for and give us some hint to who might want to harm them."

He paused and looked out over his audience, who were all feverishly taking notes. This was going smoother than he imagined. They could go down more avenues. Something would turn up he could sense it.

"Myself. I will dig deeper on this kris lead." He pointed to the blade. "There are some interesting markings on it and from what we have been told; it is usually individual to each weapon. So presumably, if we can identify the marking, we might be able to identify the owner. I will be taking a trip up to Milwaukee to visit the Public Museum, to see if they might be of service."

He fell silent for a minute while consulting his papers. The audience began moving in their seats as if they could sense that the briefing was ending. He looked up at them. "I guess that is all for now," he said. "Those of you who have been assigned specific tasks are already aware of this, and I leave it in your hands to enlist others to assist you."

"This case is our top priority!" Chief Swan called out above the sound of chairs scraping against the hardwood floor.

"Remember, if we solve one portion, we inevitably solve the other. No expense is too big here, and we have been given carte blanche financially by the city."

Everyone left for his or her respective desks or offices and soon only Swan and Teague remained. "That went well," Swan said and scratched his head.

"I thought so," Teague replied as he paged through his folder. "I decided to leave out one key element though."

"I know."

"It still puzzles me," Teague continued without reacting to the chief's reply. "If you were the only one who knew that Lindquist was operating undercover, then how did the trio know to target him? Most criminal organizations have a strict code of conduct, and it is unlikely that he would have started naming names. After all, records showed the Baz Peterson hospitalized several times without ever charged with anything, let alone rat anyone out. Why would they assume Lindquist would?"

"I think you are dangerously close here, Teague." Swan cast him a cautious glance. "Do not go making accusations, or hints of such, without the proper evidence, though."

"I understand, sir." Teague felt somewhat disappointed at his boss' disinterest in what he had to say.

"I do appreciate your investigative nose." Chief Swan placed a hand on his shoulder. "In this case, I would keep Occam's Razor in mind. The simplest answer-"

"Is probably the correct one," Teague interrupted. "I am familiar with Occam, sir."

"If The Black Diamond, or whatever it is called, is so secretive, they probably don't want any possible leak. Lindquist is young and would be quite new within the organization. If that is the case, then his trustworthiness might not have been tested yet."

"Let's play it that way then, sir." Teague grabbed his hat from the corner of the corkboard. "I have to get to Milwaukee. I hope you guys can put the room in order without me."

* * *

Martin Lindquist was not above becoming accustomed to the new routines of his life as a one-legged man. The nurses and the orderlies looked at him with pity in their eyes, and that he could do without, but they changed his linens and gave him sponge baths, even though he was fully capable of washing himself, and they changed his bandage. That was probably the lowest point of the day.

He had begun to come to terms with the fact that he only had one good leg - at least as long as he didn't have to look at his stump or try to use it. When the nurse came in with fresh wrappings and the washbasin it wasn't as easy. It was the physical contact. The woman lifting his stump from the bed and putting her hands on the spot where his leg ended. It was a wonder to him how much one missed a body part when one no longer had it. It caused him to appreciate his other limbs so much more.

There was an old thug, he had met through Peterson that the others called One-hand Molloy. He had lost his left hand to an exploding shell during the first Great War. He would still complain, some thirty years after the fact, about phantom pains in his hand. As if it was still there. Sometimes, he said, he would try to light a cigarette with the hand, only to find the hook that was in its place. HE hated it. One year later, Molloy was killed in a shootout in The Windy City. They said he had gone for his gun with the hand that was no longer there. Martin understood the old-timer now. In the morning, he was convinced he could feel the fabric of the bed linens against both his legs, and he thought it had all been a dream, but when he looked down all he could see was one leg and a stump. It was a harsh reality check for him.

This day he had been wheeled off, after his change of bedclothes and sponging, down to the basement of the hospital. He had gotten the chills as he passed the morgue and the small chapel that was down there but was grateful when he came to a well-lit room that looked like a workshop. There were all kinds of tools hanging on the walls, and shelving units filled with planks of wood of all shapes and sizes. Behind a massive workbench sat a middle-aged man dressed in overalls. He had thick glasses with a black frame, and his graying hair slicked back. The orderly who had pushed Martin there coughed ever so slightly to get the man's attention. He was leaning over a block of wood that he was sanding into some form of shape, and he paused for a second at the cough but continued to sand a few more strokes before turning his attention away from his work.

"Mr. Lindquist, I presume," the man said in a hoarse voice as he walked around the bench, wiping his hands with a rag. "Missing lower leg, if I'm not mistaken."

"That is right, sir," Martin replied and held out his hand in greeting.

"My name is Sowinski, master carpenter." He took Martin by the hand, and his grip was powerful, yet rough. The hand of a man who had used them from an early age to make a living.

"I realize that a master title might be a bit presumptuous of one who only makes spare parts for humans." The man smiled, showing off two rows of yellowed teeth. He dug in his overalls and pulled out a pack of Lucky Strikes. He pulled out a cigarette and placed it between his lips. "See you want a master craftsman to create artificial limbs. You want a leg that you can trust to carry your weight in every situation." He had grabbed a flimsy looking log from the workbench and slammed it against the edge. It splintered with a large crack. "I come from a long line of artisans, so you can count on the products I create." He sat down on a stool that he most likely had made himself - it was unvarnished and appeared to have a few splinters protruding from it. He slid his right pant leg up and struck a match against the leg underneath. "I put the same care in the work I do for others as I do with that which I craft for myself."

The orderly left Martin in Mr. Sowinski's care and said he would return in half an hour. Further back in the workshop, Sowinski had a more open space. There were parallel bars set up in the center of the room and several crash mats strewn across the concrete floor. There were also bars attached to the brick walls, and the south wall displayed a large mirror, making the room look like a dance studio. The carpenter wheeled Martin to the parallel bars and asked him to lift himself up. With some difficulty, Martin managed to do so. He had always been under the impression that an officer of the law should be in peak condition, and he had tried to maintain an enviable physical shape.

Once he had gone undercover, there was no time for hitting the weights. Most of the thugs relied on fighting dirty or the physical gifts God had given them, but luckily, he had kept enough muscle mass to pull his body up without a great deal of trouble. Sowinski asked him to keep himself elevated and balance on his remaining leg so that the carpenter could take accurate measurements. He detailed the importance of having even limbs to avoid back problems in the future.

Luckily, for Martin, the leg had been cut off at the knee so there would be little to no limp, and he could hide his peg leg under his pants. Mr. Sowinski wore his wooden appendage as a badge of honor. Like One-Hand Molloy, he had lost it on the battlefield of the Great War. Once he logged the numbers in his notebook, the man brought Martin to his workstation, poured him up a cup of coffee, and told him of life in the trenches.

He had gone to fight for the USA proudly. His parents had come from Poland when he was a baby and settled in the city after coming to New York. His father had gone to work at Mitchell Motors before it folded and had then managed to get another job at a furniture manufacturer. This had allowed them to live comfortably - a life far removed from the one in their home of Eastern Europe. It was because of this that he had so gladly signed up when the call came and that he didn't mind when they told him his leg was lost. The artisanship on his own limb - he had made it in his father's shed - had opened up the opportunity to work for the government as a maker of artificial body parts.

They had a good, long chat where Sowinski was adamant that the life as a person with only one leg was nothing to dread for the young man. Women would fall all over him knowing he had a wooden limb. They would find him dangerous and exciting and, at the same time, someone they could care for.

The orderly came and picked him up, and the carpenter told him the leg would be ready in a couple of days.

Determined to be self-sufficient, Martin refused to have his linens turned down for him and was about to order the orderly away when he noticed an envelope on his bedside table. Upon asking, what it was and where it came from, the orderly simply replied that he believed it belonged to him. It had fallen from the bed when they changed the bedclothes.

Once the man had left, he rolled over to the table, picked up the envelope and moved to the window. The hospital personnel had turned off the light so that his silhouette no longer spread out over Grand Avenue. He turned the lamp to his lap and started to open the letter with his index finger. It was a single sheet of paper without lines. The penmanship was quite beautiful, old style with big loops where appropriate. It read:

Dear Mr. Lindquist,

I have seen your beacon in the window of St. Mary's Hospital.

If you are indeed interested in speaking with me and share information that might be of interest, please light it again tonight, but cut out the eyes to make it different to before. I will contact you in a similar manner to this.

If you have no interest in speaking with me then let it be.

-DM

Martin put down the note and grabbed his scissors.

CHAPTER THIRTEEN

In 1945, the Japanese lost the war in the Pacific and surrendered. His rebels, Wayan included, and I Gusti Ngurah Rai believed that this meant freedom for Bali. Mr. Hill was also pleased, thoroughly convinced that he had come through the conflict unscathed. Little did they know that once one invading force left another would invariably take its place.

The Dutch returned to all of Indonesia to set up their old empire. The Balinese rebels decided that this was something they could not tolerate. Mr. Hill, who knew his days on the island were numbered, decided that it was time to move. Gathering his son and the tutor in the grand dining room, where Anthony had eaten most of his meals, he announced that they would be on their way in the coming months.

That turned out to be more difficult than he had envisioned. In order to leave he would have to somehow gain passage on a ship heading West. The Dutch had taken control of all the harbors and the airfields, so there was no visible means of escape.

As he had assumed the new rulers came for Mr. Hill. The rebels, now armed with weapons they had recovered from the Japanese, were stirring up trouble, making Hill less of a priority. Once they came knocking on his front door, he had all but given up. However, he was slippery and managed to talk his way out of facing the executioner.

Maybe it was his many years of loyal service before the war, maybe it was his ability to butter up the new governor, or maybe it was the fact that he was willing to give up information about the possible whereabouts of Rai and his forces. Whatever it was, they granted him a stay, and the right to remain on Bali for a year to get his affairs in order. After that time had passed, the Dutch would put him and his son on a plane for the United States, and then Mr. Hill's days as a cultural attaché would be over.

As the months passed, Wayan, donning his mask, would continue to fight the Dutch invaders on Rai's orders, and in November of 1946, they had managed to rally their forces in east Bali at Marga Rana.

* * *

Geert pulled his Studebaker Commander into the parking lot of the abandoned factory. He had received a summons the night before that instructed him to be at the building at eight. The red brick building had housed Hamilton Beach or Horlick's Malted Milk, Geert couldn't remember which. There were assembly lines running all over the open factory floor, but since they had removed most of the large-scale machinery when the building was vacated, what had actually been produced there was anyone's guess.

179

It was unfair to label it an abandoned factory. The Black Diamond had purchased the building upon first arriving in the city and had subsequently forced the occupants to leave. Geert had helped him with the actual deal without ever seeing the place. It was a strict delivering eviction notice affair - quite impersonal.

His boss had let him know that it was a clever move. Too many questions would arise if they bought or built a new factory without announcing any production. This was an economic boom period and taking up space and not hiring workers would be very suspicious indeed.

Certainly, questions were asked when the previous tenants were put out on the street and the factory turned into a warehouse of sorts, but the building was not in a prime location, and there always seemed to be vans parked outside, so the inquiries soon stopped.

Geert looked around to make sure no one was walking past. The building may be off the beaten path, but that didn't mean that people didn't live in the area. This part of the city was under development, meaning several prefabricated homes had popped up in a short time. Cookie cutter houses, placed in neat rows, directly on the ground without much for insulation and no yard to speak of. It had been a desperate measure from the officials of the city. A mass of migrants looking to fill the many industries needed homes, and in order to keep the workforce in the area, this was the answer.

The homes would house more than they should, as many as three families would live in each. Cramped, drafty and with poor plumbing, they were little more than houses found in a shantytown. Both children heading to school and their parents going to work would inevitably pass the gates of the factory, and The Black Diamond had pressed the importance that Geert not detected there.

He opened the small red metal door that was placed on the side of the building, out of sight from the street, and sneaked inside – at least, as much as his large frame would allow. The service entrance opened up right into the main open area where the assembly belts zigzagged across the floor as well as overhead. The lights had already been turned on, and the room was bathed in a yellowish glow, blended with the white light from the frosted skylights on the ceiling, which allowed the morning sun to enter.

The Black Diamond was leaning over a workbench covered in papers. He was, as always, impeccably dressed in his black tailored suit and black tie. Geert had often wondered how the man never seemed to perspire since he wore the suit no matter how hot it got. Paul began to sweat just getting dressed. In fact, he had to wipe his forehead as he stepped closer to the dark figure.

"Welcome back, sir.'" Paul wanted to get the first word in. He had found that The Black Diamond always got the upper hand by speaking first.

"Thank you, Mr. Geert," The Black Diamond said without looking up.

"I assume that the meeting with Mr. Ishimori was informative." His boss had not briefed Geert regarding the said meeting, and he was eager to hear the result. He reached the workbench and placed his hands on it to rest. His sweaty palms awkwardly stuck to a map of a train yard. He stepped backward and shook his hands to make the brittle paper drop back down. He left two handprints on the blue map.

The Black Diamond looked up at him, raised his eyebrows, sighed, and crossed his arms. "The meeting with Mr. Ishimori did not go as well as I had hoped," he said coldly. "He found my questions most insulting, and he had to be persuaded, quite forcibly, to keep our deal intact."

Geert felt as if there was something his boss wasn't telling him. Then again, on the other hand, that was how he always felt. For being the second in command, he was surprisingly out of the loop.

"The Yakuza has nothing to do with the interference in our business," The Black Diamond continued. "That was clear. I did suspect as much while on my way to Chicago, but an example needed to be set for those who might be. It has come to my attention that our nemesis dropped one of his weapons at the hospital." Geert's ears perked up at those words. "It appears to be a Javanese blade. A knife."

"So, we're looking for someone from Java?" Geert asked. "Would that be a new organization?"

"I highly doubt that we are looking at an entire group from Java." The Black Diamond paced behind the table with his hands on his back. "No, it is more likely that we are dealing with an assassin with ties to the East Indies. This particular weapon has a history throughout that very area. It is exclusive though, and the knife will most likely point us in the right direction. Once the owner of the weapon is found, the rest of the thorn in our side will follow." He stopped and turned to Geert. "I also heard that the surviving representative of our little cadre met with an untimely death." He smiled.

"Yes, sir," Geert said, beaming with pride. "It was by a hair, but we made it happen, and I believe without suspicions of foul play."

"Excellent." The Black Diamond sat down on a metal stool and steepled his hands. "We have other pressing matters to discuss though." He tried to straighten out the blueprint of the train yard on the bench and pointed to the two parallel lines that represented the tracks. "The new shipment of goods is scheduled to arrive tomorrow. We are in desperate need of it. Our people on the street have been pushing hard, and it has created a demand that we have only been able to meet due to our backup warehouse. The loss of the crates has caused us to deplete that storage, and as you know, we cannot seem untrustworthy in the eyes of our customers. If that were to happen, they would turn to another source."

"Possibly the game plan all along," Geert said as he gazed at the plan.

"Indeed," the Black Diamond replied. "Yet we can ill afford this shipment to slip out of our hands. Twice now, our enemy or enemies, whichever the case may be, have disrupted our plans. Somehow, he knows to be where we are, and we cannot discard the fact that he might be at the train yard as well. Even so, it is a chance we must take, however foolish it appears."

"I will double the number of men at the unloading then." Geert grabbed a pen and paper from his pocket and began to jot down notes.

"I am doubtful that such a measure is the answer." The Black Diamond stepped back again and looked at Geert. "I took care of some other business while I was in The Second City. I have enlisted the aid of someone to keep our goods safe."

"The Yakuza?" Geert felt that fighting fire with fire was the appropriate answer here. If your enemy was wielding

Javanese swords, then the best swordsmen of Asia might be the antidote.

"Not at all." The Black Diamond smirked. "This force is quite different. Someone especially equipped for a task such as this."

"Who might this be?" Geert was intrigued.

"Patience, Mr. Geert. It will be revealed in time."

* * *

Teague put the car in park and picked up the bag containing the kris from the passenger seat. He looked through his windshield to gauge his placement. Wisconsin Avenue was quite the street, and he felt lucky that he had managed to find a spot so close to the entrance. As he exited the vehicle, he placed the bag under his armpit and placed his hat on his head. He looked up at the grand building towering before him, constructed in a renaissance style, known as renaissance revival. Born in Milwaukee, he had lived there until the age of twelve. His father had been a police officer as well, and once he made lieutenant; he had taken the opportunity to change cities. Before he had started school, his mother, who naturally stayed at home with the children, had made a point of taking him to various public institutions of learning - the museums, libraries and theaters. To young Garfield, the public museum was the favorite stop. The taxidermy animals, their glass eyes staring at him through the windows, fascinated him.

The history of the world also held its intrigue, and his mother, who was a progressive woman, was eager to show him the wonders of evolution. The building looked the same as he remembered it. He had always felt that it looked like the palace of some European king with pillars lining the windows of the second floor, floral motif carved in the outer wall, and a large dome on top.

He walked up the stone steps, taking them two at a time. He felt as if he was in a hurry; the longer he was away from the investigation proper, the less he felt in control. The rest of the force was competent enough, but Teague had always felt as if he was on another level. They didn't have the attention to detail that he possessed or the stubborn will that allowed him to stay up late to read documents. He could just picture them loafing around, drinking coffee, and discussing the gossip of the day. He had no interest in such mundane tasks. To him, work was not a place for socializing, and he avoided it as much as possible. This had caused others to view him as an ornery old man, and thy seldom invited him to office get-togethers, which suited Garfield just fine. The downside to it was that he was never asked to represent the force at functions, and that hindered his professional position.

By all rights, he should be next in line for the position of chief, but his lack of social skills might well cause him to get overlooked.

He stepped inside the building and walked over to the reception area. Several young children, aged around seven, were standing in a line behind an elderly looking schoolteacher, and he smiled at them the best he could as he passed. He patiently waited as the teacher purchased the tickets and then walked over to the side to wait for a guide before he leaned on the desk.

"A ticket, sir?" the brown-haired woman behind the desk asked.

"No," he said and fished out his badge from his inside pocket. "Detective Garfield Teague. Here to speak to Professor Rosenthal."

The woman looked through the papers on her desk and seemed to find the appropriate note. "Detective Teague?" she said. "The Professor said he would meet you in the South East Asian Exhibit." She handed Teague a pamphlet and pointed him to a large stone staircase in the center of the building. "It is up the stairs and to the right. There will be signs."

"Thank you," Teague said and tipped his hat.

* * *

That morning, Martin Lindquist felt as if he hadn't slept a wink. Sleep almost crusted his eyes shut as the nurse came in and parted the curtains in the window. She eyed the demon silhouette, with its now carved out eyes, and made a little disapproving noise with her tongue. Martin smiled at it. He had been anxious to find out if the masked man was going to leave him a note in the middle of the night. Like a young child waiting for Santa to come bounding down the chimney the night before Christmas, he had been too excited to sleep. He had tossed and turned, waiting for the Sandman to come throw the magic dust in his eyes like he did in the Donald Duck cartoons he had seen at the movies. He had been rigid, on his back, his eyes tightly shut, almost willing himself to sleep.

Every time he could feel his body relax, getting heavy, to the point where he almost sank through the mattress, something would make a noise. A nurse in the corridor, or a gust of wind sending the branches of a tree into the window, and he would wake right up. Every time he heard one of those noises, he would slowly open his eyes - the way he used to on the morning of his birthday, trying to convince his family he was still asleep - but once his eyes were wide open he would still be alone in his room. Even though he could have sworn he had been awake all through the night, his body acted like one that had gotten the appropriate amount of rest. It was amazing how that happened. He rolled over to his side and tried to focus on the nurse, who had prepared her bowl of warm, soapy water and her sponge.

"Did you sleep well?" she asked with about as much interest in his feelings as a coyote would have in an automobile. She was a brutish looking woman. As wide across the shoulders as he, but a good foot taller. She reminded him of that actress who always played Groucho's love interest in the Marx Brothers' flicks but with a constant scowl on her face.

She didn't wait for his reply. Instead, she started washing his face. As the lukewarm water gently caressed his skin, he could feel his humanity return. She forcefully grabbed him by his neck and moved him to the edge of the bed, leaning him over her bowl. She squeezed the sponge against the back of his head, and the tendrils of streaming warmth flowed over his eyes, washing the sleep away. He held his mouth open and allowed some of the liquid to run, via his lips, inside. He spat into the bowl, trying to avoid too much of his saliva intermingling with the water. He found he could open his eyes now, and he focused on the swirling patterns the drops from his head created in the bowl.

Once his body was well and truly scrubbed by the strong hands of his nurse, he turned to sit on the bed, dressing in the fresh gown she had left him. When he swung his leg over the side, an envelope came out from under his blanket and slowly glided to the floor. Without hesitating, he halted his dressing and followed it, landing on his remaining foot and crouching to pick it up. He sat down on the floor and turned it over in his hand. His name was on it in the same script as the previous note. How had the man managed to sneak into the room without Martin noticing him? Even if he hadn't been sleeping the whole night through, he was at least in such a light state that he should have awoken to the noise of someone traversing the window. If the window had been the point of entrance, that was.

He had experienced how vigil the guards had been when he left, so a man dressed in everyday clothes walking straight through would not have been suspicious at all. The crime syndicate would have come in guns blazing, so they probably would have little attention to an average Joe entering the fourth floor.

He carefully pried open the envelope that had been glued shut. It was difficult at first, but he managed to undo one of the corners, and then he inserted his index finger and moved it upward.

The small paper gave him some difficulty, and he ended up ripping the entire envelope in two. A yellow card escaped its prison and fell to the floor. He picked it up. It was thicker - card stock. The stuff his mom used to write her recipes on. The back of it was blank, but he turned it over, his hands shaking, to see the familiar ruled look. The beautiful handwriting from the previous note was present and he held it close to the morning sun streaming through the eyeholes of his cut out in the window.

Mr. Lindquist

I am delighted that you have taken me up on my invitation.

If possible, I would like to meet you at Memorial Hall. Be there at 10 p.m.

-DM

Martin bounced the card against his chin as he pondered his next move. He had made contact, and that was what he wanted. As a police officer, he should bring in the vigilante, but what would it accomplish? He had gone undercover to bring down the drug traffic in the city. The lure of the life of crime had reared its ugly head once he had fallen in with Baz Peterson. He had witnessed the man's riches, the respect he enjoyed in certain circles, and his worldly wisdom. He had wanted part of that life for a moment.

The death of his mentor at the hands of the mysterious vigilante had turned out to be the best thing that could have happened. The illusion of glamour that a life of crime could bring him had shattered, and he was free of its hypnotic spell. Martin now focused on, what had essentially been his initial task. To bring down the crime syndicate known only as The Black Diamond.

He pulled himself off the floor with all the strength he could muster and climbed to the end table where he still had pen and paper. Wiping the sweat from his forehead, he began thinking about everything he had heard during clandestine meetings in restaurants and in cars parked in back alleys. Then he began to write.

* * *

"Detective Teague, I presume." The voice brought him out of his trance. He had followed the signs to the East India exhibit and had walked from booth to booth, taking in the riches of the islands of Southeast Asia.

The dusty old artifacts had brought back so many memories. He was once again that little boy dressed in khaki slacks and a cardigan, tightly gripping his mother's hand as the cold eyes of taxidermy animals and wax figures stared at him. There seemed to be some tradition within the museum world to keep the large rooms dark, while the subjects behind the glass brightly lit. It gave the grand rooms, with their ancient architecture, an eerie nature, an almost haunted sensation.

The chill that crept up and down his spine as he entered the halls of continents returned the moment, he set foot on the cold marble floors. In his own quiet reverence, he had moved through the foreign worlds with their strange costumes and customs. Peering at the statues of ancient deities, weaponry and homes made from indigenous materials that ranged from bamboo to ice, he became one with the worlds on the other side of the glass - as if he was standing there with the Eskimos, dressed in furs, kneeling in the snow, and hovering over a freshly killed seal. The mesmerism of the various scenes drowned out the sounds of excited kids running around, pointing to the strange looking figures and the teachers who tried to quiet them down. Occasionally he'd be cast back to reality, only to repeat the process in the next case.

Dr. Rosenthal was not the quintessential researcher that Teague had expected. He was tall and slim with a confident stride and an air of cool that permeated through the entire room. It made Teague straighten his own back to match the man's countenance. He wore his brown hair tightly cropped to his head, and his piercing blue eyes cut through the thick spectacles he wore on the bridge of his nose. He stretched out a firm hand towards Teague who tried to grab on to it with the same confidence.

"Dr. Rosenthal," Teague replied, nodding. "Thank you for meeting with me on such short notice."

"Not at all." The researcher's voice was quite high for a man and carried with it a nasal timbre. "As a scientist at a museum such as this, I rarely am too busy for anything. It is a different story for those who are out in the field. They're the ones with ulcers. I merely sit behind a desk and file the findings that they bring in. It is not the William Le Queux novel that some would make it out to be."

Rosenthal laughed at his own witticism; it went over Teague's head completely. "I don't even set up these fine displays." He indicated the cases lining the walls. "I tell them what goes where and in what way. Then they have window dressers do the rest. I guess men with degrees can't be trusted to do such things."

"I am sure they believe you have better things to do," Teague tried to comfort him.

"Wish it were so, Detective." Rosenthal removed his glasses from his face, brought out a rag and proceeded to wipe the eyepieces. "Now I believe that you had something that needed my attention?"

"Yes, that is correct." Teague was still holding the plastic bag with the kris. He hadn't even reflected on it, but when it was mentioned, he all of a sudden felt its weight and how sweaty the bag had become in his grasp. "Is there somewhere we can go?" he asked, wanting to keep the object away from prying eyes.

"We can sit down in one of the educational corners of this exhibit," Dr. Rosenthal said and put his spectacles back. "Our tours seldom venture into the East Indies." He smiled and winked at Teague.

He walked farther into the dark areas of the museum. It was true. The area felt desolate. The carpeting was nearly pristine and the bamboo decorating the wall spared the busy hands of little children. Rosenthal showed Teague to a collection of hollow tree trunks that formed a square on the floor. In the center stood a wooden stool, dedicated to the museum guide.

"When it comes to the Asian continent, the visitors seem to appreciate Japan and China more than anything else," the professor said as he motioned to Teague to sit on one of the felled trees. "I do believe that there will be more interest in the islands as time passes. At the moment, the war is still so fresh in recent memory that Americans find it difficult to deal with."

Teague nodded at this. He had cousins who had spent their tenure in the war fighting island to island. They came back broken and with night terrors reminding them of the horrors, they had witnessed. His oldest cousin, who had also happened to be his closest, had not been able to carry the weight and had ended his life, a terrible shame to the family.

"This is what we found at a crime scene." Teague handed the bag over to Rosenthal. He removed the kris and turned it over in his hand. "the makeup of the weapon is consistent with the injuries at two crime scenes."

"This is a kris," Rosenthal said without much emotion.

"We know the broad strokes of what it is and how it is used. In addition, that it is a Javanese blade. We are mostly interested in the carvings on the blade and the figure on the handle."

"It is true that the weapon is of Javanese origin." Rosenthal flattened the plastic and held the weapon closer to his face. "This particular dagger is not from Java, though. Come over here, Detective." Rosenthal motioned to Teague to come closer. "You see, this pamor, the pattern on the wilah, the blade, relates the myth of the Leyak, legendary demons of Indonesia. Specifically, Bali. To be more precise, it is about the mistress of the leyak - Rangda. Her mask often graced the village death temple and then paraded through the streets once a year. It is the same figure carved on the hilt here."

"So, the blade comes from Bali then?" Teague was intrigued.

"In my professional opinion, it does." Rosenthal handed the weapon back. "Let us venture to the display of Bali."

The professor rose from his seat and walked a few feet to a small glass case that was supposed to represent the island of Bali. There was a male figure with Polynesian features naked from the waist up standing next to some woodcarvings. The figure had a sheath stuck into a sash tied around his waist and in his hand; he was carrying a similar wavy blade as the one Teague was holding.

Behind the figure hung a mask also made from wood. Painted white and adorned with a pattern of colored lines. A long tongue hung from a gaping maw, from where large fangs also protruded. Two bulging eyes stared at him, cutting through his very soul.

"This is Rangda." Rosenthal pointed to the head. "It is easy to simply call the leyak demons. To our Judeo-Christian values, it is the obvious definition. The truth of it is that they are cannibalistic humans, deeply imbedded in black magic. The images on that blade of yours tell the legend of when the witch-queen Rangda bequeathed the Death Mask to the greatest warrior of her worshipers."

"Death Mask?"

"Right. A bastardized version of her face said to instill fear in those who harbored evil intentions."

"Isn't that a bit hypocritical when it comes to a sect of cannibals?" Teague scoffed at the proposition.

"Not at all." Rosenthal did not laugh. "To us, cannibalism is one of the most horrific acts man can engage in, but to other cultures, it is merely a way to garner the strength of other human beings. The black magic the leyak engaged in was a way to bring balance to their world. It is one side of magic; just as white magic is the other side of it."

"So, what was this mask?"

"The greatest warrior in the tribe would don it in battle or other missions. When not in use it hung in the same temple as Rangda's head. I have only seen illustrations of it and heard eyewitness accounts."

"So, it's a myth?"

"Legends and myths all have a grain of truth to them. Maybe there was such a mask that warriors on Bali would wear, but I doubt it was imbued with any magical abilities."

Teague looked at the huge head hanging next to the figure and then at the kris in the wax hands. Things were becoming more complicated than he had imagined. The description of the mask that the killer had worn would definitely fit well with the Death Mask of the cannibalistic leyak. He felt as if he had more questions than he had answers at this point.

"I hope that this has given you some answers," Rosenthal said.

"It has raised more questions, to be honest, Doctor," Teague replied and stroked his beard. "How would this weapon, with these particular markings, make its way to Southeast Wisconsin?"

"I would say that some soldier brought it over from the war. After all, it is a superior weapon."

"In that case, that person must have brought over more than one, seeing how this particular knife wasn't used in the latest attack, and we still found wounds consistent with the luk, the waves, on this kind of weapon. In the testimony we have gathered, the killer had at least two more kalis... I think they're called. That seems excessive for an American soldier to bring over."

"I agree with that assessment, but it isn't impossible. One can wonder to what end an American might want to use such nation-specific weapons. Are they sending a message, or are there other reasons? That is, unfortunately, more than I can answer, Detective."

Teague swung the bag carrying his evidence back and forth. "Well I guess that is all I need then," he said and sighed.

"Unfortunately, so," Rosenthal replied. "I might have been able to give you some information that can assist you in your investigation. It is a welcome break in the routines to help the police."

"I am sure there is something I can use. Any information is good information."

"I will see you out, Detective," Rosenthal said and placed his hand in the small of Teague's back. They began walking, but something in the case next to the one from Bali caught his eye.

The case was a jumbled mess of various artifacts, all of them vaguely Asian in appearance. He looked over the little plaque on the bottom of the window and read *The Far East.* A general enough name for objects the museum staff had no idea from where they originated. There were a variety of small jade carvings, statues of wood, weapons and even animal pelts.

What had made him do a double take was a diamond-shaped crystal resting on a turtle shell. It looked very much like the kind of diamond one found in a deck of cards, angular like as if carved to look like someone's idea of a diamond. The crystal was black - something he had never seen before. The overhead lights shining down on it almost soaked into the surface, letting nothing reflect back, and it was only by moving his head from side to side that he could see that it wasn't two dimensional. In the center of the diamond sat something very different. It was a tiny white skull.

To Teague, it seemed like there was a hole in the crystal where the skull rested but it was difficult to tell. The grinning cranium was no bigger than that of a child's, but it had the dimensions of one that belonged to a full-grown adult. Teague had seen enough craniums belonging to both children and adults in his day to spot the difference.

"What is this?" he asked and, without thinking, pressed his hand to the window.

"It's our collection of artifacts that we have yet to place in the right case." Rosenthal, who seemingly had hoped that the visit was over, sounded slightly annoyed at the interruption. "These items are constantly under investigation and research so that we might place them on the right continent. Often times we put interns on it because it involves reading old books or research papers to find similar items. It might interest an investigator like yourself."

"Maybe one day. When this whole crime business has taken its toll on me." He pointed to the diamond shape. "What is that?"

"That thing?" Rosenthal moved closer to get a good look at the object. "It is one of the bigger mysteries here at the museum. There are only three other pieces recorded here in the West. There may be others in rural communities in the East or in the collection of those interested in such objects. The crystal is a black gem, as you can see, shaped to look like a diamond. It is a great example of folk art of the region, I imagine. The only details we have regarding it are the papers it came in. We found it in the vaults of the museum, in the belongings of one of our field researchers who tragically died in the Andes. The document claims that it comes from The Far East, but not specifically where. The skull in the center is human, or human-like. Probably belonging to a member of some Pygmy tribe, although that is purely speculation. In the documents, it explains that the object comes from the temple of the god Khor."

"Khor?" Teague asked. "Never heard of them."

"No, you wouldn't," Rosenthal replied with an indignant air. "The research that we have conducted has only revealed that Khor was an ancient, forgotten deity in the East. Which specific area he belonged to is unclear. According to the findings, he had the ability to materialize objects at will. So, a form of creator god. Legend has it that he had a male child with a human woman and granted the son the same power by plucking out one of his eyes. The gem did not only grant the power of transmutation, but also incredible strength and intelligence. The son beset the gem, a black diamond apparently, in a ring and then used the power to try to take over the world, threatening to cast it into darkness and chaos. Khor, who had made the world, and all men and women in it, was not pleased and begot another child, a girl, who in the end defeated the son. This brought order to the world and ushered in a golden age for man. The ring recovered and placed in the temple of Khor. The black diamond symbolizes Khor's eye and the ring of creation, and the skull, in turn, symbolizes the dangers that it might bring."

"So, you know quite a bit about it then," Teague teased.

"I guess." Rosenthal smiled back at him. "This object is still very much shrouded in mystery. The information we have is more or less circumspect and without real basis in anything historical - most likely an amalgam of various legends from the Far East. The only time we have seen the name Khor is as a region in ancient Syria, and that does not fit the origin."

"So, this story with the ring is like the myth of Rangda's death mask?"

"Folklore? Absolutely. My dear Detective Teague, the idea of magical artifacts creating objects out of thin air and masks that supposedly strike fear in the heart of evil men is nothing more than lore."

"What was the name of the researcher who brought back that diamond?" Teague brought out his note pad.

"His name was Dr. Lansing, Timothy Lansing. A good man."

Teague noted the name. *All leads are good leads,* he thought

CHAPTER FOURTEEN

The battle of Marga Rana would forever live in the memories of the Balinese people as a horrible tragedy. It did not matter if the rebels had Japanese guns or not, they were no match for the Dutch army. Some refer to it as a suicide mission. Maybe it was and maybe not. Maybe Rai knew that there was no way they would come from the exchange, as victors, and maybe it didn't matter. The men would rather die than live under the thumb of another occupying force. Whatever the reasoning behind the attack, there was only one outcome. Wayan knew this as well, and he had sought out Anthony on the eve of the attack.

"Listen to me," he had said as they sat opposite each other in the House of Death, with Rangda's horrifying eyes looking upon them through the smoke. "I am going to fight the Dutch army, and I might not come back. If that were to happen, I want you to take the Death Mask and keep it. You use it for whatever you see fit. It is an instrument of terror and fear, especially to those in the wrong. That is why I will wear it tomorrow. I have no one else that I can hand it to. Since the day you came into my life, you have been my only son. Even though your eyes are round, and your skin is fair, you are one of us and will always be so."

They talked for another couple of hours, Wayan wanting to impart as much of his knowledge on the boy as he could before he had to leave. They walked back to Anthony's house before his adopted father turned and disappeared into the greens.

He fought valiantly on the battlefield. Taking down many of the enemies. Dutch legends tell of a ghastly figure with red bulging eyes swinging swords, impossible to hit. Death following in his wake. In the end, a bullet struck him in the belly, tearing through his intestines. A fatal shot. Wayan left the field and stumbled back through the woods, heading for his home. He wasn't trying to cheat death, he wanted it to come for him in his own village. The Dutch wiped out the entire Balinese battalion that day, and with it, the last of the resistance.

* * *

Tony was sitting on the edge of his bed waiting for the sun to sink just a little lower in the sky. It had already begun its steady descent, but it was not quite ten, and he was pretty convinced that people would find it odd if he bounced across the rooftops in his outfit, clearly visible. When he had first begun the endeavor of fighting the drug problems in the city, he had tried to figure out how he would move without detection. A person dressed in a skin-tight red and blue outfit, complete with a belt with spikes and a horrible mask was less than secretive. Running out in the open, that is to say roaming the streets, was not an option, and he was not about to start sneaking in the dark alleys like the heroes in the comic books.

He had a specific mission and a decided target, so it was easier to try to show up where he needed to be. Let the police do their job and patrol the streets. That night in the parking garage, he had just driven his car to one of the upper levels, parked it and changed there. Once he was done, he just ran back up, changed and left. It was easier. No one expected him to be there. Meeting outside Memorial Hall would be trickier, just like traversing the hospital. He had forgone the idea of taking his car there, the police might pull him over and in that situation, it might be difficult to explain his garb, but also that he was unsure of how things might unfold. He hadn't wanted to leave his car in the neighborhood as evidence. Instead, he had tried to leap from building to building as much as he could. It wasn't as easy as he at first thought it would be - the comic book vigilantes very rarely touched on this. It seemed as if everything was in very close proximity to the other.

Early on in his journey to St. Mary's, he realized that he would have to cover some ground by moving across the streets. Time and again, he would halt atop one of the buildings and look out across the street before him to make sure that it was deserted. At least Memorial Hall was only a couple of blocks to the east of his apartment, and the structures downtown were close enough that he could easily jump across them. He had dressed in the red and blue outfit already, slipped the boots on, but he left the gloves and Face off.

The grinning object was still in the wooden box that he had placed next to him on the bed, the lid wide open. The eyes stared at him as he sat there. He still felt as if it was judging him. As if it was not his to wear. That he wasn't worthy of its power. His adoptive father had placed it in his hands, had told him to be its caretaker, and to use it as he saw fit. The Face could no more than disagree, it seemed. He was not of Balinese blood. Not even close. A white privileged child, the progeny of imperialist forces. The very enemy of the island folk, but Wayan had taken him under his wing, had treated him as his own son, and in the end that was enough for Tony.

It was difficult to denounce the mask, but maybe that was the point. Maybe the intention was to cast doubt in the heart of those who wore it. That day in November - when Wayan donned it for the last time - maybe he felt it as well. Tony would never know.

He was close now, he thought. The contact with the young man in the hospital was the break he needed. It seemed as if it had been predetermined that he didn't kill him. Most men would die from losing their lower leg, but something had kept this one alive. The fates had willed it so. For some reason, they knew that he held the key to Tony's mission and that he needed to survive. He was innocent. He was on the right side of the law, and that was probably his redeeming feature.

Tony was well aware that he needed to be apprehensive when meeting with Lindquist. The man was a cop, and as such, it was his duty to report Tony and his activities. The call to him might be an elaborate trap, but he would have to take that chance. It was the best lead he had, and he was convinced that he could avoid capture - as long as he stayed on his toes.

The sun was now past the Court House building. He still had a few hours to wait. He fell back on the bed to rest; he would have to limber up before he went out, but it could wait.

* * *

The sterile room smelled of disinfectant and blood. Teague wondered how Dr. Price ever got used to the scent of human innards and waste. It was like no other odor. He knew what spoiled meat smelled like, but this was something altogether different. He imagined it had to do with the more carnivorous diet of men. That it somehow made the flesh more pungent. He would ask the good doctor some time if his theory was true.

He had met up with Chief Swan as soon as he returned to the city. Swan debriefed him on the sparse information Teague had managed to gather from the Doctor Rosenthal.

"Well that was indeed not much to go on," Swan had said in his speculative fashion. "So instead of one East Asian islander, we are, in fact, looking for another. All we did was switch from Javanese to Balinese."

He did agree that the fact that the weapon might belong to a soldier was interesting, but he was not prepared to send out officers to go knocking on every vet's door to see if they were in possession of wavy swords. They did decide that they would send a couple of detectives to the VA halls to dig for information. It might be a long shot, but it was more than they had before.

Teague decided to keep the information about the black diamond he had seen and the god, Khor, to himself. He was still uncertain what it might have to do with the case - if it had anything at all to do with it. Before he followed the chief to the forensic lab and its autopsy room, he stopped by the command center and asked the secretary, Charlotte, if she could find any information about a Doctor Timothy Lansing.

Just for the hell of it, he thought. His gut told him that this could be more than a wild goose chase.

The naked body of the thug was lying on the cold metal slab, eyes open, staring straight up at the ceiling. Its waxy complexion made it look like one of the figures in the museum, and that, coupled with the dead glassy orbs in the head, made the hairs on Teague's neck stand on end.

Dr. Price was dressed in an apron that likely had been white at one point, but now bore stains of crimson splattered with other grayish and brown colors. He wiped his hands on an already quite dirty rag and then handed it to his assistant, who placed it with other used items on a tray.

"Gentlemen," he said and removed his glasses. "Always a delight to have you here."

The body on the slab had gone through the autopsy, which was evident from the open torso. A small towel lay on the crotch so that the man would retain some of his dignity. Not that it mattered anymore.

"I take it that you are ready with your report," Swan said and paged through some papers that were fastened to a clipboard.

"All but the removal of the brain," Dr. Price replied. "In this case, I don't find it necessary. There are no visible signs of head trauma. I will get to it though since a delayed swelling of the brain might be a possible factor. At the moment, I would not say that it's the cause, but I leave no stone unturned."

"So, what can you tell us about the cause of death?" Teague produced his notebook from his inside pocket and listened keenly.

"The body has sustained quite a bit of trauma. It shows all the signs of someone bludgeoned with great force. Several broken ribs, a broken nose, and about three teeth knocked out. He also has a cut in his shoulder, here." Price rolled the body on its side and pointed to a thin incision right at the shoulder blade. "It has the same wavy pattern on the inside that matches the style of weapon we found at the scene. This was much longer - a sword if I were to guess. The blade was so sharp that it cut straight through the bone. It did, however, manage to miss several important blood vessels."

"He didn't bleed out then?" Teague inquired.

"He would have in a couple of hours without treatment, but he was found in time, and the blood was staunched." Price dropped the body unceremoniously back on the table. "Benefits of being hurt at a hospital. None of his injuries would have killed him. Unless he had managed to escape the scene and left himself untreated, but even then, that would be a stretch."

"Then what did kill him?" Swan scratched his head, following the doctor's lead. They played a game. Price danced around the answer, and Swan tried to act surprised when he actually told him.

"Well, we did take tissue and blood from the body." Dr. Price held out his hand to his assistant who handed him the clipboard Swan had been viewing. "We have the toxicology report right here, and it's quite telling."

"Just give us the information, Doctor," Teague said and gave him a satirical smile.

"Fine." Price checked over the clipboard. "You're no fun, Detective Teague."

"I know."

"According to the blood work we took from the body, he was poisoned."

"Poisoned?" Teague looked at Chief Swan who mirrored his surprised expression. "Could the weapon have been laced with it?"

"There is no evidence of it. There was nothing on the knife we found, and there is no poison in the wound on the shoulder."

"Dr. Benton did tell us that those weapons were often poisoned," Swan said.

"Not this time. The dosage that could kill a man of this age and constitution would have to be large. We would have seen evidence of it in the wound. No, the poison was ingested." Price took out a pen and pointed at the mouth. He pried it open as the assistant came in from behind with a small pin light. "Come in closer, gentlemen." He continued and Swan and Teague leaned in. "See this? See this white coating in the cheeks and at the back of the throat? It is synonymous with strychnine - potent and quick."

Swan straightened himself up again and crossed his arms with a worried look. "So, the fact of the matter, is that he would not have been poisoned during contact with our vigilante?"

"Correct. The poison works much too quickly. If the ampule were inside his mouth at that time, he would have been dead before anyone had been at the scene. No, the poisoning happened after. In my estimations, only a couple of minutes prior to death."

"That means that someone at the hospital got to him." Teague looked at Price and Swan. "Either that person managed to sneak into the building under our watchful eyes or was already there."

"Of course," Swan replied. "There were so many people moving in and out of those rooms that I'm sure keeping tabs on who everyone was would have been near impossible. That coupled with the staff and guests there from earlier."

"Are we looking at a fourth man?" Teague thought aloud. "I have a hard time believing that the information regarding a survivor would have leaked so early. It is understandable that the one employing these killers would like to get any would be squealers out of the way but being able to send someone out in such short order just seems unlikely."

"Agreed," Chief Swan replied. "There are two possible.

answers here, as I see it. Either there was a fourth man, a figure waiting in the shadows to see if the trio of thugs were successful and charged to deal with any unwanted outcomes." Then he became silent and lowered his voice

to a whisper. "Or there is a mole of some kind at the hospital or, god forbid, the department."

* * *

"Detective Teague!" Charlotte, the secretary, called to him as Chief Swan and he returned to the command center. He turned to her and nodded. He had received so many different things to think about now that he was less than interested in talking.

"Yes," he said in a short reply.

"I have found some information about the man you asked for." She was waving a light-brown folder in her slender hand.

Teague motioned to her to follow him to his desk, and with an enthusiastic spring in her step, she came away from the large counter. Teague sat down, heavily, and she placed the folder in front of him, opened it, and leaned over him.

She was standing close enough to him that he could feel the warmth of her body and the smell of her sweet perfume. As she spread the contents of the folder, she came even closer, and he felt the brush of her breasts through the softness of the silky white blouse she wore.

He closed his eyes for a moment and felt how much he missed his wife. He had seen so little of her the past few days, and any thought of intimacy was out of the question. Which was unfortunate, seeing as how they were trying to start a family. She ached for a child. It consumed every fiber of her being, and her longing infected him so deeply that he could feel her pain. Every time they had friends visiting who had new babies, her eyes would water, and he would have to look away. That constant question when they were getting ready for bed.

"Why don't we have a child, Garfield?"

Every time it was the same thing. He knew it would come, and he never knew what to say. He never said anything about it. He stayed strong and silent, like a hero in one of Raymond Chandler's books. Strong and silent.

Now as Charlotte, young and supple, with her blond hair set

in an elaborate bun, invaded his private sphere, the sensation of how much he longed for the contact of another human body overcame him. As if his own skin cried out to be touched, tenderly, warmly, and with love.

"This is what I was able to dig up on Timothy Lansing," she said and moved back to a standing position. It's not much.

Some photographs, field notes and a list of the objects that were found among his belongings."

Teague placed his hat on the desk and unbuttoned his jacket before pouring over the material. He picked up the field notes. Writing covered them- fine penmanship for someone obviously writing while researching out in the world. There were some drawings as well, mostly of flowers and rock formations. He put them to the side without looking at all of them, and then he moved on to the list of belongings. The black crystal with the skull was clearly marked, but there wasn't much else of interest at the moment. Instead, he moved over to the three photographs.

One was a portrait of Dr. Lansing himself. He was dressed in a gray suit with his hair nicely parted, posing as if he was thinking deep thoughts. Eyes staring off, beyond the camera, and his right hand gently holding his clean-shaven chin. His body tilted in that familiar angle that most portraits had, as if he was leaning to one side. Why they did that was beyond Teague. He looked young, according to the documents he had been in his mid-thirties when he went missing.

The second photograph was more sepia toned, as if it had been subject to the elements for a longer period. Unlike the first picture, it was not a studio picture. Instead, it taken in the wild. The backdrop was a mountain range overlooking a forested area with a mass of leafy trees standing close together. The kind of woods abundant with fairy tales. Standing in the foreground with their backs to the beautiful scenery were two men. One of them was clearly Dr. Lansing. He was wearing a light-colored button-up shirt, his sleeves rolled up, signaling that he was ready for adventure. His legs covered in dark pants and knee-high leather boots. With his hair still neatly parted, and with his stare confident and straight at the camera, he seemed to epitomize the idea of a gentleman adventurer, the sort of which was only to be found in books by Haggard. Next to him were two large backpacks, bursting with content. Kneeling by the bags was another man, seemingly close in age to Lansing, and dressed in the same attire but with dark hair. He must have moved ever so slightly when they took the picture, for his face was unrecognizable, blurry from the sudden movement. It created a strange effect, making it appear as if the man wore a mask across his eyes where the blurriness obscured him. Teague turned the photograph over and found a small note, too tiny to read with the naked eye. He picked a magnifying glass from his desk drawer and held it over the picture. *Malaysia 1935* it read, no more, no less. Teague leaned back in his chair after dropping the picture on the table in front of him.

"Any help?" Charlotte asked in a slightly too familiar tone. Did she think that them being so close to each other had removed the need for titles?

"I'm not sure," Teague replied and ignored her misstep. "The further this case goes, the deeper I delve into it, and the less I understand. It's not even clear if these pictures and notes have anything to do with murders, little less vigilantes who kill criminals with Balinese swords." He picked up the third photograph.

It was a picture of a chest. The old type of traveler's chest - similar to the one his great grandparents would have used when arriving at Ellis Island. The lid was open, showing it to be empty. Before it, on a blanket that looked distinctly Latin

American lay a plethora of objects. He turned the photo over and read *The Belongings of Dr. T. Lansing, 1942.*

Flipping the picture back, he once again used the magnifying glass to investigate closer. Most of the objects strewn about were nothing more than bric-a-brac. Probably endlessly exciting to archaeologists, but to his untrained eyes, it was nothing more than rocks, small figurines and old jewelry. He found what he was looking for - the black crystal with the skull insert. It wasn't front and center like he thought it would have been. Instead, placed in the lower left-hand corner.

"That picture almost looks like this drawing." Charlotte interrupted his train of thought before it had even left the station.

"What do you mean?" He turned to her.

"This drawing." She showed him a yellowed piece of paper covered in hand-drawn figures. Just as she had claimed, it was very similar to the photograph, except for a few details. Instead of the chest and the blanket, it was just the objects. It was as if the artist had drawn them in the order they had been collected, for some of the pictures were more faded then others. Every item had a little number next to it, and the most washed out figures had lower ones.

He quickly looked past most of the tiny rocks and uninteresting pieces to scan for the crystal. He found it. It was one of the last drawings. It had no other information than the number 35. Next to it something caught his eye. It was a ring. Whoever had been in charge of depicting the objects had scaled it up to make it easier to understand the scope of it.

As a ring, it seemed to be plain enough. The image drawn in ink, so there was naturally a lack of detail, but set in it was what looked like a black gem, the shape of an eye. It bore the number 36. He quickly turned the paper over, but there was no log there.

"Did you find any other papers with this?" he asked Charlotte.

"I don't think so," she said. "'t just kind of fell out when you were rifling through the notes."

"It looks as if it was part of a notebook," he said, as he looked at it closer. "See here on the left edge. It's frayed like it's been pulled out from a book. There must be a second paper, at least, and a whole journal most definitely."

"Not here."

"So where is it?" He paged through the remaining papers but found nothing that remotely looked like the paper he was holding.

"This is the only documentation pertaining to the name Timothy Lansing. I would assume that the remaining book was removed before it became part of our archives." Charlotte straightened up and posed with her fingers stroking her chin. "What I find odd is that the documents don't have any notes. No writing. There are no newspaper articles, no comments, nothing. This is all there is. Some field notes and photographs."

"Dr. Lansing worked for the Milwaukee Public Museum." Teague looked at the secretary and squinted as he always did when conferring with himself. "If there is more information to be had on him. Census counts and the like, they would be there. Maybe if we contacted the Milwaukee Police Department and County Courthouse, they might be able to assist us."

"I will get on it, Detective Teague," Charlotte said and saluted. He knew she had reverted to formalities only because of the situation, but it felt good. She gathered up the documents and

placed them back in the folder before she headed away.

"Look up anything we might have on the Milwaukee Museum as well!" he shouted after her.

Once she had vanished up behind the large desk, he spun the chair back to his desk. He moved the cigarette case in his hands while he thought deeply about the whole affair. Through most of the leads he had come across lately, there was no light at the end.

This was different. If he could figure out whom the vigilante was chasing, he might find the reason and the connection.

* * *

Memorial Hall was a beautiful building. Erected in 1924 in a near renaissance style. Columns with leafy motifs and lambs' tongues, sharp, acute angles and statues reminiscent of the old Greek gods decorated it. A gift from William Horlick, the king of malted milk. It was only one of his many philanthropic gifts to the city. He had donated an entire maternity wing at St. Luke's Hospital, Island Park and an athletic field that bore his name. He was a man of the people, even if he became one of the city's most prominent members.

Thanks to the four Romanesque pillars on the southern side of the hall, it was easy to scale the building. Tony's journey from the apartment, across the few blocks, was easy. He had jumped from rooftop to rooftop without notice by the three or so people he had seen. Once he had come to Sixth and Main, he had waited for the coast to be clear before he

214

climbed down and crossed the intersection. He had given himself plenty of time so that he wouldn't feel stressed while waiting for the green light. Now he was resting on the rectangular block right above the columns. It was like a ledge looking out over a small open area below. He had been there with so much time to spare that he had decided to have a bit of a lie down. The flat surface of the block, just below the triangular portion of the roof, was perfect for lying on one's back, out of sight from those passing by on the streets below.

He stared up at the darkening sky, now and again looking out over the mighty Lake Michigan. The sun was setting the horizon on fire, reflecting the orange glow in the calm darkness of the water, as well as bouncing off the few blue somber clouds that sailed above him. Mimicking the vessels gliding across the lake beyond.

It made him long for Bali. The place was still his first home, and whenever he felt lonely, scared or apprehensive, he longed for the lush vegetation, clear falls and warm breeze against his skin. The humid air of the city was reminiscent of that of his childhood. It made him miss his dad - not the biological one who never gave him a second thought, but Wayan, the man who raised him to be a warrior. The man who handed down his family legacy and most prized possession. The man who died fighting for the freedom of his people. He was unsure how long he had been dreaming himself back to his island paradise when he heard the sound of creaking, like ungreased wheels turning. Coming out of his trance, he realized that the sun had set, and he rolled over on his stomach and gently pushed up to a crouching position.

He scooted close to the edge and looked down to find Martin Lindquist sitting in a wooden wheelchair at the top of the steps that led down towards the lakefront. The young police officer was staring out over the now completely black water, now and again throwing glances to his left and right to avoid uncomfortable surprises. He was obviously not attempting to traverse the stairs - with either the wheelchair or jumping on one leg - but was patiently waiting for someone to arrive.

Tony made sure that his blade remained safe at his back, and then he swung himself over the edge. He gripped the ledge of Memorial Hall firmly as his legs freely hung below him, and with an easy movement from his lower body, he came close to one of the columns. Clasping it with both his legs, he gently glided down to the ground. It might not have looked particularly graceful - in fact, he imagined that it looked like a firefighter sliding down a pole - but it was effective. He landed with ease and then quickly spun around avoiding his back facing Lindquist.

He was standing at the bottom of the stairs looking up at the seated young man. He could see the same cold apprehension on the man's face as he undoubtedly wore under the mask. It was a risky gamble on both their parts. Lindquist was part of the police force, and nothing stopped him from engaging the rest of the department to ambush Tony. On the other hand, the masked vigilante had taken his leg. Who knew if this just wasn't a clever ruse to silence him. They both had reasons to be suspicious of the other.

The eight or so steps between them seemed an ample amount, at this point. Tony had his right hand at the ready, behind his back, with his fingers gently touching the hilt of his kalis. Lindquist had a blanket covering his legs, and under it, unbeknownst to Tony, was a small knife. It wasn't much -

something he had managed to steal from his lunch tray. It was dull, no more than a serving knife, but if things got hairy, he wasn't going down without a fight.

"So, you came," Tony said. He tried to articulate for he knew that the mask made it difficult to hear what he was saying.

"So, you came," Lindquist replied, almost with an air of defiance that Tony found misguided.

"I was surprised that you sought contact and that you managed to escape the guards at the hospital."

Lindquist squinted at the figure in the horrific mask, with its fangs, bulging red eyes and small horn-like protrusions. He felt it was a good thing that the streetlight didn't shine on this area too well; most of the figure was obscured by shadows. Still, he could see most of the man's body shape, lean and muscular under the tight-fitting outfit, making the covered head look disproportionate in its size. The red dots glowed eerily in the shadows, but the face held no true terror to him now.

"Those officers at the elevator and the nurses were no match for me," he replied. "They couldn't care less about a cripple in a wheelchair. In fact, they seem quite uninterested in anyone's comings and goings, but I am sure you already knew that. Seeing as how you managed to deliver this note." He held up the letter Tony had left him.

As Lindquist said, Tony hadn't experienced any issues just entering the fourth floor in the middle of the night, it must have been around four a.m. and casually walking into Martin's room. No questions asked.

"Are you planning to kill me, like those thugs you took out?" Martín boldly asked. "Did they spoil your plans?"

"Are you here to arrest me?" Tony shot back, the articulation making it difficult to give his voice any type of attitude. "As vengeance for your severed limb."

"I have information that you might need." Martin looked away, only to make things more interesting.

"What kind of information?" Tony set a foot on the first step. "Why do you think I might need it?"

"I was undercover within The Black Diamond for quite some time, and I barely knew the inner workings of it. I assume that an outsider like you would have an even more difficult time figuring it out. So, I am offering all the information that I have to you so that you can finish it."

"Why give it to me? Someone you don't even know. A masked man wanted by the police."

"You want to know why I don't just bring it to my superiors."

"Right."

"I'm pretty sure there is a mole in the department. No one knew I was an undercover agent until recently, and when that came out, killers came for me. My job as a lawman is to bring down those who prey on the innocent citizens, and if I think that is being hindered by someone who is supposed to do the same... well, and then I have to take a different route."

"Makes sense," Tony said and relaxed his hand; let it hang down in an attempt to show Martin that he was no threat. "For what it's worth, I would like to apologize about your leg."

"I get it." Lindquist moved his hand free from the blanket, trying to mimic the show of trust. "You couldn't know that I was a cop."

"And you had no idea what my agenda was." Tony took another step up. "In the end, one of us was going to get hurt."

Martin looked away again. This talk of the fight down in the parking garage a mere block away from where they were standing was causing emotions to flood over him. "What *is* your agenda?" he cautiously asked. "If you don't mind me asking."

The question ambushed Tony a bit. He had never imagined that he would have to discuss his mission with another person. On the other hand, he hadn't imagined that it would take such a long time to accomplish what he had set out to do. The idea of another person being privy to the information was daunting. What could this crippled copper do with it?

"My goal is to bring down the drug trade in this city," he said matter-of-factly. "As much as possible."

"Then I guess going after The Black Diamond is the right move," Martin replied. "I'm not going to ask you the how and why of it. I guess you have your reasons. I don't really care. If this can help then so be it, and if you die trying to do what is right, then it was a nice attempt."

He produced a sealed envelope from inside the leather jacket he had slipped on before leaving St. Mary's. He had worn the same jacket when he had first met Baz Peterson. In fact, he had put on the same cap as well, turning it sideways and doing his best Marlon Brando impression.

Tony climbed a couple more steps so that he was only one level below Martin's wheelchair. He stretched and took the envelope from his hand. He was now fully visible under the yellow streetlamps. The hairs in the back of Martin's neck stood at attention at the sight of the mask. He tried to hide the shivers he got from the piercing gaze of the red eyes and the frozen grin of the mouth.

"It's the best I can do. Information about the coming deliveries of drugs from Chicago. The next one is tomorrow night, and I'm going to guess that they are in dire need of it since you spoiled the last one."

"Thank you, sir," Tony said.

2Unfortunately, I can't tell you who is behind the organization. I don't know, and I guess only one person does."

"Who?"

"Never knew his name. Some fat, sweaty man."

"Thank you again, and once more, sorry about the leg."

"I know why you did it, but I'm not quite ready to forget about it." Martin looked away again. He couldn't look at the horrible visage anymore. "This is the only thing I will help you with. Don't contact me, and you can count on it that I won't try to find you again." There was a moment's silence, and when Martin reluctantly turned back to the stairs the figure was gone.

CHAPTER FIFTEEN

It was a testament to his stubborn will or his warrior spirit that allowed Wayan to make it back to his village, his body riddled with bullet holes. His tribe was sitting around the fire, waiting with bated breaths as they tried to listen to the gunfire in the distance. Even though Bali is a smaller island, Marga was too far away from them to understand how the battle was going. Every time there was the slightest noise, those around the fire would jump, just a little, look at each other, and then they would return to their silence.

Once the fire had burned down and only cinders and ash remained, he was there. At first, they only noticed the strained panting of someone in duress, and then one of the children pointed to the wall of trees that surrounded the glade. He was standing with his legs wide apart, to keep his balance, his arms hung at his sides, clutching a kalis in each hand, and his head hung low, his long hair shielding his face from the light of the fire. His wife called to him, but he would not move. They saw him sway gently back and forth, like a tree in a slight breeze.

After the third time calling his name without response, she rushed towards him. He collapsed in her arms as soon as she came close enough to catch him. She called to the other villagers who were watching to come and help, for her husband was very heavy. Men came running and they helped lower the body to the ground first and then lift him up in unison. Carefully, they carried him to the fire where they wrapped him in a blanket in order to keep the damp night air out. The journey from the battlefield to his home had taken everything out of the warrior, and he drifted off into a troubled sleep as the others tried to staunch his wounds to the best of their abilities. His wife pulled off strips of cloth from her dress in order to create bandages, but in a surprising moment of clarity, Wayan grabbed her arm and told her no.

"Get me Anthony," he whispered to her. "Bring him here."

She kissed him on the forehead and ran to the house of the Hill family.

* * *

To the west of Memorial Hall and the downtown area, with its storefronts and taverns, lay the sprawling mansions of the more affluent citizens. The mailboxes had once upon a time born the names of Horlick, Case and Johnson, but the families had moved to larger homes outside the city limits. Other people had bought the grand villas with their columns holding up a dome-like roof. It would be easy to imagine some of those houses on the land of a southern plantation, complete with a gentleman, moving back and forth in a rocking chair, sipping sweet tea on his wraparound porch. It was quite idyllic and a sharp contrast to the barrios closer to Spring Street, where any form of porch at all would be a luxury.

222

A Cadillac had come to pick Tony up at his apartment. He was almost a little ashamed when the fancy car stopped outside his home. Not that he had ever cared too much about riches. On the contrary - his upbringing on Bali had focused on a wealth of character and spirit.

His parents had come from money, but his father's constant change in allegiance had ruined them, more or less, forcing them to live on a minor stipend, minor to them, for the rest of their lives.

It was more due to the driver's way of looking at the brick building from where he emerged that made Tony self-conscious. He had dressed in a tuxedo, the required outfit for the evening, according to the official invitation he had received. He had purchased it the day he had gotten the job at the radio; he was that there would be functions one needed to attend. The driver, a middle-aged man with gray hair and sporting a mustache, dressed in a very proper looking uniform, opened the passenger door and gave him a quick nod. The golden buttons on his long coat, buttoned all the way up to his chin, glistened in the streetlights.

Tony gave a curt nod back, climbed in and sank down in plush white leather seats. He felt a bit uncomfortable in his garb. In order to save time, he had dressed in his red and blue outfit also – so, he was wearing two layers of clothes. Luckily, the first layer was quite thin, but it still felt as if he was wearing long johns and an undershirt, and it created an uncomfortable sensation, constricting almost. He had never enjoyed dressing in more than was necessary. Maybe it was the fact that he had grown up in a warm climate, and his body used to being as uncovered as possible, or maybe the fact that it restricted his movement. He had decided to do it after he had read the note

Martin Lindquist had given him. He had opened the envelope as soon as he had gotten home. It had two dates on it.

The first one was the following day, and the other one was two weeks later.

The note claimed that the first shipment, a load of several pounds of cocaine was due to arrive at ten p.m. It was allegedly coming in on a freight train to a little-used station in the industrial area past Spring Street. Tony knew of it from before. In the early days of the city's industry, when Malted Milk was new and there was an attempt at creating a motor industry with the Mitchell, a railroad for transporting goods had been a great idea. Now it mostly lay abandoned, giving way to trucks and large ships that could move large cargoes across the lake. It would be the perfect place for clandestine operations, especially those coming from Chicago.

The only problem was that the train was due to come in on the same night as Dr. Benton's party. There was no way he was going to miss that event, and it would be quite suspicious if he had canceled. The note said ten p.m. and the party was at six, so there was plenty of time to do both. That was why he had dressed in double layers, and the blades and Face were right behind his door, easily accessible. He had figured that he would leave the party close to nine o'clock, grab a car home and quickly sneak inside, strip off the tuxedo, slip on boots, mask and then pull the Face over his head, easy as you like.

He had allotted an entire hour to get from the party to his home and then onward to the train yard, it might be tight, but he was hoping it would run smoothly, and he was not too eager to leave earlier than he had to. It might be cutting it close, especially doing it on foot, but he felt confident, nonetheless.

The car pulled up to a large white mansion, complete with pillars and a wraparound porch. Tiki torches lined the sidewalk and from the tall windows came a warm glow that penetrated the foliage of the lush maples on either side of the steps to the porch. Night was beginning to fall, and the mansion appeared very inviting. As the driver opened the door and Tony stepped out on the sidewalk, he could hear the sounds of a brass band playing inside.

The party seemed to be in full swing already and another black automobile pulled up behind the Cadillac. A couple climbed out - a man, distinguished with his gray hair slicked back and dressed in a tuxedo, and a woman in a black dress covered by a white fur coat. Tony hung back a moment, nodded to the couple, who ignored him, and let them approach the house first. He tried to look as casual as possible, leaning on the side of the Cadillac, to the great annoyance of the driver. The couple, in their fineries, climbed the steps, painted white to match the house, and approached the ivory double doors with the shell-patterned window above. The right door opened, and they stepped inside. They belonged there; he could tell. There was no hesitation, no trembling hands knocking on the door. He was warm under the dual layers of clothes. The night was muggy, and he felt sticky and uncomfortable. Even if he had been born into a world of fancy dinner parties and formal wear, he still felt out of place. He had been so young when they left that life, and his father had never truly immersed him in it. Instead, he watched from open doors as men and women rubbed elbows with each other. A lonely child blinded by the reflective glory of the bright lights of Dutch high society.

He was more nervous about this than he had ever been going into a fight. That was his real scene; this was just a game. He was to play the role of someone he was not. Tony Hill, young radio personality about town, an eligible bachelor as it were.

He put his fingers through his hair and straightened out his bow tie. Grab the bull by the horns. He could do this. The more he became a part of this world, the more he could infiltrate it and do some good. In most people's minds, it was among the upper class that the most injustice emanated. They always wanted more than they had, and always at the expense of those less fortunate. An oppression that was not so different from the one he had witnessed as a child. A form of national economic imperialism played out on the expense of the immigrants searching for a better life.

He walked the elaborately laid stone path from the sidewalk to the Benton home. Swirling patterns reminiscent of the intricate shapes and lines found in the art of the East Indies.

He was unsure of what was going on with his head lately. More and more things, in nature as well as in fabricated objects like this, were flooding him with memories of Bali. Of home. Maybe the path of the vigilante that he had chosen lately, or something completely unrelated, had woken the feelings. Whatever it was, it was painful. He felt lonely and without guidance. The contact with Lindquist was the first real interaction with another person that wasn't a complete sham.

He had tried to walk slowly towards the magnificently detailed double door so that it would seem like he was confident. There was a gilded knocker on the door on the right side and he used it. He surprised himself at the force that the metal hit. It had not been his intention, but his nerves must have caused him to use more power than he had realized.

The door opened so quickly that it startled him, and he took a guarded step back, almost causing him to fall into a defensive stance, his hand moving to a spot on his back where a hilt would have been located. Not this time. A thin figure, bald and with a thin mustache under a hooked nose, looked at him with tired eyes. His lids were barely open, and his face bora a frozen look of disdain. He wore the uniform of a butler. Black suit with a black bow tie.

"Sir?" the man said after looking Tony up and down. Assessing him and his outfit. It was as if his penetrating gaze could see right through him. Eyes trained to calculate the measure of a person in mere seconds. "Do you have an invitation?"

Tony came out of his trance for a moment and reached inside his jacket to produce the sepia envelope that had appeared in his mailbox just the day before.

"Mr. Hill. I see," the man said. "Very good. Follow me if you would, sir." The voice was monotone, devoid of emotion. An attempt at a British accent. The man was obviously trying to hide what might be a very pronounced Midwestern dialect, and he was working very hard at keeping the illusion going.

The hallway was as grand as the outside of the building. It opened up into an impressive room. With a large staircase in the center of it that split in two, leading to a second-floor balcony. The room was a gaudy mess of cherry wood furniture, floor and detail, mixed with large mirrors in a baroque style and sprinkled with gold and brass details in a variety of places. It was as if an ancient Egyptian army had invaded the house and then vomited interior decorating all over the place.

The floor was so shiny one could have seen one's own reflection in it. Tony was afraid his new dress shoes would cause him to slip on the polished perfection. The mustachioed butler asked him to wait in the hallway and disappeared through one of the four doorways that were placed in opposite pairs to the right and left.

Tony walked over to an intricately carved vanity. Painted white with gold leafing and a large mirror in the center. He looked himself over, tried to put his hair back in place, and attempted to pat away the small beads of sweat on his forehead. The music was louder and came from the room the butler had gone into. Steps from hard-souled shoes echoing through the room as the butler returned interrupted the sounds of the rhythmic brass band. He once again asked Tony to follow him, and they walked through the doorway he had vanished through before.

It had seemed impossible at first, but the room on the other side of the threshold was even larger than the hallway. Sure, the mansion looked big from the outside as it spread out on either side with two rows of windows.

This must have been the intended ballroom when they designed the house. The rows of floor to ceiling windows spread out over one wall, looking out over the large spread of grassy land that lay beyond the mansion. The floor was even shinier here, polished to the point that one could scarcely call it wood anymore. A mural depicting frontier life around Lake Michigan covered the ceiling. A figure, reminiscent of Gilbert Knapp, the founder of the city, stood in the foreground and pointed to the Root River, with his right hand neatly tucked under his jacket, like Napoleon. There were natives trading with trappers, and pioneers building churches and raising barns.

Chippecotton was the name of the river in those days, and the outpost Fort Knapp. Great big crystal chandeliers hung from molded brackets with leafy motifs. On the opposite side of where Tony entered, a stage had been built, and upon that stage stood a ten-man orchestra with a solitary female singer belting out a popular tune. There was a long table to the right of Tony, covered in all kinds of delectable dishes. Pheasants, hams, salads, roast beef - anything one could think of - and it smelled divine. There was a pyramid of champagne glasses on a round table by one of the windows, and every glass filled to the brim with the sparkling golden fluid. It was all a bit odd. This kind of setup was, as far as Tony knew, quite unusual. Most of the time dinner parties like these were just that, dinners. No member of high society or the local country club could imagine serving food at a long table, like a garden party. Tony was convinced that the couple he had seen before were beside themselves, joking at the absence of cucumber sandwiches. There were people everywhere. Women dressed in fancy black dresses with colored accents like scarves or jewels. The men wore their tuxedos, and some wore white gloves. Tony did not agree with that. Maybe it was because he didn't feel like wearing more than he already did, or the fact that his father had always told him that only the help wore white gloves.

He moved closer to the champagne, grabbed a flute from the lot, and sipped it. He didn't have a lot of experience with alcoholic beverages, but his father had taught him enough to know a good vintage when he tasted it. He needed to be sure to nurse the drink the entire night through. Showing up at the train yard intoxicated in the slightest would not be a good idea, but a single man not partaking in free booze at a party would also raise questions.

"Hill," a hoarse voice said, and he felt a heavy hand on his shoulder. "I thought that you might have canceled." Vic Linden had managed to sneak up on him. He was not surprised to the girthy man was close to the food. He had shaved for the occasion and combed his otherwise wild mop into a part. His tuxedo stretched to its limits though, and he had been unable to button the shirt all the way up and forced the bow tie to act as the strap that held the collar closed.

'It's already six-thirty, Hill. You need to learn that when the invitation says six, you get here at five-thirty for a welcoming drink. Now you have to make the rounds and shake all these pricks' hands. It's better to be on the scene first and be the one standing still. It makes you seem important."

Linden winked at him and produced a small case from whence he produced a cigarillo "Have you met my wife before, Hill?" Linden pulled a thin woman from another conversation. She was not dressed in a little black number like the others. Instead, she wore a golden dress in the style of a flapper from the twenties. The outfit covered in sequins that sparkled in the bright light of the chandeliers and mirrored the appearance of the champagne in the glass she was holding in her left hand. In the right one, she was clasping onto a small plate with a variety of cuts of meat on it. She had obviously been a real beauty back in the days of the dress she wore. Now she was thin and gaunt looking with an excessive amount of blush and thick red lipstick smeared over pencil thin lips.

There was life in her eyes though, and she flashed rows of pearly whites at him.

"Hi, there," she said in the cracked voice of the elderly. "I am Mrs. Victor Linden. Delighted to meet you, Mr. Hill. I do so enjoy listening to you on my husband's radio station."

"Thank you, Mam," Tony replied and bowed to show his respect food and drink keeping her hands occupied. "It is always nice to hear that one is doing a good job."

He glanced over at his station manager, who was busy stuffing his face with cocktail wieners. Linden rarely praised anyone at WRJN, quite the contrary. He was quick to criticize, but if a kind word ever did come out of his fat face one knew that it was genuine.

Tony turned to stand beside Mrs. Linden, but Vic moved around them, so he was sandwiched between the couple. "So, how many do you know at this party, Hill?" he said and attempted to put his arm across his shoulder. Linden was a whole head shorter than Tony was, so in order to reach up, he had to stand on his tiptoes. After a few seconds of trying to balance, he dropped it and settled next to him instead. "Most of these guests come from old families of the area," Linden continued. "They're not like you and me, Hill. They were born with silver spoons in their mouths - some with gold ones even. Now they seem to keep them stuck up their asses - if you get my meaning." The last comment he said in a whisper so as not to offend his wife, who Tony knew came from one those older families. "Sure, some of them are self-made, but they are so aged now that they barely remember what it was like to share a bed with three siblings, not knowing where the next meal was coming from. If it came at all."

This was a side of his boss completely unknown to Tony. It also showed that Vic Linden knew little of Tony's past. The Hills were not as rich, but far from poor - probably born with a brass spoon in their mouths if one was looking to use metaphors.

There was a short silence as the conversation died, and all he could hear was the chewing of food, intermingled with the sound from the orchestra. He decided not to partake in the delicious food, for the same reason he was not washing down the alcohol like his boss. The heaviness of all that fat and protein would make him sluggish, and he didn't need the extra weight holding him down. He stayed, even as Mrs. Linden stumbled off in her high heels to hobnob with other ladies of society.

He scanned the room for other familiar faces, Dr. Benton for instance, and he caught the eye of Chief Swan, who looked just as lost as he felt. The chief's tuxedo was almost as ill a fit as the one Linden was wearing but in the opposite way. Instead of it being too tight, it was too big. It was entirely possible that Swan had lost weight since he wore it last. The job as Chief of Police was demanding, but most men in that position were rarely out in the field the way Swan was. The chief came over to stand by him, very obviously glad to see a familiar face, and a friendly one to boot.

"Chief Swan," Tony said and stretched out his hand.

"Mr. Hill," Swan replied and shook the hand with a firm grip. "And Mr. Linden." He turned to the station manager and greeted him as well. "You fine gentlemen look nice this evening."

"We clean up well," Linden said and coughed, choking on whatever he had stuffed in his face. Tony looked over at him with a concerned look. The man had pieces of meat in one corner of his mouth and the cigarillo hanging in the other. He looked like some sick kind of caricature of himself.

"Yes, well, that is true," Swan said and tried to stifle a laugh. "I heard your reporting on the radio, Mr. Hill. Very well done. It is so nice to have a working relationship with the press, keeping all the facts under wraps."

"To be honest, I don't know much about the case," Tony replied and raised his glass in a salute. "I'm not an investigative reporter. I only want to inform the public so that they can rest easy at night."

"I do believe that only criminals need to be worried when it comes to that particular case." Swan winked at Tony. "The public have plenty of other things to be concerned about. Being attacked by some masked, sword-wielding killer shouldn't be one of them."

"Completely off the record," Linden said as he wiped his mouth with a napkin singed by the cigarillo. "What do you know when it comes to the attacks in the parking garage and St. Mary's?"

"Off the record, Mr. Linden?"

"You can trust me, Chief. I am integrity itself." Linden grinned and showed his rows of yellowed teeth. Tony felt that his

eyebrow was starting to cramp from constantly rising.

"If the two of you can keep this to yourselves. Although there isn't much to go on." Swan tried to whisper and still audible through the din of the band and the conversations all around. "The two incidents are related, but they are vastly different. In the parking garage, the killer interrupted a drug deal between the Irish mob and an organization we only know as The Black Diamond. At St. Mary's, the killer instead seemed to have interrupted an attempt to eradicate a witness. The same killer did not murder the hospital staff and police officers; they instead fell to the bullets of assassins. Then they, in turn, were killed by the *vigilante* - if we use that term."

Swan sipped from his glass, which did not contain champagne, but instead what appeared to be orange juice. "Now, who this vigilante might be is a bigger mystery. Through the good Dr. Benton and the Public Museum in Milwaukee, we have been able to ascertain that his weapons come from Bali but nothing else."

Tony felt a bit uncomfortable at this. He had figured that the lost kris would be a cause for concern. It was a stroke of bad luck that Dr. Benton had knowledge of the East Indies, and that, in turn, they had garnered more information from the museum was unexpected.

"Are you any closer to figuring out motives from this killer?" Tony asked and tried to sound as calm as possible.

"Not as such," Swan replied. "There is a lot of speculating going around. One being that it is a citizen taking the law into his or her own hands, a second that another organization is trying to horn in on the drug racket in the city. We are attempting to work as many angles as possible."

"And what of The Black Diamond?" Dr. Benton chimed in. He had managed to sneak in on their conversation without them noticing at all. He was impeccably dressed in a smoking jacket, not a tuxedo. The three men were startled at his sudden appearance. "Excuse me for interrupting, gentlemen, but I have yet to welcome Mr. Hill to the soiree." He took Tony's hand and shook it, and then he turned back to Swan. "Back to the topic at hand. What of The Black Diamond?"

"Well, Doctor," Swan began. "That organization is proving to be as elusive as ever. At least with the Lehmans, we had a good picture of the family and their dealings. The rub there was catching them in the act and pinning anything to them. I guess you could say that they were our version of Al Capone."

"That is a potent comparison," Dr. Benton said with a smile. "Why do you think that is, Chief?"

"Yes, why is that Chief Swan?" Linden repeated and smirked, acting like there was some unknown issue between them. Tony could tell that his boss was noting everything mentioned.

The man was shrewd enough to know that he could use the material eventually. Off the record seldom adhered to in the press.

"The big problem that we have found is that whoever is behind The Black Diamond organization doesn't appear to have a set structure. From what we have gathered, and mind you we have only been aware of the group's existence about a year or so, it operates with independent contractors. It is as if they enlist the aid of random thugs and mercenaries through some form of third party. The result of this is that the actual criminal elements who picked up and questioned by us never have any information to give. All they ever know is the name The Black Diamond. In truth, we don't even know if that is the name at all or just some form of reference that they are given. Like a calling card. It was at least the brand that we found on the crates from the parking garage."

"That is fascinating, Chief Swan," Dr. Benton replied to the information. "You seem to know so much, yet so little."

"It must be very frustrating for you and your men?" Tony said.

"It is," Swan replied. "We never seem to get close to anything. Every time we nab someone in the act, it is always a dead end."

"Wouldn't this vigilante figure be of service then?" Tony asked with genuine interest. "If he is trying to bring the syndicate or whatever you might call it to its knees."

"If that is what he is trying to do that is. We are not too keen on the public taking the law into their own hands. Who are they to decide who warrants killing? Sure, someone can take out a big criminal network like The Black Diamond, but what then, after that. Do they attack and kill anyone who breaks the law? Those who drive too fast or are double parked?'

"Isn't that a bit extreme?" Tony unintentionally scoffed.

"Maybe," Swan said. "But how do we know that it wouldn't happen. We know nothing of this figure. Ponder it's not a concerned citizen, but another mob looking to take over the city, then what? No whatever the motive, both The Black Diamond and the vigilante need to be brought to justice."

"I will drink to that," Dr. Benton said and raised his glass. The others returned the action and they drank. "I must mingle again, the duty of a host, but I look forward to speaking to you all again." He toasted them again and vanished among the throng of dancing guests.

Once the doctor had left, the chief and the station manager also moved along. The former stepped outside, and the latter joined his wife. Tony remained by the buffet and champagne pyramid. It suited him fine, but he was also a bit lonely. Suddenly, someone tapped him on the shoulder, and he turned his head to find a young woman, around his age, smiling at him. She wore a red dress, quite the contrast to the other ladies present, and had her blond hair in an beautiful bun. It was the singer from the orchestra. The music was still playing, but he had somehow missed that the vocals were missing.

"Hello there," she said, and her full red lips parted in an alluring smile.

"Hello," Tony replied, a bit surprised.

"I noticed that your friends left, and I couldn't help but feel that you were a bit lonely." She sipped on champagne and winked at him.

Tony had never been that experienced with women. He had gone on the odd date, but it had never gone further than that. He assumed it was because the young ladies he had met with hadn't interested him, but this one with her pale skin, lush eyelashes and brashness awoke something in him.

"My name is Tony," he began and held out his hand for something like the fourth time that evening. "Hill. Tony Hill."

"Emily Chaucer, no relation. Pleasure to meet you." She smiled and placed her hand like a queen in his hand. Tony didn't know if she expected him to kiss it. Instead, he bowed slightly, like he had seen men do in the movies.

"I'm sorry," he said. "Relation?"

"To Chaucer," she replied coyly. "Canterbury Tales? The greatest English poet of the Middle Ages, maybe ever?"

"I see. I guess I didn't make the connection." Tony, of course, knew who Chaucer was. His tutor Mr. Mahr would not have been doing his job correctly if Canterbury Tales were off the syllabus. He felt like a fool in front of this beautiful woman who simply seemed to ooze charisma. "You have a lovely singing voice."

"Thank you, Mr. Hill," she said and finished off the champagne and placed the glass on the table next to her. "You have quite the voice yourself. I have heard you on the radio. You are younger than I imagined you, but that is not disappointing. Not in the least."

"Thank you for the compliment, Miss Chaucer. I assume that you are a singer by trade?"

"I am," she said. "I have been singing since I was a little girl. I won't bore you with the tired cliché that I sang before I could speak. I just think that is what people do."

"I can't remember. Possibly."

She laughed. A delightful sound, almost like a song in itself. "I have been singing professionally for about a year actually. I was going to school up in Madison, studying to be a teacher, and I used to sing on campus, at various events, but duty called here at home, and a spot in this band happened to open up. The hours suited me and that is that."

"To use another cliché instead." Tony realized that the remark might have been on the border of what was acceptable banter after he had said it. He cringed a bit inside.

"Very astute of you, Mr. Hill," Emily said and laughed again. I go on again in ten minutes. Would you care to take in the air with me? A woman should not venture outside without an escort. Especially these days," she said and winked again.

"That sounds like a good idea, Miss Chaucer." Tony held out his arm for her to grab, after having placed his own glass next to hers on the table. "One can never be too cautious."

They walked through the sea of bodies, and Tony opened one of the big glass windows that also doubled as doors. She thanked him with the subtlest of nods and smiled at him with her eyes. *She can smile with every part of her body*, Tony thought.

It was odd. In every interaction with a woman that he had ever had, there had been no different from doing the same with a man. Of course, he hadn't gone on dates with men, unless you considered having lunch a date, but that was beside the point. He noticed that his brief contact with Emily Chaucer was very different. He noticed things about her that he had never noticed in anyone else. The way she moved. The nuances in her speech, as if he could find some hint at her deepest secrets or opinions in the cadence of her speech. He felt that he paid attention to every single strand of hair on her head, as if he wanted to memorize their exact positions on that perfectly shaped head. The way it snaked around her tiny ears, complimented with hanging silver earrings, and framed her face so that those deep blue eyes became the centerpiece in her face. Her nose that some might consider a bit too long, slightly bent to one side, but it gave her character and seemed to be just right for her. It was overwhelming for him.

Never had so many impressions washed over him as he followed her through the door and gently closed it behind them.

She turned to him and cocked her head to one side, as if she could finally consider him for the first time without the distractions of the other people in the room, the sound of music, and the smell of food. Like she could finally focus solely on him. They were far from alone outside on the vast estate spread out before them, but most of them were walking quite some distance from the mansion, some were getting lost in the garden maze, and some were watching the moon reflecting in the calm water of a pond. He let her do her little body scan, but he felt a bit uncomfortable since she was silent.

Once she straightened out and smiled at him again, he walked over to her and once again put out his arm. She grabbed on to it, ever so gently. His skin tingled at the touch of her fingers, even through his tuxedo jacket.

"So, Mr. Hill," Emily said. "What brings a man like you to one these parties?"

"My celebrity status I guess," he answered.

"Interesting. I can think of several others in the city who I would categorize as more famous than a local radio host. Don't get me wrong. I'm sure you're famous enough to be here. I know that I am only here to sing. I'm not even a guest."

"I believe it was coincidence more than anything else, to be honest. I happened to be in the right place at the right time."

"I see," she said as they passed the outside of the maze, where they could hear the laughter of people trying to find their way out. "Where would this right time and place have been then?"

"You know," Tony said and looked at her. "That's a very forward question to ask someone you've just met."

"That is my cross to bear, Mr. Hill." She cocked her head to the side again. "I have always been this brash. I'm interested in you and what makes you tick. I can tell that you don't socialize very much, apart from your job, and there is a kind of loneliness in your eyes. Maybe a longing for someone to see the true you. If you would like me to back off then I will go back to the house, and we shall never see each other again.

However, from the moment I saw you, I believed that there was something special about you. Not to everyone, but to me. Say the word and I'll go. But it might be the biggest mistake that you ever make."

"I'm sorry, Miss Chaucer." He stopped and turned towards her so that they were facing each other. "I didn't mean to offend you. You are right in some respects. I am not much of a social butterfly, and the women I have met have never been like you."

"I see." Emily looked away for a moment.

"That's not a bad thing. I like it. You don't seem to know the meaning of moving too fast. You're confident, and I like it."

She turned to him again. "I've got to get back on stage." She smiled again, and his heart skipped a beat. "I'm not offended. I know who I am, and I guess that's why I don't make excuses or conform to social ideas."

"Let me take you to dinner some time," Tony said and felt that the moment was right for him to put a hand on her arm. He did, and he almost lost his breath when he felt the naked skin of her bare arm. "So, we can get to know each other. Away from all this noise."

"I'd like that, Mr. Hill." She didn't shy away from his touch. Instead, she placed her hand over his. "I'm in the phone book." She winked and began walking away.

"It was at the police station!" he called after her.

"What?" She halted and turned to him.

"The place," he said and smiled. It felt strange. "I got the invitation because I was at the police station on business. Dr. Benton happened to be there and claimed he liked my work. The host thinks I'm famous enough, at least."

She laughed her singsong laughter again and disappeared up the slope that led to the mansion. Tony stayed and put his hands in his pockets, swayed back and forth, and then headed back as well.

* * *

Teague was sitting at the dinner table in his robe. When he had come through the door and kissed his wife, a deep, tender kiss, the kind that always made her knees buckle, he had announced that he was going to take a bath. The roast was still going to be a while she said, so it was fine.

The closeness he had felt to Charlotte when she handed him the photographs had woken the lust inside him, but it had felt wrong making love to his wife because another woman had lit the fire. He was unsure where in the scope of cheating that ended up. Instead, he drew a lukewarm bath. There was no way he was going to take a cold one.

He had neatly folded his underwear and socks and placed them on the little sink, then he hung his shirt and suit on the hangers provided him by his wife. Baths had always relaxed him in a way nothing else could. Ever since he had been a child, it had been a way for his parents to calm him down. Maybe it was because they had bathed him every night before they put him to bed. Even when he had been a boy scout and had been away for a week at camp, he had taken a bath to relax, had fallen asleep, and then woken up with the water stone cold around him. He tried to avoid falling asleep this time, though his body made it difficult.

He placed a rag over his face and carefully leaned back, not wanting to shock his back with the sensation of the cold enamel. He drifted away, trying to process all the details of the case in his head. Trying to fit them together like a puzzle

242

where some of the pieces were just blue sky. He was still unclear how they fit into the grand scheme of things. He tried to arrange them on his mind's card table. He had Balinese weapons, a killer with unclear motives, a clandestine criminal organization known only by a name, an undercover police officer keeping secrets, a missing ring, a dead archaeologist, a mysterious assistant, and dead thugs and crates filled with drugs. What was the big picture in all of this?

Once out of the tub, he slipped into his striped pajamas and then his robe. His wife was a bit surprised that he had chosen to dress in his nightwear so early, but he assured her that he had no interest in going anywhere else that day so he might as well be comfortable. She smiled and kissed him on the cheek and told him that it was a good thing the ladies from her book club had decided to move their meeting to a different date then.

Dinner had been delicious. Roast with mashed potatoes and peas with a gravy sauce. He had eaten two full servings and was now sitting at the cleared-off table with notes and papers spread out before him. He stroked his beard with one hand and fingered the cigarette case with the other. It wasn't working. He wasn't seeing it.

"That case is going to be the death of you, dear," his wife said as she sat in a chair across from him. She also looked over the documents and photos.

"I know," Teague said and leaned back a bit. "As it stands now, I am just going to assume that it's going to end up a cold case."

"Why?" She had a concerned look on her face.

"There is just too much missing. Too many parameters that we don't know. If we knew anything about The Black

Diamond, then maybe we would know why the killer is targeting them. If we had any witnesses who actually could give us any information, then that would help as well."

"But isn't it so that you are dealing with criminals killing each other?"

"That is true. What are you thinking?"

"Does it really matter if criminals kill each other?" She winked at him with those brown eyes that he loved so much. "Less work for the police to deal with."

"I understand what you're saying, dear, but I am fairly sure that this isn't the end of it. The killer isn't done, and the criminals he is killing will most likely retaliate. Too many innocent people have already died because of his actions. We can't afford more. We have to stop him. Both of them, in fact."

"Well, what if it is over?" She rose from her seat and rounded the table. "What if there is no more and he disappears?"

"Well, then I would go crazy not knowing the truth," Teague replied. "I need to solve mysteries - that's my job."

"What about the mystery of us not having a baby yet?" She came close to him and put her fingers through his still-damp hair, pressing her body to him.

"Well, that's a mystery I think I can solve," he said and stood up to kiss her. First, just a peck, then a longer one, and then another. She parted her lips and invited him in. His hands glided over her white blouse and freed the bottom of it from the checkered skirt. One hand wandered up under the blouse and caressed her soft skin, while the other unbuttoned the skirt. He kissed her neck, and she moaned with pleasure. He got lost in the moment, closed his eyes, and let their bodies almost meld together. It became a blur, as if everything just melted away - the room, the furniture and work. They were all that remained. She put a finger to his lips and halted him for a moment.

"The bedroom," she whispered.

* * *

"I see you're admiring the Far East collection." Tony's trance was broken, and he turned around to Benton smiling at him with a martini in his hand and a young lady in a black dress on his arm. She kissed Benton on the cheek and sauntered off after a word in her ear from the doctor.

Tony was tired of just standing around listening to the orchestra play. He was not famous enough that people immediately recognized him, so no one came up to him or gave him a second glance. Vic Linden and Chief Swan, the only two people he had any form of connection to, had disappeared - either gone home or were just hobnobbing with someone else.

For a while, it was enough to just stand in a corner and watch Miss Chaucer sing her heart out on stage. Every now and then, she would look over at him and wink, batting her eyes at him. Then it felt like he was the only person in the room and her words were directed at him. It was foolish, he knew. They had only just met. Literally just met. For some reason, he felt that instant connection with her. Not as if they had known each other their entire lives - more as if she was an enigma that he needed to unravel. She was the question and he had the answer. Something like that. He didn't know if it even made sense. In the end, it could just be that she was the only one to approach him in a room full of strangers. Maybe his need for human interaction made him so needy that any form of it made him desperately grab on to it and refuse to let go.

He had grown weary of standing there, and since the night was still young, he had decided to wander around the mansion. He wanted to get an idea of what measure of a man Dr. Benton was. He had returned to the grand hallway and looked up the elaborate staircase, but he decided not to climb them. It was likely that the bedrooms were on the second level and that was too private.

Instead, he had taken the first door to the left of the entrance and ended up in the kitchen. It was noisy and chaotic. Men and women were running back and forth trying to make sure to keep the buffet tabled filled. He had retreated and taken the first door on the right, instead. It was the library or study. In contrast to the rest of the mansion, it was more subdued in its furnishing. Dark wood shelves crowded with large tomes lined the walls, and a large oriental rug lay on the floor. Art deco lamps placed in the corners of the room, casting the room in a dim glow. A desk stood against one of the big windows, facing the street. It was probably pleasant to gaze out over the street while working, but one's back would be to the rest of the room, leaving yourself open to surprises. He had perused the books a bit. They were of a great variety, but mostly books about medicine, mixed with the odd fictional title. The darkness and almost claustrophobic sensation he got from the oppressive books made him leave.

He tried the final door, second on the right. Lights that shone inside glass cases, very similar to the way a museum organized their artifacts. Someone had divided the cases into regions on either side. There were no windows, so there was plenty of room for storage. It almost created a corridor of cases, and on the far wall hung a very elaborately woven tapestry of a world map. He passed cases with artifacts from South America, Europe and the Arctic. He had remained by a case filled with medieval weapons, some that looked far more brutal than his kalis. There might even have been blood on some of them, and that was when Benton had startled him.

"Yes, it's very nice, Dr. Benton," he replied once his pulse had slowed back down. "You seem to be an avid collector. It is quite impressive."

"Please, call me Jack." Benton moved up alongside him and they both faced the display case.

"Jack," Tony echoed.

"I spent quite some time in the Orient in my younger days, as you may be well aware of by now. Fancied myself a bit of an adventurer even though I was mostly researching the plant life there and herbal remedies to bring back. More like a modern-day Carl Linneaus than an Alan Quartermain, in all honesty. The Asians are far more advanced than we are when it comes to medicine, and I did return with more than I bargained for. Did I understand that you were acquainted with the area?"

"My father was stationed on Bali and worked in Batavia, and I was born there, so the East Indies are not unfamiliar at all."

"I see." Benton appeared genuinely impressed. "Your father was an ambassador of sorts then?"

"A cultural attaché to be more precise. We lived through the Japanese invasion but returned to Great Britain once the Dutch reclaimed the island."

"'re your parents still overseas?"

"No, my mother died when I was very young, and my father passed a mere year after we had left the island. They sent me here to live with my aunt and uncle and then attended college to study broadcast journalism. I do miss it though. I spent my formative years as a young child and adolescent there."

"Well, then you might enjoy this." Benton placed his hand in the small of Tony's back and led him further down the wall, past samurai suits of armor and Chinese vases until they reached the far corner, and placed between two statues of Indian deities was another large cabinet filled with objects. "This is my Indonesian exhibit, as it were."

Tony slowly walked up to the grand piece of furniture. Benton sneaked past him and opened the glass doors to allow him a closer look. The walnut shelves covered with bric-a-brac of varying degree. Everything from hand-carved little figurines to brightly painted woodcuts, but it was the collection of Balinese masks that caught his attention.

"I see that you are eying my pride and joy in this collection," Benton said and put his hands on his back, bobbing on the balls of his feet. "My assortment of Indonesian masks, and this one is, of course, my favorite." He pointed to one that Tony recognized very well.

"May I?" he asked with his hands hovering above it.

"Please do." Benton smiled and took a sip of his martini. "As a native of Bali, I am convinced you recognize the Queen of the Leyak: Rangda."

Tony did. He gently picked up the mask that was roughly the size of a basketball, but twice as heavy. Constructed from some form of lightweight wood, the natives had decorated with dark hair, and painted in white with swirls of pink across it.

There were huge fangs protruding from a snarling mouth and two great eyes staring straight at him. A long tongue hung from between the fangs and almost touched the floor as he cradled it in his hands. It was very similar to the one that had hung in the Hut of Death in his adopted father's village.

"This one I believe used to hang in a Death House in a Balinese village."

"They usually would," Tony said dreamily. "I was in one such hut once, and it is quite an intimidating sight to see a mask like this hanging there. In the dark, with the smoke of the eternal fire obstructing one's vision."

"I can only imagine. I bought this one after a festival where they had taken it out of its home. The person who sold it to me claimed they could make a new one."

Tony gingerly put it back in the case and rose again - he could feel the layers of clothing stretch as he moved. "It seems like artifacts like these are your special interest."

"True." Benton turned to look at the rest of cases standing in their neat rows, like soldiers before their general. "There is something very intriguing about perceived magical objects. As I mentioned, I have traveled extensively around this world, and I have seen so many things. Things you might not believe that I scarcely believed then. Sure, the scientists of today will tell you that there is nothing supernatural or mystic in the world, that there is only logic, but they have not been where I have been or taken part in what I have been part of.

There is one particular incident, I will tell you about it sometime, which came to shape me. It also woke my obsession with ancient lore and artifacts. My lifelong mission has been to find the magic in this world."

"And how has that worked out?" Tony let just a little bit of sarcasm escape from his mouth.

"You'd be surprised-" Benton smiled at him. "There is something to be said about the power of suggestion. Most of the artifacts that I have come across work like some form of placebo. Something that one such as I, being in the pharmaceutical business, is quite familiar with. They only have imagined powers. This usually pertains to objects with purported healing capabilities. On the other hand, there are certain objects that have been imbued with the power of belief over the centuries that it has come true."

"How do you mean, Doctor?" Tony looked at him in surprise that such words would come from the mouth of a man of science.

"I am talking about a unique object. One of its kind that has

such cultural significance that they pass it down from person to person, through decades, centuries, maybe even eons. Every time new hands touch these objects a little bit of that person's belief seeps into it, making it stronger and stronger."

"Do you believe that?" Tony understood this thinking all too well; after all, he was in possession of an artifact that had some magical powers.

"I have seen enough in my days to convince me of it." Dr. Benton took another sip from the martini.

"Dr. Benton," Tony began. "This has been a great party, but unfortunately, I must be going."

"So soon, Mr. Hill?"

"Yes. I have had a good time, but as you must be aware, I am somewhat out of place."

"I couldn't help but noticing that." Benton smiled, and when he did, his entire face lit up. "You, your boss and the good chief gravitated towards each other. The outcasts, as it were."

"Yes, well we come from the same place I guess." Tony blushed as he said it. "They also seemed to leave the festivities early."

"They did, and without saying goodbye. Quite rude, if you ask me."

"I was raised with better manners than that." Tony bowed. "I would like to thank you for the delicious food and fine drinks, Doctor Benton."

"We must get together some other time, Mr. Hill," Benton replied without sarcasm in his voice. "At parties like these, one seldom gets to visit with the guests they find most intriguing. I'll have the car brought around for you."

They walked out of the room together, and into the grand hallway, Dr. Benton picked up a phone and called for the driver, who promptly came out from the kitchen door. Tony walked over to the entrance to the grand ballroom, but he hesitated on the threshold. He had wanted to say his goodbyes to Miss Chaucer, but he could hear her singing on stage. For a moment, he considered waving to her from the back, but he decided against it. For the first time, he felt that his inexperience in these kinds of social situations was a hindrance. He felt awkward in a way he hadn't since his childhood days. He followed the driver, bid farewell to Dr. Benton, and then left the din of the party, still in full swing.

CHAPTER SIXTEEN

Tony ran towards the village faster than his adopted mother had run to his house. Her absence during the rebellion had gone unnoticed. The Hill's home had fallen into disarray and even begun to fall apart in places. Crumbling stone and rotting wood. Mr. Hill, in his drunken state, had become disinterested in keeping up appearances to the outside world. Whom did he need to impress anymore?

He was not much of a cultural attaché, more a traitor. A turncoat that danced after the flute to those who played the loudest. He was torn. For he knew what he was, but his survival instinct, call it American capitalist ideals, forced him to survive, no matter what the cost. The conflict made him drink even more and eat less.

The wet grass felt cool against Tony's naked feet as he traversed, first the rolling hills and later the jungle. His nightshirt ensnared in the vegetation, and branches cut his tanned legs, but he ignored it. He slowed down when he saw the torches of the village, and once he entered the circle of huts that surrounded the central fire pit, he slowed to a walk. There, on one of the crudely made benches, lay Wayan, surrounded by tribesmen. He was completely still, only the movement of his chest visible as he breathed.

His hands were on his stomach, and he was gripping something tightly. Tony came close to him and whispered his name. The warrior opened his eyes ever so slightly and looked at his adopted son. The corners of his mouth curled up into a smile, and he moved his head, indicating that he wanted Tony to move in closer to him. The young man knelt next to his head and placed his hands on his shoulders.

"My son," Wayan spoke softly. "Take the mask from my hands. It is yours to keep now. I feel that our time on this island is soon at an end. Our way of life will soon give way to modern ideas and ideals. In this mask rests the history, traditions and magic of our people - now your people as well. It cannot fall into the wrong hands, or even be hidden away from the world. Care for it and do with it what you see fit. Use it for good or just keep it safe." Trembling, he raised his hands and held up the Face to Tony, who took it carefully. "Flee from this place. There will be nothing but pain here for you from now. It is not safe."

"Do not leave me, Father," Tony said and rested his head on Wayan's chest, tears welling in his eyes.

"I love you, son," Wayan replied and put a hand on his head.

They remained in that position. Tony listening to the gentle heartbeat of the warrior. His head moving in symbiosis with the falling and rising of his chest until it became slower and the beating fainter. Wayan's body became colder and the hand on Tony's head heavier. The women around him wept, and the men sighed.

* * *

The train was right on time. The driver prided himself on the fact that he remained punctual. Scheduling was very important to him. Everything was in the right place, at the right time. It was something he had learned in Catholic school, and it translated to his adult life.

He was very popular within the board, but his colleagues viewed him as a bit of a brown-noser, casting the rest of them in a bad light. He didn't care. If being punctual and doing one's job well made one a brown- noser, then so be it. The fact that he was so good at his job had also given him freelance work - something that was unheard of in the train driving business, but there it was.

A few months earlier, a sweaty round man in an ill-fitting suit had approached him. The man had thrown a briefcase filled with money at him. In return, he had to promise to transport crates from Chicago to Wisconsin. The distance wasn't very far - it only took about forty minutes or so.

He arrived at a train yard in one of the more clandestine harbors of Chi-town, looked over the engine and waited as silent shapes loaded the crates on the freight cars. He had assumed on the first-round trip he had done that the crates contained something untoward. Why else would they load them here among discarded containers and rusty fishing vessels?

The dollars that the man with the Dutch-sounding name had handed to him came at the right time. His wife was ill and needed medication, and his children kept asking for money. It didn't matter how long ago they had moved away from

254

home. They still came to the house with their bags of laundry and palms stretched out. It had bled him dry, so this job had come as a godsend.

His insurance did not want to cover the treatment his wife so desperately needed. It had struck them both very hard. That day when they sat on the other side of the doctor's desk. That man, with his thick, black-framed glasses and pristine white coat, looking down his nose at them. His wife in her floral housecoat, and he in his dirty overalls. Tears in her eyes at the death sentence. At that moment, it all seemed so dark. How were they going to pay for it all? That night, he had visions of her wasting away before his eyes while he was trying to feed his no-good kids and desperately fighting the agencies for help.

He had been sitting at a bar on Milwaukee when the fat man had taken the stool next to him. He had asked him why he looked so glum and was noticeably fiddling with a briefcase. They struck up a conversation, and his heart had opened like a faucet and his feelings had been the water spraying forth. The fat man had listened carefully. Had not interrupted, only the occasional nod, and once the story finished, he came with an offer. An organization needed help with transporting goods once a month, maybe more often if everything went well, and the preferred method was by train. It was a "you help us, we'll help you" situation.

Maybe it was the drink, maybe it was the desperation, that compelled him to carry that case home that night, but he did it. It was with a satisfied grin that he could shove the check in the doctor's flushed face, and they treated his wife that same week. She never questioned how he afforded it. Maybe she guessed that something wasn't on the level, and in the end, maybe it didn't matter. Business hadn't picked up any. He still worked once a month. He walked to the harbor under the light of the moon, checked over the engines, and when the loaders finished up, he took off. Alone on the train in the night as the landscape of the Midwest flew by.

He pulled into an abandoned train yard in the industrial area. It was like a small courtyard in between tall brick buildings. It had been a car factory- the failed Mitchell Motors. His father had always raved about Mitchell Motors when he was young, and his mother used to sing *Give me a ride in your Mitchell, Bill*, whenever the topic came up.

How his father, had he still been alive, would have been jealous now if he could see him pull into The Mitchell Lewis building on 815 Eighth Street. When the company folded in 1923, the building had passed through a few hands - Nash Motors, J.I. Case, and finally, the Massey-Harris company who manufactured tanks during the War. With great enthusiasm, he had researched the history of the plant by reading the county records.

This evening, the loading had taken a bit more time than usual. It was if the loaders had been waiting for something or someone. It had made him worry. Rumors abounded round the Windy City that the Japanese mob was dissatisfied with illegal substances transported through the railroad, believing that they owned the mass transit line. Since he was only on the sidelines of these illegal operations, he didn't have his ear to the ground, but it made him antsy nonetheless.

Nothing had come of the delay, more than just that, and as soon as he heard the doors close to the freight cars and the familiar banging on the side, he rolled on.

He brought the train to a slow halt in the center of the courtyard. The wheels made a screeching sound, and steam rose all around. He had found it oddly exhilarating that he would be driving an older style engine. He had been somewhat concerned that it might bring too much attention to the operation, but it hadn't. Steam engines were still common enough that no one noticed. As soon as he stopped, lights came on in some of the lower windows of the old plant. Through the steam, he could see shapes moving around in the light, and he heard the opening and slamming of doors, as well as the familiar sound of the storage door rolling open.

* * *

Tony was crouched on the roof of one of the plant buildings, once the home of the proud Mitchell Motor Company. The trip back home had taken longer than he had expected. He hadn't counted on the one-way streets forcing the driver to take a different way to the apartment building. It had, him late, and it forced him to run up the stairs and grab the bag with the Face, boots and gloves. He dressed quickly, and while running to the window, he strapped the kalis to his back. He looked out the window to make sure that the car had rounded the corner, and then he climbed out the window.

Like the previous night, it was already dark, and the journey across the rooftops had been without incident. He was trembling as he scaled the side of the factory gates, already sweating from the mad dash across town. It was not the ideal starting point, but it would have to work.

As he had pulled himself over the rod iron spikes, he heard the whistle from the distant train as it crossed the nearest intersection. He had crouched on the top, trying to avoid impalement as he did so. From his perch, he had followed the train tracks from the street outside as it wound through the red brick buildings. Tony wondered why The Black Diamond had not chosen to cancel the shipment. Had desperation to get the product out clouded their judgment?

Others heard the sound of the whistle and came running towards the gates. Tony then quickly moved to one of the nearby buildings. That was where he had remained as the gates opened and the transport slowly rolled inside in a billowing cloud of white steam. He took the opportunity. Shrouded in the cloud, he jumped to his feet and ran to the edge, leaping off the roof. It was as much a leap of faith as anything else. He had only the faintest idea of where the train was. He had no sense of how many cars it consisted of or how fast it was moving, he just felt he needed to get on top of it.

He extended arms and legs to his sides and tried to flatten his body. He knew that he was not going to be able to land on his feet. Injury was a distinct possibility, and if he tried to roll when landing, he might well roll off the train. It felt as if he was hanging in the air for several minutes, and he tried to avoid bracing for the impact. Instead, he relaxed his body completely and then hit the roof flat. He tensed his fingers and attempted to grip the curved metal to avoid bouncing off. He had the wind knocked out of him and he gritted his teeth against the pain in his abdomen. He couldn't afford to get hurt now, not when he was so close.

He tried to scan his body as his adopted father had taught him. With his eyes closed, he let his consciousness move through him, feeling every fiber of his body. His ribs were a bit tender, but there was nothing broken at this time. He would have to be careful so that there was nothing hidden.

The wheels of the train screeched as the brakes hit, and a moment later the entire machine jerked to a halt. Tony rolled over to his back and moved to a seated position.

Big puffs of steam still rose from the engine, and he slowly moved through it. He saw the figures who had opened the gate move wheelbarrows, and more men emerged from the buildings. He counted six of them. An easy match for him. Only two of them appeared armed at that. As soon as they all had their attention turned to the train cars and began unlocking the doors, he made his move.

Flying through the air, he did a somersault and landed behind the men. He winced a bit as he landed. He had tried to come down on his toes. It seemed as if his body was not listening to him completely yet - perhaps it was still recovering from the landing earlier - so he came down on flat feet.

The impact reverberated through his legs and up his spine, making him all too aware of the tenderness in his ribs. He had gone undetected though. The sounds of doors sliding open and the rumbling of the train drowned out whatever noise he made. The dual kalis slid from their wangarakas silently, and he advanced on the men from behind. They were all dressed the same - denim bibs, white shirts and caps. Some had cigars or cigarettes sticking out of their mouths. They were regular laborers, most likely unaware of the evil machine they were working for.

He felt a pang of guilt at what he must do, but in this war, there would be casualties, and they were but mere soldiers. The closest man was pushing a wooden cart, and he never knew what hit him as the blade sliced its way down his back. The man collapsed at his feet.

Tony moved towards the next one when he heard a shout and the sharp noise of a gun firing. A bullet struck next to his foot, and sparks came from the blacktop. He stepped back and raised his head. An elderly man dressed in dark overalls was leaning out of the engine with a pistol trained on him. Another shot rang out, and he ducked just in time. He thought he felt it pass by the mask.

The other workers now alerted to his presence, the one in

front of him tipped over the cart and hid behind it. He was out in the open. There was nothing to take cover behind. He threw a glance over his shoulder and all he could see was brick wall. He felt cornered. One of the armed men climbed up in an open car, while the other one remained behind the cart. They opened fire and Tony it forced to move from side to side to avoid the bullets. The smoke all around him was protecting them from the effects of the mask, but it was also making him difficult to see. Instead of backing up, he dropped to the damp ground and rolled towards the cart. One of the shots grazed him across the back. Once at the turned over cart, he shoved the kalis through the wood and could feel it cut through human flesh. A voice cried out on the other side and the blade came back stained with blood. The cart splintered as several shots hit it.

He tumbled to the side and came out from behind the cover. A boot to the side met him. He stumbled to his feet as the man advanced on him with a fist. He parried with his sword and the steel cut in between the man's second and third knuckle, down to the wrist. He placed his own boot on the man's chest and kicked him to the ground. At the same time, two more fists hit his head. One of the men wrapped his meaty arms around his waist and pulled him down. Tony held on to his weapons with all his might, but it was difficult. The man climbed on top of him and attempted to pin down his arms with his knees, all while the other worker kicked his legs. The man stunk of stale alcohol and old sweat, and beads of perspiration rained down from his forehead. Suddenly he froze. Tony had ceased his squirming, letting The Face do its work on the man. His eyes widened and his mouth fell open in a twisted look. It was enough of an opening for Tony, who raised his left shoulder off the ground, giving him enough room to swing the kalis at his attacker's back. It wasn't enough to do any great damage, but the sharp edge of the blade cut the man across the shoulder and down his side.

The effort twisted Tony's wrist and forced him to let go. The kalis clattered to the ground and the man rolled off him, whimpering as he tried to staunch the flow of blood with his free hand. Tony rolled back and came to a standing position, grabbing the blade in the process. He leapt in the air, towards the kneeling figure, and came down on his left foot while kicking his opponent in the face with his right. With a groan, the worker went down. His friend, temporarily paralyzed at first, advanced on Tony, who spun around and kicked him in the gut with his left heel. As the man doubled over, Tony let his blade slice through his throat in one fluid motion. A crimson flood poured from the wound as a gargled noise escaped the man.

Tony paused for a moment and surveyed his surroundings. He dodged a couple more shots coming from the open train car and noticed how the last unarmed man turned and ran.

Swiftly, he unsheathed one of his kris and threw it at the fleeing figure. It landed deep in the man's shoulder and he collapsed without being able to catch himself. He went to fetch the dagger from the man's body. He was forced to step on his back for leverage, because of how deep it had cut. Then he turned to the last worker. The man in the car.

Shots had stopped coming from the engine, and he assumed that the driver had run off some time ago. The smoke had begun to evaporate, and he could clearly see the figure hiding in the dark trying to load his revolver. He could tell that the mask was in plain sight now, the figure's hands were shaking uncontrollably, and bullets kept falling to the floor of the car. Tony moved slowly, centering himself. Taking each step slowly and deliberately, he moved closer to the train so that he moved along it, feeling the warmth from the steel against the side of his body.

Without warning, the door to the car he was walking next to flew open. He spun around just in time to see a body fly out from the dark. In the yellow lights that hung from the side of the factory buildings, he caught a glint of steel, or something else shiny, before two boots crashed into his chest. It sent him back and he tumbled, both weapons dropping to the ground. He ended up on his stomach with his arms extended in front. His chest was on fire and he was finding it difficult to breathe.

He looked up to see who or what it was that had attacked him. From the lingering steam, covering the wet, black asphalt rose a figure straight out of one his adolescent sci-fi magazines. It had the seductive shape of a muscular woman, dressed in, what appeared to be a dark bathing suit, open from the waist up to form a vest-like appearance. The figure wore gloves and boots, and covering its eyes was a domino mask where the top part pointed upward to give the impression of two horns. Brown hair framed the face and cascaded, in full locks, over the shoulders. Where there should have been bare skin there was what looked like banded metal. It was what had glistened in the light, but what caused Tony to do a double take was the mouth beneath that mask. A maw filled with rows of razor-sharp metal teeth, set in a steel jaw. This woman, this thing, seemed to be more machine than human.

It walked towards him, picking up speed as it did so. Tony got up and pulled out his kris once again, his swords out of reach now. He waited for her, bouncing on his toes, ready to pounce. The Face did not appear to have any effect on her, so he would have to rely on his fighting skills instead. The woman extended her fingers and blades grew from the tips of them, and when she was merely six feet or so from him, she made her move. She dove, the way a cat would attack an unsuspecting mouse. He vaulted over her and landed where she had been standing. He spun around and threw the kris at her. She had also turned to face him, only to have the dagger bounce off her chest with a metallic clang. Tony did a handspring off to the side and grabbed one of the kalis from the ground, but as he was about to touch down, the woman swept his feet from underneath him with one leg, and he crashed to the ground.

With feline quickness, she tried to impale him with her nails, but he rolled away before she could. He came to a crouching position, blade still in hand. She eyed him cautiously for a second and then moved again, her right hand reaching for him, and him parrying with the sword. An action that normally would have severed the hand of any opponent only caused a spark of steel on steel as she moved past him.

The weapon vibrated through his hand, sending shock waves up his arm. He slowly stepped back from the impact.

The woman moved closer, took two quick steps forward, and then swung her bladed hands at him. He dodged both of them but could have sworn that he felt the tips of the knives graze his abdomen. He sent his right foot at his attacker's knee. It felt as if he had stepped on a rock, but it caused the leg to buckle. While she was on one knee, he kicked her in the face with his left leg. His shin landed squarely on her jaw, and she toppled onto her back. He circled around from the momentum of his movement. If kicking the knee had felt like stepping on a stone, then kicking that steel chin hurt even more. His left leg felt weak, as if he had broken his shin, but he had no time to investigate it further. This was life or death.

He capitalized on her position and aimed his kalis at her neck to sever the head. She was ready for him though. Maybe it had been the momentary pause from the pain in his leg, or that she was playing possum, but she caught the blade by crossing her finger knives above her face, and his sword became tangled between her weapons. Tony tried to free it by twisting. He stepped on her chest hard and heard breath explode from her, but she seemed unfazed and instead jerked her right hand upward so that his sword twisted out of his grip and clattered across the courtyard. She hit him with her palm on his thigh, and he backed off her from the impact. Now he was unarmed. He made a quick assessment of the situation and made sure he had all his weapons accounted for. They lay spread out in a triangle with the enemy in the center of it. She did a flip up onto her feet and turned to him. Tony stared at her and tried to focus as much as possible on her, her eyes... those two dark pinpoints behind the domino mask. There was something different with this person. Either she wasn't human at all or she had done nothing wrong in her own mind.

She moved her head from side to side, as if she was working out some kinks from his kick to her face as she moved towards him with deliberate steps. With a few quick movements, she was upon him again. He tried to swerve to the side, but she landed a stiff punch to his gut, one that caught his lower rib. A second fist came from the left and embedded itself in his chest. He could feel his ribs compress from the force and felt a wet snap. He staggered to the side and fell onto his right knee, clutching his side. She continued to move towards him. Not quickly this time, but with purpose.

He was breathing heavily now, struggling to catch a deep enough one so that he could continue fighting. He felt a hand gripping his shoulder. It squeezed. Pinpricks of sharp nail dug into his flesh. He sent an elbow into her stomach, but she refused to let go of him. He followed the first one up with three more in rapid succession, and he quickly rose. She was still holding on. As he moved, he hit her on the jaw once again. This time with the top of his head. The impact made his ears ring, and he struggled to find his bearings.

It was her turn to stagger back. She fought to maintain her grip on him, but he pushed off her arm with his. The nails extended as they tried to keep him and tore his flesh. He saw a stream of blood splutter in the yellow streetlights. He gave her a side kick to the chest, and it sent her into the brick wall behind. There was an unmistakable sound of metal against stone, like a duller version of his swords landing on the blacktop. His antagonist shook her head and struggled somewhat to release herself from the bricks.

Tony took the opportunity and tumbled across the ground, grabbing one of the kalis as he did so. He came to a standing position over by the train car, skipped over one of the bodies, and came to a halt by the car. His ribs were burning from the pain, and he tried to take deep breaths, but he just couldn't.

She came at him again, her steel boots echoing off the ground. With one great bounding leap, she cleared the overturned cart and made ready to send her claw at him. Tony flipped backward, and he passed her in the air. He landed inside the car as her fist crashed through the metal and wood where his head had been. On his feet once again, he took the opportunity and kicked her in the face once more. The woman had caught her arm in the train, and she fought to be free of it. Tony followed up his initial kick with several more, ran back to the opposite end of the car, bounced off the wall, and came in with a baseball slide at the prone face. Both feet slammed into the forehead of the enemy and with a nasty tearing sound, she flew back. He saw her tumble, but she rolled to her knees. She gently moved her arm, making sure that everything was in one piece. It was difficult to make out any details, but Tony was convinced she was not showing any signs of bleeding. Any normal person would have surely broken their hand crashing into the car, or at least dislocated their shoulder pulling it free.

He remained in the car, looking at her through the open door, swinging his blade back and forth, indicating that he was ready for her. The movement hurt like hell, but he gritted his teeth and continued. She, on the other hand, paced back and forth, assessing the situation and planning her next move, very much like a cat toying with a mouse. She backed up, keeping her eyes on him while doing so.

She stopped by the stairs that led to the factory building, and Tony crouched in an effort to be as ready as he could possibly be. With a sudden movement, she grabbed one of the fire barrels flanking the stairs, held it over her head and with a great cry, flung it at him. Tony dove out of the car as the cylindrical fire container came at him. He heard it crash behind him. He tumbled forward as he saw the second barrel fly overhead. One of the dead bodies halted him but managed to steamroll it before coming to his feet. The second barrel had broken through one of the other cars and flames now engulfed both of them. He spun around and received a fist in the side of the head. It struck his temple, and the force continued his rotation. He lost his equilibrium briefly but managed to center himself again.

She was getting frustrated, or she would not have missed such a prime opportunity. Another fist came at him, and he dodged it with ease. She overreached, and he took the chance. Tony stepped on her knee from above, causing it to buckle. Then he sliced at her waist. She parried and pushed back. Tony quickly took several paces back so that her next move would miss, and it did. He was now at the wall again and leapt at it, pushed off with one foot, and soared over her. She came at the bricks and placed her hands on it to stop herself from crashing into the stones. Tony was behind her now. He ran towards her with as much speed as he could muster and dropkicked her with both feet. She had turned towards him already and the boots landed on her chest sending her back. She made a second imprint in the wall.

Tony rolled back to a crouching position, managed to recover his Kris, and then ran over to his second kalis. He didn't need to leave any more evidence behind. Armed with two blades now, he was ready for her attack. She was limping, her right leg not quite able to support her full weight. She could get hurt after all. He ran at her, she swung, and he slid under her arm and clipped her legs with the swords. She toppled, landed hard on the ground, but bounced back quickly. It was becoming increasingly difficult to breathe and move. He needed to end it, but even though he had now understood that he could hurt her, she was too durable to take down in one move. He needed to incapacitate her and fight another day. She was also breathing heavily. Took two steps and pushed off with her left leg, flying at him from above. He spun around and met her with a stiff kick to the midsection. The force from her and his kinetic energy collided, and shivers reverberated through his extended limb.

Tony collapsed as he saw her fly back, and her head hit one of the metal wheels of the train. He rolled around on the ground, making ready again, but she was still. The impact had knocked her out cold. He was motionless for a moment. Flames from the train rose against the night sky. The entire thing was now up in flames, and he needed to flee before the fire department or the owner of the goods in the train arrived. Gingerly he rose to his feet. He winced at the pain in his side and fled business unfinished.

* * *

That night, Tony sat with his head leaning against the cold tiles in his shower. His hand was covering the purple bruise that had spread across the side of his torso, and hot water was raining down on him from the nozzle in a hard stream. He had carelessly undressed and left The Face and the rest of his outfit in the hallway and had then stumbled into the bathroom. The water worked well on his tight muscles, yet it stung on the sore patch on his side.

He found that he had begun to shiver, not from any chill in the air though, for he had turned the water as warm as it could possibly be. It was something different. A sensation that crept through his body that he had not felt since he had first taken to the streets. When he had fled Bali as a child.

Maybe it was because he barely escaped with his life there, in the courtyard of an abandoned factory. Maybe it was the fact that The Face had not affected the woman with the claws or that his mission might fail. It began as a twitching in the skin, like involuntary spasms shooting up and down his body and through the muscles, like the corpse of a dead frog manipulated by electricity. Then the shaking became more violent, and it forced him to stand up, place his hand on the tiles and push in an attempt to make his body focus on something else.

The water went from hot to warm, to cool and then cold. He didn't know how long he stood there or how little sleep he got after crashing, still naked and wet, into his bed. However long it was, he felt it wasn't enough when his alarm went off.

CHAPTER SEVENTEEN

Anthony slowly walked up the white steps that led to the porch where his mother had watched him play as a small boy. At that moment in time, it felt as if it had been another lifetime. He barely remembered her. He had a sense of who she was, but he could not conjure up her image before his eyes. His mind could hear the sound of her rocking chair moving back and forth, creaking in time to the wood beneath it as her voice softly hummed, and he could recall the warmth of her skin.

He stopped and leaned against one of the columns and stared at the spot where the chair had once stood. Mr. Hill had ordered it destroyed several years earlier. To him, it was as if she was still sitting there, judging him and the life he had chosen to live after she had passed. The front door opened and silhouetted by the light from the inside stood Mr. Mahr, waiting for him. As the young man approached, Anthony could see the compassion in the old educator's face. He knew how important Wayan had been. He stepped aside and let Anthony saunter past. Mr. Hill stood in the hallway, in front of the grand staircase with its mahogany railing and lavish velvet rug. He was dressed in a black suit, was clean-shaven for once, and his blond hair was carefully combed. Anthony had not seen him so put together for many years.

"We must away, son," he said in a hard voice. "Our time in this paradise is over."

Anthony didn't know what to say about it. Bali was the only place he had ever known. His father had never spoken of another place where they might one day go back. He knew little of the past. Mr. Mahr had taught him geography and the history of Europe, as well as the Americas, but not how he related to them. There was no room for discussion or disagreeing; suitcases of various sizes filled the first floor, and he had removed all of Anthony's belongings from his room. Before he knew it, they had piled onto a bus headed for the airfield. They only brought what they could carry; Mr. Hill assured them that the rest of their things would come by boat to New York, to join them. He had connections there. It was in the middle of the night as the small plane took off, and Anthony stared out the window with tears in his eyes.

He saw the lights from the torches surrounding the village where Wayan's remains lay on the pyre, and in his hands, he clutched a wooden box containing a mask. Invaders raided and burned their home to the ground soon after they fled. The only thing remaining of their lives there would be a solitary cross looking out over the ruins of the mansion on the hill.

* * *

"What's new?" Garfield Teague asked as he came into the police station the following morning. It was a routine question. One that he had asked every single morning of his working life. At least, since he made detective. Whoever was standing behind the reception desk at any given morning were aware of this and never answered. Instead, they handed him the typed-up reports from the previous night. Teague flipped through domestic disturbances, misdemeanors and other miscellaneous crimes or events. There was no early morning call and that had been some relief - at least no more violent attacks perpetrated by masked vigilantes, not yet. He stopped at a report of a fire at a factory, but apparently, the company had taken care of things themselves before the fire brigade had arrived at the scene.

He fanned himself with the papers for a moment and looked around. His co-workers were filing into the office, a new workday was starting, and he would have to see if there were more dead ends or if he would make any progress.

* * *

Paul Geert, the rotund middle-aged man, was standing in the courtyard of the factory and warehouse that acted as a front for The Black Diamond's distribution center. He kicked at the charred remains of the train cars that had gone up in flames the previous night. The two cars that had burned were still smoldering. It had ruined over half of their goods. The dealers were running low on product and this was supposed to replenish a great deal of it. Now they it forced them to scrape the bottom of the barrel to keep the customers happy.

Maybe they could cut corners, maybe they would never notice, not the ones who were far-gone. The more private clients would be another story. They might have to be placated some other way.

Several workers were unloading the remaining crates and carrying them up the ramp to the warehouse behind him. It had been hectic. He had received a phone call in the middle of the night. One of the workers, who had remained in the building, as his friends were out to obtain the goods, had noticed a commotion in the courtyard. He described a figure with a horrible face killing off his colleagues - most likely the same man who had been the roadblock at every turn so far.

Geert had called in back up, and once they had arrived on the scene, the train was already on fire. The man who had called him was not much help in that matter, although he had also claimed that there was someone else there. Another figure. However, he had not been able to make out their appearance. Thank God, that Geert had brought enough reinforcements and that the factory had its own security system. Like a fire commissioner, he had organized his troops to put out the fire and remove the dead bodies that lay scorched on the ground. Naturally, the fire department had arrived as well - late, but they had come. He had been very convincing in the role of factory manager and with a bit of grease, in the form of currency, the firefighters were sufficiently satisfied that he had the matter well and truly at hand.

Black smoke rose against the morning sun as he tried to assess the damage done to the train and the contents. Two out of four cars were intact, along with the engine, which was singed, but in good enough shape. The driver was missing. Geert had hired the man himself. He was quite proud of the fact. It would be a shame if he had perished in the fire. He would have to find someone else to return what remained of the transport to Chicago without raising suspicion.

"The Black Diamond wants to see you inside," a short, wiry man with horn-rimmed glasses told him. Geert had not seen him at first, and the man had been able to come up to him without a sound. He had a receding hairline, which he tried to hide with a comb-over, and under his pointed nose, he sported a thin mustache in the style of Clark Gable. He was one of The Black Diamond's many accountants. Bland figures who often melted into the background. Once again, his boss had heard of this latest development without Geert contacting him personally. He had also entered the factory undetected. Maybe he had been there the entire time. Whatever the truth of the matter was, it was very disconcerting to Geert.

"I'll be inside right away," Geert said in a short, sharp manner, unhappy with taking orders from the likes of wiry accountants.

* * *

Dressing was painful, and Tony was no stranger to pain. When he had first trained to fight as a young boy, Wayan had not been merciful on his body. He needed to be tough, to fight through the pain, to learn how to ignore it, or even use it to his advantage. Many a morning he had wondered how he was going to make it out of bed. When the alarm went off, bright and early, he felt worse than he had when he had crashed on top of his bedclothes.

With some difficulty, he rolled off the bed so that he landed on his feet. There was no other way he was going to get out of it, let alone stand up. He touched his side but quickly pulled away his hand at the sharp pain that accompanied the movement. The bruise was comprised of all the various shades of purple one could think of. He tried to straighten up, but his body wanted him to stay hunched over. It felt better.

He hadn't checked himself over before going to bed, he was too preoccupied with the broken rib or ribs. He had various cuts and bruises all over his arms, legs and torso. He felt around on his face, but nothing was sore. At least he could look presentable going out to face people.

Without attempting to dress, he moved to his dining area and cautiously sat down. He leaned on the table with one arm while dabbing at the bruise with his opposite hand. He was going to have to power through. There was no way he could stay home from work now, and he could not let up on his mission. The mysterious woman in the armor and claws was a stick in his spokes for sure. He had incapacitated her for the moment, but he had not stuck around to finish her - there was no time for that. Once at the office, he could check the police wire to see if there were any reports of her arrest, but it was likely that she had managed to escape the scene.

He looked around the apartment as he tried not to breathe too heavily; every movement by his lungs cut into him like a dagger. His outfit lay strewn all over the floor of the hallway, his three remaining blades dropped next to it. The Face was lying closest to him and staring up at him like the head of a bearskin in a log cabin up north. It was judging him. Looking at him with that familiar contempt. Telling him that he was a failure. This mission had taken too much time already. When he had arrived in the city as a younger man, straight out of college in Madison, it was without the goal of fighting a criminal organization. It had been solely for work, but he had fallen in love with the city on the lake, with the lively river running through it. He loved the red brick buildings, the industrial area, and the beautiful lakefront homes with their columns and balconies. Such a juxtaposition to the wild untamed land he had grown up in as a child.

The Scandinavian heritage that flowed through the city like blood through veins reminded him of the European cultures that had influenced his time on Bali. It had felt like home the instant he had driven off the I94 and towards the city center. He had been blissfully ignorant of the goings-on among the underworld of it all. It became clearer as he read the evening news to the public seated in front of their radio sets that not all was well.

He had arrived at the tail end of the criminal war that had raged between various criminal families. That was when he had decided to do something about it all. He had gone into his closet and donned his ancestral mask. He had used it while at the university, so the outfit was ready and tested, but only against petty criminals. He hadn't even been required to use the swords. He had tried to do his part, even though it seemed as if the criminals took care of each other. He managed to take out the odd gangster, but it had gone by undetected. What was another few dead bodies in a turf war, even if they bore cuts instead of bullet holes?

Once the war was over, he had been confident that he would not have to dress up again and take to the streets. He had obviously been wrong. The rise of The Black Diamond had somehow passed under his watchful eye. It was the kind of news that did not make the bold headlines at the top of the paper or the news. Instead, small notices from the police tucked away on the last pages hinted at criminal activities in the outskirts of the city. Those places where respectable people did not venture. Where the Mexicans, Asians or Eastern Europeans lived in their own small communities.

Where the elite could forget about them or the fact that not too long ago their ancestors had been in the same situation. One of those notices that had caught his attention, and one night, dressed in a trench coat and hat, he had walked towards the water tower off State Street to see what was going on.

He had spent several nights there. Seeing the Mexican women rise before the sun had gone up to work in the bakeries, the smell of freshly made tortillas making his empty stomach growl with hunger. The trucks arriving to pick day workers for the fields, and children running to school. He also saw clandestine meetings on the street corners. Hands quietly touching hands, moving something between them. He made friends with a young man by the name of Tavio, who he frequently encountered during the wee hours of the night. He told Tony of a new player in the drug business coming to the city, and he explained that there was a new product flooding the underworld - bad stuff. Different stuff. Several young people trapped in it already. In the lure of the culture, but he only knew of the name: The Black Diamond. Nothing more. He had produced a business card, a black rectangle with a white skull set in a diamond shape. Tony still had the card in the nightstand next to his bed as a reminder. Three weeks later, Tavio was dead. Found floating in the river, a bullet wound to the head, and in his pockets were small plastic bags with remnants of a white powder. It was what had alerted the police to the problem, and it was then Tony had resolved to take down the The Black Diamond.

It had been tumultuous since that day, dead ends and false leads, but he had managed to sort through it all. Yet he had never gotten a lead on the leaders behind the name or symbol. This was the first true roadblock, and it had nearly derailed him.

He tapped a finger on the matte finish on his second-hand kitchen table. Officer Lindquist had mentioned a mole within the police department, and he had witnessed someone sneaking into Chief Swan's office when he was in there. Maybe that was where he needed to direct his efforts at this time. A mole gave up information through pay or some other form of extortion; maybe it was easy to coerce him. He might just need to pressure the person a little to get a lot.

Once again, Tony looked at the scattered outfit in the

hallway. He would have to slip the Face over his head again, but hopefully, he wouldn't have to fight. He didn't know if he could do it. Heck, he didn't even know if he could dress in his suit to go to work today. The station downtown would be his first stop though.

* * *

"Any new information from Milwaukee, Charlotte?" Teague had hung his coat and hat and then headed to the cafeteria to pour himself some coffee. With a casual air, he was now leaning on the command center desk where Charlotte was answering the phones.

"Not so far, but it is early," she replied, parted her red lips and smiled at him, and added just the slightest wink.

"Well, let me know as soon as anything comes across the wires." He tapped an imagined brim of a non-existent hat.

"Will do."

He was in a better mood this morning, and the people around him didn't seem to annoy him as much as they usually did. Charlotte never got on his nerves, though. Sometimes it made him nervous - the tension that arose between them. He hadn't felt that other than with his wife. He could never act on it though. His would-be family meant too much to him and Charlotte probably had too much character to let him even try.

Smiling to himself, he walked over to his desk with hopes that the Milwaukee police department would be quick about their reply. It was the only lead he had at the moment. Not much, but maybe he could solve the case by way of Dr. Lansing or whoever had been with him on his trips. The kris had been a dead end so far, but the skull artifact might help. He sat down at his desk and looked around. There was something different this morning. He was meticulous when it came to cleaning it when he left the office in the evenings. Now it seemed to be in some sort of disarray. Several objects, the typewriter, the stapler and a heart-shaped paperweight his wife had bought him were all slightly askew. As if someone had moved them to make room on the surface. The brown folder he had put aside, in line with the corner of the desk was now sideways instead. He raised an eyebrow in confusion. Had he been so tired and confused from the case that he had not put everything in its rightful place? Impossible. He would not have been able to sleep if that was the case. He could barely leave the house if his clothes were not uniform - it messed with his balance.

He put down the coffee cup on one of the coasters he kept in his top drawer. The four coasters, which usually lay one on top of the other, were also scattered all about the drawer. He leaned back in his chair and tapped the desk. He called Charlotte over, who quickly came over to him, notepad in hand.

"Charlotte," he said in a loud whisper. "Did you close up last night?"

"Yes, sir," she replied in the same tone, reading the situation well. "Several high-ranking folks were at that party over at Dr. Benton's house. The pharmacist, you know."

"Right," Teague answered. "Was anyone over at my desk after I had left for the day?"

"No. After you went home, most others had already left. When I closed up, the room had been empty for nearly an hour. Why?"

"Not sure." His tapping on the dark wood surface quickened. "It seems as if I might have left things a bit of a mess when I left."

"That is unlike you. Usually, you won't head home without making sure everything is just so." She giggled at this, and he nodded his head in agreement.

Teague scooted forward on his seat and picked up the folder. He opened it only to have the photographs and papers slide into his lap. They were in disarray, not the way he had left them; pictures arranged by size and then the documents. There had also been a paper clip holding everything together, but it seemed to be missing. There was an indentation in the corner of the folder to indicate that it had once been there, yet it was nowhere. He looked around to see if it had fallen out when he picked up the documents, but it was not visible.

"Have the cleaners been here yet?" he asked the secretary.

"They don't come in until this evening," she replied. "At least, not into this room. They are busy in other areas. Do you think someone has been tampering with your papers?" She was sharp.

"Maybe," he said placing the folder and its contents on the desk. "Or maybe I am beginning to lose my mind. Will you be a dear and head down to the forensics department and get me a fingerprint set?"

* * *

"Excuse me, sir, I did not quite catch that," Geert said as he entered the room that took up the entire third floor of the building. Huge lead-framed windows set in an art deco pattern ran along the walls, giving a view of the entire factory grounds. The room was completely empty except for a desk standing off to one side and a blackboard covered with numbers.

"I said that I am beginning to get quite annoyed, Mr. Geert," The Black Diamond said in a sharp tone as he stared out one of the windows that looked over the courtyard. His hands were behind his back, and he didn't as much as glance over his shoulder as his second came up the stairs. "All I'm trying to do here is to run a business." He slowly turned around. "We have clients to consider."

For the first time, his boss was slightly askew. It wasn't much. Just his otherwise neat hair hanging in his face, limp and lifeless. "The incident with our truck was a complete failure. My hubris took control and I assumed that the experience from the hospital had given us an edge over our enemy. So why are we now standing with only two train cars of goods?" His voice rose at the end and cracked just a little.

"I do not know, sir," Geert said in his trembling voice. "We were certain that the train would sneak into the city undetected like it has always done. I equipped what I saw as the appropriate number of men, armed of course, but it wasn't enough, I guess."

"You guess it wasn't enough?" The Black Diamond walked towards him, his hard-soled shoes echoing through the empty room. "Maybe I expected too much. Getting the shipment into the city was vital for our business and I hoped the trap we set would have eliminated our vigilante problem. Half our load incinerated down there in the courtyard, along with half a train. Our operation was almost revealed by the fire department, and now we have to find a means to replace and return our mode of transportation, and you guess it wasn't enough?" He was furious; he was gesticulating wildly with his arms, and his voice was reaching a level that Geert had never experienced before.

Are you cracking, sir? Are you losing your grip? Geert thought with some form of satisfaction. *The great Black Diamond is finally showing some humanity.*

"I don't know what to say, sir." Geert put two sweaty palms up in defense.

The Black Diamond halted his movement and turned his body slightly. He raised a hand and suddenly a flash of light flew from it. The light struck Geert clear in the chest, and it felt as if he had been kicked by a mule. The energy sent him flying across the room, and he crashed into the metal railing attached to the staircase he had walked up. The iron bars rang like bells as his large frame hit them, and he flopped on the dirty concrete floor, out of breath, but seemingly intact.

"I am tired of your excuses, Mr. Geert," The Black Diamond said. Geert was uncertain if he had lost any time or consciousness, but the man had come to stand in front of him very quickly. "I have given you chance upon chance, upon chance. My worry is that you have a difficult time seeing the big picture."

"There was someone else out there last night," Geert replied, straining to speak. His lungs felt compressed by the force. "That man was not alone. He had help."

The Black Diamond laughed. "No, not help," he replied. "One who made sure that we did not lose everything. My trap." He snapped his fingers, and from the shadows of the blackboard emerged a figure. She had the telltale curves of a woman, dressed in some form of banded metal, except for a dark blue bathing suit, gloves, boots and a domino mask. Her chestnut hair cascaded from her head and onto her shapely shoulders. She came to stand next to The Black Diamond.

"This is Miss Iron Claw," he indicated. "We have been associates for many years, and she has assisted me on many troublesome cases."

Geert came to a seated position, leaning on the railing, still panting heavily.

"Miss Claw has been out of the country on private business, but she has finally come back to the family. When she heard of our troubles, she was eager to help us get rid of whoever might come in our way."

"How will we find the person responsible?" Geert asked cautiously, not wanting to incur the man's wrath again.

"I am thinking that our little mole in the department has been playing us for fools. I think he believed he could get the best of both worlds." The Black Diamond paused. "He has been a valuable commodity, and without him, we would not have the leads we do, but it is time that he is taken out of the equation, and Miss Claw will do that for us." The Black Diamond smiled and indicated that Geert could leave the room.

Every single step that led to the third-floor offices of WRJN pained him. It seared through his body, cut deep into his ribs, and hindered his breathing. It felt as if he was sweating right through his navy-blue suit, and his hair lay plastered against his scalp, but once he reached his destination and hid in the washroom, he could see that he appeared fine. The reflection that stared back possibly hinted at some fever since his eyes appeared glazed over, and he was paler than usual, but that was all that gave his discomfort away. After splashing some water on his face, he left to join his colleagues in the break room.

As soon as he had closed the door behind him, a tall woman dressed in a black and white dress suit, complete with long white gloves and a wide-brimmed hat on her head, stopped him. She looked like Audrey Hepburn in Breakfast at Tiffany's.

"Mr. Hill, fancy meeting you here," she said in a soft, melodic voice.

"Miss Chaucer," Tony replied with a smile. "I have a suspicion you are not at all surprised at seeing me at my place of work."

"Whatever do you mean, sir?" She feigned shock by placing a hand on her chest. "Are you accusing an innocent woman as myself of seeking you out?"

"I might be," Tony answered and leaned against one of the glass doors that lead from the hallway to the corridors. "Maybe I am just so convinced that I made an impression on you that you could not help yourself."

"Well, sir," she said and touched his shoulder. "It is fortuitous that we meet like this. I will not deny that you did make an impression on me, but I have been invited by your station manager to sing live on the air.”

“Well then, I stand corrected.” Tony was not quite sure where he was getting this flirtatious attitude. Maybe the battle from the previous night had scrambled his brain a bit. He was normally uncomfortable with this form of banter. “May I escort you to your

destination then, Miss Chaucer?”

“You most certainly may, Mr. Hill,” she said and produced a small business card from her clutch. “According to this, I am supposed to be in Studio One.”

“You’re most likely performing on the Charlie West Lunch Hour,” Tony informed her with a smile and held out his arm for her. “It is a variety show for those having their midday break. It actually goes on for two hours, but no-one has ever bothered to change the name.” She laughed at this, obviously a fake one to make it seem as if he was clever, but he took it.

“So, Mr. Linden snagged you at the party then?” He continued as they walked through the building towards the big studio at the end.

“He did,” she replied. “It was between two sets. He said that there had been a cancellation, and since I didn’t have any prior engagements today, I was only going to sit alone in my room. I thought it would be a great way to get heard.”

“With your voice, I’m surprised you are not on the airwaves all the time.”

“Flattery will get you everywhere, Mr. Hill.”

“Call me Tony.”

“Only if you call me Emily,” she said in return.

"Emily." He let the name roll around in his mind and rest on his tongue as he said it. It felt nice.

"I have been on various radio stations around the country, but it has always been small stations such as these. It never goes anywhere. I continue to sing at functions and the like. I would really like to get into the pictures. A musical of some sort, but I have two left feet, and most singers need to be able to dance as well. Be like Ginger Rogers."

They strolled down the corridor arm in arm, as several staffers passed them by and turned their heads at the jovial pair. Tony imagined that they found it quite odd that he was so lively. In their eyes, he was probably very reserved, and with good cause. Ever since he had taken the job with WRJN, he had tried to stay clear of personal interaction. It interfered with his nocturnal movements, but also it never interested him.

Since leaving the island of Bali, it had been difficult for him to adapt to the Western lifestyle. They were not foreign to him - his father, tutor and the upper class all came from Europe or America - but it was different once one was immersed in that society. The coldness of people put him off. How they refused to say what they truly meant. He was used to loud arguments, raucous laughter and getting things off one's chest instead of carrying it around so that it may fester and ruin a relationship completely. It had caused him to remove himself from interacting with others - they became like stone statues that he was unable to read. Emotionless which made him uneasy.

Through college, he avoided the parties and tomfoolery of his classmates. The men branded him a surly loner while the few women who attended UWM found him extremely interesting, and he did get quite a bit of interest from them, but he was not interested.

In a way, he liked dealing with criminals instead. At least he could tell what they felt towards him and that was why he had enjoyed the barrio. The Mexicans were like the tribesmen in the small village where Wayan lived. They were loud and boisterous, spoke their minds, and weren't afraid to burst out in song whenever they felt like it. Through the hardships that he witnessed it made him smile. Maybe that was why he had chosen to act on their behalf. No one was speaking for the voiceless on the outskirts of the city when drugs threatened to break the community. Like the oppression of the imperialists to the natives, this too was a form of oppression, a cultural one.

Once the drugs found their way to West Boulevard or the North part of the city, once they found upper middle-class children dead from overdoses in alleys downtown, would they scream for action.

"This appears to be my stop," Emily said as they approached the large double doors adorned with Studio 1 in big bold letters. They had engaged in polite small talk, not saying anything important, just speaking of the previous evening. The walk still hurt, but he found that it was less painful when walking with a beautiful young woman at his side. Even so, he twitched every other step or so. He tried to hide it from her, but he was convinced that she noticed it.

"I am afraid I will have to leave you here, Emily." He smiled and knocked on the dense door.

"That is a shame." She smiled back at him, a darling smile, with rows of pearly white teeth beneath those ruby red lips.

"Would it be too forward of me to ask you on a date, Emily?" Tony said and felt that his voice was not fully devoid of a tremble. He didn't quite know why those words had left his lips. He had been on a date or two in college but had done so because it others expected it of him. The women he had gone out with were nice enough, but there was nothing else, and it had never amounted to a second one - it was probably for the best.

Emily, on the other hand, had cast a spell on him. There was something about her, like a magnet drawing him in. All he could think about was those lips, to touch that waist, to hear that voice, or drown in her blue eyes. He had wanted to see her again. He realized it once he saw her standing there in that black and white, and he wanted it to happen again. It was as if something forced him to ask her out.

"We are already on a first name basis, Tony," she replied coyly. "So, I would not claim that it is too forward at all. I will gladly go on a date with you while I'm in town." The doors opened and a short, stocky man wearing a tuxedo opened it. He saw Emily standing there and his eyes lit up. He waved her inside.

"Here, take my card." She quickly let go of Tony's arm and produced a small business card. She also produced a pen and wrote down her room number at the hotel where she was staying. She then slipped into his inside pocket. Tony winced at her touch and jerked. "Call me, and we'll work something out." She winked at him, came in close, and softly blew in his ear. He felt the warmth from her cheek against his, and for a moment closed his eyes to get the sensation of her being.

"I will," he whispered in her ear in return. She vanished behind the door, and the short man gave him a quizzical look before he also did so.

* * *

The fingerprint kit came in a wallet-style case made from durable fabric. Teague unfolded it and looked over the tools he had at his disposal. There was a round plastic box of white powder, a brush and some plastic tape. When he was on the beat, he had taken prints on cases that did not require any greater forensic investigation. The odd break-in where the alleged perpetrator was already in custody or times when he had recovered various weapons. Therefore, he was well versed in the art of lifting prints.

He decided to wait until most of his colleagues were out to lunch since he was not interested in fielding questions regarding his decision to investigate papers on his own desk. Only Charlotte remained at the command center, operating the phones, and she already knew what he was doing. From his desk, he produced a pair of rubber gloves that he slipped on his hands.

He was well aware that the documents must have passed quite a few hands on their journey from the archives to his desk, but maybe he would get lucky and find one that was out of left field. One that just shouldn't be there. He gently unscrewed the top of the plastic container and then took a breath. The first time he had done the task; he had exhaled a bit too hard and sent the powder flying all over the scene. He found no prints on that surface. Luckily, his partner, a grumpy old sergeant by the name of Otto Waldow, managed to recover them on a windowsill.

289

He dipped the brush in the powder, carefully shook off the excess, and let the brush ever so slightly dab the photographs and the papers. He had spread them out across his desk, as well as the desk opposite it. He let the white powder cover the items like a second layer. Once done with that, he moved his garbage can over to the end of the desk and let the powder glide off the papers and into the bin. He softly blew at them to assist the process. He held the papers sideways to let the light hit them just so. He found several prints and circled them with a Sharpie. That done, he meticulously placed the adhesive over the marked fingerprints. He patted it down with as gentle a touch that he could master, and then he peeled them off. He collected them all on a separate piece of blank paper so that they became clearly visible. When he was finished with the entire process, he cleaned the area with just enough time to spare before everyone returned.

He was sitting in the break room snacking on a sandwich that Charlotte had ordered from Lee's Deli on Washington. It was very kind of her to think of him - he had just spent his entire lunch break chasing something that might not pan out. It was an Italian sub, three kinds of meat, Thousand Island dressing, and all the vegetables he liked. She knew him very well. Better than anyone else at the department. The reason was that she was the only one he actually conversed with. Most colleagues he only met at the bubbler and they, of course, exchanged the customary pleasantries - how their favorite sports teams were performing, the latest weather, and what happened on the episode of some radio show. It was a ritual that he was little interested in, and in truth, he was incapable of performing in any convincing fashion.

In Charlotte, he had found a person that he could talk to about important things. They had a rapport he had been unable to find since Waldow had left the force to move to his cabin up north. It wasn't as if they engaged in longer conversations over food or in clandestine meetings in seedy hotel rooms. It was enough to chat at the command center, in the corridors, or leaving the office at the end of the day. It was all he needed. A quick back and forth about something important to them - it was what made a true friend.

With his sandwich in hand, he passed by the lab to drop off the prints with the analyst there - an Asian man by the name of James Bae. He had been at the department for many years, and the talk around the bubbler was the speculation on his retirement date. He was one of the best in the Midwest, and Teague assumed that he was difficult to replace. Probably why he stayed in his little cubby where he could analyze prints in private.

Teague had asked if he could put it through quickly, and Mr. Bae had nodded and then said something in Korean before vanishing behind the door. By the time he had finished the sandwich and washed it down with a cup of black coffee, the analysis was done. Mr. Bae placed a Manila folder on the folding table in the break room and smiled at Teague.

"Here are your results, Detective," he said in English peppered with a Korean accent. "It was not that difficult since there were very few sets of prints on the documents. All were accounted for."

"Thank you, Mr. Bae," Teague replied. "And here is a little something for your troubles." He produced a box of cigars Charlotte had been kind enough to procure from the tobacconist down the street.

"Thank you, Detective Teague." The little man in the lab coat nodded at him and then walked away, opening the box and sniffing one of the cigars.

Teague opened the folder and leaned over the table. The paper with the prints was still there. Bae had numbered them, and the same numbers showed up next to several of the prints. To his surprise, there were only three sets of prints. So, this was going to be easy – especially as the analyst had said that all the prints were accounted for.

He stopped to think of what that might mean. If all the prints were on record at the department, then there were only two options: the one who had messed with his documents was an alleged criminal that they had taken prints off during booking, or the person was part of the department. Every time the police employed a new person, they registered their prints. It was not customary, but Chief Swann had insisted it done as a fail-safe so that they could eliminate certain prints from contamination.

He was getting into some uncharted territory. At the same time, he was on the precipice of breaking this case wide open. He slid the report out from behind the print sheet. It consisted of tables of numbers and names in the scratching of the Korean analyst. He read his own name and Charlotte's as well, but the third name... His finger halted as it began to slide over the black ink. His head dropped, and he shook it in disbelief. It was obvious, really. Somewhere deep down he had suspected that the person would be an easy target for criminal activity. His character was weak and easily mislead. *Gregory Glade* it read.

There was no reason he would even know what Teague was investigating. Not this angle. The man had always been first at every crime scene, which in itself was not suspicious, admirable in fact, but it was an anomaly for him. On other cases, he seldom showed up on time. He was the last one to see the only surviving assassin alive, and he was heavily involved in the case. He was going to have to pay Detective Glade a visit and confront him. Not here though. He'd have to go to his home. This day was shaping up to be quite shitty.

* * *

"I heard you have a hot date coming up." Vic Linden, big and boisterous, startled Tony as he peeked his red head around the corner and into his office. He was smiling.

"Excuse me?" Tony replied quizzically and spun his office chair around.

"A little bird told me that he saw you hobnobbing with Miss Chaucer in the corridor." He came to stand in the doorway, occupying the entire space. "That you asked her for a date no less. Good for you, son. It is not healthy for a young man such as

yourself to be alone. I have said so many a time to Mrs. Linden."

"Thank you, sir." Tony smiled back at his boss. "It was a bit nerve-wracking. I am not an experienced dater, to be honest."

Linden pulled out a stump of a cigar, damp and well chewed on one end, and stuck it in his mouth. "Be sure to bring flowers. Pick her up sharply at the time you decide," he said as he lit the stogie. "She will make you wait anyway, so make sure your reservation is half an hour later. Complement her outfit, but don't ogle her, and take her someplace nice.

Dinner and dancing should do it. Take her to the Hobnob. It has great music, food and an amazing view of the lake."

"That sounds good," Tony replied. "We haven't even decided on a date or time yet."

"Well, don't let this opportunity slip between your fingers. The girl is heading out on tour soon, and then it might be too late." Linden winked at him and grinned behind the billowing puffs of smoke. "Strike while the iron is hot. She might forget you otherwise. Make sure she has a reason for coming back here."

"Will do, sir." Tony saluted him.

"How is the script coming along for the four o'clock segment?" The man's tone was quite different from the usual sharp and loud one he had. It was as if Tony's proposed date had softened his attitude towards him. Like he saw him as a person all of a sudden.

"It is going well at the moment." Tony shuffled through the papers on his desk. "Not much developing in the big case as of yet. At least, not what the cops are letting us know. A fire down in the industrial area without casualties, but that is about it. More sports and weather though."

"Excellent." Linden turned to leave. "I'll make a call to Chief Swan and see if he can give us anything more, but if not, just go with what we have." He vanished, leaving a trail of smoke lingering behind.

Tony turned back around and rested for a moment. He had tried to finish the paperwork as quickly as possible so that he could focus on the next step in his own mission. He had decided that he was going to try to find the mole in the department. The difficult part was how that was going to happen. Lindquist knew of the person, that much was clear, but it was also obvious that he did not know who it was. Tony was convinced that if he were on the case, and he knew about it, then he could have figured it out. The only personnel that he knew by name was Chief Swan and Garfield Teague. It was unlikely that Swan was the one leaking information to The Black Diamond, but not impossible. Teague, on the other hand, was a wild card. He knew nothing about him other than that he was the lead investigator. As such, he would have access to every single piece of information pertaining to the case. He could also slow down the process, losing information or placing out red herrings.

To Tony, it was obvious that he was the most likely candidate, but he needed to be completely certain of it before confronting the man. Injured or not, he was going to have to sneak into the police department again and see if he could find evidence among the detective's things. When visiting the building, he had observed that each employee had their name on a little plaque on the desks strewn about. It would take only a moment to find the right one and go through it. He sighed and touched his side again. He was going to have to be extra careful this time.

* * *

Paul Geert was sitting in the restaurant on the first floor of the Racine Hotel in his usual booth. This time he was alone with a bottle of whiskey. It was still early in the day, but he had already made it halfway through the brown liquid. The radio had been blaring music, but it now broke for the four o'clock news.

"This is your radio friend WRJN," it said. "It is time for the news report with Anthony Hill and Gabriel Posner." He tuned out, uninterested in what was happening both

295

internationally and locally. He downed another shot instead, refilling the glass in one smooth motion. He was trying to dull the pain in his massive body - as well as the growing pit in his stomach. That woman The Black Diamond had brought in to solve their problems was about to kill one of his friends, and he needed to forget about it for the moment.

He stared straight ahead towards the glass doors that led to the restaurant from the reception area. It was a very pleasant place to rest the eyes. The doors made from that heavy maple wood present all around the hotel.

The glass intricately decorated with a floral motif, repeated in the carpeting in the dining room area. The doors opened, a woman dressed in a white and black dress, dark sunglasses, and a wide-brimmed hat swept into the room. Her lips were a deep red, and blonde hair flowed from beneath the hat. By her sheer presence, she owned the entire room. She removed the glasses with a gloved hand, revealing two of the bluest eyes Geert had ever seen. They were of such a color that they almost appeared iridescent.

She scanned the room and noticed that he was staring at her. She smiled and winked at him before she headed to the bar and took a seat on one of the stools. Geert tapped on the table and eyed her. She was one of the most stunning women he had ever seen - as if she had stepped right out of a Hollywood picture. He sighed. There was no way in hell that he would ever develop a meaningful relationship with such a creature. Sure, the women he usually drank and chatted with were nice and all, but they were of a certain caste and not like this stunning beauty. It made him realize that he most likely would die alone. Nothing he possessed was endearing. He was overweight, sweaty, and had the charisma of a block of wood.

The only reason women even spent time with him was because of his money or rather, that he spent money on them.

When he was standing there on the Day of Judgment, he would have nothing going for him, and the moral path that he had chosen would doom him for all eternity. He emptied the glass again and dried his lips on his sleeve. He was ugly on the inside and the outside. He continued to rest his eyes on the perfect shape of the woman at the bar and refilled his glass.

* * *

Movement was as difficult as he had imagined it would be. The climb up the side of the police department building in order to find an open window was like a lengthy torture session. Every reach for a handhold and every push with his legs sent waves of cold sharp pain through his torso. As a child, he was convinced that arm and leg strength were the keys to power, but that was only one minor detail. Wayan had taught him that his core strength was the most essential part of a warrior's body. He made progress as his fingers found cracks and crevices in between the bricks - the place where the mortar had withered or the natural indentations in the material. This night, the staff had remembered to close the windows, and it was not as simple to gain access to the inner sanctum of the law enforcement agency of the city. Once he had finally reached the flat roof, he rolled onto his back and panted heavily.

He stared up at the night sky as he felt the cold from the concrete material of the roof leak through his outfit. It was still early. The sun had just disappeared over Lake Michigan, and there was still a hint of fire on the horizon. He knew that the building emptied around five-thirty, and then a skeleton crew

297

remained. Maybe it was foolish of him to attempt a break in so early in the evening, but there was a sense of urgency about things. It might have been his fear of failing, the Face goading him on, or his belief that he should strike while the iron was hot. The Black Diamond had lost part of another shipment, he was sure of it. The organization was most likely in a state of disarray and were likely to make mistakes. A mole might be willing to spill the beans if pressured. He could wait. Wait for his ribs to heal up, wait for the police department building to settle even more, or wait for The Black Diamond to cover their tracks. No, he needed to catch them while they were on the run. There was no time to wait and see. He got to his feet and found a vent. When he first decided to take to the streets, he had spent time in the Heritage Museum, pouring over the blueprints of the most important buildings in the city. One could never know when one might need them. Be prepared, his tutor had said, like a mantra. It is just as important to keep your mind as toned as your body.

He knew that the roof had several vents, and he knew exactly where each one of the metal tubes led. He pulled out his kris and gently stuck it into the grate that covered the vent. Without much effort, it popped off, and he caught it before it came clattering down to the ground. The quick movement caused him to cringe, but he bit his lip and closed his eyes in order to fight the pain.

He did the same as he pulled himself up and swung his legs down the shaft and then slid down. Pressing his hands against the flat sides, he attempted to slow his movement. Had he been at one hundred percent, there would have been no issue, but instead, he came down with greater speed than he had wanted. He landed on the bottom of the shaft harder and left a small dent where his feet struck. Crouching down, he tried to listen for voices on the other side. After a couple of minutes, he figured that it was all clear. No one had detected him.

Tony crawled through the vent and counted quietly to himself. He had tried to figure out how long it would take him to reach the command center. He had not figured that he would be slower when he actually needed to use it. This vent hung suspended high above the rooms of the first floor. There were others, which ran inside the walls or along the floor, but they would force him to move through the building. This was perfect for covering his tracks.

When he was done counting, he was still several feet from the grate that would lead him to the room. He opened it, and the metal hatch swung down - this one on hinges so he didn't need to be concerned about it making noise. He tried to follow it with a controlled roll forward, using his core to slowly lower himself down, but the pain was too great, and he came through the opening too fast, forcing him to use all his finger strength to not fall. He gritted his teeth as he came to an abrupt halt, swinging back and forth in tune with the hatch. They were opposite each other like two trapeze artists. Tony looked down over the grand room, dark below his swinging feet. He was slipping. He was the one making mistakes. He had not taken the time to peek down to see if the room was empty. He hadn't listened for footsteps in the corridors outside. Instead, he had dived right in and now he was carelessly swinging, in agony, just waiting for someone to find him there. He was in luck. No one was in the room and before anyone entered, he dropped to the floor and rolled forward, stopping behind one of the desks. He cocked his head to the side to listen, but everything was silent. He got to his feet and looked about. He identified the command center desk at the far end and Chief Swan's office along one of the walls. He picked up the plaque placed on the desk next to him. It was the wrong one. The streetlights outside the large windows of the room cast a white glow at the empty workstations and made it easy to read the names. After a few minutes of traversing the maze of identical desks, he found the one with name Garfield Teague on it. It was clean and everything placed in perfect symmetry. Many other desks drowning in piles various papers, coffee cups and pens - the telltale signs of someone working at them. This one looked unused. Like a showroom piece at an exhibit. Tony quickly glanced over the top. There was a folder lined with the corner, a typewriter in the opposite one and a few pens in a straight row. If Teague were the mole then he would most likely not place evidence of his crime on top of the desk. Tony began questioning if a mole would even have such things at their workplace. He shuffled over to the drawers and began opening them. Like the desk, things formed neat rows and stacks. Larger papers on the bottom and small ones on top, creating flat pyramids. Tony picked up the stacks and looked through them. Most of them had nothing to do with his case. Older ones and copies of reports. It was the same in the center drawer, but in the bottom one, there was something of interest.

The envelope placed out in the open. Teague had placed it, inconspicuously atop a stack of unused stationery. He picked it up. In blue ink, someone had written; *Open in the case of my disappearance or death.* Tony turned it over to find that the envelope was not sealed. He opened it quickly to find several sheets of lined papers. His eyes scanned the handwritten note. It was everything Teague knew about the case. Tony found that the detective knew a lot more than he had imagined. Some things that he hadn't figured out yet. He knew who Lindquist was for instance. It also contained details about what he thought Tony was, The Black Diamond, and where the drugs came from. It also mentioned a Dr. Lansing and an actual black diamond. It perplexed Tony, but he continued. Finally, he found mention of the mole. Garfield Teague was going to confront him. He was certain he knew who it was and that he was the key to breaking it all wide open. He went on to profess his love for his wife, and what he wanted her and Chief Swan to do if something happened to him at the confrontation. Tony looked at the name - Greg Glade. He didn't know that name and had no idea where he might live, but the command center was sure to have a phone book where he could find that information. He felt like he needed to be there, at the confrontation. Teague was an ally in the war on The Black Diamond, and he might need his assistance, but more importantly, Tony might be able to get there first and could squeeze information out of him. Teague would wait to make sure that Glade was home and alone. That meant that he might stake out the place for a while before going in, and that was Tony's window. He headed for the phone boo

CHAPTER EIGHTEEN

They arrived in New York after a harrowing journey across the water. Mr. Hill had forgotten how ill he always became whilst traveling that way. Young Anthony was excited since he had never been on such a big boat before. Since they were United States citizens, and Mr. Mahr naturalized some years earlier, they had no trouble entering the country. Mr. Hill had filled out the proper paperwork regarding Anthony's birth and sent it in. The first few days they stayed at one of the more upscale hotels in Manhattan, but there was no money in the bank account, everything seized as they fled, and it forced them to leave. Mr. Hill had relatives in Chicago and that was where they would go until he could get back on his feet.

The plan was to find some government job by using one of his many contacts. Mr. Mahr, the old tutor, reluctantly made the decision to leave the household at this time. The apartment on Manhattan, which already housed a family of four, was not big enough for Mr. Hill, Anthony and him. It was time to move on. He checked into a hotel close by, but after only a few days, he was at the apartment handing in his notice. Anthony would always remember how the gaunt figure of the Englishman stood in the small kitchen, silhouetted in the morning light, as his father sat at the dinner table, smoking a cigarette, still in his robe.

It wasn't solely about the accommodations. It was a financial decision. There had been no salary from Mr. Hill in the past few months. Only promises that he would get back payments once they arrived in the States. He could ill afford to stay at a hotel for any extended period, and he had no interest in moving to Chicago on yet another promise of payment coming in on time. He cared for the boy, that was not an issue, but a man had to live as well.

Mr. Hill begrudgingly let him go, and Mr. Mahr walked over to Anthony, who was playing with a second cousin in the hallway.

"Master Anthony," he said as the boy looked up at him. "I have to leave now. I have not taught you all that I know, but I am convinced that whoever takes over your education has a good base from which to build."

For the first time in their relationship, they embraced and Mahr's eyes teared up as he wrapped his arms around him. He left the trunk as a memento. He had packed two kalis and kris underneath the pile of clothes he had also left in it. Anthony would find them once they unpacked in Chicago, and he smiled, remembering the old man.

Mr. Mahr continued to tutor children of the well-to-do until he returned to his family home in Northern England. Every morning, he would walk past Hadrian's Wall. He would lean on the cyclopean ruins and gaze out over the rolling hills. As the chill burrowed through his skin and set in his bones, he imagined being back on Bali. He never forgot Anthony Hill and often wondered what became of the child who was a product of two cultures.

* * *

Gregory Garrison Glade, his parents had loved alliterations - his younger brother and two sisters all had some combination of Gs in their names, stumbled out of Ivanhoe's and stopped himself from toppling over by grabbing on to one of the street lights. The pub and eatery was his regular stop before going home for the night unless The Black Diamond needed him for some after-hours patrolling.

Its placement on Main Street was not far from his own home farther up on the same. It was what he liked about it. Often his guilty conscience was nagging at the back of his head, and a combination of whiskey and beer was the only thing that would silence it. As was often the case, the kind bartender had decided when it was time for him to leave. He did so without argument, well aware that they might not allow him to return if he created a scene in the establishment. The pub was a popular watering hole for many in the city and having an officer of the law getting into it with the staff would reflect poorly on his record.

That and the fact that the owner, Mr. Richter, was a retired prizefighter and not one to argue with. Many a rowdy guest had found this out the hard way. Several of Mr. Richter's prizefighting friends would stop in on their travels across the country so that on any given evening the place might house strong men who used their fists to talk instead of their words. The world was spinning around him more than usual. He had overdone it this time, he felt. It was that sensation one got when not completely in control of one's faculties.

304

He rested his collarbone against the cool metal of the post and felt the low hum of power run through it. His head lolled back and forth, as he attempted to find his bearings. His mouth hung open, trying to collect as much fresh evening air as possible. To those who drove by, it probably looked like he was going to be sick on the pavement and maybe he would be. At this moment, it was all up in the air.

Once he had punched out for the evening, he had headed to the post office box to check for any messages. There had been none, so he was free to do as he pleased. It was but a few minutes' walk from the post office to Ivanhoe's, and with purpose, he had perambulated towards the sweet relief of alcohol. Now he regretted it. Not the kind of regret he felt when his alarm clock threatened to blow out his eardrums, no this was instant. He placed a sweaty palm against his cheek and pressed his beard down convincing himself that if he could get some feeling back to his face, he might be able to make it home. Time went by. How much it was anyone's guess, but he heard patrons leave the pub behind him. They took little interest in him, once or twice, he felt a pat on his back, but that was it. He opened his eyes wide and let them scan the area before him. He kept his head motionless and focused solely on what his eyes could see. The only thing was the concrete sidewalk. At least it was clear enough so that he could make out the cracks and rough surface of it without issue. To Gregory Garrison Glade, it was enough to convince him that he could make it home.

He pushed himself away from the post, nearly tipped over the other direction, found his balance, and then, swayed a bit before he turned towards the direction of his house. It was odd how it always seemed to be so far from the pub once it was time to go home. He needed to pass Memorial Hall, the library, the post office, and the parking structure where that masked vigilante had first interfered with his life. Even if he dealt with a lot of guilt over his actions on a daily basis, it had allowed him to live a comfortable life. The big house overlooking the water was his pride and joy. A true upgrade from the rat-infested hovel out in the countryside his parents had raised him in and the chicken coup of an apartment he had lived in by himself. Now he had so much room that he didn't even know what to do with it all.

He bought antique furniture just to fill up the space. It was as if the void compressed his body, like the black guilt inside him. Filling the holes with objects neutralized the sensation. After buying the house, he spent all his ill-gotten gains on decorating it. The idea comforted him. It was like nesting - that thing women did when they were with child - but in his case, it was all about trying to prepare the house for an eventual family, one that he could never seem to start. Instead, he would sit in his grand living room, with its bay view windows facing Lake Michigan, alone with a drink in his hand. Those were the loneliest times in his life.

He had believed that the money and material things would bring him some measure of popularity or social importance. His neighbors paid him no attention. It was as if they could smell his family lineage on him. His mother trying to wash their clothes in a washbasin, and his father trying to put food on the table by fishing in the river. Greg and his siblings selling bait to wealthy men in fancy clothes, probably the fathers of those he was living next to now. Yes, he had tried to dress well and speak eloquently as he picked up the papers in the morning at the same time they did, but still, there were no invitations in his mailbox. Instead, they turned their noses up at him and eventually he had stopped caring. He had stopped hiding his drinking behind his curtains. On more than one occasion, he had vomited in their well-kept bushes or pissed on their rod iron fences with statues of lions. Served them right. When he stood there and let his steaming urine decorate the plaster wildlife in the middle of the night, with the moon's reflection in the water as his only company, he felt satisfied with himself. That he was doing the right thing in betraying the city. It was rotten anyway.

These fancy people in their fancy houses ignoring the plight of the real people they trod on to get where they were. Sure, they could throw fundraisers to help the needy, but in the end, it was only like putting a Band-Aid on a festering wound, it was too late. At least, he had chosen a side. He didn't wear blinders; he knew what reality was like. He had seen it firsthand and it had put his mark on him. He knew why angry fathers harmed children, he knew why drunk husbands beat women nearly to death, and he knew why daughters walked the streets at night or sons numbed their pain with drugs.

In the evenings, by his fire, he made no pretense about what the world was like. He had seen it. He had decided to buy in to the corruption. He couldn't fight it, and he chose not to ignore it. He became part of it. Greg continued, walking clear of the downtown area and towards the grand houses lining Main Street. He would be home soon. Then he would piss on one of the lion statues again, maybe even vomit on that low brick wall symbolically keeping pedestrians away from the lawn.

* * *

Teague was spinning his cigarette case frantically in the dark of his car. He had parked it on a side street - 9th to be precise. Glade lived along Main Street. Not actually on Main itself. One had to turn a corner to get to Lake, which was the street that overlooked Lake Michigan.

Teague had never been invited to Greg's home after he had moved, and he had come to realize that he didn't know where his colleague lived. He was aware that Glade had moved from his bachelor apartment a couple of years back. When Teague looked up the address in the register at the station, he had been surprised. He had cross-referenced it with the payroll and come to the conclusion that Glade in no way could afford a home on Lake, not even on a detective's salary. It was all beginning to add up. Glade had not said anything about wealthy relatives passing away recently, and Teague knew enough of his past that there was no such thing in the Glade family. He had never cared for the nervous figure with the unkempt facial hair who always seemed to wear suits not tailored to his shape, but he had not expected him to be a traitor to the force.

On the drive over, he had reflected on if there was something, he could have done to hinder the treachery. Had his cold shoulder caused the anxious man to seek comfort and warmth in another, like a jilted lover on the rebound from a relationship? The entire force often ousted, no one having the patience to deal with him. Naturally, that could cause a man to look for acceptance somewhere else. Maybe the money was just too good to pass up.

The great depression had left an entire generation with a variety of issues, Teague was all too aware of it. He was frugal, and his wife was quite the opposite. Both of them had grown up in the shadow of the great shut down and had lived with the consequences of it.

The pressure was getting to him. It felt as if he was sweating right through his suit, and he had even taken out a cigarette from the case and placed it in his mouth. Luckily, he was fresh out of matches or any other means of lighting one. He had wanted to confront Greg as quickly as possible. He expected the spineless coward to give up the goods right away, but then he would spend hours explaining why he had done it. It was going to be a long night anyway, so it would have been nice if he could get it started as early as possible.

Glade had unfortunately not been home when he approached the mansion-like building overlooking the lake. The massive doors on the white brick house bore large iron knockers in the shape of gargoyles. Teague had raised a skeptical eyebrow at the gaudy decorations, and while he waited for someone to answer his knock, he looked around, only to notice more ostentatious objects littering the yard. There was a fountain, complete with Triton swinging a pitchfork above his head as water sprayed from the mouth of the giant seahorse he was riding. There were other mythological beings randomly placed on the unmown lawn. They stuck out of the ground like those statues on Easter Island he had seen in magazines. They weren't half-buried like those objects, though. The grass had just grown so high that they appeared to be sinking. Teague was not surprised at Glade's inadequacy when it came to yard work, but if he had the funds to make the place look like a museum then he obviously could afford a gardener.

No one came to the door, and Teague decided to walk around the house to see if he could peer through a window to see if the man was home. Without any luck, he returned to the car and waited. After what felt like an eternity, and with several passersby giving him the stink eye, he noticed a figure in the streetlights. At first, it was just a stumbling shadow moving in the faint glow, but as it came closer, he could clearly make out the ill-fitting brown suit and the familiar hat askew. He was obviously drunk, for no sober person swayed the way the figure did.

Teague sank down in the driver's seat as Glade sauntered.

past. He was not interested in confronting his colleague out in the street. It would reflect poorly on both of them if they caused a scene. Added to it that whatever evidence he could gather at this point might not be admissible later. Ideally, he wanted Glade to spill the beans to him, maybe break down so that he could call the station and have two uniforms come and arrest him. He wanted as little confession as possible immediately. At the moment, there was only a letter in his desk revealing where he was and that would only be opened after he had died or vanished. Chief Swan would undoubtedly chastise him for going alone, but he was still only working on a hunch and circumstantial evidence and that was not going to be enough at this time. Once Glade had turned the corner onto Lake, Teague exited the car and checked his pocket for his revolver. He looked around to make sure he was alone then checked it for bullets. He had no idea how this was going to end, but one way or another it was going to.

* * *

310

The home of Greg Glade was perfect for sneaking up on. The man had not cut his grass in quite some time, and oddities littered the grounds. Tony easily traversed the yard by running from statue to statue and then crawling through the grass. The dark was his friend as well, and before he knew it, he was at the back door. He couldn't open it, so he was forced to scale the wall to reach the roof. That was more difficult due to his injury, but he made it. He crawled over the two-story building so that he came to the balcony right above the front door. He arrived just in time to see a figure walking along the sidewalk. He was moving erratically, as if he was not completely in control of his faculties. Just as he was about to turn onto the stone path which led to the house, he turned, unzipped his pants, and urinated on a statue of a seated lion which looked to belong to the neighboring house.

The figure was talking to himself in a growling manner, as if he was angry with someone, but Tony could not make out what he was saying. As the figure was doing his business and looking over his shoulder in the process, Tony felt he should take the opportunity to enter the premises. Crouching, he slowly moved towards the glass double doors that would grant him access inside. It wouldn't budge, but he used the kris to jimmy open the door by sliding it in between the doors. With a soft click, it opened, and he got ready to move inside. He was unsure what he was going to do in there, maybe just listen and observe the conversation between the two detectives, or he could head Teague off at the pass. He would have to improvise.

He slid inside in the dark of the second floor. He crawled across thick carpeting, came to a halt and looked around. It was a bedroom. Closets stood along the walls. They were all of different sizes, shapes and ages. There did not seem to be any rhyme or reason behind the decorating of the room. The bed, a queen-sized sleigh bed with a canopy around it, stood in the center and there were clothes strewn about. In the light of the moon, Tony could see swirls of dust flying through the air as he moved. Whoever lived here was not very good at cleaning. Obviously, a bachelor lived here. Not because of the collected dust on every surface, but because there were no women's clothes around and nothing connected to the fairer sex.

Tony felt he had little time to do any reconnaissance of the area, but at the least, he had learned that this was a household of one, without the luxury of a house cleaner or butler. There were no family photographs on any of the walls either. He moved from the room, wading through clothes like he had traversed the lawn outside.

* * *

"Greg, we need to talk," said a voice behind him as he was trying to fish his house keys from his pocket. They had tangled up in the lining and were fighting him. Everything always seemed to go against him in his life. He turned around to see his colleague Garfield Teague. The detective was dressed in his dark blue pinstriped suit. He held his hat in one hand and came to place the other one on Greg's shoulder. He looked sweaty and uncomfortable. His hair and beard had a slight damp shine to them.

"What do you need, Garfield?" He managed to say without slurring too much.

"Let's go inside instead." Teague motioned to the door.

Greg pulled out the keys and felt how part of the fabric tore as he did. On the third attempt, he managed to insert the key in the lock, and they moved inside.

Teague was amazed at the size of the house. It looked huge on the outside, but it was nothing in comparison to how it looked inside. From the hallway that they had entered, it extended in two wings. In the center, a large staircase led to the second floor, with a balcony that wrapped around the first one. There were things everywhere. Cabinets, chairs and end tables covered with knick-knacks in every available space created a claustrophobic sense. Everything covered in dirt and grime, making Glade appear as some old baron, the only surviving member of a noble family. Impoverished so that he would be unable to care for his inheritance.

"Can I get you something to drink?" Glade asked Teague once he shut the door behind them and placed his hat on the rickety coat rack, weighted down by various coats and jackets.

"No, thank you, Greg," Teague replied. "Is there someplace we might be able to sit down and talk?"

"Sure, in the living room," Glade replied and walked past him to show him the way. They moved through a maze of furniture and objects, Teague careful not to step on the things which had fallen over and not been picked up. There were unwashed dishes seemingly just dropped on the floor and never cared for. As if the price of new dishes was not an object.

"This is your first time here, isn't it?" Glade said as they walked. Not even glancing over his shoulder and supporting himself by placing his hands on the stained walls. Dark handprints were like tracks along the corridors.

"You have never invited me, Greg," Teague commented. *And with good reason,* he thought.

"Well, you know how it is when one moves into a new house," Greg said. "You work to get it all in order, and before you know it an entire year has passed."

"I completely understand," Teague replied. Deep inside they both knew why there had been no invitation to the mansion-like house on Lake Street.

The living room was not as cluttered as the rest of the house. There was an unnecessary amount of furniture there though, but at least Glade had allowed for an open space in the center of the grand room. A wide couch stood before a fireplace, facing the bay windows. The stained carpeting lush, luxurious and a bit too soft for Teague's taste.

"Can I get you anything to drink, Garfield?" Glade asked again and headed to a turn of the century armoire.

"I am good thanks." Garfield walked over to the windows. "This is quite the view you have of the lake." The moon hung lazily above the calm waters. It lit up the yard that stretched out from the house. It was like a picture of the wild nature of Cambodia, with ancient statues standing vigil in the dark. It was a haunting, unintentional beauty. Teague felt a chill run down his spine.

One of the windows was slightly ajar, which he found odd. He had walked around the house on the little pebbled path, and he had not noticed anything open. Of course, there was only the natural light of the night and he had probably overlooked it.

"So, what did you want to talk about?" Glade was holding a tumbler of scotch in his trembling hand.

"This is serious business, Gregory," Teague said and walked toward the couch, placing his hands on the back of it. "I need you to be honest with me now."

"Alright, but I am sure I don't know what you are talking about. I have kept my head low and not gotten into any trouble."

"I'm not so convinced that that's true." Teague shook his head as Glade took a swig from the tumbler.

"What do you know of The Black Diamond?"

"Nothing." The glass in his hand began to shake even more, golden liquid spilling on the already tainted carpeting. "No more than anyone else at the department."

"Greg," Teague began. "We both know that you're lying. I have evidence that you tampered with my folders the other day."

"That manila envelope that was on your desk?" His voice was now almost completely free of the slurring of a drunk person. "I was looking for something and happened to move it. The papers inside fell out and I gathered them up. That is all."

"There is more than just that. There are many things that don't add up. The fact that you have been first at all the crime scenes pertaining to this case. You were the last one seen with that assassin before he died. This house on a detective's salary. There is just too much pointing to it. I have it on good authority that there is a mole in the force, and it all comes back to you."

"Why would I do anything even remotely close to that, Garfield?" Glade's voice was calm and collected, but his body said the opposite. "The fact that I am trying to do a good job by being early to a scene should not work against me, or that I happened to be with a man as he drew his last breath. I find it unfair."

"Come on, Greg." Teague threw his hands in the air. "You have never been a good policeman. Not as long as I have known you. All of a sudden, you show up on time and then only on cases that aren't yours. It doesn't add up."

"I don't know what to tell you. I have nothing to hide." Glade walked over to the door they had entered. "I think I would like you to leave." He placed a hand on the doorknob.

"I am going to present my findings to Chief Swan, and he will have to make his own assessment, but don't think that this is over, Greg." Teague walked towards the door. He lightly touched it with his fingertips but turned to Glade. "Don't forget that you took an oath once. That you promised to keep people safe, and if you are playing both sides then you are not only breaking that oath, you are betraying the people you have sworn to protect."

Glade was just about to answer when the door flew off its hinges and came into the room at breakneck speed. It struck Teague in the shoulder and the side of his head. He tumbled sideways and rolled across the acrid smelling carpet until the couch halted him. Glade had moved to the center of the room as well, instinctively moving away from the entrance. Teague looked up and tried to stop the room from spinning by focusing on something. A shape stood in the doorway. A female figure covered in banded steel. In Teague's daze, she looked partially covered in a bathing suit, with her eyes hidden behind a domino mask and claws protruding from dark blue gloves. She walked with purpose into the room, looking around carefully.

Teague tried desperately to pull the pistol from his pocket, but he landed on the side where he kept it, and he was still too stunned from the blast to his body to pull it out. Glade shouted something at the woman and threw the tumbler at her. She swiped at the flying object and it shattered in midair.

Tony had been crouched on the landing, listening to the conversation between Teague and Glade. In a way, he had been satisfied with the outcome. That Glade would not give in to his friend; it meant that Tony was free to do his thing next. He had kept an eye on the door to the living room at the bottom of the stairs, when a shadow flew through the corridor and slammed into the door, blowing it inward. That was quite a feat since it opened the

other way. He pulled out his kalis and bounded down the steps.

Teague attempted to roll over to his other side without being too obvious at what he was attempting. He managed to pull it from the holster and fumbled with the trigger. The woman was still, in a crouching position, hands extended to her sides, like a cat ready to pounce.

"Get out of here, Garfield!" Greg cried over the sound of bullets exploding from his gun. The woman flipped to the left, avoiding every single shot, leaving holes in the wall behind her.

Teague had gotten his weapon out and fired from his position on the floor. Three shots, one went wide and struck the fireplace, while the other two caught her in the right leg. She buckled but didn't seem to take too much damage. She dodged a few more shots from Greg but ran up to Teague and with a stiff kick knocked his pistol across the room. She put a foot on the couch and leapt in the air, somersaulting over Glade and coming to land, gracefully behind him.

Teague peaked over the couch and saw Greg turn around to face her. He had his gun tight to his vest and fired. The woman jerked twice before sending Glade back on to the couch with an uppercut. Blood sprayed and colored the ceiling in a fountainous pattern. She flicked her wrist so that the blood flew from the claw.

Teague looked for something to use as a weapon, but all he could find was shards of broken glass. Something flew past him, also springing off the couch. Two feet crashed into the woman's chest, catching her off guard. The attacker vaulted backward from the impact and landed next to Teague. The woman flew back into one of the bay windows, but she did not go through it. Instead, the mass of broken glass and wood trim caught her. Her backside was hanging outside while the rest of her was trying to wiggle free. Teague looked at the figure next to him. It was a lean, muscular man dressed in a tight-fitting red and blue outfit. A spiked belt sat at his waist, and covering his face was a hideous demonic mask with protruding eyes. Teague fell over and crawled backward, cutting his hands on the glass in the carpet. The vigilante paid little attention to Teague, but he could sense that he knew he was there. With a roar, the woman pulled herself free from the window, and as she came to a standing position, the masked man moved swiftly and drop kicked her on her already injured leg. Once again caught by surprise, she crashed to the floor.

Tony tried to adopt a fighting style that would involve his ribs as little as possible, but it was difficult. He tried to stab one of the kalis at the prone body of the woman, but she rolled to the side, and all he caught was carpet. She came to a crouching position and swung a claw at him. He jumped back and kicked at her. She blocked with her left arm, still crouching. She pushed him away so that Tony rotated a full 360 around, and as he did, she attacked with her right claw. Tony sidestepped, and as she overextended her body, he placed a hand on her back, assisting her in the forward motion. The claw penetrated the wall, and she was stuck.

Teague came away from the wall where he had been cowering and watched the fight progress. He saw masked man swing his blade at the woman, still stuck in the wall, and he heard the sound of steel on steel. Sparks flew in the air, and the woman fell backward. The blades of her right-handed claw still deep in the drywall.

Tony kicked her in the chest, planting his shin hard. He kicked once, twice, three times, and she staggered. He winced behind the mask at every kick, his own chest on fire in the process. It was becoming increasingly difficult to catch his breath, but he continued.

The woman pulled free from the wall and jumped into the air, landing a punch in Tony's face sending him back. He was completely rattled. She followed it up with a high knee to the chin, and he backed away even farther. She gained ground but stopped in her tracks. She looked over at Glade motionless on the couch. Blood was pouring from the cuts on his face, but he was still very much alive. She leapt at him and let her left claw sink deep into his gut. Glade cried in agony. Teague popped up, and he punched her in the face as she was trying to free herself from the flesh of his colleague. It was like hitting a brick wall. She barely reacted. Tony picked up Teague's pistol from the floor and threw it at the detective. Teague noticed the weapon fly at him just at the last second, caught it and without thinking fired it at the woman. Free from Glade's body she avoided the shot, that otherwise would have hit her square in the face. Instead, it caught her in the shoulder. She turned and caught a boot to the face from Tony.

He swung his remaining kalis at her throat, but she dodged it with ease and shoulder tackled him hard in the ribs. Tony toppled over and rolled on the floor, clutching his side. The pain was too much to bear.

The iron-clawed woman, chased by the bullets from Teague's gun, leapt out the bay windows and disappeared into the wild backyard. Teague came around the couch and stopped by the shattered glass, continuing to fire the weapon until it clicked. He turned around to see a river of blood bubbling from a nasty looking gash in the abdomen of a pale Greg Glade. He was desperately trying to staunch the wound with his hands, breathing heavily and quietly whining. Teague dropped the pistol on the floor and slowly walked towards the couch. He knelt by the man and put a hand on his knee.

"Let me see it, Greg," he said and tried to move the man's hands.

"It's bad, Garfield," Glade said quietly. "I'm not going to make it."

"I know," Teague said. There was no point in trying to deny the obvious. Glade's hands relaxed and Teague could move them with ease. The wound was deep. The claw had ripped clean through the fabric of the vest and shirt and shredded the stomach with three jagged cuts. Matching the lines across his face.

Tony crawled over to the corner closest to the broken windows, still clutching the kalis with one hand and his ribs with the other. He stared at the two detectives, listening, not trying to interfere, and just observing the conversation. Teague could hear the masked man move, but he ignored it, not taking his eyes off his colleague.

"You've got to give us the information we need, Greg," he said and took the man's hands in his, trying to soothe him. "Don't die in vain."

"You're right, Garfield." Glade coughed and crimson saliva moistened his lips. "This is what I deserve for betraying the city and my duty." He started panting heavily, and his eyes went wide, like he was struggling to hold on to something. "A man came to me and offered me so much money. More than I could ever spend. It was just so much money, Garfield. I had never had that kind of cash before. I worked day in and day out for this city, and for what? Peanuts. I just wanted to make my way up in the world."

"Who was it, Greg? Who is The Black Diamond?" Glade was starting to fade, his eyes slowly closed, and his breathing came in softer and softer rhythms. Teague shook him to keep him awake. The eyelids opened again.

"I don't know who the man is," he whispered. "I never saw him in person, only heard his voice or read letters from him. The man I met with on a regular basis was a man named Paul Geert." He coughed again.

"Paul Geert?" Teague echoed.

"Yes. He lives in the Racine Hotel. That is all I know." The color kept draining from his face as crimson liquid flowed from the wound and stained the couch. "I'm so sorry, Garfield. So sorry."

"I know you are, Greg." Teague rose and looked at his hands and then at the man before him. He was hardly moving now. Only the barely visible movement from his chest revealed that he was still alive. He had little sympathy for him. Everyone had a reason to turn, to betray those who trusted them. Something in their childhood or a climactic event in their life. To him, there was no excuse though. He was not going to be able to forgive Glade. He would always say his name with some contempt. He had made his job so much more difficult than it had to be.

"I am going to call this in now," he said without turning to the vigilante. "If the neighbors haven't called the police already. I should arrest you in the process."

"There is no need for it," Tony said, trying to distort his voice as much as possible. He had never considered the possibility of having to speak to people. If he had, he might not have gotten a job in radio. He sheathed the kalis he was holding and moved to recover the other one.

"I guess I should thank you for saving my life." Teague continued to stare at his blood-soaked hands.

"We are fighting the same enemy, Detective Teague," Tony replied without acknowledging the comment. "Might be that we are doing it in different ways, but the truth of it is that we are on the same side."

"You kill without mercy. How is that the same as what I do?"

"Just different ways of reaching the same end."

"What are you?" Teague was not interested in getting into a debate over law and order.

"Just a citizen who wants to change his city and happens to have tools that the police lack to do so."

"I will not arrest you tonight. Not after what you have done for me and my family, but that does not mean that I will let you off next time."

"You need me, Detective," Tony replied. "There are things that I can do which the police cannot. The Black Diamond and the iron woman that he has working for him possess powers that are way beyond the capabilities of the police. You would be no match for them. At least, I have skills to combat them."

"You might be right, but that does not change the fact that what you are doing is against the law."

"Do you have any other leads than this Paul Geert?"

"Nothing solid. What about you?"

"The same. Every lead has been a dead end."

"I guess I will see you at the Racine Hotel then." Teague was turning his cigarette case again.

"I guess so." Tony backed away and with some difficulty slithered out the broken window into the darkness.

Teague waited a bit until he was sure that the masked man had left the room. He turned around met by a cold breeze from the outside. He walked to the hallway where he had seen a telephone, his hands still stained with blood.

* * *

Gregory Garrison Glade heard the conversation between the two men in front of him. His eyes were only partially open, but once Teague had left the room, he let his eyelids fall. He sighed. This was how it was going to end. He was fine with it. He only hoped that this would be the end of The Black Diamond as well and that he, in the end, did enough good to make up for the path he had chosen. He took one final br

CHAPTER NINETEEN

The transfer from the cramped apartment in New York City to Chicago was not as smooth as Mr. Hill had hoped. His connections had landed him a job as a foreign affairs consultant to a large business. Anthony and he moved into another apartment overlooking the river, but it was also claustrophobic. Not because they had to share it with another family this time, but because it only consisted of two rooms and a minor kitchenette. Father and son shared a bedroom and at first a bed, but as time passed, they would furnish it more and more and it came to feel like a home.

Anthony hated the cold oppressive walls closing in on him. He was used to being free and running wild. He longed for the house on Bali, where the doors and windows always stood wide open so that the warm breeze would come in and mess with his hair while he was studying. It would call to him to come outside and play. To run to the village and continue his training to become a warrior. Instead, he was stuck on the fourth floor of a square structure devoid of life. He seldom ventured outside. The concrete jungle, the synthetic wilderness, was not inviting at all and instead, he felt the sensation that they wanted him to stay away. Life was hectic here in the city. People were always on their way to some place, and they always appeared to be late for it. They were in a hurry, red-faced and angry at the world. His father enrolled him in a school and had to follow their rules.

Mr. Mahr was structured and meticulous as it pertained to education, but he made learning fun and would always show the deeper value of what they were discussing around the dinner table. Here the structure was of a different kind. It was as if they were products molded in a factory, hell-bent on producing similar figures. The teachers less interested in adapting the lesson plan to individuals, and more into testing. Some of the things that they taught Anthony knew very well already, but others Mr. Mahr had not spoken of. Not because he did not find them important, instead, it was part of a greater plan - he had assumed that Anthony would be in his care for the duration. There was little time for physical activity, and in order not to have his skills deteriorate, Anthony practiced what Wayan had taught him in one of the parks on his way to and from school. When winter came, he tried to do it in the apartment instead, while waiting for his father. The cold and snow kept him indoors, not familiar with the season at all.

He would sit in his room, Mr. Mahr's trunk open, weapons on the floor, clutching the case with the mask. He thought he could hear it speak to him. Telling him that he needed to move on. That he could not stay in Chicago. It was all he had left of his childhood; it became his only solace. The other children at school found him odd and some had attempted to bully him, but he had put them in their place quite easily. Since that day in the schoolyard, as Michael Adams and Stephen Strong lay on the wet ground with their noses bloodied, they left him alone. No one said anything to the principal for fear of what he might also do to them.

Mr. Hill also had a difficult time adapting. Life on Bali had been leisurely and slow. Most of the time he had been able to wander from building to building reading various reports and sitting in meetings, while the evenings were mostly parties of a varying kind. Here they expected him to come in at nine and work until five. Parties were unheard of - if it was not a Christmas one - and people mostly engaged in mundane conversations. It felt as if they took even the smallest aspect as a serious matter. He consulted on overseas negotiations and trade deals and had to sit in endless meetings. It bored him. He continued drinking, though he avoided it on the job. Once he came home, he could finish off a bottle of cheap whiskey.

At first, he felt guilty. His son often fended for himself and ate whatever might be in the house; Mr. Hill had stopped eating, only business lunches, so he tried to keep food in the house. As his bank account filled up again, he hired a girl to take care of Anthony, who had grown into a tall teenager, not the gangly and insecure kind he had been, but rather a broad-shouldered one. He attributed it to growing up on the island and all the outside activity he had taken part in. Mr. Hill became more and more reclusive and brooding. He went to work and did what they asked of him, only for his son's sake, and when it was time, he sent the boy off to college in Madison. An odd choice Mr. Hill found, but they had no real relationship - if they had ever had one - so he gladly paid for the move. Anthony would come home for Christmas and a week in summer, but they would see less and less of each other.

* * *

Teague did not wait around for the officers and forensic team to arrive at the house on Lake Street. He told the man on the other end of the line that he had left a letter in his desk that explained it all and that they needed to tell Chief Swan to meet him at the Racine Hotel.

Once he had hung up the phone, he called Theresa, told her he loved her and that he might be home late - after she was already in bed. He did not want her to wait up for him, and he would update her the following morning. He got to his car and headed towards the hotel, which was not located far away. Also located in the downtown area, it would only take him a minute or so to drive there. Unfortunately, the masked man had a head start, so he needed to drive as fast as he could to get there. He sped through the dark streets, met the black and whites on Main going the opposite direction with their sirens blaring. He came to an abrupt stop on the street outside the majestic structure. He looked over his pistol, it was empty, and he filled it with bullets from the box in his glove compartment.

The street was quiet and still. It was a work night after all, so people were likely home and getting ready for bed. There was no evidence of unrest, so either it was too late, and the vigilante had taken care of the suspect already, or he had yet to arrive. Teague removed his hat from his head and threw it in the backseat of his car. He placed the pistol in his pocket again, careful to put it in a position so that he would not need to struggle with removing it. He grabbed a handful of

327

ammunition with his left and put them in his left pocket. He was as prepared as he could be.

* * *

The station called Chief Swan at his home just as he was getting ready to crawl into his striped pajamas. He usually enjoyed reading the evening paper in front of the fire, in his favorite chair before getting to bed. As a member of law enforcement, he was in the thick of the news on a daily basis, but there were other things going on in his fair city, and he wanted to know the good things, not only the bad.

His wife had only just put the children to bed when the phone rang, and she picked it up after having descended the stairs. He listened to her speaking in a soft voice while he was taking care of the dishes in the kitchen. They had given the maid the night off, she apparently had a date, so he did her duty. He enjoyed the everyday tasks and quite missed not having to do them, but his wife had been quite adamant that they should get help - they could easily afford it and their station in life demanded it. Swan came from simple folk and was not used to being waited on hand and foot and he did not particularly like it. So, he avoided the maid like the plague. It made him appear aloof and ornery, but he did not care about that fact, which was in sharp contrast to his natural instinct to be pleasant to all those around him.

His wife Jessica called him into the hallway and handed him the phone as soon as he had stepped across the threshold.

"It is from the station," she said in her angelic voice, her big brown eyes had a worried look in them. She tried to smile,

328

but he was all too familiar with her facial expressions to know that it hid something.

It was one of the secretaries on the other end. She informed him that Detective Garfield Teague had called in a murder in a home on Lake Street. The victim was a cop, she said in a trembling voice, and cars were already en route to the location. Teague was no longer there. Instead, he had taken it upon himself to head to the Racine Hotel to apprehend the perpetrator. Swan told her to have a squad of officers meet him at the hotel as soon as possible.

"Be careful, my love." Jess put a hand on his chest as he put the phone back on the hook. "You haven't been out in the field in years. Make sure you come back to us." She bit her lip to stop it from quivering.

"Don't worry, my dear." Swan placed his hand on hers. "I am sure it will be all over when I arrive." He gently kissed her on the forehead and then proceeded to dress in his overcoat and hat.

* * *

Teague entered the hotel through the Mandalay Lounge. He had been there on a few occasions in the past. He had taken Theresa there on their first date and then tried to do it on every anniversary. The food was nice, and the interior was contemporary with a rounded bar which stretched across the entire back wall.

The place filled with patrons, nicely dressed young men and women sitting at the bar or in the booths placed along the opposite walls. A man in a pair of glasses with thick, black frames, dressed in a white shirt with suspenders, was serving up drinks. He nodded at Teague, who nodded back.

He tried to look as inconspicuous as possible as he sauntered up to the bar and placed a hand on the polished wood top. He leaned in to indicate that he needed special attention from the barman, who read the sign loud and clear.

"What can I do for you, sir?" he said in a low voice.

"My name is Garfield Teague of the Racine Police Department." Teague cast a glance over his shoulder to make sure no one was eavesdropping. "I am looking for someone."

"Who might that be, sir?" The barkeep raised an eyebrow. "You are, of course, aware that we who work at the Racine Hotel are very particular as it pertains to the privacy of our guests."

"I am well aware of this," Teague replied. "There has been a murder of one of my colleagues, and I have reason to believe that a key person in solving this case is staying here. In a few minutes, the Chief of Police will be here with a squad of officers. It would be a shame if we closed this place down in order to raid it. Quite the scandal."

"I get your point." The barkeep straightened up. "It is not really my place to give out this information. I would look to the manager."

"Might you at least be able to inform me if Mr. Paul Geert is staying at this hotel?"

The man nodded slowly, as if he had been expecting this.

"He was in this very lounge earlier today, but he has probably relocated to his rooms. He usually spends most of his evening here, but he is late tonight. The front desk can assist you further."

"Thank you for your co-operation, sir." Teague tapped the bar and looked around before he headed towards the glass doors that led to the hotel reception. He strode over to the desk where two well-dressed men were busy talking to each other. They wore trademark uniforms of hotel porters in blue and gold. The older of the two, a man with sprinkles of gray in his otherwise black hair, turned to Teague as he came towards them.

He was the manager on duty, and Teague merely needed to inform him of who he was and what he needed. The man was keen to avoid a big commotion, so he gave the detective the room number of one Paul Geert, who had not left the hotel in the past few hours.

Teague took a description of the man, finding that the manager was surprised that he did not know who the man was. He had apparently been living at the hotel for several years, and he seemed to be some form of high roller eager to flaunt his money. They had thought that he was an important executive or a captain of industry in the area. They afforded him the utmost privacy and never discussed his job.

Teague, who had never heard the name Geert before, was starting to piece things together. It would make sense if the suspect were some form of 'higher up' in The Black Diamond organization. He would have quite a large amount of disposable income to throw around and would not have to leave the hotel if he did all his business in the city. Without a permanent address, he would be difficult to track as well.

He had decided to take the elevator to the room. The description of Geert made him assume that he was averse to taking the stairs. He had asked the manager to stop people from going up to that particular floor and to send Chief Swan up as soon as he arrived at the premises.

As soon as the doors slid shut behind him and he heard the light bell of the elevator indicating that it was moving on, he began to feel nervous. He put one hand in his left pocket and felt the cigarette case, and the other hand slowly slid the pistol from the right one. He was all alone now. He had been fairly confident that Glade was not going to turn on him, so the nervousness he had felt then was one of actually being right. This was uncharted territory. There was no way he could predict what he was going to find on the other side of the door.

He moved slowly through the corridor, being mindful not to make too much noise. Luckily, the floor had carpeting so it masked his approach. As he advanced on the door to the suite at the end of the corridor, he turned and put his back to the wall. He raised the revolver at the ready and pulled back the hammer. It still smelled of gunpowder from when he had unloaded it earlier. Once at the door, he hesitated. Should he knock and announce his presence or spring in like a surprise, catching whoever was on the other side unawares.

The manager had given him the master key, so he decided on the latter and slid the key ever so slowly into the hole, trying to avoid touching the lock itself. The key hovered in the hole. He was doing it with his left hand and it was awkward. When he was convinced that it was in place, he quickly turned it and pulled the door open, pistol at eye level.

The door swung open with more force than he had expected, and it crashed into the wall and bounced back at him. He put out his foot and stopped it from slamming into him as he entered the room.

"Paul Geert!" He shouted. "I am Detective Garfield Teague of the Racine Police Department. Remain where you are with your hands above your head. I will come towards you." There was no reply. He paused for a moment and leaned against the door that led to the bathroom off the hallway. "Geert?" He called again.

He was afraid that he might be too late. That woman might have gotten to him already. Maybe she had realized that Glade was going to reveal what he knew. As he crept along the wall, he could see a larger room ahead of him. A blinking light threw shadows upon the walls around it. It made him concerned. He took a deep breath and swung around, went to a knee with pistol aiming somewhere. It was some kind of living room, bigger even than his first bachelor apartment he had lived in. The hotel had furnished it like a real living room than an imitation one so common in such establishments. There was a large couch against one wall, flanked by love seats. All of them were facing the large windows gazing out over Lake Michigan with that moon hanging above it like a big Wisconsin cheese. There was art deco artwork in dull colors and angular shapes hanging on the walls and statues of stylized naked women holding orbs and flowers strategically placed in corners and at the end of the seating. Across a glass table lay knocked over lamp, blinking.

The room was empty, apart from a lone figure standing in the center of it, feet planted on the Oriental rug on the floor. It was the masked vigilante, his silhouette flickering in and out in the blinking light. He was still, head turned away from Teague, arms limp at his sides, both hands clutching those wavy swords that matched the dagger they had found at St. Mary's.

"He is not here," the masked man said, still facing away from Teague.

Teague kept the pistol trained at the man. "Did you dispose of him?" he asked.

"Not this time," was the reply. "He managed to get away before I arrived. I found the place like this." He gestured at the room in general. There were a couple of doors open and the lights were on in them. "I have been through every corner of this room to no avail. I have found nothing. He somehow sensed that we were on our way."

"The front desk claimed that they had not seen him leave for the evening." Teague was getting fatigue in his arms from holding the gun.

"They could be covering for him, or he took the fire escape at the end of this floor."

"Another dead end," Teague said in frustration and lowered the gun.

"Agreed," the masked man, said. "We come so close and yet so far away."

"I should place you under arrest." Teague shook his arm to get some blood flowing in it again; a sharp tingling went up and down his limb as it started to wake up. "You have broken the law on several occasions and obstructed justice."

"I do not think that it would be a wise decision to make, Detective. As I said, you and I are on the same side in this. We might go about it in very different ways, but I can go where you cannot, and in return, you are privy to information not available to me."

"You suggest that we are some sort of team?" Teague scoffed at the claim.

"We could be, at least on this. We both want to see The Black Diamond shut down and brought to justice. To me, it matters little if the responsible parties go to jail or die. If we compare the information, we both have gathered, we might be able to find the common denominator."

"Maybe. That does not mean that we become partners going forward. I will still take you down once The Black Diamond is gone."

"Alright." The vigilante turned toward Teague, and then he saw the true horror of the mask the man wore. It was as if a force attacked him. Teague had to back away, away from those protruding eyes, the nasty grin with its rows of sharp teeth and the horns atop the head like a Minotaur. He started to shiver and tried to avert his gaze, but those eyes, those hideous eyes beckoned to him. He steeled himself and straightened up.

"You are stronger than most, Detective," the man said in his deep, muted voice. "This Face is designed to strike fear in those who have a guilty conscience. I see that you are uncomfortable at the sight of its power, but your soul is clean enough to not become incapacitated by it." He walked closer to him. "In one of the old factories, the Mitchell Factory, the one that had a fire yesterday, The Black Diamond has a warehouse. I stopped part of a shipment from coming out on the street. Unfortunately, I could not do more at the time. Go there and shut it down."

"I have been digging into the origins of The Black Diamond symbol," Teague replied, still trying to look away from the mask. "It has something to do with a Dr. Lansing, but I am awaiting answers from other departments."

"I found this ledger in one of the nightstands in the bedroom." The masked man held a leather-bound book in his hand. "Take it. It details all of the shipments that have come into the city this past year, and as far as I can tell, it contains the names of those who distribute the product in this area. The book mentions two places - one the Mitchell factory and the second, another similar building.

I assume that Geert is hiding in one of them. We find Geert and we can bring this whole operation down, but we still need to be stealthy about it. This organization has eyes everywhere, and if we go in with an entire squad of policemen, they will without a doubt find out, and we will have lost them forever."

"How do we get in contact with each other?" Teague hesitated.

"I will find you if need be, but you may contact me with this number." He handed Teague the ledger and atop it was a strip of paper with a number scrawled upon it. "This number goes to my phone, and I will trust that you do not use it to catch me. We have to work together, and when all is said and done, I will vanish, and hopefully, that number will vanish with it."

"You have my word,' Teague said as he grabbed the objects. "You are putting quite the trust in someone that you do not know," he said and smiled, the power of the mask was dissipating.

"If you can't trust the law, then who can you trust?" the man said. "Let us each go our separate ways now, Detective, and start fresh in the morning. We do not know if Geert has fled because he thought that we were on to him, or if he felt he needed to hide. As long as we don't chase after him tonight, he might feel safe."

"I will raid the Mitchell building tomorrow morning and head to the other one alone."

"Good. I will meet you there."

"Now go." Teague cast a glance over his shoulder. "I can hear the chief and his men coming through the corridor."

"I will see you later, Detective," the masked man said and headed to one of the other rooms. Teague remained and walked to the center of the room, standing where he had come upon him.

* * *

They put out an APB on Paul Geert as soon as they got back to the station. The forensic team stayed behind at the hotel in order to do a clean sweep of the rooms. Chief Swan and Garfield Teague sat themselves down in the break room, each with a cup of tea in their hands and waited in silence. The death of a fellow cop, no matter what the reason might be, was something that struck everyone hard. Greg Glade had not been the most popular man on the force, but he was a brother in blue, the only thing that mattered now.

"You know, Garfield," Swan said after a while. "I am not particularly pleased with how you handled the situation. You should not have kept this information to yourself."

"I know, sir," Teague replied after taking a sip of tea. "It just all happened so fast. I did not think that the fingerprint analysis would come back so fast, or that it would reveal Greg having tampered with the folder." He had detailed the events leading up to Swan and his men finding him in the hotel room, alone. He had omitted the fact that the very same masked vigilante that they were chasing had assisted him.

"Tell me more about what happened," Swan demanded.

"There is not much more to say than what I have already reported," Teague began. "Upon getting the report back showing Glade's fingerprints all over my folder, I went to his home to confront him. There were so many details that fell into place once I read his name on that paper."

"Such as?"

"Being first on each scene which in some way was connected to The Black Diamond. Him being the last person to see the only surviving St. Mary's assassin alive and so forth. There were so many unanswered questions, and I needed to hear the story from him personally."

"You believed there might be some logical reason behind this? The fact that he was an officer of the law."

"Of course." Teague sipped the tea. "I did not want to get the force involved if he had a reasonable defense."

"I have a feeling you had already made up your mind about him before going to his home on Lake Street." Swan bit his lower lip.

"Maybe. I just needed a break in the case so bad that I could not think straight-"

"Or follow proper procedure?" Swan was never this serious, but the death of a man under his command was too much for him. "What of his killer? You claim that it is not the vigilante. The one who keeps tripping up our investigation."

"I must claim that they are two different figures." Teague leaned back in the chair. "Every description we have of the masked man with the wavy swords is that he is indeed a man. This was without a doubt a woman. I saw enough of her to make that assessment. She did not wield swords either, she had claws."

"And she spared you but took out Gregory."

"I believe he was her primary target. I feel that this is another cause to implicate him in the dealings of The Black Diamond."

"That and his dying confession, which led us to the Racine Hotel and this Geert character." Swan stroked his chin. "I believe I have met him on occasion. A large man prone to spending money about him. I would observe him sitting in The Mandalay Lounge, and may have spoken to him as well. He claimed to be an investor in various local companies, having inherited his wealth from his parents. Dutch family. Never investigated it because I thought little of it at the time."

"It feels as if we are close now." Teague was fingering the ledger he was carrying in his pocket. It felt wrong to sit on it, but the masked man had a point. At the risk of Geert fleeing the city, they needed to have him feeling a false sense of security. "The Black Diamond must feel that we are on to them, and if that is the case, they are bound to make mistakes."

"I believe the organization is cleverer than that, but you might be on to something none the less."

"We will have to see what the forensics team can lift from the murder scene and the hotel room. I would assume that the latter has quite a bit of information to give us."

"I hope so." Swan stared off in the distance. He knew there were a few phone calls that would have to happen. Glade's parents, the press and the mayor. The death of a police officer was difficult enough to deal with, but when he was also an alleged mole for a criminal organization, things became even more complicated... He sighed. He wasn't going to release that particular information, but it was bound to come out one way or another. "Go home and get some rest, Garfield," he said. "You look like you need it."

Teague nodded. If this end was in sight for the Black Diamond, then there was not going to be much chance for sleep in the coming days.

* * *

Geert was pacing the floor of the empty warehouse. The stink of fire still hung in the air. He had ordered the men to fumigate the area, but one could only do so much when it came to burnt wood and melted steel. This was the first place he had thought of running. He was unsure of why he had decided to flee. It was a sensation, a kind of anxiety building up in the pit of his large gut. One he was unable to shake, like something tugging at him from afar, telling him to beware of something.

Iron Claw was taking out his best informant, and he was worried that Detective Glade might have documents pointing to him. It was best to get out of the hotel room and assess the situation from a distance. It was the safest thing. Surrounded by the vast, sterile concrete building did not ease his mind, but he was fairly convinced that no one would find him here. They had no reason to look for him, but if they did, and they went to the hotel, they would only find him gone. He was certain he had not left anything behind.

He walked from abandoned room to abandoned room in the offices of the warehouse. There were a few thugs dressed in trench coats and armed with machine guns patrolling the hallways, otherwise, there was a minimal amount of activity in the building. If it was devoid of product it would have been empty, but since they had not distributed everything yet, a skeleton crew stuck around. It made Geert feel somewhat safer, knowing that he was not entirely alone.

One of the rooms, which at times functioned as a break room for workers, had a comfortable couch, and he decided to make it his bed for the evening. With any luck, The Black Diamond would contact him in the morning. The man had an uncanny knack of knowing where Geert was. By that time, they would know if the detective had turned against them. If the Iron Car had been too late or if she had managed to put him away and destroy whatever evidence he might possess.

It was not uncommon for untrustworthy people like Gregory Glade to keep information hidden away, a form of security. If this were the case, Geert would be in deep trouble. The various branches of The Black Diamond organization knew little of each other, functioning as separate entities. Glade would never have encountered The Black Diamond himself, but he had visited with Paul. If this came out, then his head would be the next one on the chopping block. He might not survive the night after a visit from Iron Claw.

He slumped down on the couch and placed a briefcase on the cushion next to him. He had refrained from packing anything too heavy - only the essentials - but he had made sure to pack the envelope. Closed with a wax seal, and inside were papers detailing everything he had learned over the years. Everything about the operations of the criminal group known as The Black Diamond.

There was more information scrawled upon those papers than his boss was aware of. Geert was tired of being used as a punching bag by a man who did not trust him enough to reveal his identity. He would love to see the look upon the man's handsome face when the police were standing on his doorstep. Geert would surely be dead by then. At least, hopefully.

He swung his massive legs up on the couch and used the briefcase as a pillow. Lying there in the invasive light of a single light bulb hanging from the ceiling, he thought about his life up to this point. Most folks would say that he had wasted it on morally questionable activities. For a man of his frame, not blessed with the best things in life, there was not much else to do. He had used the cards dealt to him in life and made the best of things. Geert could claim that he had come out on top. He had made more money than most people could dream of even hearing about. He had eaten the best dishes, had the best wine, and had the most beautiful women on his arm. All of it thanks to money acquired by nefarious means, but did it truly matter how one got the win? Wasn't winning alone the true goal?

* * *

Tony knew he had promised Detective Teague that they would go inside together, but he couldn't wait. He had seen Geert head into the warehouse by himself. He was on the run. Probably only to be safe. He was likely unaware that Glade had named him. Tony was back in his apartment trying to recover from the encounter with the masked woman. She had appeared more vulnerable this time and had taken several bullets. He could hurt her, but he was hurting as well and the next time they faced each other one of them must surely break. There was little time, and he had to make haste. He was still going to get Paul Geert in the morning, but he was not waiting for the detective. Geert would feel safer in the morning, and that was when Tony would strike.

CHAPTER TWENTY

Anthony had lived in Madison for two years when his father passed away. After his son moved out, his health had deteriorated rapidly. The drinking had become more excessive. He had taken to doing it during the day as well and would often leave work after lunch. His employer wanted to avoid a scandal, gave him a nice severance package, and let him go. This gave Mr. Hill the excuse he needed to spend the entire day drinking - until he one day collapsed in the living room and was found by the housekeeper.

Anthony did not travel for the funeral and made all the arrangements through the family attorney. He had brought everything he needed with him to his small apartment on campus. His father's money had afforded him the luxury of not staying in the dormitories, and he had no need of returning to the Windy City. He immersed himself in journalism, English literature, and social studies. His aim was to be top of the class.

At this time, a mysterious predatory figure began stalking young college women and attacking them in the parks of the city. The police were on the case, but the man, described by his victims as dressed in a dark suit, dark coat, hat and face covered by a dark scarf, kept eluding them. One night, Anthony woke to a noise from his closet. It was a loud banging coming from behind the closed door. He imagined it to be nothing more than a rat having made its way into the apartment and figured it would stop once the rodent realized there was no food there. The banging continued, and he decided it would be best if he took care of it before it chewed through his clothes. When he opened the door there was silence. The creature must have been startled and run away. Then he heard the muffled sound of something speaking. He looked around, but there was no one near that could have made the sound. Instead, he realized, it came from the wooden box placed on the floor before him. It was The Face, calling to him.

He crouched down and removed the lid. It lay still, staring up at him with those big eyes. Lifeless in the loneliness of the box. *Why are you not doing your duty? It seemed to ask him. Protect those who need protecting. Help the people who cannot fend for themselves. It is your calling as the keeper of Rangda's Mask.*

It was echoing in his head, like the repetitive beating of a drum. He did not want to listen. The city of Madison in Wisconsin was a very different place than the jungles of Bali. Who was he to take justice in his own hands, to do the job of the police? The words continued to repeat themselves in his head. He did not sleep that night. He sat on the carpeted floor of the closet with the box open in front of him and the mask speaking to him. As the first rays of the morning light came in through his window, he had relented. He had a duty to perform.

* * *

The sun was barely setting the horizon on fire when Tony climbed atop the main building of the Mitchell Motors warehouse. He could still see the dark, charred stain left by the burning train car in the center of the courtyard. The tracks warped from the heat making the steel curl like a snake slithering across the concrete. He had taken a power nap and was as rested as he was going to be that morning. He was stiff, his body ached from the encounters of the previous two days, and the three blades he carried weighed heavy on him.

He was going in blind. He had no idea of how many men might be patrolling the building or where Geert was located - if he was even in the building anymore. He would just have to do the best he could to find the man. The night before, he had stuck around long enough to see lights turn on in the windows of the third floor, so that was where he would start. He leapt over to the main building and then dropped down to one of the third story windows. As silently as he could, he broke the glass. He rolled inside and came to a crouching position on the floor, kalis at the ready. He waited in the dark for a minute, listening, scanning the room.

He had entered into a corridor, devoid of anything. No one appeared to have heard his entry, so he relaxed. The route was straight forward, so he moved along the wall, taking every step carefully on the dusty wood floor. It all looked like the hallways of a hospital ward - sterile with walls painted white. Grime and dirt caked the trim, revealing that the place empty. He peered around the corner of the hallway leading to what he had assumed was the room he was looking for. A man dressed in a trench coat was making the rounds. He had his back turned to Tony, so he took the opportunity, ran on his tiptoes and pounced.

The man never knew what hit him as the blade cut into his back and came out through his chest. With an audible moan, he collapsed on the floor. Tony slid the weapon free at the same time as two other guards came through one of the doors. They shouted at him, but he raised his head and looked at them. They averted their eyes at the mere sight of The Face and backed off. One of them, still keeping his gaze away from him, opened fire. Blindly letting the bullets skirt across the corridor. Tony dropped down and rolled to the side. The bullets came at him waist high, so he easily avoided the spray. With the spell temporarily broken, the other guard looked up and noticed him. Before he could react, Tony had tumbled forward and cut him right above the knee. Steel grinding against bone, the man cried out in anguish and dropped the weapon. The first guard had now turned and trained his gun at Tony, who dropped flat on his back and kicked the weapon out of the man's hands. The injured guard was down and bleeding out on the floor. He clawed at Tony and pulled him down. Tony was pinned under the heavy, lifeless body of the man and tried to wiggle free. The first man, paralyzed for a moment, tried to decide if he should go for the machine gun on the floor or go for the pistol in his pocket.

He decided on the latter, but by then it was too late. The Face sent fear through his skull, and he staggered back against the wall. Tony, in a great deal of pain, managed to roll the body off him. Covered in blood and with his ribs screaming at him, he stood up. The man's face had gone completely white.

He was sweating profusely as he tried to avoid the bulging eyes of the mask. Tony stumbled towards him and without a sound punched him, first with his left and then his right. The man's head snapped back and crashed into the wall behind. He fell to the floor, lifeless.

A bullet whizzed by his head, and he spun around. At the other end of the passage were three other men. One large dressed in an ill-fitting suit and a tie barely sitting around the thick neck. Men in dark suits flanked him, one of them with a gun aimed at Tony. They too shied away when he turned towards them. The men tried to fight the horror of The Face and fired their weapons at him. He hurried at them, bounced off the wall with one leg and kicked one of them in the head. The man spun in the air and landed hard, still conscious, but incapacitated. The fat man had already begun running away from him. Tony dispensed of the second opponent by slicing his abdomen wide open, so the air became filled with the stench of blood and internal organs.

He was in pursuit but not needing to run. The final man, obviously Paul Geert from what intelligence he had gathered during the night, couldn't move very fast. He turned to one of the doors but was unable to get it open. He cast glances over his shoulder, each time met by the gruesome visage closing in on him.

Geert desperately fiddled with the door but without success. Locked, jammed or something like that. He wished he had turned back into the break room instead. At least, he knew he could get inside and lock the monster out. He was out of breath, soaked in sweat, and had begun to weep uncontrollably. He turned around and tried to push himself through the massive wood of the door.

The masked man had come to stand right in front of him. The eyes of the mask were penetrating his very soul. It was as if they knew his every secret. Every dastardly deed from childhood until that very moment in time. Everything else melted away. The only thing he could see were those glowing eyes. The figure came at him and kicked with both feet so they both broke through the door.

The fat man was whimpering, which was understandable after his large frame split the hardwood as if it were mere particleboard. He was stirring slightly as Tony found himself between the man's feet. The landing had been harder than he had imagined it would be, and he struggled to get to his feet. Luckily, there didn't seem to be any more guards in this part of the building, so he could take his time getting up.

He tried to listen for commotion outside, but there was nothing. The police were not here yet; it was still early. He scrambled to his feet and climbed up the frame of the prone person lying in a pile of debris. The man's eyes were rolling in the back of his head, and the whimpering had turned into wheezing. He was clearly concussed, blood trickling from several cuts in his forehead and saliva flooding from the side of his mouth. Tony grabbed him by his collar and pulled him, with some effort, into the room. The room was a storage closet. Filled with old junk from when the warehouse was still part of the car manufacturing plant. Metal billboards with pictures of old automobiles stood against the walls, covered in cobwebs and dust. A hidden tribute to the former glory of the automotive history of the city. He grunted as he flung Geert against the wall. He was now sitting on the floor, back against one of the billboards, still unresponsive.

"Paul Geert?" Tony said in a cracked voice. The man stirred at the mention of his name. Tony said it again.

"Yes." The man coughed. "That's me." He kept his eyes shut, hiding from the eyes of the mask.

"Tell me where I can find The Black Diamond," Tony said and placed the point of his kris against Geert's throat.

"You can threaten me all you want." Geert smiled. "It would be nothing compared to what he would do to me once he found out I talked."

"We can do this the hard way or the easy way, Geert." Tony pressed the point harder against the skin, drawing blood. Geert winced.

"It doesn't matter. I am damned anyway." He opened his eyes slightly. "You or him. Either way, I will not see the end of this day. It would be a stretch to say that I have lived a full life, but for a while, I envied no man. I was on top of the world. No matter the cost. It wasn't for me, though. The constant paranoia, the fear of getting caught, or the fear of reprimands from the man himself. I was never a good criminal. I was weak and easily led - a patsy."

"Are you going to tell me or not, Geert?" Tony was losing patience. He was so close again, and now this tub of guts was stalling. Was he waiting for someone to rescue him?

"I give in," Geert replied and pulled out a revolver from his jacket pocket.

Tony looked at it and placed his hand on the gun. "It is over, Geert; there is no point in trying to get out of this."

"I know. In my inside pocket, there are documents detailing everything I know about The Black Diamond and its routines. The shipments and all the buildings they own all around the city. I was in charge of all the operations. Fact is he never trusted me with was his name."

Tony's shoulders slumped. It was a start. Maybe the document could point him to where he needed to go.

"But I figured it out," Geert continued. "He thought he was so slick, that he was untouchable, but I will have the last laugh. The only one who could run such an operation under the nose of the police department, who had the proper channels and the funds."

"Who is it Geert?" Tony said through gritted teeth.

"Dr. Jack Benton." He smiled through bloodied teeth.

Tony rose to his feet. *Dr. Benton,* he thought. *Of course.* The man ran the largest pharmaceutical company in the Midwest. He had all the tools needed to import and distribute illegal narcotics and right under his nose. He benefited from both legal and illegal substances. He needed to find him. At this hour, he was most likely still in his home off Main Street.

"The police will be here soon, Geert." he told Paul, who was still breathing heavily and was staring at the revolver still in his hand. "Hand over the documents to them and maybe they will let you off easier. Maybe they can protect you?"

Geert sighed as Tony left the room. He was not going to kill the man today. It would be too easy of a punishment. He began moving down the corridor when he heard a single gunshot come from the room. He hung his head for a moment, and then decided to move on.

* * *

Teague came into the station extra early the following morning. He had never set a time with the masked man, and they had not ironed out any details concerning if they were supposed to wait for each other at the warehouse or not. The department was already bustling with activity, and Chief Swan was in his office going over documents with Dr. Price. They had set up a round table close to the command center. On it was a framed photograph of Greg Glade, complete with a black ribbon on one edge and a candle burning next to it. Teague was unsure about what he was supposed to feel. The man was a traitor, a criminal who had worked against them, but he was part of the force. He tried to convince himself that his colleagues needed to grieve. Eventually the truth would come out.

"Detective Teague!" Charlotte called from the desk. "This came from the police in Milwaukee." She held an envelope in her hand. Placing it on the surface, she slid it towards him. He nodded a thanks and was about to vocalize his gratitude when he was called into the office by Swan.

"I have received a preliminary report from the forensics department concerning both Greg's home and the hotel room of Paul Geert," he said as Teague approached. "We are still waiting on the analysis from the blood at the murder scene, but so far there seems to be nothing to go on. Geert's rooms were clean apart from some notes, nothing that links him to any crimes. We need to find him."

The notebook in his pocket burned, but Teague remained silent.

"The only thing we have to go on is the report you gave about Glade's dying words," Swan continued. "It's not enough to detain him or even arrest him. It was difficult enough to motivate the APB."

"So, you're saying that the words of a detective aren't strong enough?"

"Well, apparently the detectives around here are proving to not be trustworthy." Swan's words came back at Teague like a slap in the face.

Teague was not quite sure how he was supposed to reply to the comment. His integrity was in question here. After all the years he had been working on the force, he was getting this reward. It would not have hurt so much if there hadn't been some truth to it. He had gathered information from Lindquist and had made a deal with a hunted vigilante, kept information, vital to the investigation from his reports, and worked questionable leads. It was all for the greater good, but it was also morally wrong.

He had to take a step back and gather his thoughts for the next move. Did he want to prove Swan right by going off to the Mitchell Motors factory by himself to see if he could find Geert, or did he want to do it by the book?

"Give me one moment, sir," he said and walked to his desk. Swan nodded and turned back to the papers he had been perusing.

Once he was back at his station, he opened the envelope. It contained pictures of Dr. Lansing and a folder with basic information about him. Nothing that he had not seen before. There were newspaper clippings as well, detailing his excursions from various parts of the world. The photograph he had seen before, the one of Lansing with another man. The face was still blurred, but there was a caption. He ran his finger across it as he read, *Dr. Lansing, shown left, next to his ever-present assistant in the hills of Mexico.* This did not give him any more information. If the assistant was ever present then he must show up in other pictures, Teague reasoned. He continued to shuffle through the papers until he found another newspaper clipping. It was a story about a fundraiser the Milwaukee Museum had set up several years earlier. He quickly read the opening paragraph, which said that several of the personnel of the museum were showing off various relics they had gathered on their excursions.

The main photograph was of a crowd of well-dressed people sitting around tables eating dinner. The story continued on page five and by a stroke of luck, it was attached via a paper clip. He pulled it off and saw the text in full, but there was a picture in the bottom corner of the article. It was of Dr. Lansing holding a vase of some kind, next to him stood a younger man, well-groomed with a wide smile on his face. The man was holding the diamond artifact with the skull inlay. Teague's heart skipped a beat. He recognized the man but checked the caption to confirm his suspicions. *Dr. Timothy Lansing holding an early Mayan vase (left) and his assistant, Dr. Jack Benton, holding the legendary Black Diamond.*

Teague looked up. Benton. The Black Diamond. It was too much to be a coincidence. He marched over to Swan's office and pulled out the ledger as he did so. Swan turned to him as he entered the office. Teague held out his hand and presented the book to the Chief of Police.

"This," he said, "is a ledger I found at Geert's hotel room. I must be getting forgetful in my old age. I had completely missed that I picked it up when I was looking for him." Swan raised an eyebrow and was just about to speak when Teague cut him off. "It is filled with locations and numbers regarding the drug trade in the city. I have cause to believe that he is hiding at the old Mitchell Motors factory - the one that reported a fire but refused to allow the fire department access."

"I guess I do not want to ask you any further details about this," Swan stated. "I will send a squad with you immediately."

"No." Teague put up his hand. "You go there. I have another tip I need to investigate. It is just a hunch, but a strong one. One that may very well break this case completely. I need to investigate it myself. I will take a few officers with me, but they will have to wait."

"I guess I can agree to that," Swan replied. "Keep your radio alive so that we may be in constant communication."

"Will do, Chief." Teague turned and headed to gather two of the best officers he could think of. This might be all over, and if the vigilante were waiting for him at the warehouse, Swan would trap him as well.

CHAPTER TWENTY-ONE

Tony was well aware that lurking in the undergrowth on campus grounds was an oxymoron when one was doing it to catch someone lurking in the undergrowth. That afternoon he had stood in front of his full-length mirror, dressed only in his underwear and slipped the mask over his head. Wayan would have gone into battle with nothing more, but the climate in Wisconsin did not exactly permit such things. Tony felt he needed something more. He had fashioned himself an outfit made from a skin-tight fabric he had come across in one of the stores downtown. It was stretchy and pliable, something he could easily maneuver in. A bit revealing but was going to have to do. He had decided to use the colors of the Balinese seal to honor his adopted heritage. Blue and red mostly, leaving out the gold and white parts as they were not available in the fabric he wanted. Mr. Mahr had stressed the importance for a gentleman to know needlework. One could not always trust to have a woman by one's side or a manservant for that matter. Tony had not taken to it, and his suit had gone through several stages of problems - so much so, in fact, that he ran out of material, causing the finished product to have one red leg and one blue and the same with the arms. It would do for now he had thought.

He had decided to bring the swords. They were a bit too much in the event that he got stopped by the police. Instead, he armed himself with a kris and stuck it in the spiked belt Mahr had packed in his trunk. He sat still in the shrubbery as he watched young men and women pass him by, and it was not until it was late at night, closer to midnight, that he saw suspicious activity.

A figure came walking through the campus park, dressed in an overcoat, which was suspicious in itself since it was late spring. His face hidden below a wide-brimmed hat, casting shadows from the lamplights. The figure was smoking a cigarette, the white smoke curling up towards the night sky. He was moving from post to post, waiting, watching, being watched. There was a sound of people talking. Of heels on the stone path that wound through the park. The figure backed into the shadows, only the glow from his cigarette still visible. Tony gripped the hilt of the kris and made ready to move.

Two young women came into view under the light. They were engaged in vigorous conversation about a party they had just attended. They had listened to the advice of the dean, walking in pairs in order to be safe, if they must venture out at night. Several of the young women at the university had made a point of not being scared into staying indoors. They would fight, they said. They would take back the night.

The man came out of the dark as they passed his hiding place. He threw the cigarette to the ground and opened his coat. In his hand, Tony could see a blackjack, held at the ready. There was no doubt in Tony's mind that this was the perpetrator, and he had pounced. Before the figure had been close enough to take out the first woman, Tony was on him. He had caught the man's arm as it was in the air and twisted the limb to the point of breaking. The attacker had cried out, dropped the weapon, and the two women had turned around. They had screamed and covered their mouths with their hands but froze in place. Tony had held the man so that he got a good look at the mask in all its glory. The blast from The Face had been too much for him to handle, confronted with all his crimes, all color melted from his face, and his eyes rolled back in his head. He collapsed in a heap on the ground. Tony did not turn to the women, afraid of what the mask might do to them. Instead, he vanished back into the night.

Campus security heard the screams and were there to arrest the man, who was guilty of four separate assaults and quickly confessed to all of them.

* * *

Tony once again found himself pausing for a moment. He took a deep breath. Let the sharp pain in his ribs ground him for a moment. Blood from his latest victim still covered him. It had already dried up, and it made the fabric of his outfit stiff. A stark reminder that he had taken a life less than an hour ago. It was still early in the day, and the sun hung above the rooftops, bathing the city and the lake. He was hiding among the bushes in the yard of Dr. Benton's mansion-like home. There was no time to lose. Benton would soon head off to work, if he hadn't already, but more importantly, he would soon be aware of the break-in at his warehouse and the death of Geert.

Tony assumed that the head of The Black Diamond was not one to run. He would fight and probably have that woman with him. Tony didn't know if he could manage another battle with her. He had been standing in the yard for a good twenty minutes, assessing the house and the area. Did Benton have guards with him? Those who visited the doctor might find that odd. Why would the head of a pharmaceutical company need armed men? He was wealthy, and that might be reason enough.

The grounds looked very much the same as when he had walked them a couple of nights prior. He had not thought to scout them then, but there was an open path from where he was hiding to the great windows of the grand ballroom. Things were not going to get easier, and once Detective Teague arrived at the warehouse and found the body of Geert and his documents, he would come here with the entire police department. Then it was all for nothing. He rolled his shoulders to get some movement into them and kicked at the ground. He took one last deep breath, and then he ran towards the house.

He was not going to crash through the window. He would have the element of surprise. What if Benton was nowhere near the ballroom? Then Tony was the sitting duck. Instead, he ran up the white wall and grabbed on to the top of one of the windows. He tried to peek through the window as he leapt, but all he saw was his own reflection and the glare of the sun. He curled up and managed to find a small ledge for his feet. Pushing off, he came up to the second-floor balcony and crawled over the railing. He waited a moment to listen, but he heard nothing but the rustle of the wind in the large oak trees and the chirping of birds. The balcony was of a classic half-moon type, reminiscent of the White House. A set of double doors provided his way inside, and he pulled out both kalis as he headed for them. They were unlocked, which worried him somewhat. For some reason, Benton did not feel it necessary to lock his doors at this time. There could be several reasons for this. Maybe he had been out on the balcony earlier that morning, he had armed guards to protect him, he was expecting a visitor, or his butler had unlocked the doors. All of these options were a distinct possibility, but Tony was just going to have to take a chance.

Once inside, he moved as slowly as possible. The floors were wood, not covered with carpeting, and they were going to creak as he moved along them. He could do nothing about it; only tread as lightly as possible. He tried to listen for the sound of voices coming from the various rooms in the house. It was a mansion, so it might be impossible to tell where noises came from. The room he had entered only seemed to be some form of lounge. There was a roll top desk and an office chair off to one side. A bookcase stood against the wall in front of him. He didn't have time to investigate the titles on the shelf, but he did see several names like *Mysteries of the Orient* and *Asian Mysticism.*

There were doors on either side of this room, but Tony opted to take the one to his right since the opposite looked to be a bathroom. He kept his back to the wall and pushed the door, slightly open. It didn't make a sound, as if the hinges had been oiled that very day. He was at the top of the stairs leading down to the hallway. Now he could hear voices. He crouched down and sneaked forward, trying to peer through the bars in the railing. The voices were right below him. He figured he was too high up to jump down and surprise them. If he had been at one hundred percent maybe, but with injured ribs and weary from not sleeping it was not a great plan. He tumbled forward so that he came closer to the top of the stairs. He needed to get a better look at the people down there.

Suddenly a door opened, and he looked up. Dr. Benton's butler was standing there, carrying a silver tray. Tony leapt at him and sliced his blade across his chest. He tried to grab the tray before it fell to the floor, but he was a fraction too late. Tray, coffee pot and cups landed hard and shattered. The voices were silent, and Tony looked down the stairs only to see the woman who had killed Gregory Glade standing at the foot of them. She stared up at him and coming up beside her was Dr. Jack Benton himself. He had a look of smug distaste on his face and said something in her ear. He did not cry out for anyone, nor did he run and hide. There were no other guards in the building, Tony assumed, only the three of them. Perfect. The woman extended her claws and moved up the steps. Tony ran and jumped up on the banister. He slid down, like a surfer catching a perfect wave. The weight from his blades created a balance and he bent his legs ever so slightly to get the correct speed. He came at her so quickly that she didn't have time to react before he pushed off, spun in the air and landed a stiff kick to her jaw.

She crashed into the opposite banister, and he heard the wood crack. She was still upright, clutching to the railing, but was clearly dazed. Now he noticed the bandage around her upper right arm, wrapping up towards her shoulder. A target to be sure. He had landed in the center of the staircase giving her no time to recover, sending her over the railing with a pump kick to the chest. He heard her body thump against the marble tiles beyond. He turned towards Benton, who was still looking at him. There was no concern on the man's face, only that smile. He raised one hand and turned the ring he bore on his ring finger.

Tony could not quite see what it looked like, and he did not care. Instead, he came towards The Black Diamond, who pointed the ring at him. A yellow flash came from it and slammed into Tony's body. He flew back and hit the stairs, the steps rattling his spine as he met them. He still held on to the swords, but his breath flew out of him on impact. He raised his head to look at Benton, who was still at the bottom of the stairs, hand raised and palm towards him. A blue light glowed around the limb like a halo.

Tony tried to focus his energy on the man, but he did not seem to react to the horror of the face.

"The Mask of Rangda," Benton said calmly. "Designed to cast fear into the hearts of the wicked. The lost eye-jewel of Khor can conjure anything I wish. A force field to combat the effects of Rangda is but a fraction of what I can imagine." He looked over to his left as the woman came limping from the shadows. Her claws extended and she twisted to look at Tony.

"It seems as if you have figured out who The Black Diamond is. I'm not surprised. I always assumed I hid in the open. The police in this city were just too dimwitted to put the puzzle together." Benton gave a nod to the woman in Tony's direction. "I will not get my own hands dirty. I have tried that once and found it disgusting. Iron Claw here will finish you off."

She pounced at Tony, who rolled to the side as she crashed her clawed fist into the stairs. She wiggled free of the wood splinters, but as she did so, Tony once again gave her a stiff kick to the chest. She tumbled backward down the steps but landed on her feet at the bottom. Tony followed her through the air and planted his two feet on her face. Her head snapped back, and he heard a slight crack from her neck joints, but she was still standing. She swung her claws at him, left following right. He evaded by moving his entire upper body back and to the side. He swung one kalis at her head, and she parried with her banded metal arm. He swung low with the second kalis, and she jumped over it, coming down on her left leg and trying to step on him with her right.

He spun to the left as her foot hit the floor hard. It would surely have broken more of his bones if it had found its mark. He flipped backward and landed right in front of a vanity. She charged, he somersaulted over her, and she stopped right in front of the piece of furniture. Iron Claw saw her own reflection in the oval mirror and saw Tony aiming his kalis at her. She turned as the blade flew through the air. It missed and shattered the mirror. The distraction made, Tony performed a baseball slide at her legs, knocking her off her feet. She rolled and managed to avoid the impact of the floor by tumbling forward. She turned and they were now facing each other a few feet apart. Breathing heavily. For the first time, she was looking straight at him. At the Face. Tony concentrated on her and sent wave after wave of energy her way. She averted her gaze for a moment, and he ran towards her. He swung the blade at her midsection, connecting and sliding the sharp edge against her body as he passed. She doubled over for a moment but seemed only slightly fazed by the action. Blood covered Tony's kalis, but she was still upright.

He could see that the wavy edge had cut through the fabric and even the metal underneath. It had left a slit the width of her waist, but whereas it would have cut another person clean in two, it had only left a red gash. She roared at him and leapt towards him again. This time she caught Tony off guard and came upon him hard. He staggered back, trying to control the snarling maw of the woman. He held his sword up in an attempt to do so. She contorted her body and clawed at him so that he could feel every cut through the fabric. He dropped the sword but kept his left arm against her throat to keep her at bay. With his free hand, he repeatedly punched her in the wrapped shoulder.

She clenched her jaw at the pain but continued to push him back and up against the front door. He was relentless. His fist ached from the contact with her body, but he would not stop. He sent his knee into the wound in her gut. She let him go with a shriek.

He paused a moment to regain his breath. He turned his head to see where Iron Claw stood. She was clutching at her stomach, doubled over. He saw Benton standing behind her, one step up on the staircase, keeping an eye on them, his palm still up. Tony bent down, picked up his kalis, and walked towards the woman. She looked at him, and the eyes behind the domino mask narrowed. He spun his blade, trying to convince her that he was still in fighting form. She came at him with a claw, missed as he sidestepped, once again planting a knee in the open wound. She fell to her knees, and he kicked her so she fell over, whimpering on the marble.

He turned to Benton, who was no longer smirking. His eye also narrowed, and his hand formed into a fist. From the ring came a green dragon-like shape that flew towards Tony. He sliced at it, but the vaporous creature ignored it. The mouth of the beast opened to reveal rows of hideous teeth then snapped shut, the head crashing into his body. His world erupted in a world of green. The creature might have looked like a fog-like projection of a dragon, but it felt as real as a brick wall. The winged lizard pushed him back with such force that he went right through the front door, and they took the entire front wall with them. He tumbled across the stone path leading up the mansion and lay still on the well-manicured lawn.

* * *

Teague had decided to take the car even if he could easily have run the distance from the station to the Benton house. Every second counted he thought, and as he flew down Main Street, he kept an eye in the rear-view mirror to make sure that officers Blake and Murphy were along for the ride. He didn't know why he felt in such a hurry. The evidence pointed to Benton, but he had no hard evidence, only circumstantial, unless the warehouse and Geert's testimony could assist them. He stopped about ten feet from the house and climbed out, motioning to the officers to stay behind as he walked towards the large building. It was a tranquil spring morning. It all looked quite idyllic, and for a brief moment, he envied people who could afford to live in such a lush environment.

He turned onto the stone path leading to the mansion when there was a sudden explosion. The front of the building blew out with wood and brick flying in all directions. The front door came bounding towards him, and he barely dodged it as it rolled past him and crashed into a car on the other side of the street. The massive wood tore the vehicle in two. Green smoke rose to the sky, and debris rained down on the lawn. He called for Blake and Murphy who were already advancing with their guns drawn. Teague brought out his weapon also and approached the building. He could clearly see the masked vigilante try to rise from the grass on the side of the path. His outfit had torn in several places, and he was bleeding from cuts and wounds in various parts of his body. Somehow, he had figured out the identity of The Black Diamond as well and had arrived first.

Teague instructed the police officers to ignore the vigilante for the time being. Whatever had destroyed the facade of the house was a bigger threat. In the opening, he could see a figure dressed in black pants and a white shirt. It was Benton. His wry smile and devilish good looks were unmistakable, even from a distance. Teague aimed at him.

"Dr. Jack Benton," he cried. "You are wanted for questioning in the affair of The Black Diamond criminal organization." He waved Blake and Murphy forward, who both crept along the path. The smoke had dissipated, and dust filled the air dulled the rays of sunshine.

Tony stumbled to his feet and saw the officers walk towards Benton. He tried to call out to them, but he was having a difficult time articulating his words. There was a flash of red, and a large spear flew from the house and impaled one of the men. He fell to his knees, clutching at the weapon protruding from his chest. The spear disappeared into a red mist, and the man toppled.

Teague couldn't believe his eyes as he saw Murphy face down on the ground, a pool of blood gathering under him.

Blake was trying to lay as flat as possible and opened fire against Benton. If nothing else, they had him on a count of murder. He had no idea how one proved it without a weapon, but he'd get him now. A blue shield appearing out of nowhere stopped the bullets from Blake's gun. Teague opened fire as well and it forced Benton to move out of the way, dropping the shield towards Blake and concentrating it on Teague. He couldn't focus on two things at the same time - this was clearly the weakness. Teague had to figure out how to use that fact.

"Forward, Blake," he called, and Blake reloaded his weapon and proceeded to fire and move towards the house. Teague did the same from his position. Benton baked up the stairs leading to the second floor as he tried to avoid the bullets.

Tony leapt up, ignoring the pain and rushed towards the house. He passed the cop Teague had called Blake and tumbled forward before he reached the house, moving to the side of it instead of going through the opening. If Benton was busy with the police, he could potentially be an easy target from another angle. He needed his blades. All he had was the kris now and he didn't know what kind of help it would be against the power of the ring on Benton's finger.

Blake and Teague flanked the opening. They looked around the corner and sent a few shots inside but turned back behind the wall as a barrage of arrows came towards them. They had noticed the vigilante fly past them, but they had no time trying to detain him. He had his own agenda surely.

Teague should have sent one of the officers back to the car to call for help, but it was too late now. Teague reloaded again. He hadn't counted on there being so much gunfire, and he was almost out of ammunition. Blake must be in a similar situation. They desperately needed backup.

Tony broke through one of the windows on the side of the house and crawled inside. He was in a dining room and quickly ran through. He stopped at a cabinet of fine dinnerware and grabbed a serving bowl made from bone china.

He gently opened the door that opened onto the hallway. He could hear the sound of gunfire and the crackling of what must be magic on the other side. He slipped through the crack of the door, and as soon as he saw Benton standing on the staircase, he threw the dish at him. It struck the man in the side, and he lost his footing on the stairs. Tony dove to the floor and found one of his kalis among the splintered wood and broken stones. A force pushed him across the floor. Benton had his fist trained on him. He shot something at him, but Tony sidestepped again, losing his footing in the process, his leg buckling under him. His body was fatigued. A razor-sharp blade flew past him and embedded itself in the floor before turning into vapor.

Teague took the opportunity as Benton's attention was elsewhere, and he fired off three shots. Two went wide, but one hit Benton in his left arm. Benton went to a knee and winced at the pain, turning his body to Teague and Blake, who were now standing next to him. He sent a blast of fire towards them. Both of them were cast backward, Blake's uniform engulfed in flames, and he rolled himself on the ground, attempting to extinguish them. Benton turned and ran up the stairs.

Tony tried to get up but something grabbing his ankle. He looked down and saw Iron Claw holding on to him. Her mask partially torn from her face and revealed dark eyes staring up at him. She snarled and clawed her way up his leg.

"Get him, Detective!" Tony cried and tried to kick at her with his free leg. She took several kicks to her forehead before she released him.

Teague checked on Blake who was badly burned but still alive. He picked up his weapon and headed inside the building. He felt his entire body working against him. He could hear sirens in the distance, coming ever closer. His revolver was empty, and he tossed it to the side, checking the bullets in Blake's service gun. It had five good shots left. He took the stairs two at a time as he saw Benton turning left and ducking through a door.

Tony also heard the sirens coming. He didn't care. He was standing, swaying back and forth, his kalis at his side. Iron Claw was up to her feet, blood flowing from her body, domino mask on the floor. The top of her face was like any others. Pale skin, clearly defined eyebrows, and high cheekbones. Her jaw was made of steel, making her mouth look like a digger. It must be another mask, Tony thought, otherwise she would be part machine, like that tin figure from Oz. She was panting, struggling for breath. She was done for they both knew it. There was no way she was coming back from the wound she was sporting.

Saliva ran from her open maw, and she extended her claws, the ones on her right hand still nubbins from when Tony had cut them. She moved on him. He swung his kalis at her, and she batted it to the side with such force that it made his arm numb. She might be dying, but that didn't mean that she couldn't take him with her. She tried to catch him with the claws on her left hand, and he evaded and tried to kick her.

She parried again. It felt as if he was kicking a metal post. He felt her power through his shin, threatening to break.

She came at him again. He took a jump back, and she came off balance, woozy from the blood loss. He spun around and let the back of his fist crash into her jaw. He felt something give but felt the bones in his hand break. He spun again, this time letting his foot come around in a roundhouse kick, landing it flush on her jaw again. On the third rotation, he allowed his knee to connect with her side. She fell towards the staircase, breaking several of the spindles. He stopped, watching her broken body, her lower jaw hanging limply from her face. She was barely breathing now. He could hear a soft gargle coming from somewhere deep inside her, like Mr. Valdemar resting on his chaise-lounge, consumptive and near death. He stumbled. Looking around for his weapons, he managed to locate them both. He had seen Teague and Benton run up the stairs. He would try to cut them both off on the other side. He moved back from where he had come.

Teague slowly opened the door, gun held at the ready. He had already done this too many times in the past week. The room was some form of library. There was a large desk against the far wall in front of large windows. Books and an oriental rug on the floor occupied the rest of the room. There was a door to the left, ominously placed between two bookcases, and Benton was probably hiding there.

"Come out, Benton," he called. I know you're hiding here. You might as well give up. The rest of the force is here, and there is no way you can get away. He sneaked farther into the room and moved towards the door. He knocked on it and put a hand on the doorknob. "I'm coming in, and I expect you to have your hands raised when I do." He took a deep breath and made ready. From the corner of his eye, he could see something stepping out of the shadows.

Benton had been standing next to one of the tall windows, the light streaming in hiding him. He threw something at Teague; a red knife struck him in the hip. Teague cried and grabbed at the object, which vanished at his attempt. Blood flowed from the wound, and he fell over. He tried to squeeze off a round, but it went wide as he fell. Benton cracked his knuckles and moved closer to him, still far enough away from the detective to feel safe from kicks or punches.

"All things must, unfortunately, come to an end, Detective," he said in a low voice. "I have quite enjoyed the chase and always being one step ahead of you. To be fair, I am certain you would have come close if it had not been for the man in the mask. It is sad to think you would have had to arrest him as well for acting outside the law.

However, you will not be arresting anyone today since you will be dead. I will set up shop somewhere else. It is amazing how one has the world at one's fingers when wearing a ring such as this." He wiggled his right ring finger at him. The black diamond shaped as a skull glinted in the sun. He pointed it towards Teague, who refused to look away.

There was a loud crash, and Benton toppled forward, sending a wave of something red past Teague. It set the bookcase on fire. The masked man was on top of the doctor. He had come crashing through the window, leapt off the desk and landed on Benton's back.

Benton turned, and Tony staggered back. He grabbed onto a shelf to retain his balance. Benton saw his opening and was just about to blast him with the power of the ring, but Tony kicked his hand away. He fell towards him and focused on him with the rest of his energy. The Face sent wave after wave of horror at Benton who cried out in agony. It was too much to handle for him; his eyes went wide and bloodshot, his jet-black hair streaked with white.

He kneed Tony between the legs, so that the spell was briefly broken. Teague shot at him and hit him in the leg. Benton spun around, flicked his wrist and sent Teague twisting in the air and into the books behind him. Shelves came crashing down around the detective as he fell to the floor. Tony punched Benton in the stomach, who doubled over. He gritted his teeth at the shock flying from his fist and up his arm. His hand was broken there was no doubt. Even though the impact to Benton's abdomen was not full force due to the break, it still had the desired effect. Tony sent another punch to Benton's jaw, and his head snapped back violently.

Benton tried to raise the hand with the ring, but Tony grabbed his wrist with his left and twisted until he could hear an audible crunch. Benton cried out in anguish, and Tony silenced him with a well-placed elbow to the bridge of his nose. Benton tumbled backward and scooted towards the desk. Tony watched him move at a speed that he would have thought impossible for someone with an obviously broken nose. Blood poured from Benton's face, and there was fear in his eyes. Fear and something else. Teague was sitting up, his back against the charred bookcase. The fire had died down almost as quickly as it had started. Singed pages were falling around him like leaves on an autumn day. He searched for and found the revolver. He could clearly hear the voices of other police officers on the first floor, and he imagined that they were debriefing Blake and surrounding the building.

"We need to stop him!" Teague called to the vigilante, who nodded his reply.

Benton had crawled up the desk and as Teague aimed at him and Tony came towards him, he raised his hand and a blue explosion erupted from him. The sound was deafening, and it threw them both back. Tony's ears were ringing, and everything enveloped in a blue mist. He couldn't tell which way was up, where he was facing or what was happening.

As the smoke cleared, he noticed that he was still facing the desk where Benton had been standing, but he was gone. He ran towards the window, the only place he could have escaped through. Teague hobbled after him, still pointing the revolver towards it. The window was shattered, the way Tony had left it as he came crashing through. There was fresh blood on the jagged pieces of glass, and white fabric from Benton's shirt stuck to the wood frame. They looked out at the yard, but he was gone. Teague screamed in frustration as he emptied the revolver through the window. The Black Diamond had escaped.

"My colleagues are surrounding the area as we speak." Teague tossed the gun on the floor. "There is no way he will escape us. He is injured and alone." He turned to look at the room they were standing in. The smell of scorched paper hung in the air, and the blue mist still surrounded his feet. It was all over.

He sighed and allowed himself to feel the pain his body was in. He started to shiver uncontrollably, the world started to spin, and he had to grab onto a shelf to avoid collapsing. He glanced over his shoulder, but the masked man was gone.

CHAPTER TWENTY-TWO

Dr. Benton did manage to escape, contrary to Teague's belief in his own police force. By the time they had surrounded the building, he was long gone. Chief Swan had found the body of Paul Geert in the old Mitchell Motors warehouse, and he had found a letter in his pocket. It was a detailed account of everything Geert had been involved in. From how he had been contacted by The Black Diamond to the attempted murder of Martin Lindquist at St. Mary's Hospital, to the distribution ring of the organization. He named Jack Benton, in particular, and several low-level thugs.

Every single location the organization had used detailed in the ledger Teague had handed Swan, and he could easily corroborate it with Geert's confession.

Swan had rushed to Benton's house after leaving a small force to sweep the warehouse. On the way to Main Street, he had gotten the first reports of gunfire in the area, and he knew then that Teague was there. They swept Benton's home for evidence, but nothing was found. His prints were picked up in several of the locations mentioned in the ledger instead, linking him to the actives of the criminal group.

In the coming weeks, the police conducted several raids in the city and neighboring towns. Hundreds of men brought into custody, and thousands of dollars' worth of product confiscated and later destroyed. Teague could not take part in it. Instead, the police physician forced him to recuperate in his home, nursing wounds from his encounter with Benton. His leg would never quite heal, and he walked with a limp for the rest of his life. Once he got older, he had to use a cane, a blow to his ever-fragile ego. Swan allowed him to come back to work early if he promised to sit behind a desk, and he did, desperate to see the progress the force was making in the case.

In a huge announcement to the press, Swan claimed the organization The Black Diamond was no more and that the city was once again at peace. Teague sighed at the statement. He knew that someone would come in and attempt to fill the criminal void left by such a big machine, but he also realized that he would be without a job if crime all of a sudden vanished.

Theresa had an announcement of her own, and as he lay in the hospital, she told him that he was going to be a father. The news filled him with joy and he wept for the first time since becoming an adult.

Tony Hill returned to work the next day. Vic Linden raised a bushy eyebrow at his appearance, wondering where he had been the previous day and complaining that Posen was not equipped to run the newscast by himself. Tony moved gingerly from one place to another, not comfortable in any position. His body still ached, from the cracked ribs in his side to the broken hand and the cuts and tears all over his body.

Once again, he had managed to avoid bruising to the face, whether it was the mask acting as extra protection he did not know.

He did his contractual duty and then went home to rest. He did call Emily Chaucer and arranged for a date the following Friday. He picked her up at the Racine Hotel, and they ate at the Mandalay Lounge in the same building. They made polite conversation, and Tony tried to hide his aches and pains as best he could. He winced occasionally, when he thought she wasn't looking, but she saw it and opted not to speak of it. They had a pleasant time, and when it was time to say good night at her room, she kissed him romantically on the mouth. Girls in her line of work were often considered to be of a certain type, but she was not - as difficult as it might be among the pressures of entertainment.

She placed a hand on his chest and told him that she had already stayed too long in the city waiting for him to call. She had to move on to the next place, the next venue. Her job entailed touring, and she was running low on funds. She would return if he wanted her to, and they could pick up where they had left off, for she was not ready to leave something so promising as their relationship. Tony said he would wait for her, and he had an extra spring in his step as he walked down Sixth Street towards his apartment.

That night he sat in the dark, dressed in only his pajama bottoms, with the trunk Mr. Mahr had bequeathed him open in the center of the kitchen. His outfit had been torn to shreds and badly he needed a new one. The kalis and kris lay neatly wrapped in fabric to keep their edges sharp, and The Face stared at him but was silent. *What now?* He thought.

For a long time, he had a purpose, a calling to change the world. To make things better. His body was broken but healing from attempting to right wrongs. There would always be crime in the city, it was undeniable, but did he have to dress up in an ancient mask to fight it, or was there another way to help? The Black Diamond was still out there – despite what the Police Chief said.

All evidence pointed to him fleeing by way of the harbor to South America. The harbor police had not been able to find him or had just been too late. Tony was not going to pursue him. One day he might return, and he would deal with him then. He would fight injustice another way he convinced himself, closing the lid to the trunk and hobbling over to his window to stare out over the city as the streetlights cast their yellow glow over the blacktop. It was beautiful in a way. Not like the nature of his beloved Bali, but beautiful, nonetheless.

Teague was sitting at Ivanhoe's with the rest of the department. They had chosen a booth and were celebrating the conclusion of the case. Teague had revealed everything he had done behind their backs in order to crack it, as well as the great assistance from Charlotte. She winked at him with her seductive eyes, and he raised a glass to her and smiled. They played a dangerous game.

He left the involvement of the masked vigilante out of the story, apart from where others had witnessed him. They were still looking for him. Yet they made no great effort in trying to find him. They were well aware they might never have brought The Black Diamond organization down without him.

Swan held a minute of silence to Greg Glade whose picture now prominently graced the bar. They all knew what Glade had done, but he was one of them, and no matter the crime, he had once been a fine cop. As the night progressed, the patrons filed out and soon all that remained were Swan and Teague. The chief pulled on his overcoat and placed a hand on the table.

"You going to be alright?" He asked.

"Yeah, I'll be fine," Teague, replied. "Just exhausted after everything we've been through."

"I understand," Swan said. "Go home to Theresa and get some rest. Tomorrow we will be honored by the mayor, and you do not want to face the press or him with dark circles around your

eyes."

Teague scoffed. "My body is already a mass of bruises and cuts, what would circles matter?"

"So true. Go home, though. It's an order." Swan gave him a nod and walked out into the night.

Teague leaned back in the booth. He picked up a piece of paper from his pocket. On it was the number of the vigilante that given to him at the hotel. If he called it, someone would pick up. It would probably be the man himself. Policeman's curiosity wanted him to call and find out who it was, but he had been trusted with the number, knowing full well what might happen. He downed his beer, grabbed his coat and left the bar. He looked up and down Main Street, tossed the paper to the right, stepped on it as if were a cigarette butt, and walked to the left.

Epilogue

A figure stood atop Memorial Hall, silhouetted against the moon. She had long white hair flowing in the breeze coming in from the lake. She wore a skin-tight outfit made from leather, and where her face would be was nothing more than a skull. Empty sockets looking out over the city, twin hints of light in their center and a permanent grin on her white face.

About the Author

C. Marry Hultman is equal parts Chicano and Scandinavian.

An expatriate Wisconsinite currently residing in Sweden,

where he spends most of his days teaching, podcasting.

and writing. He lives together with his wife Marie, daughters Mina and Maia, and a huge cat named Fizzgig.

Find him online and follow his writing at:

https://linktr.ee/C.MarryHultman

https://wisconsinnoir.wixsite.com/wisnoir

www.ingramcontent.com/pod-product-compliance
Lightning Source LLC
La Vergne TN
LVHW091656190726
843493LV00001B/29